FAYRENE PRESTON

"An exquisitely polished writer, Ms. Preston gifts us with a unique, silken sensuality that will heat your dreams up to fever point."
—*Romantic Times BOOKclub*

"Fayrene Preston surrounds her appealing lovers with her trademark highly-charged sensual ambiance."
—*Romantic Times BOOKclub*

"A master storyteller, Ms. Preston creates an enchanted ambiance that will cast a spell of sheer delight over her fortunate readers."
—*Romantic Times BOOKclub*

Dear Reader,

The editors at Harlequin and Silhouette are thrilled to be able to bring you a brand-new featured author program for 2005! Signature Select aims to single out outstanding stories, contemporary themes and oft-requested classics by some of your favorite series authors and present them to you in a variety of formats bound by truly striking covers.

We want to provide several different types of reading experiences in the new Signature Select program. The Spotlight books offer a single "big read" by a talented series author, the Collections present three novellas on a selected theme in one volume, the Sagas contain sprawling, sometimes multi-generational family tales (often related to a favorite family first introduced in series), and the Miniseries feature requested previously published books, with two or, occasionally, three complete stories in one volume. The Signature Select program offers one book in each of these categories per month, and fans of limited continuity series will also find these continuing stories under the Signature Select umbrella.

In addition, these volumes bring you bonus features...different in every single book! You may learn more about the author in an extended interview, more about the setting or inspiration for the book, more about subjects related to the theme and, often, a bonus short read will be included. Authors and editors have been outdoing themselves in originating creative material for our bonus features—we're sure you'll be surprised and pleased with the results!

The Signature Select program strives to bring you a variety of reading experiences by authors you've come to love, as well as by rising stars you'll be glad you've discovered. Watch for new stories from Janelle Denison, Donna Kauffman, Leslie Kelly, Marie Ferrarella, Suzanne Forster, Stephanie Bond, Christine Rimmer and scores more of the brightest talents in romance fiction!

The excitement continues!

Warm wishes for happy reading,

Marsha Zinberg

Marsha Zinberg
Executive Editor
The Signature Select Program

SWANSEA LEGACY

FAYRENE PRESTON

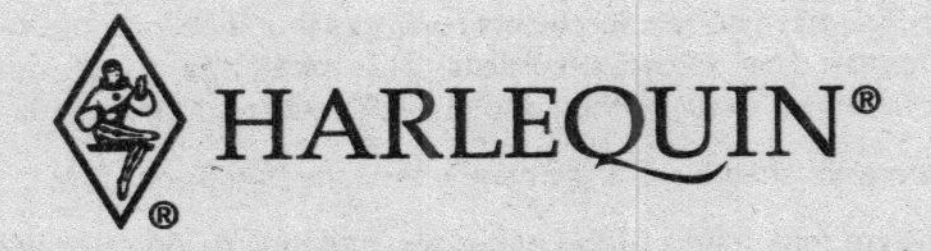

TORONTO • NEW YORK • LONDON
AMSTERDAM • PARIS • SYDNEY • HAMBURG
STOCKHOLM • ATHENS • TOKYO • MILAN • MADRID
PRAGUE • WARSAW • BUDAPEST • AUCKLAND

ISBN 0-373-28517-5

SWANSEA LEGACY

This edition published by arrangement with Harlequin Books S.A.

www.eHarlequin.com

Printed in U.S.A.

CONTENTS

SWANSEA PLACE: THE LEGACY 9

SWANSEA PLACE: DECEIT 193

Dear Reader,

When I finished writing *SwanSea: The Destiny,* the historical prequel to the SWANSEA PLACE series, about Jake Deverell and Arabella Linden and the Great House of SwanSea, I found I absolutely could not let them go. The characters and the house were simply too alive and too compelling for me to let them go out of my life at that point. It was akin to being caught up in the middle of a raging love affair, and I had to stay.

And so I wrote four more books. This time, though, they were contemporary, but each with a historical preface that goes back in time and gives more information about the people and the history of SwanSea. In addition, each book reveals a new mystery about SwanSea.

In this 2-in-1 collection from Harlequin, I am thrilled to be able to share with you the first two of those books: *SwanSea Place: The Legacy* and *SwanSea Place: Deceit.*

I so hope you enjoy.

Fayrene Preston

SWANSEA PLACE: THE LEGACY

PREFACE

1894

HE STOOD WITH HIS BACK to the ocean, his gaze on the great house before him. *SwanSea.* Edward Deverell smiled. The house was truly a monument...a monument to him.

He had heard that next year in New York City, Mrs. Cornelius Vanderbilt would open her five-million-dollar house on Fifth Avenue. And it was said that Mrs. William C. Whitney was also planning a grand residence on Fifth Avenue. But he had commissioned the great Chicago architect, Louis Henry Sullivan, had worked closely with him, and he was satisfied that when people spoke in superlatives about a house, they would speak of SwanSea. Here on this wild, beautiful, windswept shore of Maine, the house would stand forever, a symbol of his life's accomplishments.

The morning sun rose behind Edward, spreading its golden warmth over the house. Like a giant fan-shaped seashell, the house symbolized the ocean that he had crossed to reach America. The back was narrow, softly rounded, and faced the sea. From there it fanned outward, northwest and southwest, in a series of horizontal structures that mirrored the waves behind him and offered an unobstructed view of the sea from the majority of the rooms. The front was a broad, curving expanse with a long, graceful skirt of white steps. Elegant curvilinear ironwork formed the balcony railings, and friezes of flowers and twisting, trailing vines decorated the facade.

Its four main stories represented the four decades of his life thus far: the next four decades would be his glory.

He had been nothing more than a deckhand when he had first sighted this shore from the railing of a merchant ship. He had brought nothing with him but a strong back, a keen mind, the name of his birthplace, SwanSea, and a terrible burning within him. A burning that wouldn't let him rest until he had obliterated all memories of the dank, frigid Welsh coal mines where he had labored as a boy.

In a month he would wed Leonora Spencer, a young woman he had chosen with meticulous care for her breeding and social connections. They would be married here at SwanSea in the immense ballroom that seventy-five florists would turn into a bower. Leonora would wear diamonds in her hair and on her gown. Special trains would run between New York and Boston, carrying their guests. From Boston, a convoy of coaches would bring them to SwanSea. Society would be talking about this wedding for years.

He was pleased. The marriage would not only accomplish the feat of bringing society to his doorstep, but Leonora would also provide him with sons.

Without warning, a cloud skimmed across the sun, blunting the light that had been shining on the house, turning its stone cold and its windows dull and opaque. A chill shuddered through Edward. No, he thought. *No.* This wasn't right. Deprived of the sun's golden warmth, the house had no heart, no life; it looked like a mausoleum.

Leonora had said much the same thing when she had first seen the house. For some reason, when she gazed at the house, she couldn't see what he saw. But he was confident that with time she would. Once the house was filled with furniture, art and guests, it would be everything he had ever dreamed it could be. As if to prove his point, the cloud passed on, and the full strength of the sun's light poured over the house again. Edward felt soothed. Everything would be as he planned.

He had made his fortune. Now he would establish his name. His destiny would be his children. He would give them the best of everything, and in return, they would make their marks in business, politics, and academia. Society would open its arms to him and his family. Presidents would come to him for advice.

From SwanSea he would launch a dynasty that the world would come to respect, if not revere. Through SwanSea and his children, he would live forever.

CHAPTER ONE

The Present Day

SHE STOOD WITH HER BACK to the ocean, her gaze on the great house before her. *SwanSea*. Caitlin Deverell smiled. She'd been born in this house, lived her first six years here. During that time and when she'd visited in the years since, she'd always had the house pretty much to herself. But now, painters, plasterers, artisans and gardeners swarmed in and around it.

Her great-grandfather Edward had had the dream and built SwanSea. Her grandfather Jake had made SwanSea a legend. The walls of the house had seen birth and death, pain and joy, love and hate. The bright and the beautiful, the famous and the infamous had all passed through its doors. But to Caitlin it had always been home.

Now after a long sleep, SwanSea was reawakening. And she felt a thrill of pride that under her care and direction, SwanSea would be restored to its former splendor and glamour.

Caitlin lifted her face to the sun-warmed ocean breeze. It lingered around her to tease the skirt of her sundress, lifting the hem then sending it rippling in sensuous undulations against her legs. Traveling on, the wind softly embraced the house before rustling through the majestic pines that lay just beyond.

The sun, the wind, the ocean and SwanSea. Caitlin sighed with contentment, thinking there was a rightness about the day, a sense that all was in its proper place.

Then, unexpectedly, a cloud scudded across the sun, and the wind shifted. Catching a flicker of movement in her peripheral vision, she turned, and immediately her attention was arrested by a tall man who was approaching.

He moved with controlled grace that would have reminded her of a natural athlete if it wasn't for the slightest hint of stiffness in his gait. Black jeans molded his long legs, and a lightweight white sweater stretched across his broad chest. The casual outfit took on an elegance that made it seem as if the jeans and sweater had been designed especially for him. Unable to look away, Caitlin stared, rapt by the strong aura of earthy sensuality radiating from the man. The thought flitted through her mind to wonder what it would be like to be made love to by him.

And still she had no sense of anything out of place.

He stopped in front of her, and the sensation that he was dominating all the space around her came over her suddenly. *Odd.* His thick coal-black hair and pale olive skin drew her gaze; his strong-jawed face interested her; his dark brown eyes riveted her. *Unusual.*

"Caitlin Deverell?"

She'd been so caught up with her thoughts about him that the sound of his deep voice nearly made her jump. "Yes?"

"I'm Nico DiFrenza. A man named Haines said I'd find you here."

"Mr. Haines is my foreman."

Without taking his eyes off her, he indicated the house with a movement of his head. "It has an amazing strength to it."

She stared at him, taken aback yet strangely pleased to hear from a stranger something she'd always felt. "I know."

"Yes, I suppose you do." The walk out to the bluff had taken more out of him than he had expected, Nico realized, and looking at Caitlin Deverell while in his weakened condition wasn't helping. Her eyes were an unusual green tinted by flecks of gold, and he felt the potent effect of them to his spine. Outlined against the vivid blue sky, with the wind blowing her cinnamon-colored hair and the skirt of her gold sundress, she was beautiful. He wondered why he hadn't anticipated the impact she might have on him. Not that it mattered.

"Is there something I can do for you, Mr. DiFrenza?"

Another time, another place, the possibilities would be endless, he thought, and in spite of his weariness, a slow smile spread over his face. "Yes, you can do something for me. You can let me stay here for a few days."

She was reflecting on the notion that the sensuality of his smile hadn't been deliberate when the meaning of his words crystallized in her mind. She stared at him blankly. "I beg your pardon?"

Dammit. His approach had been too abrupt. He curled his fingers inward until he had unconsciously made a fist. "I'm sorry. Let me explain. Like practically everyone else in the country, I've heard of SwanSea. Then just recently, I read that you were turning the house into a resort."

"That's true, but it will be months before it will be ready for guests."

Come on, sweetheart. Don't make this hard for me. I'm just not up to it. This time his smile was quick and meant to take her breath away. The slight widening of her eyes told him it had worked. He forced his fingers to relax and slipped his hands into his pockets. "At least hear me out. Please."

She blinked, realizing he said "please" the way another man might caress. Softly. Persuasively. With a certain charm and seductiveness.

"I'm on a leave of absence from my job, and this morning I headed up the coast."

"That's all very interesting, but—"

"You're not listening."

"Sorry." In the next moment she fought back the urge to laugh. Why was *she* apologizing? He was the trespasser.

"My heart is set on a room with an ocean view, and under ordinary circumstances, I'm sure I wouldn't have any trouble getting one. But there's an insurance convention in Portland, and all the really good places are taken."

"So you thought you could stay here?" She smiled with regret. "No, I'm afraid not. Look, Mr. DiFrenza—"

"Please call me Nico, Miss Deverell."

With a toss of her head, she sent shining cinnamon strands flying behind her shoulders. Nico followed the motion with a concentration that gave her pause. She'd probably tossed her head in that way thousands of times in her twenty-six years, but no man had ever narrowed his eyes at the gesture in quite the same way as Nico had. It was almost as if her action had caused some inner disturbance in him. A funny little shiver went up her spine. She wrapped her arms around her waist. "It's a shame that you couldn't find anything to suit you, but you can't stay here."

His dark brown eyes warmed with a smile, and Caitlin realized that she had never met a man who knew how to smile in so many ways. But she wasn't sure if she'd seen a sincere smile from him yet.

"I've tried one place after another, and I'm tired of driving. A little while ago, when I realized how close I was to SwanSea, I decided it was an omen." His glance darted to the house. "As I said, I really had my heart set on an ocean view." He felt guilty, deceiving her like this, but he had to stay at SwanSea.

She turned toward the sea, giving herself time to think. Up to this moment, she'd thought all the truly compelling men were in her family. But this man... He intrigued her. He attracted her. He definitely made her want to do as he asked. She sighed. She couldn't.

She looked back at him and was surprised by the expression of pain on his face. In the next instant, the expression passed, and she decided she had been mistaken. "I suggest that you drive back to the little town you passed on your way here. There's a lovely tearoom there. Have something to eat, then drive on up the coast. I'm sure you'll find something to your liking."

He shook his head, his impatience barely restrained. "Surely you have a room somewhere that I can use, perhaps in a section of the house where the workmen haven't yet started."

She did. On the northwest side of the house on the third floor, where she was staying. "You don't give up, do you?"

"Hardly ever."

She swallowed against a thickness in her throat. The dark intensity of his gaze was stirring up warm quivering sensations inside her that threatened to push aside her common sense. "What you're asking is impossible."

"Nothing," he said, "is impossible."

"It is, Mr. DiFrenza, if I say it is."

So there was steel beneath the beauty, he thought, and silently applauded her. A woman in her circumstances should be cautious. Except in this particular instance when her caution stood in his way.

He ran his hand along his waist to his side and felt the tenderness. For a moment, he struggled with himself. Under normal circumstances, he would never expose a weakness—but in this case, he might be able to use it to his advantage. "I haven't been entirely honest with you, Miss Deverell. I told you I'd taken a leave of absence from work. What I didn't say is that I've been ill..."

"Oh, I'm sorry."

As he had hoped, her guard began to melt away, to be replaced by sympathy. He nodded. "I was discharged from the hospital yesterday after being advised that I might recuperate better away from Boston."

Curious though she was, good manners kept her from asking the nature of his illness. But she failed to imagine what could have put him in the hospital. Even with the faint pallor beneath his olive skin, he exuded an astonishing power. It made her wonder what he'd be like when he was entirely well. And, a small voice whispered, if she gave him a room, she'd find out.

In truth, letting him have a room for a few days would cause her very little inconvenience. SwanSea had over fifty bedrooms. And though it was true she knew nothing about him, she also wouldn't know anything about most of the people who would be arriving to stay when SwanSea officially opened. Still, her instincts told her that none of those guests would come close to moving her in this strange, inexplicable way. "I've been living in Boston in recent years. Maybe we know some of the same people."

Only an inherent self-discipline kept him from groaning aloud. She was going to probe. Why did she have to be beautiful *and* smart? "Boston is a big town, I doubt it."

She persevered. "There's a wonderful family-owned department store in Boston by the name of DiFrenza's. Are you by any chance related to the owners?"

He hesitated. He had a circle of close and trusted friends. Outside that circle, he didn't talk about himself. Protecting his family was his first priority, but he had to stay at SwanSea, and to do so, he had to gain Caitlin Deverell's confidence. "Elena DiFrenza is my great-grandmother."

Her eyes widened. "She's a legend in Boston."

"She deserves to be a legend," he said, gratified to see Caitlin relaxing. "She's a remarkable woman."

That Elena DiFrenza was his great-grandmother was reassuring, and it was a fact easily checked. But a doubt Caitlin couldn't quite name continued to niggle at her. "I understand DiFrenza's is about to open a second store in Beverly Hills."

"That's right."

"I shop quite often at DiFrenza's. Are you in the family business?"

"No. In general, I leave the store to my father and my sister. My father heads the store, and my sister is a buyer."

Studying him, Caitlin at first found it difficult to put this obviously rugged man together with the delicate Angelica DiFrenza. Through her frequent patronage of the store, Caitlin had struck up a casual friendship with Angelica, and she often relied on the woman's impeccable taste when she needed something to wear for a special event.

"I know your sister," she said, "and you look nothing alike." Then it struck her. While it was true that Angelica's waist-length hair was dark brown, not coal-black like his, they had the same eyes. Some people called that particular dark-brown shade and velvety texture *bedroom* eyes. Now why was she thinking that?

"I guarantee that Angelica would hate it if she resembled me," he said. Though his words were meant as a joke, his patience was thinning by the minute. "And I wouldn't take it too kindly if I looked like her. Anyway, Mother Nature knew what she was doing when she created Angelica. She's just about perfect."

"She is lovely," Caitlin agreed, reflecting that he was saying all the right things. Why then did she continue to sense something irregular and uneven beneath his smooth manner? Something that made her want to keep digging. "Your sister wears a ring I've always admired."

He'd be amused if it weren't for the fact that he was suddenly so tired. "Yes, it's a Colombian square-cut emerald. Her birthstone." He felt the slight tremor in his limbs. Giving a silent, crude curse, he whipped out his billfold and held out his driver's license for her inspection.

A quick look showed her a stern, unsmiling picture of him and informed her that his name was Niccolo DiFrenza, that he lived at a good address in Boston, that he was six feet tall and had brown eyes.

On a certain level, she was reassured. Everything was checked. But on another level, something told her Nico DiFrenza couldn't be so simply and neatly explained by fitting him into a slot on the DiFrenza family tree. There was nothing simple or neat about this man.

"Look, Miss Deverell, please reconsider about the room. I really don't think I can drive one more mile."

His pallor *had* increased, she noticed with concern. "It's just that I'm not sure this is the best place for you. We aren't set up to offer any service. Ramona, my mother's housekeeper, is with me helping out, but all the workers you see are involved in the renovations."

"So you do have other people staying here?"

"I phrased that poorly. Only Ramona and I are actually staying here. The workers come in from the surrounding towns each morning."

"I wouldn't expect room service or someone to bring me fresh towels and make up my bed in the morning. All I need is a bed. Period."

"And an ocean view." She turned slightly to look at the house. "Well, thanks to my great-grandfather Edward Deverell and his Art Nouveau seashell-shaped design, there aren't many rooms in the house that don't have an ocean view."

He saw that she was softening and pressed his advantage. "I promise I won't be a bother. I'll even drive into the town you mentioned for my meals."

"Ramona would have a fit," she said dryly. "As soon as she found out you're recovering from an illness, you'd be lucky if she'd let you lift your own glass of water."

"Then I can stay?"

She was tempted to say yes, but in the end, caution won. Reluctantly, she shook her head. "No. But I will give you a bed for a few hours so you can rest before you start out again." He accepted her verdict in stony silence. "All right?" she asked.

"That would be very kind of you."

NICO STEPPED BACK to allow Caitlin to precede him through the massive carved black-walnut front doors, then followed her into the grand entry hall with its forty-foot ceiling and majestic staircase that climbed a story, then branched in opposite directions to climb another story.

Nico lifted his gaze to the top of the stairs and inhaled sharply at the sight of the twenty-foot stained-glass window there, crafted in vibrant greens, purples, golds and blues.

"Louis Comfort Tiffany designed the window to represent a peacock's head and body," Caitlin offered. "And the marble mosaic of the landing and stairway below it portray the tail."

Nico's gaze followed the vivid plumage of the peacock's tail as it fanned out in the breathtaking jewel-colors of the window to spread down the stairs to the hall floor. "The staircase is a work of art," he said, his voice hushed.

She nodded, pleased with his reaction. "The whole house is." She cast a glance at his pale face. "I forgot to ask you about your bags. Will you need them to freshen up?"

"Probably. They're in my car. I'll get them later."

"Fine." She gazed at him worriedly. He really didn't look at all well. "I think we'd better take the elevator."

His lips compressed. "I can manage the stairs."

Without a word, she took his arm and led him to one of the two gilded elevators tucked beneath the stairway. On the third floor, they walked down a wide hall.

If he were going to be allowed to stay only a few hours, he had to make the best of the time, Nico thought, trying to focus on the layout of the house. But all the doors that led off the hall were closed, and he couldn't summon his usual excellent sense of direction. "Is your room on this floor?"

"Yes, I'm a few doors down from the one I'm lending you, and Ramona's room is at the end of the hall. Traditionally, the family's private rooms are on this floor, but I'm planning on converting a series of suites on the fourth floor into rooms to be used exclusively for the family. That will give us more privacy, and we'll always have rooms available when we want to come and stay."

His strength dwindling rapidly now, Nico stared down at the Persian carpet, concentrating on putting one foot after the other. He had to learn the general arrangement of the place, he told himself, but later. For now, rest was the top priority.

She stopped in front of a door and opened it. "I put this room in order in case my mother decides to drop in."

He threw an unseeing glance around the large room. "Are you expecting her anytime soon?"

"I never know. Mother's a restless soul, and she travels a great deal."

He noticed a slight edge in her voice, but he didn't look at her face. He focused on the big bed, its tall headboard done in marquetry work of dark stained wood with inlaid ivory and mother-of-pearl. He crossed to it and eased himself down onto the cream-colored satin coverlet.

She walked to the French windows and opened them. "I'm not sure where my mother is at the moment. She has homes in both Paris and Boston, but the last postcard I received from her had a picture of the Great Pyramid of Giza on it." A tiny frown creased her forehead. "No telling where she is now." She swept her hand in an arc before her. "Well, there it is. An ocean view, as ordered." Turning, she found him sprawled on the bed, asleep.

She stared at him for a moment. Against the pale satin coverlet, his features seemed harder, his skin darker, his whole being more sensual and masculine. Like granite against silk, the contrast brought out the best of both.

She slowly shook her head, bewildered. She didn't think she'd ever had such a strong reaction to a man, and she couldn't explain it. But for some reason, she wasn't particularly bothered.

She pulled a blanket from the wardrobe. At his side, she started to bend over him with the cover but then stopped. His sweater had separated from the waistband of his jeans, and the lower a part of a large bandaged had been exposed. Immediately her heart went out to him. He hadn't been lying when he said he'd been ill. Actually it appeared that he'd either sustained some sort of injury or that he had had surgery. Speculation aside, whatever had been wrong with him, he'd obviously been through the mill.

With special care, she spread the cover over him, bringing it up to his chin. Straightening, she looked down at him. Exhausted though he obviously was, he still managed to maintain a certain wariness, a measure of control, even in sleep. There was no doubt about it. She was fascinated by him.

To be held spellbound by a powerful attraction could be dangerous. But it could also be exciting, pleasurable, fulfilling.

What was she going to do about it? she wondered.

STILL HALF-ASLEEP, Nico stretched. Pain in his side brought him wide awake to a dark room. A check of the luminescent dial on his watch informed him that he'd been asleep four hours. Damn. He had meant only to rest, not fall asleep.

He tried to recall what had happened. He remembered lying down, he remembered Caitlin walking to the window... Her voice... Her graceful movements...

He rubbed a hand over his face. He couldn't allow her to distract him. Swiftly he went over what he knew about her. Since earning her B.A. from Harvard, she'd held an executive position with Deverell, Incorporated, the family business in Boston that was run by her cousin, Conall Deverell, a shark of a businessman. She had an uncle who was chairman of the board of the company, another uncle who was a powerful United States senator. A third uncle had died a hero in the Korean War. Last year, she'd inherited SwanSea from her grandfather Jake Deverell, the distinguished diplomat and statesman. She had beauty, wealth, social position—and SwanSea. In poker that would be called an almost unbeatable hand. Fortunately, he was very good at playing poker.

Mindful of his wound, he carefully reached for the switch on the bedside lamp. As he sat up, a blanket slid off him, and he saw his two bags sitting on the floor beside the bed. The idea that someone had been in his room while he slept fired him to action.

He checked his bags to make sure nothing had been disturbed, then stripped off his sweater and jeans. In the bathroom, he flipped on the light and discovered a stack of thick white towels and washcloths piled beside a black-marble basin with gold faucets in the shape of swans' heads. Nice, very nice.

The house was astonishing, and its mistress...

Looking into the mirror at himself, he shook his head. *No, Nico. No.*

Deliberately, he dropped his gaze to the two large gauze-pads on the left side of his upper body, one over his ribs, the other below his heart. He peeled off the bandages and studied the healing wounds, a grim expression on his face. He supposed he should be grateful that Nathan Rettig hadn't been a better shot. A half inch more to the right and one of the bullets would have punctured his heart. As it was, the first bullet had grazed a rib, and the second had nicked his spleen. The result had been two hellish weeks in the hospital, with only policemen to keep him company.

He owed Rettig, Nico thought, and he was going to see that he was paid off in spades.

"HELLO," Caitlin said as Nico walked into the kitchen. She was sitting at the big walnut table in the center of the large room, drinking coffee. And until she saw him, she hadn't admitted to herself that she'd been waiting for him. "You're looking a little better."

"I feel better," he said honestly. He'd showered and changed into another pair of black jeans, along with a long-sleeved blue-and-black-striped shirt. He'd left the collar open and rolled up the sleeves to his forearms.

Sexy, she thought, then caught herself. "Next time you tell me you need a room, I'll respond very quickly."

The teasing glints in the green-gold eyes caused a tingling along his nerves. He ignored the sensation. "Sorry to conk out on you like that, but I guess the drive took more out of me than I realized."

"Don't apologize. I understand."

I hope not, he thought. "By the way, my bags were in the room when I woke, and I was wondering who brought them in."

The wariness in his seeemingly casual question brought her head up. "I did."

He concentrated on excluding all tightness from his expression. "Does that mean I can stay?"

The answer was on the tip of her tongue, but she forced herself to consider the situation one more time. She folded her hands on the table in front of her and stared at them for a moment. He was already here. She'd taken his bags upstairs herself. And there was her incredible fascination. *I've got to be crazy.* "I'd hate to see you have to start out this time of night and try to find a place."

"Is that a yes?"

She met his gaze. "I guess it is."

"Thank you," he said allowing himself to relax a degree. "Then please call me Nico."

"Fine, if you'll call me Caitlin."

Caitlin. The sound of her name rebounded softly through his brain, hitting all sorts of pleasure sensors. But then he remembered. It wouldn't pay to get too close or to become obligated to the people in this house. His plan was to get in, spend some time, accomplish his tasks and get back out. Smooth. Without causing a ripple. "I meant it when I said I don't intend to be a bother."

A small smile lifted her lips. "I know, and believe me, I don't have time to wait on you. But as it happened, it was no trouble for me to bring up the bags. Now, why don't you sit down, and I'll get your dinner."

"Dinner?"

The two men she'd been closest to in her life, Jake and Conall, were both formidable men with wide streaks of stubbornness and pride, so the objection Nico was about to make didn't deter her. She pushed away from the table and stood up. "Ramona made a huge casserole for the two of us tonight, and there was quite a bit left over. She left it warming for you."

She grabbed a hot pad, bent to pull the dish from the oven, and set it on the counter, talking all the while to distract him. "Remodeling this kitchen is going to be a hellish job. I really dread it. But in order to hold the type of up-to-date professional equipment we'll need for the resort, we're going to have to rearrange the kitchen and knock out a couple of walls to make it large enough. That one—" she pointed to a wall "—and the one beyond that. We'll lose the original servants' dining hall, but there are so many other rooms down here that we can connect into a dining room and lounge for our employees, we won't even miss it."

"Caitlin."

The sound of his iron-hard voice made her turn and look at him. "Yes?"

"I won't allow Ramona or you to go to extra trouble for me."

She shrugged. "You'll have to take that up with Ramona. I never tell her what to do." She scooped a large portion of the casserole onto a plate and set it in front of him, along with a basket of hot, crusty French bread.

"Beef bourguignonne?" he asked.

"Yes. Coffee?"

He nodded, thinking that there probably weren't a lot of people who would call beef bourguignonne a casserole, but his brief glimpses of the house had already begun to teach him that there were the rich, and then there were the *rich*.

Ignoring the food, he watched Caitlin as she moved around the room. Unfortunately he couldn't find a thing about her to fault. The sundress left her arms, throat and back bare, and revealed skin the color of ivory with a tantalizing undertone of gold. She was too damned beautiful for his peace of mind.

"Did you have any trouble finding the kitchen?"

He shrugged. "A little. I took the elevator down to the first floor, then headed in the general direction of the back of the house. It should have been simple, but it wasn't. I had no idea how huge this place is until I made a few wrong turns. And it hadn't occurred to me that the kitchen would be in the half basement." He took the cup of coffee from her outstretched hand and waited until she sat down again. Now was as good a time as any, he thought, to get a little information. Mainly, though, it would give him something else to think about beside her—something he badly needed. "What's the general layout of the place?"

There was a coiled alertness in him that seemed to have come out of nowhere, and it presented her with a moment's unease. She wondered if his controlled energy was natural, or if it came and went with each new difficult situation. No, she thought. This wasn't a difficult situation, and it was normal that he would want to learn how to get around the place where he'd be staying for a few days. She was being too suspicious. She smiled. "Knowing the layout would make it easier for you, wouldn't it?"

He nodded, his gaze dropping to the fullness of her curving mouth. She wore no lipstick, but a delicate sheen of moisture had been applied to the natural soft pink color of her lips. He'd like to kiss his way through that sheen of moisture to the taste and the texture beneath. A strong surge of hunger shook him; he picked up his fork and tried hard to dredge up interest in the beef bourguignonne.

"Okay, I'll give you a rundown on the highlights. Here in the half basement there's the kitchen, its pantries, which are quite extensive, service and storage rooms and the servants' dining hall. On the first floor, there's the great hall and staircase, of course, and all the formal rooms. The drawing rooms, a banquet hall, a smaller dining room, plus a library and the study are also on the first floor."

To his disgust, he was having trouble keeping his mind on business. He was finding Caitlin infinitely more absorbing than the information she was giving him, and he had to have the information. So far, nothing had worked out as he had planned. No, that wasn't true. His first objective had been accomplished. He was now an official guest at SwanSea. He'd just have to come to terms with this incredible attraction he had for Caitlin. He *had* to, because he wasn't sure ignoring her would be possible. "Study? That was your grandfather…Jake's study?"

"That's right, and it was also Edward's. The ballroom, a billiard room, a music room and more sitting rooms are on the second floor. I'm going to turn most of those sitting rooms into meeting areas. The third floor contains bedrooms, dressing rooms and sitting rooms, as does the fourth floor. Neither the third nor fourth floor has enough bathrooms or closets, so dressing rooms and some sitting rooms will be converted for those two relatively modern conveniences."

"What about the attic?"

"Storage and servants' quarters. One of these days soon, I've got to get around to going through all the trunks and boxes up there."

Interest quickened in him. "You don't know what's stored there?"

"Some of it I do. I used to play up there as a child. But a great many new things have only recently been transferred to the attic from rooms currently being worked in."

"I'm surprised you didn't store it."

"All the really valuable items *are* in storage. And a lot of the furniture has been sent off to refinishers. A first-floor sitting room, the study and the bedrooms on the third floor are practically the only rooms left with all of their furniture."

Having gotten a few of the answers he needed, he finished eating, then leaned back in the chair to study Caitlin. He could afford the luxury just this once, he assured himself. After all, greater knowledge could help him deal with her.

She was a woman who had had the best of everything all her life. She could coast through life on her beauty alone, not to mention her wealth, but by all accounts, she could have become a vital part of the Deverell organization if she'd stayed. Instead, she'd taken on a new and different challenge. "I'm curious. What made you decide to turn this place into a resort?"

She smoothed her thumb and finger around the porcelain rim of her coffee cup, a gesture that unexpectedly brought life to his lower limbs and made him shift uncomfortably in his chair.

"In college, I'd majored in business because it seemed like the thing to do at the time, and it was relatively easy for me. When I graduated, I *naturally*—" she grinned, giving the emphasized word significance and charm "—went to work at Deverell's. I was in the public relations department, and I'd begun to feel restless when I inherited SwanSea."

"Restless about where you were in the company?" he asked, totally engrossed in what she was saying.

"No. Public relations wasn't the problem. I could have worked in any department I chose, including assisting Conall, my cousin. But I had found a certain confinement and rigidity to the business world that had begun to chafe."

"Even in a company where you must have had a certain amount of power?"

"Yes, because I would never have abused that power."

Somehow he'd known that, he thought.

"Your family must have hated the idea of you turning your back on the business." His had, in spades. The fights between him and his father had been terrible.

"They called me crazy at first," she admitted. "They couldn't see the practicality. But they have their own warm feelings for SwanSea, and now they can't wait for the grand opening."

"But running SwanSea will be a business, too."

The sudden luminosity of her expression caught him unaware and caused a tightening in his gut.

"Yes, but SwanSea is different somehow. This place has been a part of me all my life. It was my first home. And even after my mother and I left and lived in Boston, I always considered myself a part of it. I know exactly what's right for it, and I've thought things through very carefully. The style of life Edward Deverell had in mind when he built the place is no longer practical. When I inherited SwanSea, I had several options, one being to open it for tours. But it would have been too dispassionate to have groups of tourists tramping through its rooms."

"Dispassionate?"

She grinned. "You probably think that's a funny way to speak of a house, but I can't be unemotional when it comes to SwanSea. Remember? You noticed its strength. The house is almost a living force."

He nodded, recalling the strange feeling that had

come over him at his first glimpse of the house. It had seemed to have a rhythmic energy. Even more strange, it had seemed to be welcoming him. He'd chalked up the reaction to his weariness.

Then there had been his reaction to Caitlin. As much as he had tried to ignore it, he had been strongly attracted to her. He hadn't expected that with simply a look, a gesture, or a smile, she could make his insides catch fire. He'd slept, awakened rested and found he still wanted her.

The burning she saw in his eyes gave her momentary pause, a burning that singed her to her fingertips. But was the heat really there? she wondered, or was she seeing something she wanted to see?

"I also decided against giving SwanSea to the government or the state." Her lips twisted wryly. "The truth is, I'm selfish. The romantic side of me wants always to be able to call SwanSea home, to come and stay whenever I want, to have a part in its future; hopefully in the years ahead, my children will take over for me. The practical side of me wants to see that SwanSea is preserved, but preserved in such a way that it's not simply another sideshow or an empty monument. By turning it into a resort, I'll be able to control what happens to it for as long as I live." She stopped, no longer able to doubt the expression in Nico's dark brown eyes. The look was a sensual wanting that left her weak.

"You're quite a lady, Caitlin Deverell," he said softly. "Romantic *and* practical. You've figured out how to safeguard and protect the house and, at the same time, how to give it back its life."

"SwanSea deserves loving attention. This is a gracious house, and I want to give other people the opportunity to come to know SwanSea the way I do, to stay here for however long they can, to rest, to draw energy from its atmosphere, to love and be happy within its walls."

He gave a short laugh, attempting to break free of the web of desire that bound him tighter with her every word, his every breath. "I guess it's a good thing I'm seeing the house now. When it opens, I probably wouldn't be able to afford to stay."

She frowned, taking his lighthearted words seriously. "I wish we weren't going to have to charge so much, but I'm afraid the value of SwanSea's contents along with the high costs for renovation, insurance, upkeep and staff dictate high prices. The resort will be *very* exclusive, but that's the compromise I've had to make to accomplish the things I want." Suddenly a puzzled look came over her face. "What do you mean you couldn't afford to stay here. What about DiFrenza's?"

"My family's business, not mine." He gave her a smile meant to divert. "I forgot to ask how much you're going to charge me, didn't I?"

Feeling a warmth in the pit of her stomach, she returned his smile. "Yes, but I wouldn't worry about it. With SwanSea so far from being finished, I can guarantee your bill will be very affordable."

"You have quite a task in front of you."

"It's a labor of love. SwanSea is one of the best surviving examples of Art Nouveau in America. Everything from the design of the house to the door handles, panelings and moldings creates a unity." Suddenly she had to swallow against a dry throat. Unable to go on any further, even about a subject she loved so much, she sat back, aroused, excited and unsettled. She was used to the passion she felt for her birthplace, but the turbulence

Nico had created within her was something she wasn't sure how to cope with. She tried again. "I'm really sorry you're not seeing the house at its best. You'll have to promise to come back when the restoration and renovations are completed." She gave a husky, uncertain laugh. "I'll give you a special rate."

He heard her uncertainty and understood she was drawn to him. He had far too much experience not to know that with a little effort he could have her. He shifted uneasily in his chair. The idea played with his mind, seducing him.

He brought his thoughts to a halt. If there was one thing he'd learned over the years, it was that hardly anything was simple and straightforward or what it seemed. Caitlin obviously hadn't learned that lesson yet, and he wasn't sure how he felt about being the one to teach her. There was an openness and a warmhearted quality about her—the complete opposite of himself.

Damn this edginess, he thought angrily. Coming here *had* seemed like the perfect plan. "I think I'd better call it a night."

It was a shock for Caitlin to realize she didn't want Nico to go. In her twenty-six years, she'd been through the normal ups and downs with men that most women of her age experience. But the strong, instant response to him was unique. He had made no advances to her, but a look from him was as potent as a kiss from any other man she'd known. Involuntarily, her gaze was drawn to his lips. They were strong and firm, and he would know exactly how to use them on a woman. "I'll go up with you, to make sure you have everything you need."

He closed his eyes against the sight of her, but he couldn't close down the functioning of his brain, and his imagination sprang into overdrive. What would it be like to reach across the table, pull her onto its top, and climb over and into her? Heaven, his body told him. Heaven.

He stood so quickly he bumped the table. The plates rattled, and an empty glass toppled over, then rolled off the table and crashed to the floor. The sound of the shattering glass was earsplitting in an atmosphere of aroused senses. "It's not necessary to come up with me. I have what I need, and I can find my own way."

Disappointed, she walked around the table and reached for his plate.

"I'll get it," he murmured and brushed her hand as he too reached for the plate.

Her gaze locked with his, and for a moment, Caitlin forgot everything but the strange aching need in her. "I'm just trying to help, Nico."

Lord, but her eyes were beautiful, he thought, even with the slight glint of hurt he saw in them. "I know," he whispered and wondered why he felt he was fighting the inevitable. He lifted his hand, intending to touch her cheek, but quickly dropped it to his side before he could brush the inviting softness. "It's just that I'm not used to being waited on."

"You live alone then?" It was a question she should have asked sooner. But then again, she couldn't believe his heart could belong to another—not with the hungry way he looked at her.

"Yes." He wasn't sure, but he didn't think he'd ever wanted to kiss a woman as badly as he wanted to kiss Caitlin. To lick, bite and taste her until he was sated. To take her, fill her, empty himself into her. And then do it again.

The tantalizing scent of her skin floated into his

brain, momentarily blocking caution. This time he touched her as he lightly stroked his fingers across one bare shoulder. Velvet. The urge to crawl inside her scented velvet skin was almost overpowering.

He closed his hand around her arm and pulled her against him. Everywhere her soft, curving body touched his, he felt heat. A muscle clenched in his jaw. He was going to take her.

In the next instant, he released her, unsure why.

Sanity. Training. A sense of self-preservation.

Whatever the reason, he was intensely grateful—and fiercely disappointed. "Good night, Caitlin."

"Good night."

A few minutes later, in his room, he carefully settled himself on the bed and covered his eyes with his forearm. Maybe if he couldn't see, he wouldn't be able to think. And if he couldn't think, he wouldn't be able to remember. But his senses were working overtime, and he could still feel her skin against his fingertips.

Damn whatever this thing was between him and Caitlin. Something in him ignited whenever he came near her, and she obviously felt the same way. It was almost as if each of them had exactly the right elements within them to strike sparks off each other. But sparks led to fire, and fire led to danger.

Slowly he lowered his arm. He couldn't let anything happen between them. No matter how much he wanted it. No matter how much she wanted it.

He was in no position to get involved with anyone right now, much less Caitlin Deverell. He just had to keep reminding himself: Caitlin wasn't the reason he was here.

And when the pain came and he couldn't sleep, he told himself it was from his wounds, not from wanting her.

CHAPTER TWO

LORD, HOW SHE'D WANTED Nico to kiss her last night, Caitlin remembered as she left the elevator on the first floor the next morning. She'd wanted it so much that when he'd told her good-night, she'd felt as if he'd inflicted a wound deep within her.

Nice going, Caitlin, she told herself, *and so much for all your caution.* She clicked her tongue in disgust. She should have saved herself a lot of time and trouble and agreed to let him stay as soon as he'd asked her the first time. And then, after all her turmoil, she'd spent most of her night trying to put yesterday and Nico DiFrenza into perspective.

She'd been spectacularly unsuccessful.

All her instincts were telling her that there was more to him than met the eye. Secrets. Parts that he wasn't showing. But deep inside, she felt a powerful pull toward him that she didn't understand and couldn't seem to fight.

A new feeling sparkled inside her, a feeling that was part excitement, part dread. She felt as if she were holding a hand grenade, and she wasn't sure who held the pin: she or Nico.

She sighed loudly, unaware that more than one stare followed her, curious at her unusual self-absorption. She felt nothing but impatience with the day's work that awaited her, but her list of things to do was long, and the first order of business was to speak with her foreman. She found him supervising several workers in the main drawing room. A huge room, it involved painstaking work to restore the original Art Nouveau style of the elegant swirling movements in the wood, metal and marble surfaces.

"How are things going, Mr. Haines?"

"Fine, Mistress Caty. Just fine."

His response brought her back to the reality at hand, and she hid a smile. Jeb Haines, a tall man with steel-blue eyes and a shock of gray hair tucked under a cap, had lived all his life in the small town five miles beyond the gates of SwanSea. Like so many of the men who were working here now, he had known her almost from the first day of her life. Mistress Caty had been his pet name for her, and he was a man set in his ways. But she didn't mind. The continuity of SwanSea and the people around it comforted her. "No problems?"

"Not any more than what you'd normally expect." He squinted at a young man perched high on a ladder, who was methodically and patiently stripping away several layers of varnish from the carved molding. "You take care up there, Richie. That molding was here before you were born, and if you treat it right, it'll be here after you're gone, too."

Richie threw the older man a grin. "You worry too much. Morning, Miss Deverell."

"Morning, Richie." She turned back to Jeb Haines. "He's right. You do worry too much. But I can't tell you how much I appreciate the conscientious work you're doing."

He lifted his hat, smoothed his hair, and replaced the hat. "Well now, I guess I do worry. But you know, this house is one of my earliest memories. I was a young boy during the times of your grandfather, Jake, God rest his soul. And your grandmother, Arabella—my, my, but she was a high-spirited lady. Me and my friends all had crushes on her, and we weren't the only ones, let me tell you."

Caitlin grinned. "That's what I've heard."

"Well, you heard right. And this house fairly glittered when they lived here. You can't see the house from town, but we used to make up all sorts of reasons to come down the road and have a look. 'Course, eventually the house was closed up, but I still loved to look at it. It was like as long as it was here, everything was all right. You know what I mean?"

"I know," she said softly.

"Then when we were building the church—oh, that must have been about twenty-five, twenty-six years ago now—I could see the house from the roof. What a sight that was."

"It must have been," she said, wondering fondly why Jeb Haines had missed the news that New Englanders were supposed to be taciturn. She glanced at her watch. "Conrad Gilbert will be here in about an hour," she said, naming the architect who was working with her on the restoration and conversion of the house. "Can you join us?"

"Just tell me where."

"Probably one of the second-floor sitting rooms. I'll come get you." She paused. "By the way, have you seen a tall black-haired man this morning?"

"Sure have. Said he was staying here."

"That's right."

"I think I saw him going into the study."

"Thank you."

As she strolled slowly toward the study, she told herself that there was no earthly reason why she should be seeking out Nico. As a matter of fact, there were probably several reasons why she shouldn't. But disturbingly erotic thoughts of him had kept her tossing and turning all night. She'd never seen that particular combination of danger, physical weakness and compelling power in a man before. She wanted to see him, to be near him, *now*.

Knowing very well that she should stay away, she went to him anyway.

She opened the study door and discovered Nico bent over the big desk. When he looked up and saw her, he closed a drawer.

A troubled line creased her brow as she gazed at Nico. With his self-assurance and inherent poise, he seemed to belong behind the desk with its commanding, rhythmic lines and its rich, exotic citron wood. And yet she couldn't shake the sense that he'd been searching for something. "What are you doing?"

With the manner of someone completely worry-free, he straightened and eased a hip down onto the desktop. "Good morning. I expected to see you in the kitchen when I came down, but Ramona told me you usually skipped breakfast."

"Ramona? You've met Ramona?"

"Terrifying lady."

"Terrifying?" Did he really mean that? Ramona had worked for her mother for twenty-four years, and never in all that time had she been frightened of her.

"She wouldn't let me cook. When I tried to insist, she threatened to bring me breakfast in bed tomorrow."

"Yes, I can see why that would terrify you." She spoke slowly, distractedly. Though his words seemed easy, unforced, she still couldn't help but feel something wasn't quite right.

He shrugged. "I gave in and let her prepare my breakfast."

She crossed the vast expanse of parquet floor to the front of the desk. "What are you doing in here, Nico?"

One dark brow rose. "Oh, I'm sorry. Is this off-limits?"

"No, of course not." She looked around the room. The morning sun heightened the golden tones of the furniture, the paneling and the floor. The overall effect was one of harmony and warmth. She felt neither of those things, but couldn't explain her unease.

Nico cursed silently. Her obvious disquiet at finding him riffling through the desk made guilt twist uncomfortably through him. Guilt was a new emotion to him. He didn't like it, and in this situation, it could be extremely bad. "You don't have a pen I could borrow, do you? I was writing a letter to my great-grandmother, and mine ran out of ink." He walked to a chair and side table by a window and picked up the pen lying across a piece of stationery half-filled with writing. He scratched the pen in circles over the paper, but no ink came out. "I thought maybe there might be a pen in the desk."

Caitlin let out a sigh of relief and hoped he hadn't noticed. How stupid of her to jump to the wrong conclusion. "I don't know about a pen, but there are probably crayons in the desk. I used to spend hours there, drawing pictures."

"What kind of pictures?"

She laughed. "Badly drawn pictures, I can assure you. And to answer your question, no, I don't have a pen, but I keep some in the kitchen. I started out working in my bedroom, then the paperwork spilled over into the kitchen. Yesterday, Ramona told me bluntly that I was crowding her out." She laughed lightly. "I'll be moving everything in here tomorrow."

He nodded while carefully phrasing his next words. "I couldn't help but notice the desk was pretty empty…."

"The desk hasn't been used for business in years. All of Jake's and Edward's personal papers are stored away."

"Here in the house?"

"For the most part. Just more things I have to go through." She drew a deep breath. Her earlier suspicions had prevented the awkwardness she'd expected after last night. But now she was suddenly uncertain what to say next. "How are you this morning? Did you rest well?"

She was wearing a sleeveless, white, curve-skimming shift that ended above her knees and made the ivory hue of her skin, the green-gold of her eyes and the cinnamon shade of her hair more vivid, more desirable. "I slept very well," he lied smoothly. "As a matter of fact, I thought I'd take a walk in a little while." What he heard himself say next shocked him. "Could you come with me?"

She hesitated and glanced at her watch. "I have a meeting in about an hour. After that, I'm free."

He told himself that it was only practical to ask her to join him on the walk. For instance, she might drop some small bit of information that he would find useful. "Why don't we meet in the kitchen? Ramona more or less ordered me to come back at about one for lunch. If I don't show up, I'm afraid to think what she might do." His comment was lighthearted, but Caitlin was looking at him with eyes so wide and an expression so serious, he decided he had to smile or kiss her.

His slow smile made her pulse race. *Caitlin, Caitlin, what are you doing?* she asked herself.

"ARE YOU GETTING TIRED?" she asked, interrupting what she'd been telling him about her plans to convert the carriage house into a guest house.

"No, actually I'm feeling much better than yesterday. It must be the sea air and my ocean view."

She laughed as he had intended. He enjoyed watching her laugh. And he enjoyed watching the way the sun seemed to touch her skin with a gentle golden color. And he just plain enjoyed watching her. It bothered him like hell.

She waved to two gardeners. "In Edward's day, there were over a hundred acres of gardens, all extensively landscaped. It wouldn't be feasible, though, for me to try to reclaim all of the land. Besides, I like the new thickets of pines that have grown up and the meadows of wildflowers that you find in the spring. But at least part of the grounds are on their way back to how they were in Edward's time."

There was that mix of the practical and the romantic, he thought, disconcerted because of how much he was intrigued. "I'm glad you're not going to try to reclaim all of it. Nature's way is usually best, not only for the people but also for the animals. We have quite a few that make their home at my great-grandmother's country house."

"What kind?"

"Oh, deer, squirrels, rabbits, raccoons." The corners of his mouth lifted slightly. "When I was a little boy, I'd spend hours trying to get the deer to eat from my hand."

"Did you succeed?"

"Yes. I had all the patience in the world then. I wonder where that patience went to."

"You don't feed the deer anymore?"

He hesitated, suddenly wondering why he'd even mentioned the deer. "On occasion I try. But if they don't come to me within a reasonable amount of time, I toss the oats where they can see them and leave."

"You know what I think?"

He shifted his weight from one foot to the other, uncomfortable at how easily he'd let this conversation slip out of his control. "I can't imagine."

"I think you might not suffer fools or your own weaknesses easily, but I bet when it counts, you still have patience, especially with people you care about."

He was utterly stunned by her assessment of him. As right as she was, it would be wrong for him to allow her to think too kindly of him. He wanted to snap back a retort, but much to his surprise, his answer held a tinge of sadness. "You don't even know me, Caitlin."

Staring at the sharp angles of his profile, she realized he had a point. But something inside her insisted that she did know him. She wasn't sure she trusted him, but she trusted herself, and being with him felt absolutely right. Nearing the edge of the bluff, she turned so that she faced the sea and the wind.

At any rate, her feelings for him weren't serious. Not yet. The pull might be strong, but they hadn't even kissed. No real damage had been done, she told herself, conveniently forgetting how she'd felt last night.

Inhaling the tang of the salt air, she gazed at the sight before her, a sight almost as familiar to her as her own image in a mirror, one that soothed and calmed. The gray water glistened in the early-afternoon sun. A lone fishing boat was silhouetted against the blue sky as it cruised past the island. Seagulls called and circled overhead.

"Who owns the island?" Nico suddenly asked.

"I do. It's part of SwanSea. There's a cottage on it."

"Does anyone live there?"

She shook her head. "When I was little, Mother and I used to sail over and have picnics. I need to check on the place soon."

"Exactly how long has it been since anyone from your family has been out there?"

"Years, probably. Ben Stephenson has been the caretaker here for as long as I can remember. He goes over once in a while, although there's nothing left of any value in the way of furnishings or paintings." She thought for a moment. "But the island is wonderful. I've visited islands all over the world, and I like that one best."

"Why?"

She considered the island with slightly narrowed eyes. "I think all its rocks and pines give it character and a sort of hardy, tough beauty. White sandy beaches and tropical flowers are nice, but—"

"You want more than a pretty postcard picture?"

"Definitely." She gazed up at him. "And what do you want?"

You, naked, beneath me in my bed. The unexpected thought hit him like a blow that was all the more brutal because he hadn't had a chance to prepare a defense.

"What do you mean?" he asked carefully.

"What would you like to see next?"

The answer was the same, he thought achingly. He had all the normal sexual needs and desires of a healthy male. In the past, he'd always taken care of his body's requirements in a prudent, discreet and uncomplicated manner with women who understood that affairs were nothing more than a game. But the needs and wants Caitlin made him feel were abnormal in their power, scope and demand. With her, a recklessness threatened to take over, and that wasn't good. He wanted her, but he couldn't have her, and the whole situation made him mad as hell. "It doesn't matter. Whatever you like."

"Then let's walk over to the tennis courts. I want to check on the progress of the work over there."

"Fine."

She glanced curiously at him, wondering why he suddenly sounded so abrupt. Finding no clue, she followed an impulse and took his hand.

He looked down at the hand she had placed in his. It was probably the most unthreatening gesture that had been made to him in his recent memory, and he found himself wishing he hadn't convinced her to let him stay.

"You know, Caitlin, some people think that Jack the Ripper was a member of the British royal family."

"Yes, so I've heard," she said, startled by his off-the-wall comment.

"The point is, you based your decision to let me stay here on the fact that I'm Elena DiFrenza's great-grandson."

"That was part of the reason," she said slowly.

"You realize, don't you, that I could be her great-grandson and still be an ax murderer in my spare time."

"In your spare time?" Amused, she asked, "Are you?"

"No."

"Then why bring it up?"

Sighing, he scrubbed his free hand over his cheek. "I'm sorry."

Her amusement faded as she realized he'd been serious. "Why would you say something like that, Nico? Tell me. I really want to know."

"Maybe, I was trying to warn you. I'm not an ax murderer, but, Caitlin, I'm a lot of other things that aren't so nice."

"Okay, then. You want to tell me about those others things?"

"No." He pulled his hand from hers. "And as a matter of fact, I think I'll go up to my room and rest for a while."

"I thought you said you weren't tired."

He wasn't, he thought, gazing down at her, feeling the need he'd begun to associate with her pound through his veins. Fortunately, he also felt the control he'd always depended on and a strained but still connected thread of decency. In his line of work, he didn't often encounter the basic sweetness and goodness Caitlin possessed. He had learned that her beauty was both inside and out. She didn't deserve the grief he might bring her, he thought. And, actually, dammit, neither did he.

"You said my being Elena DiFrenza's great-grandson was part of the reason you let me stay here. What was the other part?"

"When you stretched out on the bed yesterday, your sweater pulled up enough that I could see the bottom of your bandage."

"You saw my bandages?"

"Bandages? I saw part of one bandage."

A muscle in his jaw tightened, relaxed, then tightened again. "What else did you see?"

"You," she said softly, "asleep."

Nico read the sensual awareness in her eyes with a sinking heart and a hardening body.

He could not let whatever this was between them blossom.

Unable to prevent it, his gaze dropped to her breasts, and he saw her stiffened nipples outlined against the white bodice. She shouldn't be feeling those things, he thought with despair, even as a corresponding primitive reaction rose up inside him.

Fortunately there was something else. She had her doubts and uncertainties about him. He sensed them, heard them, as if she'd spoken them aloud.

Hold on to your doubts, Caitlin, he silently urged. *They may be your only salvation.*

SOMETHING AWAKENED NICO. He tensed, trying to orient himself to his surroundings. Raising up on his elbows, he scanned the darkened room until he was sure he was alone, then collapsed back onto the pillows and drew a hand across his sweat-soaked brow. He had been dreaming of lovely green-gold eyes and ugly copper-and-brass bullets.

Immediately after dinner, he had pleaded fatigue and retired to his room, badly needing distance between Caitlin and himself. Once in bed, he'd fallen into a deep sleep. But now he heard something….

Music. A lilting melody drifted through the open windows and into his room with the night air. What was that tune? It sounded familiar, but he couldn't place it. And who was playing music at—he checked his watch—midnight?

He rolled off the bed, reached for his pants, and dressed so quickly that he left the room without taking time to button his shirt.

Following the music, he made his way through the halls and rooms of the huge house. He walked through shades of darkness and shadows overlaid by shadows, and he didn't once think of his reasons for coming to SwanSea. It was the music that drew him. Or so he told himself.

Downstairs in one of the drawing rooms, where dust-covers took on the odd shapes of the furniture beneath them, he discovered the source of the music—an old upright Victrola phonograph with a 78-rpm record playing on it. And outside the open doors on the veranda, Caitlin stood at the balustrade.

"Caitlin?"

She turned, her absorbed expression clearing as she saw him. "Hi. What are you doing up?"

"The music woke me."

She looked startled for a moment, then glanced up to his room. "I'm sorry. I didn't even think about being on the same side of the house as your bedroom."

"It's all right." He slid his hands into his pockets and strolled toward her, his gaze roaming intently over her. She was wearing peach satin lounging pajamas, with the legs wide at the bottom, a lacy camisole, and her hair like fire against the overjacket.

She looked too beautiful, too desirable.

He felt too much on edge, too full of desire.

He should return to his room, he thought, and in the next moment gave in to his curiosity. "What are you doing up?"

"Oh, I don't know. It just seems to be one of those nights when I'm finding it hard to go to sleep."

"Do you have many nights like that?"

"Occasionally…when the events of the day refuse to be still and rest until the morning."

"That's an interesting way to put it."

Was it? she wondered. Actually, she was too caught

up in him to be sure of what she'd said. She had only to cast her eyes to the enticing space between the edges of his unbuttoned shirt to see the fine black hair that covered his chest. And she had only to inhale to breathe in the masculine scent of his flesh. "What about you? Do you ever have trouble sleeping?"

"Not lately," he said, a tinge of self-disgust in his tone. "I put my head on the pillow, and I go out like a light."

She laid her hand on his arm in a gesture of comfort. "It won't last. You'll get better."

He glanced down at her hand, feeling heat from her touch instead of the comfort she'd intended. Casually, he moved his arm and dislodged her hand.

He was trying to do what was right with her. Lord knew he was trying.

"I'm already better," he said. "I've always healed quickly, and I had a feeling that as soon as I could escape from that damned hospital, I'd improve rapidly."

"Escape?"

"A figure of speech." The peach satin of her outfit took on added luster in the silvery moonlight. He reached out one finger and touched the shoulder. Nice. But he was sure that the sensuousness of the material was nothing compared to her skin.

"You know, I haven't asked what you do for a living."

He stilled. After a moment, he said, "I'm a lawyer."

"A lawyer? That's interesting."

"Not as interesting as whatever happened today to worry you so much you can't sleep."

She supposed it would sound strange to him if she told him that since their meeting yesterday, he had begun to dominate her thoughts to the point that the normal course of her life seemed to be altering. It sounded strange, even to her. She settled for part of the truth. "I received another postcard from my mother. This one had the Taj Mahal on the front of it."

"So she's visiting India. Why should that worry you?"

Her mouth twisted with rueful humor. "India doesn't bother me. Neither does Egypt. What does is that she's been flitting from one country to another for years now. She can't seem to stop. It's as if she's searching for something."

"And she's done this for how long?"

"She started at the same time I entered college. We lived in Boston during my school years, and she was there for me. Back then it was just the two of us, along with Ramona, of course. It was only later that she became so restless."

"What about your father?"

"I don't have one."

He nearly came back with a lighthearted comment about how it was biologically impossible not to have a father, but the serious expression on her face kept him silent. He reached out to her, meaning to comfort her as she had tried to comfort him, but with his hand on her arm, her expression changed, and his heart skipped a beat. Desire and need—emotions he'd been attempting to keep banked down inside himself—were plainly written on her face. She wasn't as aware of the possible repercussions as he was. She was simply a woman who wanted a man.

How long had it been since anything had been that simple for him, he wondered, beginning to harden and hurt. And why shouldn't he allow himself the pleasure of basic simplicity where nothing mattered but the two people involved?

Why? he asked himself. Let me tell you why, Nico.

A tremor shuddered through him as he tried to control his unraveling resolve. He had no idea how long his fevered mind had shut out the dull, rhythmic, scratching sound, but he heard her say, "It's the record. I'll get it."

She disappeared through the high-arched doorway into the drawing room, and he eagerly seized the short time she was gone to take himself in hand. But the music began again—slow, melodic and haunting. And then Caitlin reappeared, bringing her own melodic and haunting qualities into the air surrounding him. He drew in a deep breath and smelled her fragrance and femininity. What could he do? He couldn't stop breathing. Was he destined always to have her scent with him, in his lungs, in his pores?

He concentrated on the music. "What is that song?"

"George Gershwin's 'Someone to Watch Over Me.' It's one of my favorites. My grandfather saw to it that I cut my teeth on Gershwin and Cole Porter. *Literally*." She laughed softly as she remembered. "He sang songs like 'Isn't It Romantic,' and 'Embraceable You' to me as lullabies, and later, when I was older, he danced me around and around the ballroom to 'Night and Day' and 'Begin the Beguine', with my feet on his."

For years, Jake Deverell's pictures had filled newspapers as he troubleshot one world crisis or another for the government. Nico tried to imagine this powerful, formidable man dancing with his granddaughter while she balanced on his toes. He found he liked the picture. But even more, he liked the image of her in his own arms.

She laughed again, and the silvery sound stroked his spine.

"It was quite a sight, I can tell you. I was such a gawky, awkward young thing."

"You must have been a beautiful child, because you take my breath away as a woman."

Suddenly, inevitably, her body was burning for his touch. "Dance with me," she whispered huskily.

At first he wasn't sure he had understood her. "What?"

She moved to him and put her arms around him. "Dance with me."

A shock of heat ran through him and told him everything he needed to know about why he had been so careful until now to avoid holding her in his arms. Instinctively he had realized how it would be to have her against him. She was satin, sweet-smelling skin, and soft curves. Everything lovely and desirable. And inside he was dying with need for her.

She stared up at him, her head back, the long line of her throat exposed, her hair streaming down her back. He put his arms around her and pulled her closer. Clouds of music and moonlight, drifts of sea breezes—and most of all Caitlin—threatened his common sense. But Nico was beginning to wonder why he was bothering to resist. She wanted him, and he sure as hell wanted her. He was playing with fire, but he had never had a burn that didn't heal. Where was the harm?

Somewhere in the back of Caitlin's mind, she was aware that they weren't dancing. Not that she had really wanted to dance. If she'd had a conscious thought at all, it was that she wanted to learn the feel of his hard lines, strong arms, firm lips. *Him.*

"Nico," she whispered.

Slowly, methodically, he wrapped long silky strands of her hair around his hand until his hand was tight against her scalp and he controlled the position of her head. "Yes," he said. "Yes." Then his mouth came down on hers, and his tongue thrust hotly into her mouth.

She gave herself up to the kiss and to him as a low moan escaped her throat. She'd imagined this kiss, yearned for it, but she wasn't prepared for its reality. His tongue made outrageously intimate forays into her mouth that inundated her senses with new sensations. Her knees threatened to buckle, but he held her tightly to him, so tightly, it seemed that he was trying to make her part of him. The idea didn't frighten her at all.

He parted her satin jacket, then delved beneath the camisole and closed his hand over her breast. She was fuller than he had thought, more perfect. And the rigidity of her nipple thrilled him. He rolled the taut peak between his fingers, thinking he could spend hours lavishing attention on her breasts and nipples and never grow bored. He salivated to have as much of her as possible in his mouth. He could almost taste the honey-sweetness of her now. And she wouldn't protest. This sure knowledge nearly drove him past the edge of reason. But he held on. He wanted both her and reason, and he wasn't yet ready to admit that was impossible.

Passion unfolded in her body and spread, taking possession. His hands and mouth had an extraordinary sureness that brought her nerves alive. He was seducing her with ease, but the moment seemed too right for Caitlin to resist. His actions and his obvious arousal left no doubt that he wanted her.

In a corner of her mind, she realized he completely controlled her. The idea carried excitement with it, yet the steel-hard control he kept over himself bothered her. Still, she skimmed her hand inside his shirt, along the smooth flesh of his back. Muscles rippled beneath her palm, giving her some sense of his strength, making her tremble with passion. A feminine hunger raged within her to touch all of him—every dip and rise of his body, every plane and curve. She wanted to learn him intimately, and she let her hand rove freely, but when she encountered the tape securing one bandage, she hesitated.

And then he was pulling away.

"The record."

She blinked as if she'd suddenly come from complete darkness into a brilliantly lighted room. "What?"

"The record's over," he said gruffly.

Confused, she stared at his dark expression, trying to decipher what was wrong, and it was a moment before she became aware of the insistent scratching of the needle as it tracked against the record. Her limbs quivering with weakness, she walked into the drawing room, turned the Victrola off, then leaned against the tall mahogany cabinet for support.

She'd never in her life experienced anything like what had just happened between her and Nico. A touch of his lips had sent her out of control—an experience he obviously hadn't shared. *Okay*, she thought, rubbing her forehead, *what now?*

She was torn. She was beginning to wish desperately for something more to develop between her and Nico than a brief brush with passion, although she sensed it would be foolish of her to try to pierce the mystery that surrounded him. But in the final analysis, like the tides and the seasons, some things were inevitable, and she felt she had no choice.

When she came back to the veranda, she found Nico leaning against the balustrade, his shirt buttoned, his arms crossed over his chest. He appeared very hard, very closed.

She halted beside him, facing in the opposite direction, and folded her hands on top of the ornamental barrier. "Did I touch a tender spot?"

"No."

"Were you afraid I would?"

He glanced at her. She was gazing out at the night-shrouded ocean, and the confusion he saw on her face filled him with anger—an anger directed solely at himself. "No."

She ran her tongue over her bottom lip. "I was just wondering.... When you were kissing me, you seemed so guarded."

No woman had ever sensed that he was holding part of himself back during any phase of his lovemaking. He wasn't sure he'd been aware of it himself. Not until now. Caitlin was too perceptive for her own good. "You're mistaken."

"I don't think so."

He ground his teeth together in frustration. Why didn't she just leave it alone? "Maybe I feel it wouldn't be a good idea to become involved with you."

"Is that because you're involved with someone else?" Her heart beat very fast as she waited for his answer, and it seemed a long time coming.

"No."

"Then why, Nico?"

He shot out his arm, clasped the side of her throat, and pulled her in front of him. Each word he spoke carried a biting emphasis. "It could be I'm afraid to lose control with you, because if I did, I wouldn't know where it would end."

She swallowed hard. "Do you really believe that?"

He stared broodingly at her, his thumb stroking up and down the sensitive cord at the side of her neck. "Maybe."

"You're a difficult man to get to know, Nico Di-Frenza."

"And you, Caitlin Deverell, are too damn easy to want." Like a junkie needing a fix, he pressed a hard kiss to her lips. It seemed a long time before he released her. But once he did, it seemed too short a time.

He waited for her to say something and cursed the continued silence. This kind of tension couldn't continue. Something had to give between them, or there would be an explosion. "You didn't put on another record."

She folded her shaking hands on top of the balustrade. "No. That's the kind of music I love, but I wasn't sure if you liked it or not."

"When I listen to music, it's usually classical or opera, but I liked what you were playing."

She shifted slightly, so that she could see him better. His answer had been curt, but at least he was talking to her, telling her something about himself. "You don't seem the type of man who would like opera."

The slight upward curve of his mouth surprised her. "Your grandfather raised you with Gershwin and Porter. My great-grandmother raised me with Puccini and Verdi. She's from Italy, and to her, music is opera." His smile slowly faded. "My mother died when I was twelve, but even before then, Elena was a strong force in my life. Now she's ill. Her nurses call me whenever she's having a particularly bad day. It makes her furious when I show up, because she doesn't want me to worry about her. She fusses at me, calling me by my full name, Niccolo, and telling me all the reasons why I shouldn't have come."

An expression of incredible tenderness came over his face, causing Caitlin's breath to catch in her throat.

"I put on *Madame Butterfly* or *La Bohème,* then I sit with her and hold her hand. It never takes long for her to settle down, and soon she begins to talk to me in her native tongue of the times in Italy during the First World War. It was the hardest time in her life, but also the happiest. When she was seventeen, she met and married a young man who was working in the Italian Underground. A year later, he was killed, and she was left widowed and pregnant." He paused. "She goes on and on about those times. Sometimes I wonder if she knows what she's saying. But her mind seems very clear, and somehow talking of those times seems to soothe her."

"I'm sure a lot of it has to do with your being there."

Caitlin's soft voice drew his gaze to her, and he remembered. She was an innocent in all this, a pawn. She had trusted him...opened up her home to him. And he was a first-class bastard, a bastard who could easily fall in love with her if he wasn't careful. "We've always been close."

She misinterpreted his flat tone and raised her hand to his face. "I know how you feel. My grandfather's illness was very hard for me to watch. He'd always been such a vital man, but he didn't mind his going as much as I did. He was eager to see Arabella again."

He closed his fingers around her wrist, but he didn't pull her hand away. "His wife?"

She nodded. "I wish I could describe his expression to you—when he drew his last breath."

"You were there?"

"All my life he'd been there for me. I wouldn't have forgiven myself if I hadn't been there for him. And I was glad I was. He seemed so at peace, so happy. I knew without a doubt that he was with Arabella, so I grieved only for myself then."

Why, oh why, did she have to be such a special person? Feeling momentarily defeated, he gave in, drew her into his arms, and just held her.

Caitlin pressed her cheek against his chest. No matter what he'd told her about himself, she was certain there was much, much more to learn. He was a difficult, enigmatic man, but she was beginning to feel just as puzzled about herself. What were these sad-happy, confused-clear feelings she'd been having?

She'd had what she supposed could be termed a few "relationships" over the years, and along the way she had lost the normal number of illusions. She'd learned that fairy tales weren't real and that love could be confusing, sometimes even painful. None of her lessons in love had been traumatic, but now she realized that what she'd experienced in the past was milk toast in comparison to what she was going through with Nico. He shook her to the marrow of her bones.

She lifted her head and brushed a warm soft kiss across his lips. She felt him stiffen, then slowly relax and gather her closer to him. The control was still there, but so was the heat.

And the taste of Nico lingered on her lips long after he'd abruptly and quickly broken off the kiss and gone upstairs to his room. And still she found she couldn't sleep.

IN HIS ROOM, Nico dialed and waited. When the sleepy sound of Amarillo Smith's gravel voice came on the line, he said, "Rill, it's me."

"'Bout damn time you called. Where are you?"

"SwanSea."

"Good. I was afraid you wouldn't be able to get in."

Nico's mouth firmed. It might have been better if he hadn't. "I'm here. Anything new?"

"Not so far. Just lie low and get well."

It sounded so easy, he thought grimly. "Right."

"Are you in pain, Nico?"

"No."

"I just wondered. Your voice sounded funny there for a minute."

"I'm fine. Have you looked in on Elena?"

"She's doing well."

"Did you check to make sure she has everything she needs?"

"Of course." The acerbic tone of Amarillo's drawl indicated Nico had been stupid even to ask.

Nico's lips quirked. Amarillo had been raised in the oil fields of west Texas, and his frontier mentality made him a law unto himself. No one understood why he was in Boston, but he was as hard and as tough as they came and always got results. And he was the one man Nico trusted with his life.

"Got a pencil, Rill? I'll give you this number."

CHAPTER THREE

RAMONA, A BIG-BONED WOMAN with shoulder-length salt-and-pepper hair and a no-nonsense manner, filled Caitlin's cup with steaming black coffee, then stood back and fixed her with a critical stare. "Why do have shadows under your eyes? Aren't you feeling well?"

"I feel fine."

"What about those shadows?"

"The sun isn't out today, and the light is probably making every one of us look ghastly." She smiled. "Except you, of course. You always look wonderful."

"So do you...usually. And you can quit trying to butter me up."

She sighed. "I'm telling you, the rain is giving the light a gray cast."

"I don't believe a word of it. If you don't start taking care of yourself, young lady, I'm going to have two patients."

"Which you'd love. Come on, admit it. The great sorrow of your life is that you don't have enough people to fuss over."

Ramona's lined face took on a pensive expression. "I always thought Julia would marry and give you brothers and sisters. It would have been the best thing for her."

"I agree." Caitlin's words were sincere, but today she

wasn't in the mood to listen to a rehash of what she'd heard time and again. She changed the subject to something she did want to hear. "How's Nico doing? I haven't seen him today."

Since their encounter on the terrace she'd done some serious thinking, and she now realized that Nico was the one who always pulled back when their encounters threatened to become too intimate or, as on the terrace, too passionate. She didn't know why he was reluctant to become involved with her, but she was coming to understand that with all his mystery and passion, he represented a danger to her well-being. And she was no clearer how she felt about him.

Except, she was very much afraid that, in spite of her better judgment, she was falling in love with him. The thing was, she'd inherited the Deverell pride. She'd never in her life pursued a man, and there was no reason why Nico DiFrenza should become the first.

Except she couldn't stop thinking about him. Or aching for him.

"Nico is getting better every day," Ramona said. "By the way, do you know what kind of surgery he had?"

"No." Caitlin smiled ruefully. "In fact, he's never admitted to surgery, just some vague illness. But I'm surprised you haven't asked him."

"Actually, I did. And he told me about his condition. But you know, I don't think he ever answered my question."

"I wouldn't worry about it. Like most men, I think he's just very sensitive about being ill. Anyway, whatever was wrong with him has obviously been taken care of."

"I suppose."

Caitlin glanced at her watch. "I better get moving.

Conrad Gilbert is due soon, but before he gets here, I want to run up to the attic. If I remember right, there's a chair up there with upholstery I want duplicated for a suite of rooms in the northwest wing."

NICO RESTED on his heels and rubbed his neck. He'd been in the attic for over two hours, and he'd only managed to search two trunks. He had thought that over the years, a family like the Deverells would have devised a more systematic way of storing their things. Apparently though, they were a family who tended to move forward, rather than spending time reflecting on the past. Admirable, but not at all helpful to him.

The creak of footsteps on the attic stairway took him by surprise. Quickly and quietly he shut the lid of the trunk he'd been searching. By the time Caitlin entered the musty room, he was standing by an arched window.

"Nico. I didn't expect to find you up here."

And he sure as hell hadn't expected her to come up here, he thought, eyeing her warily. She was wearing a jade-green tank top with a lacy appliqué on the front and crisscross straps in the back. Her faded denim shorts had a formfitting waist and full, flirty legs that made it resemble a sexy little skirt. Perfect outfit for mucking about an attic on a rainy day. Perfect outfit for driving him crazy.

His expression revealed none of what he was feeling but reflected the innocence of a small boy caught in a harmless prank. "It's the rain," he said by way of explanation. "It always makes me want to seek out an attic."

She smiled somewhat nervously as she noted that being away from him for a time hadn't changed the way his presence made her heart race. As startled as she'd been to encounter Nico and despite her recent resolution regarding him, she was very glad to see him. "How long have you had this condition?"

"Since I was a kid. Didn't you tell me you used to like to poke around up here?"

"Yes, and as you can see, I still do."

"Are you poking around for anything in particular?"

"Yes, a chair. I thought I remembered it being in this room, but I'm not sure."

She'd accepted his explanation without question, and he felt as if he were the worst kind of con man. He couldn't leave SwanSea yet, but there was a part of him that half wished she'd throw him out. "Maybe I could help you search for it."

"If you like. It's a pear-wood armchair with curved arms and legs, and cream-and-yellow upholstery."

"I haven't really looked around much, but it could be here. We could each search a different area if you like."

"Okay, but there's no rush." She lifted her tightly linked fingers in an awkward gesture. "What were you doing? I mean, have you been up here long?"

He shrugged. "No, not really. Did you know there's a great view from this window, even with the clouds and rain?"

She weaved her way around trunks, boxes and an assortment of furniture until she reached Nico's side. "You're right," she said, gazing out the window. "I'd forgotten how much more you can see from up here than down on the bluff."

Driven by a compulsion stronger than his will, Nico studied the pure line of her profile and discovered that her dark lashes feathered against her cheeks when she blinked. *Charming*. And her finely pored skin appeared luminous, even without makeup. *Beautiful.* And her lips parted slightly as she breathed in and out. *Tantalizing.* As he had all day yesterday, he relived the feel of her in his arms.

Without his being able to prevent it, she had gotten under his guard the night before last. He'd told her things about himself and his great-grandmother that no one outside the family knew. The people he could really talk to were so few, he'd been left wanting to tell her more. But that was impossible.

He'd kissed her and hurt to go further. And of course that too was impossible.

On impulse, she unlatched the window and pushed outward on the frame. It didn't budge.

"Stuck?" His voice was slightly husky.

She nodded, trying again. "It hasn't been opened in years."

"Let me see if I can do it." He gave the window one good shove, and it swung outward.

"Thanks. I thought the room could stand a little air." She turned and looked at him, and the smile on her face slowly faded as she took in the intensity of his eyes. She shouldn't read anything into the expression, she told herself. He just happened to be a man with intense eyes.

So he'd kissed her. He wasn't the first.

So she'd melted when she'd never melted before. It meant nothing.

What's inside you, and why do I care so much? she asked him silently. There were layers to this man that no one would discover unless he allowed it—she'd learned that much. And she had resolved that if something developed between them, he would have to make the first move.

But his nearness was sending jittery little thrills skittering along her nerve endings; she stuck her hand out the window and let the gentle rain cool her skin.

Before the cooling was done, he drew her hand in from the rain and brought the inside of her wrist to his mouth. He pressed his lips against the nearly translucent skin and felt her pulse race. Then his tongue darted out to lick away the rain.

"I missed seeing you earlier," he heard himself murmur. What the hell, he thought wearily, he was simply trying to divert her. And licking rain from her wrist was as good a way as any. How could he have known how delectable he would find her flesh?

"I was busy," she said with a catch in her voice.

"That's what Ramona said." He brushed his lips back and forth over the sensitive underskin of her wrist and heard her intake of breath. *Oh, Caitlin, why do you have to be so damned sweet?*

"She told me you were feeling better this morning."

He dropped his arm, taking her hand to his side. "As soon as it stops raining, I thought I'd try to jog a little."

Protest sprang immediately to her lips. "You shouldn't. You'll hurt yourself."

"I said a *little*." His dark gaze fixed on her lips, and he bent and placed a kiss at the corner of her mouth. It was as much as he would allow himself. "Don't worry," he whispered, his breath fanning her lips. "I'm very good at taking care of myself." He traced the outline of her lips with his tongue, then again kissed the corner of her mouth. It was enough, he thought. After all, he was just playing. But her shudder tore through him.

"I'm glad."

He'd accomplished what he'd set out to do, he thought. She was distracted. He wouldn't have to kiss her again. He straightened, reached for a lock of her cinnamon hair and wove it through his fingers. "How about you, Caitlin? Are you good at self-preservation?"

She gave a shaky laugh. "I suppose I'm adequate. I couldn't have reached twenty-six if I wasn't."

"You're just a baby."

Her tongue moistened her bottom lip. "How old are you?"

His gaze followed the action. "Thirty-four." He released her hair and skimmed the pad of a finger across her moistened bottom lip. "But most of the time I feel eight-four."

Any minute now, she was going to lose track of their conversation, she reflected. All she could think of was how close he was standing to her and how much he seemed to be touching her. "Why would you feel that old?"

"Life, Caitlin," he said roughly. "Life. Take my advice and stay the same age as you are biologically, for as long as you can."

"H-how would you recommend I do that?"

His jaw clenched until he felt pain shoot up the side of his face. "Stay away from me."

"Stay…" To her mortification, tears filled her eyes. "What?"

"Damn." He jerked her to him and crushed his mouth to hers. His tongue found the hot velvet of her mouth, and need exploded in him, nearly undoing him. Thoughts crowded into his brain, thoughts of taking her down to the floor with him, undressing both of them, locking their bodies together, and learning her from the inside out. It was a bad, bad idea. It was the wrong time, the wrong place, the wrong person…. But Lord, how he wanted her.

Lightly he grated his teeth along the length of her tongue, eliciting a moan from her. Caitlin had no thought of holding back. He'd jerked her to him as if wanting her had gotten the better of him. The idea thrilled her, and at the same time she understood. Maybe there was a reason why she should fight against him and the way he made her feel, but if there was, she couldn't think of it.

He thrust both hands upward beneath the wide legs of her shorts and the lace trim of her panties and took hold of the rounded contours of her bottom. The sensation of kneading the firm flesh satisfied him for only a moment. Everything in him was clamoring for him to bury himself inside her and seek relief for this fever that was driving him crazy. Without relinquishing his hold on her, he lifted her against his pelvis, then pulled her into him hard, so that she could feel the strength of his desire. When Caitlin wrapped her legs around his hips and tightened her hold on him, he nearly came undone.

The fresh smell of rain came through the window and mingled with the scent of their need. They strained together as a dark fire blazed in and around them.

Caitlin felt as if she were balancing on a precipice and the uncertainty made her feel helpless.

Nico had an intense driving need for her, and the certainty made her feel strong.

Uncertainty. Certainty. Helplessness. Strength. Whatever... She couldn't, wouldn't let him go until the hunger growing inside her was assuaged.

The muscles in his back shifted and moved beneath her hands as he began lowering them to the floor.

"*Caitlin.* Caitlin, are you up there?" Ramona called.

Nico stilled and muttered a curse. Then, before she

could protest, he set her on her feet and almost ripped her arms from around his neck.

"Caitlin?"

"Yes?" she said, but her voice was too weak to reach Ramona, who she knew was standing at the bottom of the attic stairs.

"Caitlin!"

"Answer her, dammit," he ordered in a harsh whisper.

Nico's eyes were burning with an anger that bore right through her. She cleared her throat and called, "What is it, Ramona?"

"Conrad Gilbert is here."

"Tell him to make himself comfortable, and I'll be down in a few minutes."

"All right." There was a brief silence, then, "Are you okay? You sound—funny."

She bent her head and rubbed her temple. "I'm fine. I'll be down shortly."

The rasping of their heavy breathing sounded loud in the quiet attic room as Ramona's footsteps receded. Caitlin could feel the heat from Nico's body on her skin, but the continued silence between them stretched out until she couldn't take it anymore. Uncaring that her eyes revealed all the hunger she was feeling, she said, "I'll tell Conrad I can't see him today, Nico. I'll—"

"No."

"But—"

His teeth ground together as he reflected how close all his fine resolutions had come to being blown straight to hell. "I said it before, and I'll say it again. Stay away from me."

"What are you talking about? Something just happened between us—"

"Something that damn well shouldn't have." A hard dark mask descended over his face. "Stay away from me, Caitlin, and I'll stay away from you!" He wheeled and stalked from the room.

Caitlin bit her lip and wrapped her arms tightly around her waist. Devastated, she stood very still, knowing it would hurt to move, to think, to recall what had just happened. Long minutes passed, but no relief came.

Finally, slowly, with heavy automatic movements, she began her search for the chair. The sight of the trunk gave her momentary pause. The lock hooked in the hasp wasn't completely closed.

"That's odd," she murmured aloud. "I thought all the trunks were locked."

THE NEXT FEW DAYS blurred for Caitlin. She dealt efficiently with crises as they arose. The morning after the scene in the attic, she discovered that the wrong wallpaper pattern had been put up in one bedroom. Much to the consternation of the workmen, she ordered the paper stripped. The next day, she caught a painter about to use too bold a shade of peach in the main drawing room and had to explain to him that the Art Nouveau period was one of rich but muted colors and that she wanted a softer color. She knew she was being a perfectionist, but where SwanSea was concerned, everything had to be just right.

Obsession with work blocked out thoughts of Nico—sometimes for minutes.

She went out of her way to avoid him, not because he had told her to but because she felt seeing him again would be like exposing an open wound to more injury.

But by the time the electricity blew on the third day,

she had begun to be annoyed with herself. Since when had she become so fragile? she asked herself. *Since Nico came to stay,* she answered.

After discovering that a mistake had been made when the new wiring was installed, she put in a call to the electrical subcontractor. Then she realized Nico needed to be told they would be without electricity for a while, perhaps even a few days. Her first thought was to send Ramona to find him, but she quickly vetoed the idea. *Enough of this,* she decided. She had a strong backbone, and it was time she used it.

NICO CAME to a sudden stop by the marble fountain in the center of the conservatory and lasered a sharp gaze around the immense iron-and-glass building. He heard nothing now, and he knew that he was alone. But…just for a moment there, he had thought he heard laughter, like a haunting echo of long ago.

He shook his head, puzzled by the intense interest he felt for the great house, its land and its buildings. SwanSea was built on the detailed and opulent scale nearly unbelievable and almost impossible to achieve in present times. But his interest went deeper than the awe that was natural upon seeing for the first time the wonders of this century-old house.

But it was as if the house had reached out and taken possession of him, so that slowly he was coming to understand Caitlin and her fierce feelings for her inheritance.

Procrastination had never been a part of his makeup, but this afternoon he had decided to explore more of the grounds of SwanSea instead of continuing his investigation of the attic as he'd promised himself.

He'd taken a stroll over to the pool house, large

enough to accommodate a couple of families easily. According to Caitlin, it had been built in the 1920s after her grandfather had taken ownership of SwanSea. Nico had spent some time wandering through its bowling alleys, squash courts, the gymnasium, the Turkish bath and the fabulous indoor swimming pool. Then he had made his way here.

Sinking onto a wrought-iron bench, Nico exhaled heavily. The sun was setting on the west side of the conservatory. Golden light flowed through the big glass panes, filling the inside of the nearly translucent building with currents of sunshine that coiled and curled around the statues and the orange trees growing beneath the crystalline roof.

His recuperation was coming along nicely, but in a call to Amarillo he had learned it wasn't safe for him to leave SwanSea—too many people were still looking for him. And in a call to his great-grandmother, he had promised her that he would continue his search.

How much longer could he stay here without losing his sanity? He'd had many opportunities over the last few days to watch Caitlin from afar. He'd envied every man at whom she'd smiled. He'd been jealous of anyone with whom she'd spoken. And worst of all, as he lay in bed every night, the knowledge that she was in her room just down the hall chafed at him until he felt raw.

His desire for her had grown daily until he'd almost become used to the pain. That day in the attic had nearly been his undoing. Since then, a lot of his time had been taken up with remembering the way the tantalizing scent of her skin could wind around a man's body until he thought he'd suffocate if he didn't have her.

He had to stay away from her.

"Nico?"

His head jerked around as she made her way along a path between flower beds newly readied for planting. At the sight of her, his body tensed and his chest began to hurt.

Nearing him, she nervously smoothed her damp palms down the full skirt of her sleeveless jade-green sundress. "You're a hard man to track down," she said.

He sensed her unease, but he couldn't smile easily to reassure her, and he couldn't take his eyes off her. Her sudden and unexpected presence had heightened and intensified the aching pain he'd felt these last days—and the sensation was the difference between holding his hands toward a fire and feeling its warmth, and thrusting his arms into the fire.

He came to his feet. "Was there something in particular you wanted to see me about?"

"Yes. We've had some trouble up at the house and—"

"Trouble?" Alarm turned his muscle to steel.

She eyed him warily. "I'm afraid so. We have no electricity." She shrugged, trying for nonchalance. "I'm not sure what happened. Something blew something. The electrician will be out first thing in the morning. Tonight, though, and maybe for a few days to come, it will be candlelight. I thought you should know."

He exhaled slowly. "Thank you. I appreciate your coming to tell me."

"No trouble," she said shortly and laced her fingers together. "I needed to check out what they've done in here anyway, and it looks like they're making real headway. I see they've carted away the debris, replaced the broken panes and cleaned the windows. They'll probably start on the fountain next." She shrugged awkwardly. "Well, I need to get back. I've got work waiting for me."

An inexplicable panic seized him, and he anxiously searched for something to keep her with him a little longer. "I've never seen anything quite like this building. What exactly is it used for, anyway?"

She was pleased by the genuine interest in his tone. "Originally, it was built to be an indoor garden for people to stroll through, to rest in, to read in—anything, really. But there have been wonderful parties here, and I can guarantee you, there will be again."

His appreciation for the confidence and joy she felt in the great house of SwanSea was newfound. But his pleasure at simply being near her was an ancient, primitive reaction.

There was a tightrope he'd had to walk for many years. Often he'd had difficulties. But he'd never had to remember to keep his balance as he did now. "You plan to rent it out for private functions?"

She nodded. Without her being aware, the subject of SwanSea had given her pale, stiff features a lovely animation. "Yes. And I think it would be perfect for the hotel's regular afternoon tea, with a pianist playing Gershwin and Porter. Or for special dinner parties or events… The possibilities are endless."

Her excitement over her plans flushed her skin with luminosity, and Nico decided he'd never seen anyone quite so exquisite and desirable. The sun had been lowering in the sky while they talked, so that the golden light appeared silken and tinted with crimson. To lie down in the light and make love with Caitlin would be the ultimate sensual experience.

"The conservatory has always reminded me of a glass castle," she was saying. "Doesn't it you?"

His mouth twisted with humor. "That wouldn't have been my first thought, no."

Caitlin's gaze went to his mouth, and she was forcibly reminded that her attraction for him was as strong as ever. But unfortunately nothing else had changed either, and the fact that they'd managed to talk companionably for a few minutes didn't alter the fact that she meant nothing to him.

She swallowed against a dry throat. "It looks like some sort of iron-and-glass fantasy to me. The weblike ironwork appears so delicate, yet it supports all of that glass. Using structural ironwork as part of the decoration of a building was a trademark of Art Nouveau."

Good, he thought—a topic that would take his mind off the desire building inside him. "I guess you're an expert on the period."

"It's part of my heritage, just like DiFrenza's must be part of yours, even though you don't work there."

"I suppose so," he said, unaware that she'd managed to change the focus. "It's true I never developed an affinity for the clothing business, but I did work in the store every summer when I was in school." He grinned slightly. "It made my family happy."

"What sort of jobs did you have?"

"All sorts. I even learned to dress windows."

"Really?"

"Really," he said huskily, "and I also learned fabrics. For instance, I could tell you what your dress is made of." He paused as he realized what he was about to say and do, and then he plunged on. "But I'd have to feel the material."

"All right," she said as a tremor began within her.

Two of his fingers slid beneath the edge of the scooped-out neckline and touched her skin as he grasped the shimmery material of her sundress. The sudden heat from the contact made her gasp.

He heard her and experienced a corresponding quickening. The tactile sensation of her skin and the soft material made him linger, rubbing the material back and forth between his thumb and fingers. He was torturing himself, he thought, but he couldn't stop. "It's a silk-linen blend," he murmured.

Caitlin had come to life at his touch. Her pulses were racing, her sense whirling. But no matter what, she knew she couldn't betray what she was feeling. Not this time. She managed to indicate he was right with a slight nod.

With more care than was warranted, he withdrew his hand. "Very pretty."

"Thank you." Her pounding heart sounded in her ears. She moved a few steps away from him and gave the fountain her complete attention. "You know," she said casually, "I don't think you ever told me what type of law practice you have."

He gave a brief prayer of thanks that she hadn't been looking when she asked the question. Otherwise, she would have seen him go rigid. "I'm a criminal lawyer."

She risked a glance over her shoulder. "That must be interesting."

"It's a job."

She contemplated his terse remark, running her hand over the cool marble of the fountain. Nico didn't strike her as the kind of man who would enter a profession about which he didn't care passionately. Otherwise, like his father and sister, he would simply have gone into the family business.

She turned back to him. "But you must enjoy it. You did have other options."

"Not really." He looked away. His fingers still tingled as he remembered the feel of her skin. "Caitlin..."

"Yes?"

He gripped his bottom lip with his teeth until all the color had been squeezed from the flesh. Then and only then did he trust himself to speak. "Did Ramona tell you what time supper would be?"

Instinct told her that his inquiry about supper had been an afterthought, but instinct also told her not to probe. He knew as well as she that Ramona would serve him whenever he showed up. "Around seven. Are you hungry?"

He returned his gaze to her, and his throat constricted at the sight she made in the gathering dusk, her cinnamon hair a vivid contrast to the jade-green dress. "Yes," he murmured softly. "Yes." He cleared his throat, taking a moment to get himself together. "I am hungry, but I can wait. I think I'll go back to the house, though, and wash up."

"I have to get back, too. I'll walk with you."

They moved at the same time and bumped against each other. The contact was minimal, but the result was magnified by their charged state.

Nico pulled a deep lungful of air into his body, attempting to clear his mind. But the air was filled with sweetness—newly turned earth, orange blossoms and the knee-weakening fragrance of the woman beside him. Nico closed his hand around her arm and pulled her against him. The taste of her mouth brought a growl from the back of his throat. He deepened the kiss, seeking the warmth and the heat that he had craved every minute of every day since he had last kissed her.

A violent tremor shook Caitlin. The passion of his kiss—the fire skimming along nerve endings, invading the lower part of her body—was heaven, was hell.

She wanted this man, and it would be so easy to give in and surrender to where the kiss would lead. But there were too many things she didn't understand. The memory of his rejection in the attic played like a warped record in the back of her mind.

It wasn't that she didn't have the strength to risk his rejection again. She did. But why should she?

And she could stand the pain she knew love sometimes brought. But only if she had a reason to accept that pain.

Crushed against his body, Caitlin could feel the power of his need for her, yet just days ago he had told her to stay away from him. That meant he didn't *want* to want her.

But his mouth was devouring hers, and his hand was caressing her breast with urgency. She could conclude only that he wanted her in the same way he would want any reasonably attractive woman and that she meant nothing special to him. She had too much pride to allow any man to make love to her when his entire heart, mind and soul were not involved. Heartsick, she pushed against him.

He felt her hands against his chest, but her resistance was slow to penetrate his raging need. Once his mouth had touched hers, control had vanished, and now his body was set and ready for just one thing—to make her his. He wanted her with a strength that involved every cell of his body.

When he finally realized something was wrong, he could hardly believe it. With an angry sound, he wrenched his mouth away from hers and brought his head up in one movement. His dark brows drew together in a scowl as he concentrated on reassembling the broken pieces of his willpower, and waiting for the pain that held his body in its grip to subside.

"I'm sorry," she murmured. "It's my fault."

"What?" he asked, totally without comprehension.

"You told me to stay away from you. I should have sent someone else to find you. But I thought..." She'd thought she would be able to carry on a casual conversation and that if he touched her, she'd be able to hold back all signs of a response. She'd been wrong.

Nico's mind cleared, and suddenly he saw what had happened. He had hurt her badly that day in the attic, but he'd been so caught up with his own agony, he hadn't been able to see it.

Initially, he'd known that just by coming to Swan-Sea, he was taking advantage of her. In his world, right edged toward wrong, but the end always justified the means. He'd intended to get into the house, fulfill his promise to his grandmother, and then get out again without fuss or bother.

But the complications of the situation had been apparent from the start. He wasn't sure if he had been too weak from his wounds to see the complications or if the impact of her green-gold eyes had made him ignore the truth. He also wasn't sure why he now felt such an overwhelming need to protect her. But whatever the reason, he knew what he had to do.

"Caitlin, nothing is your fault."

"But—"

He clasped her shoulder. "No, I mean it. *Nothing* is your fault. You were kind enough to let me stay here when I needed a place to rest and regain my strength. I'm much better now, and I promise you I'll leave as soon as I can make other arrangements."

She couldn't keep the dismay from her voice. "You're going to leave? But, Nico, is it really safe for you to leave so soon?"

Hell no, he thought, but it would be easier to face the type of danger Rettig and his men offered than risk staying. And he didn't dare risk the danger of hurting her—one more time. He dropped his hand to his side. "I'm better, Caitlin, and I need to leave."

"Very well." Her dignified bearing did not quite disguise the shakiness of her words. "You know what's best for you. When you've made your plans let me know."

"I will."

"Good. I'll see you back at the house."

Unable to trust himself to speak, he nodded.

And then he was alone in the great iron-and-glass building, the silence and the emptiness engulfing him. Guilt weighed so heavily on him, and he had to sit down.

Sometime later, he heard the sound of someone softly weeping. The sound grew and grew until it rebounded through the conservatory, surrounding him, and he covered his ears.

"RILL? IT'S NICO."

"Hi. How are things?"

"My recovery is going fine."

"Uh-oh, I hear a *but* coming."

"But I've got to leave here."

Amarillo's voice changed from laconic to tense in a split second. "Rettig?"

"No, no, nothing like that. It's just that... Look, if you don't want me to come back to Boston yet, make arrangements for me to stay at another safe place until I can."

"Nico, I thought you were crazy when you told me you were going to try to get into SwanSea, but now that you're there, it's turned out to be perfect."

"I'm glad you're so satisfied with the situation," Nico said, irritation making his words razor-edged.

"I know the waiting is hard—"

"*Hard,* Rill? It's damned impossible."

"Since when has impossible stopped you? And as long as you're in a bad mood, I might as well tell you I faxed photos and rap sheets of Rettig and his key people to the local police, just in case we're right."

"Dammit, Rill! I told you from the start I didn't want the local people in on this."

"I saw it differently, so save your breath. It's done."

Nico let out a fluent string of curses that accomplished nothing, not even making him feel better. "Just get back to me with a place, Rill, and don't be too long about it, or I'll strike out on my own."

"You do, and I'll come and kill you myself," Amarillo said, his tone quite pleasant, quite serious.

CHAPTER FOUR

CAITLIN LEFT the study and shut the door behind her with a vicious tug. A few minutes before, she'd glanced out her study window and seen Nico jog by. Against her will, she'd watched him for a time, noticing the natural athleticism that had emerged with his healing. She remembered wondering what he'd be like when he recovered. Now she knew, and she wished she didn't.

She had no idea how long it would take him to make other arrangements but she knew it was just a matter of time before he left. She had only one question: How long before she forgot how close she'd come to surrendering everything to him? Her mind, her body, her heart.

"What's wrong, honey?" Ramona asked, coming up behind her. "You don't look like you feel well."

Caitlin turned to her. Seeing Nico's white sweater in Ramona's arms, she pressed a finger to her right temple where the pain of her developing headache seemed to be centered. "Where would you like me to start?" she asked wryly.

"That bad, huh?"

"It depends on how you see another twenty-four hours without electricity, and that's an optimistic estimate. To top it off, Rowan's Plumbing has just delivered twenty-five Victorian-style tubs to us."

"Victorian?"

"Boxy with claw feet," she said succinctly. "What makes me so angry is that there was just no excuse for this mistake. I've spoken directly with the company's president several times about my design that called for a tub with flowing, curving lines. He assured me it would be no problem and sent me a refinement of my sketch for approval."

"What are you going to do?"

"I've already called Rowan's. The Victorian tubs will be picked up tomorrow."

"When will our tubs be delivered?"

"Good question, but I'm through worrying about it for today. In the meantime, I'm going to change into a swimsuit, then walk down to the cove. I've got a little headache I'm going to try to swim away."

"That's a good idea." Ramona patted Caitlin's shoulder. "Swimming always makes you feel better. Oh, as long as you're going upstairs, would you mind putting Nico's sweater in his bureau for me? I mended it for him."

Caitlin hesitated. The last thing she wanted was to run into Nico, but she'd just seen him outside, so… She took the sweater. "I'll be glad to."

A SHORT TIME LATER, Nico wiped his sweat-dampened face with the end of the towel draped around his neck and opened his bedroom door. And he froze.

Caitlin held a 9-mm automatic in her hand, the muzzle pointed toward the ceiling.

Quickly taking in the open bureau drawer and the sweater lying on the floor, he instantly grasped what had happened.

She stared at him, a look of betrayal on her face. "Why do you have something like this?"

"Put it down, Caitlin. It's loaded."

"I know that. What I don't know is why you brought a loaded weapon into my home."

Holding her gaze, he walked to her, took the gun from her hand, and replaced it in the drawer.

"You didn't unload it," she said.

"No."

"That means either you're expecting trouble or you are the trouble. Which is it, Nico?"

He regarded her cautiously. "You're one tough lady. Many women would have reacted as if they'd found a snake."

"But it wasn't a snake. Answer my question."

Just one more thing that hadn't gone as planned, he reflected wearily. "Sit down."

She didn't move. "Are you about to tell me something I'm going to hate?"

His lips quirked. "I can almost guarantee it."

With hammering heart, she sank onto the end of the bed and drew the tie of her short terry robe tighter around her waist. "Okay. You told me you weren't an ax murderer. I have to say, I'm really hoping you didn't lie about that."

"I'm a cop."

It took a moment for what he had said to sink in. "I thought you were a criminal lawyer."

"A lie of sorts, Caitlin, and a truth of sorts. I do have a law degree, but I've never hung out my shingle. In my job, I practice criminal law every day."

"I see, and are you going to leave it at that, or are you going to flesh out the particulars?"

He saw beneath her calm facade the smoldering anger. He tugged open another drawer and from beneath a pile of underwear pulled out a black leather case. He flipped it open and handed her his badge. "I'm a detective with the Boston Police Department, Caitlin. For months now, I've been involved in the investigation of a drug lord. I got too close to him."

She smoothed a finger over the badge. "Someone shot you, didn't they? And that's why you were in the hospital. How serious was it?"

He hesitated, choosing his words with care, his habit of playing things close to the vest not easily broken. "It could have been far worse than it was, but it was bad enough."

"Well, that certainly explains a lot." Shaken, she slid off the bed to her feet. "Why didn't you tell me all of this at the beginning?" she asked, her nerves beginning to show.

"Training. That and the fact that I never expected to...become involved with you."

She tried a laugh and failed. "*Involved?* Is that what you'd call it?"

Obsession would be closer to the mark, he thought. "I came here because I needed a place to rest and recuperate." And, he added silently, *I needed to search your house.* Self-condemnation roughened his voice. "I'm sorry, Caitlin. I never meant to hurt you."

Her chin lifted. "Hurt? No, Nico. Try mad as hell."

"I know this has been a shock."

"Definitely." She turned away from him, her mind in a spin as she attempted to gain some perspective on the matter. So he'd lied to her by omission. What was so terrible? So she was sure there was more he wasn't telling her. Did that give her the right to yell at him and pound her fists against his chest as she wanted to? She turned back to face him. "This person who shot you—did you catch him?"

"That's police business, Caitlin."

She felt as if he'd hit her. "If this person is still out there looking for you, it's *my* business too. You're in my house, and if he comes looking for you—" She saw the odd expression that flitted across his face. "He *is* out there, isn't he? You're still in danger!" Her eyes misted with tears. "Damn you, Nico, you're still in danger!"

"Trust me, Caitlin. You've never been in any jeopardy."

"Trust you?" Her breath caught on a sob; her chest was tight with a strange new kind of pain. She stared at him, realizing he'd completely misunderstood her concern. His gray workout clothes were soaked through with sweat—under his arms, around his waist, and beneath his throat. His black hair lay in disheveled waves on his head. Dampness burnished his olive skin. I hate him, she thought, brushing moisture from her eyes.

"How many times were you shot?" she asked coldly.

"It doesn't matter, Caitlin. They didn't kill me."

"No. But maybe next time…"

He shook his head with impatience. "I can't think of things like that."

"Why not? It seems like a sensible thing to be concerned about."

He laughed shortly. "Now you wish I'd turned out to be an ax murderer, right?"

"Not quite." She folded her arms across her breast. "But I am curious as to why someone with a law degree would join the police force."

"Dammit, Caitlin, why can't you just accept what I've told you? I'm not very good at this sort of thing, explaining or talking about myself, I mean."

"Obviously not," she said, sarcasm lacing her tone. "You know, I remember thinking not too long ago that you weren't the kind of man who would enter a profession you didn't care passionately about. I want to know, Nico. Why are you a detective for the Boston Police Department?"

"It's not that uncommon for a lawyer to become a policeman."

"No? I would think it would be more common for a policeman to become a lawyer."

"What does it matter, Caitlin?"

"It doesn't. I said I was curious, that's all."

Damn. Some information about him could be used by his enemies against him and he made it a practice never to reveal the secrets of his soul. But she wasn't his enemy, he reminded himself. He cared about her, and had been able to give her so little. He'd put her through a lot, and truthfully she wasn't asking for much.

Staring at the wall across the room, he tried to find words for something he wasn't sure he'd ever verbalized, even to himself. He started haltingly. "I had a brother. Antonio—Tony. Four years younger. He died when he was nineteen."

Her sympathy was instant. "I'm sorry."

"Yeah, me, too. When I was in my first year of law school, he was in his first year of college. He was a great kid, but he was hard on himself. After his death, I learned that he'd always used me as a measure. Unfortunately for him, I was good in school and athletics, and I knew exactly what I wanted to do." He rolled his shoulders as if he carried something heavy there. "For as long as I could remember, I had this burning in me for the law. Looking at me, Tony must have felt rudderless."

"That wasn't your fault."

"No. But I could have paid more attention to what was going on with him. Maybe if I had, I could have helped him. As it was, he went away to college, and for the first time in his life, he was away from the family, without our support, feeling as if he had no particular ability."

"A lot of kids are like that," she said, wanting to help him.

"Right, but they give themselves time, and eventually they find themselves. Tony was too hard on himself. He didn't see the promise we all saw in him. He put this terrific pressure on himself to succeed, and he got involved with drugs. Within six months, he burned out like a comet. By the time we realized something was wrong and reached out for him, he was gone. He was found dead one morning in his room in the dorm. Cocaine overdose."

His bleak tone tore at her heart. "You weren't to blame, Nico." She put her hand on his arm.

"So I've been told," he said, instinctively flinching away. A touch of comfort to a man walking a tightrope might affect his balance and send him toppling. He couldn't chance the fall. Circumstances beyond his control had set his path, and no matter what, he had to take that path, even though it led away from her.

She withdrew her hand, this rejection added its weight to his other rejections.

"At the time, I felt so damned helpless," he said, continuing on with determination. "I went to the school, looking for a villain, someone I could focus my rage on. What I found enraged me even more. The availability of drugs astounded me, and I discovered that the trails to the people responsible were like a giant cobweb made out of hundreds of tiny easily broken threads. Initially I was looking for a neat ending. Something to make it bearable for me and my family. Instead I found a totally hopeless situation where I could do nothing."

"But you've been trying ever since," she said tonelessly.

"Yes."

"And you'll go on trying," she said, wondering at her sinking heart.

"Yes. I win more than I lose, Caitlin."

It was the idea of him losing at all that bothered her, she realized. Then it hit her. *She loved him.*

Stunned, she took a step back. Despair welled in her heart. *No.* Loving him would be one-sided, hopeless, and agonizingly painful. She couldn't—she wouldn't love him!

She saw him looking at her oddly and realized she must have gone pale. "You're in serious danger, aren't you?" she managed to say. "You were told to leave Boston for your own safety, weren't you?"

"I can't talk about that, Caitlin, but there's nothing for you to worry about. I'll be leaving in the morning."

"In the morning," she repeated softly. "In the morning. Right."

"Caitlin—"

"Then just leave," she said, her vision clouding with a red mist, "and the hell with you. I've made a fool of myself over you for the last time, but no more." She began backing out of the room. "No more."

"Fool—wait, what are you talking about?"

"I'm talking about *you,* you self-contained, iron-willed bastard!"

SHE CUT CLEANLY through the waves, anger, frustration and heartache making her strokes sharp and powerful. She wanted to forget.

The physical exertion gave her a sensation of freedom. Out here, she was part of a mighty force, and she felt renewed. Here there were no wrong deliveries or paint colors. Here there were no headaches. Here there was no Nico.

Something brushed against her leg. She sliced through the center of a wave, kicking vigorously, reflecting that battling the Atlantic was infinitely easier than loving a man who didn't know how to open up, even when he kissed her passionately and held her as if he had no intention of letting her go.

The water was cool, providing exhilaration, forgetfulness and peace.

Long fingers snaked around her arm and jerked her around. Fear seized her, and she screamed.

"Caitlin, it's me!"

She couldn't believe her eyes. In her surprise, she inadvertently swallowed a mouthful of water and briefly choked. "Nico, what are you doing?" Kicking to maintain her buoyancy, she glared at him. "What are you *doing* out here?"

"Come back in," he yelled, his face set with a hard dominance. "You're too far out."

Her legs tangled with his as she tried to tread water. She went under and came up sputtering in an explosive mood. "What are you talking about? I'm fine, or at least I was until you came out here. Now you're trying to drown me!" She pushed as hard as she could against him, but his hold on her was like steel.

"Just come back with me, Caitlin. It's too dangerous out here."

"Dangerous?" Concentrating on him, she didn't see the wave until she felt it wash over her. She surfaced, coughing and furious. "Dammit, Nico, let me go. I've swum here all my life."

"At least swim closer to the shore."

"No," she shouted. "I won't. I like it out here." Enraged, she gave one hard jerk and freed herself.

An iron band came over her shoulder, crossed diagonally over her breast, and yanked her against him with such force that she lost her breath. "Nico!"

"Just shut up," he said, starting toward shore with her clamped tightly against him.

She fought him, kicking and hitting out, but her blows connected awkwardly.

Nico's lungs burned as they tried to pump sufficient air through his body. When his feet touched the sandy bottom, he dragged her to the water's edge, then collapsed, pulling her down with him to the sand.

"Are you *crazy?*" she demanded, flinging her wet hair behind her shoulder. She saw he was wearing only a pair of briefs. The white knit was plastered to his hard male form, and the ridge of his manhood pressed against the almost transparent briefs. She couldn't tear her eyes away. He resembled a sculpted masterpiece. The water had laid an olive-toned patina of sleek satin over the corded muscles and sinews. A fire rushed through her, momentarily debilitating her. She wrenched her gaze away to see his discarded clothes lying several feet away, next to her towel and robe.

"You were so angry when you left that I came after you," he said, his breathing slowly returning to normal. "Then I saw you swimming out to sea." He took in the heightened color in her cheeks, then his gaze dropped to her breasts mounding perilously above the skimpy top. One good breath, and her nipples would break free, he thought, his stomach clenching, his loins heating.

"Out to *sea?* Lord, how can one man be so stupid? Look at you—" keeping her eyes above his waist, she gestured to the two brilliant red scars across his torso

"—you're just out of the hospital, probably not even healed properly yet."

"I'm fine."

"And you scared me half to death out there, coming up behind me like some sea monster, nearly drowning me."

"Me drown *you?* If you hadn't fought me—"

She uttered an exasperated sound and pushed against the sand to get up. He grabbed her. Off balance, she fell against him. The contact sent shock waves through her.

"You're not leaving yet," he muttered.

"Oh, that's really rich," she cried, her eyes alight with an inner fever. Her skin felt uncomfortable, as if it were too tight, too hot, too full of nerves. "I just love the way you give orders. First you tell me to leave you alone. Now you tell me to stay. I'd say make up your mind, Nico, except I don't care anymore."

"Caitlin, listen to me."

"I've listened and listened, but you don't say anything."

"Then maybe we shouldn't talk at all."

He felt as if all control had been stripped away from him, leaving him a primitive man, raw with knife-sharp desire and blazing need.

Adrenaline pumped furiously through her veins. There was something untamed in the way he was looking at her, and at that moment, she'd never felt more alive. Or more frightened.

"Leave me alone, Nico."

"Don't you see, I've tried to do all the right things and ended up doing everything wrong."

"I don't see anything—"

"Then I'll have to show you." With a quick, smooth motion, he wiped the moisture from her brow, then tangled his fingers in her wet hair.

"Stop, Nico!"

"Sweetheart, if the world came to an end right this moment, I could not stop."

A small cry escaped from her as a hot weakening coursed through her body, shattering all coherent thought.

He reached behind her, and within seconds, the top of her swimsuit fell to the sand. Then she was fighting to pull air into her chest because his gaze was on her breasts and his expression told her he was starving for her. Her nipples were already erect, and her breasts began to throb—for him.

Bending his head, he caught one tip in his mouth and sucked so hungrily and with such raw eroticism that when he pressed her back on the warm sand, she couldn't even think of protesting.

Water quickly dried on their hot flesh. Her swimsuit bottom and his briefs came off. He kneed her thighs apart and came over her. She clutched at his shoulders. The savage expression in his eyes made her realize there would be no leisurely foreplay, nor did she want it. She was frantic for his possession.

He braced himself on his elbows and gazed down at her, the skin of his face drawn taut with powerful male lust.

"Caitlin," he said, as though her name had been dredged up in an agony of wanting from his gut. Then he surged into her—so easily, so naturally, it was as if it were meant to be.

Filled completely with him, she held his gaze, unable to look away or close her eyes. This moment was too electric for less than all her senses. She wanted to see the changing expressions on his face as he moved in her. She wanted to hear his rough sounds as he felt her tighten around him. She wanted to feel the way his muscles bunched as the ecstacy grew. She wanted to know the taste of his mouth as he thrust into her time after time with a passionate violence.

He showed her no mercy, but he also showed her no control.

The sun, the wind, the surging ocean and Nico—unyielding elements that couldn't be fought, not now at any rate. No matter how she might wish it were different, she loved him.

He thrust again, and red-hot pleasure flooded through her. She cried out and arched up to him, taking him deeper into her.

The ocean sent its waves spilling to the shore, its lacy foam curling around their feet. He wrapped her legs around his waist, binding her to him in a wild primitive rhythm, and they crested together, hard and intense, their cries mingling and filling the deserted cove.

Time passed, waves rolled into the shore, a bird glided out to sea on a current of air. Finally, Nico rolled to her side but kept his arm around her.

Only then did she close her eyes and lay motionless, willing her body and mind back to normal. It took a while, but her breathing evened and her senses steadied. Passion died; anger and hurt returned.

She could call herself stupid all day long, she told herself wearily, and it wouldn't change the fact that they had made love. Besides it had been inevitable. But now their storm of desire had passed, and she had to deal with its aftermath.

With the warmth of his body against her, she was tempted to turn her head, bury her face against his chest, and spill her heart and soul to him. She resisted.

Nico might be holding her to him at this moment,

but at any minute, he would push her away. It was his pattern. And if his rejection had hurt before, what kind of pain would she have now after experiencing his love-making that had left no part of her untouched?

She drew free of his arm, got to her feet, retrieved her swimsuit, and quickly slipped on both pieces.

"Caitlin?" He raised up on his elbow and frowned. "What are you doing?"

"I don't see what difference it makes," she said, bending to scoop up her robe and shrug into it, "but if you must know, I'm going back to the house."

He wasn't sure what he'd expected, but it was definitely not this cold, indifferent attitude. "I don't understand."

"Then let me explain. In spite of your attempts ever since you've been here not to get too intimate with me, we've just made love—if you'll excuse the euphemism. I'm sure you're embarrassed and sorry about the whole thing, but don't be." She picked up her towel and neatly folded it. "You were already planning to leave in the morning. To my way of thinking, you couldn't ask for a neater, less complicated ending than that."

"Caitlin—"

"I've got to go now. I'm sure we'll see each other again before you leave, perhaps at dinner."

Nico sat up and braced his arms on his upraised knees. He stared out at the sea, not trusting himself to watch Caitlin as she climbed the steps to the top of the bluff. He wanted with everything that was in him to run after her, stop her and bring her back. His body throbbed mercilessly to have her again. And his heart felt as if it were breaking apart.

To stop himself from going after her, he made himself think of Rettig and a long-buried secret—two things that could hurt her if he stayed.

TWO SIX-BRANCHED SILVER candelabra sat at either end of the walnut kitchen table, their candles sending a white-gold pool of light over Caitlin, Nico, and Ramona. Six other candelabra stood on the sideboard behind them, their candles ready to be lit. Caitlin stared at her empty plate, trying to recall what she'd just eaten. She supposed it was possible that for once in her life, Ramona had slipped up and given her an empty plate for dinner. Possible, but not likely.

I am not going to lose it, she thought fiercely. She put down her fork and reached for her water glass. All she had to do was concentrate on tomorrow when Nico would be gone. After he left, she'd be fine.

Peering over the edge of the crystal rim, she studied him from beneath her lashes. He'd been quiet during dinner, speaking only to answer Ramona or to compliment her cooking.

"I think I'll drive down to Boston next week," Ramona was saying. "There are a few things I should check on at home, and—"

"Home?" Nico interrupted unexpectedly.

"I live with Julia, Caitlin's mother," Ramona said. "She has a home in Boston, and, as a matter of fact, so does Caitlin." She turned to Caitlin. "I'll run by your place, too, honey."

"There's no need. The security firm's watching it for me."

"I know, but it's no bother, and I'll feel better."

Caitlin smiled at her. "Thank you."

"You're welcome. And now that I've met you, Nico, I think I'm also going to do a little shopping at DiFrenza's. I've been in there a time or two with Julia, but I've never—"

"You mean Caitlin is going to be left all alone in this big house?" Nico asked, interrupting again, this time in a more strident tone.

Both women looked at him, startled. "I've stayed here by myself before," Caitlin said. "When I was in college, I'd sometimes drive up to get away from everything so that I could concentrate on studying."

"And there is Ben Stephenson, you know," Ramona said. "He's always around."

"That's not exactly reassuring," Nico said grimly.

Caitlin blinked, uncertain why Ben Stephenson would bother him. "Why not?"

"The man has been around forever. I ran into him on one of my walks around the estate, and we talked. He's very nice, but the fact is, he's an elderly man, overdue for retirement. I don't know how he's managed to look after this place all alone for as many years as he has."

"He's had help," Caitlin said defensively. "We've always paid a special fee, so the county sheriff's department would keep an eye on things for us. On those occasions when vandals have threatened, we've hired off-duty sheriffs for security until the problem's passed. The main thing Mr. Stephenson has done for us over the years is keep us alerted to trouble."

"That's all well and good, but how can he alert anyone to trouble when he's out in his cottage and you're up here alone?"

"I'll be fine," she said quietly. *Heartbroken and lonely,* she thought, *but fine.*

"She really will be, Nico," Ramona said. "Now I'd be afraid to stay here by myself. I'd never get a minute's sleep. There are just too many empty rooms, strange shadows and unexplained noises for my taste.

But Caitlin is a child of SwanSea. She knows this house, and this house knows her."

"It's not the house that bothers me," he said, staring broodingly at Caitlin.

"I wouldn't leave her here alone if I wasn't sure she'd be all right," Ramona said in a tone that made it clear she felt she had brought the subject to an end. "Now, would you like some more wine?"

He shook his head and pushed back from the table. "I think I'll explore the library for a while and see if I can find a book to read."

"By candlelight?" Caitlin asked in surprise.

"Sure. Why not?" Anything to try to get his mind off her and his leaving her in the morning.

Ramona waved her hand toward the candelabra lined up on the sideboard. "Take a couple of those with you."

"One will be fine." He cast a glance at Caitlin. Her head bent, she was studying the crystal goblet in front of her. What was she thinking about? he wondered bleakly. Had he made her hate him?

He shifted slightly. A current of air waved outward from his body, and the candles flickered, sending ripples of white-gold light through the cinnamon strands of her hair. But Caitlin didn't move.

"Good night," he said.

CHAPTER FIVE

CAITLIN'S SHADOW WAS her only companion as she paced the length of her candlelit bedroom. Sleep eluded her. Thoughts of Nico filled her mind. Initially, he had attracted and intrigued her. Then he had evoked sympathy, desire and full-blown passion. And finally he had made her fall in love with him.

Remembering those times she'd had an uneasy feeling about him, she paused by a table crafted in an exquisite marquetry floral design set in front of drawn silk-embroidered drapes. The silver candelabrum she had placed there that resembled a six-bud rose tree held tall cream candles. She had been surrounded by beauty like this all her life and assumed that Nico, being a Di-Frenza, had too.

He'd spoken of his great-grandmother, told her that he was a police detective and why, but there was still so much she didn't know about him.

She knew what had happened between them from her point of view—she had fallen deeply in love with him, in love with the vulnerable and passionate man she'd sensed beneath the enigmatic surface.

But if he left in the morning without her trying to talk to him one more time, she would never have a chance to find out what had happened between them from his point of view. She stiffened with indignation. Maybe he would never return her love, and maybe she'd never see him again, but she'd be damned if she would go through her life wondering why he hadn't been able to love her.

Intent on setting out to find him, she turned sharply and struck her hip against the side of the table, sending the candelabrum tumbling.

NICO STOOD OUTSIDE Caitlin's door, his hand raised to knock. It seemed as if he'd been frozen in that position for an eternity, his reason warring with his feelings. But peace of mind refused to come regarding what would happen if he knocked on the door and she refused to answer. Slowly, he lowered his hand.

Seeing Caitlin now wouldn't be fair. He had absolutely nothing to offer her, nothing other than a raw, aching need that wouldn't let him alone. Nothing more than a love that because of the less than honorable circumstances under which he was in her house, he didn't feel free to confess.

She deserved honesty and one hundred percent of him, and right now, he couldn't give her either.

He stuffed his hands in his pockets, and with shoulders hunched, turned to go. Then he heard her cry out.

He opened the door, rushed in, and in that moment learned the true meaning of fear. Flames were steadily eating their way up the length of one set of draperies and onto another. To his horrified eyes, Caitlin appeared completely defenseless in her bare feet and skimply pink satin chemise, trying to fight the angry red fire with only the coverlet from her bed.

Intent on battling the flames, she didn't realize Nico had entered the room until he lifted her and carried her to safety by the doorway.

She struggled against him. "The fire, Nico. I've got to put it out."

"*I'll* take care of it. *You* call the fire department."

She tried to push past him. "By the time anyone gets here, the whole house will be cinders."

He took a grip on her arms to hold her still. "Then, dammit, do exactly as I say. Stay right here, and I'll put it out."

"But—"

"You're wasting a hell of a lot of time, Caitlin."

Immediately she took a step back and held up her hands. "Do it. For heaven's sake, just do it."

The sob in her voice spurred him to action. He ripped the drapes down and hurled the coverlet over both sets. He made a few stomps over the mound, then dragged the blanket off the bed and jerked more draperies from the walls, throwing all of them on the pile. Gradually the fire was suffocated until there were only smoke and the acrid smell of burnt textiles.

"Are you all right?" Caitlin asked at his side.

"I thought I told you to stay over there."

"Let me see your hands. Oh Lord, you've burned them."

"No, they're just dirty."

"Let's run cool water over them to clean them, and then we'll be able to tell." Shock and the trembling that came with it had started to set in, but tending to his wounds was uppermost in her mind.

"In a minute. First, I want to open these windows and get this smell out of here, then make sure the carpet's not smoldering somewhere that we haven't seen yet." Soon a fresh ocean breeze was blowing through the room. He kicked the burned pile of curtains out to the balcony and inspected the carpet. Finally, he was satisfied, and he gave Caitlin his full attention.

Her eyes were wide as she watched his every move.

"You shouldn't have put yourself in danger like that," she murmured.

"Me?" He had a great urge to shake her for putting *herself* in such terrible danger. "Look at yourself. You're nearly naked, and you were trying to put the fire out with your hands."

"I had the coverlet."

He wanted to take her in his arms, hold her tightly against him, and let her sweetness flow into him so that he'd forget the sight of the fire rising behind her like some menacing monster. He settled for returning to her side and venting his frustration. "Lord, Caitlin, what if I hadn't been passing by? What if you'd fallen and hit your head and been knocked unconscious? You could have died of smoke inhalation, maybe even burned to death."

He must care, she thought absently. She was still somewhat numbed by the near disaster, but he must care at least a little about her. But was *caring a little* enough for her? "None of those things happened."

"No. Not this time, but this is exactly why you shouldn't stay here by yourself next week."

"Then stay with me," she said abruptly.

Her quiet request was like a sudden punch in the stomach. He closed his eyes and shook his head. "I can't, Caitlin."

"Why?"

When he looked at her again and saw the shock that lingered in her eyes, he groaned. "Lord, what am I thinking of?" He swept her up in his arms and strode out of the room. "You need to be wrapped up and put in bed."

"I don't have any more bedrooms made up."

His arms tightened. "That's all right. You're staying in my room tonight."

NICO'S BEDROOM WAS QUIET, all its sharp corners and edges were softened by shadows. Candles rising from a tall silver candelabrum emitted a pale glow that spread over the bed's cream satin coverlet and lapped at the surrounding circle of dark.

He still cradled her in his arms, and to Caitlin, there was something infinitely right about the way her body fit against him, as if in some far distant past, they had been made from the same piece, separated and were now together again. It was the same feeling she'd had this afternoon when he'd thrust into her.

"Why did you bring me here?" she asked in the hush.

He felt her warm breath against his cheek. Without choice, his hold on her tightened. "You've had a shock. I think the best thing for you would be to get into bed and cover up."

She considered that. "And you? Where will you be?"

"Downstairs, somewhere, on a couch."

They had had hot passionate sex on the beach, but she had never spent the night in his arms, and now it appeared she never would. The idea was strangely unacceptable.

But she had to accept. She *had* to.

Her gaze dropped to his jaw and the muscle that briefly flickered, then returned to his taut profile. "At least let me see to your hand."

Slowly he eased his hold on her and let her feet slide to the floor until she stood without his support. His arms felt curiously empty. The pink satin chemise followed her body's shape, skimming over her breasts, catching on the tiny outward jut of her nipples, making a slight indentation at her waist before caressing the rounded curves of her hips and ending at her thighs. "You're going to get chilled," he said, his voice husky.

"Being chilled is not my problem."

Her whispered response went straight through him like a scorching wind that left him parched for the taste of her. And when he looked into her eyes, he saw the shimmering reflection of a candle's flame. Almost desperately, he reached for the fast-fading remnants of his strength. "I'm only trying to take care of you, Caitlin."

"I know that, but why?"

Out of thin air, he created a reason. "Because you took me in when I needed a place to stay."

"Oh. So you're grateful to me?"

Caitlin in this mood was as dangerous as any gun he'd ever faced, and his tone was wary. "That's right."

"Then since you're so grateful, give me something I need."

"What?"

"Help me understand you."

A sardonic smile lifted a corner of his mouth. "Trust me. Understanding me wouldn't help a thing."

"I think it would."

She was tenacious, and he could tell that she wasn't going to give up easily. He felt assaulted by her questions and her sensuality, and he badly needed a reprieve from her. In her bare feet, wearing a scrap of nothing, her hair tousled in silky waves around her face, she looked too soft, too sweet, too sexy. In short, too damn much like everything he'd ever wanted.

And though he no longer held her, he could feel the heat coming from her body in waves, battering him, bruising him with need.

"You're right," he muttered. "I should do something about my hands."

He disappeared into the darkness of the bathroom, and she heard him turn on the tap. Staring after him, she tried to recall the moment after the fire when the idea had occurred to her that he might care. She wondered if she'd been right. Obviously he had been concerned for her safety. But was it only the concern one would feel for someone owed a favor? At this moment, she didn't have a clue. Only a newfound hope. She might be setting herself up for another fall, but it did seem that he had held her longer than necessary once they'd reached this room.

"Let me see your hands," she said when he returned.

"They're fine."

"Then you won't mind if I check them, will you?" she asked mildly, taking his arm and leading him to the candelabrum. In the brightness, she smoothed her hand across his, straightening his fingers to look for any sign of burn.

Her touch was as light as the brush of a butterfly's wing, its effect nearly catastrophic.

Tentatively she pressed a finger against the hard flesh of his palm. "Does that hurt?"

He swallowed hard. *Not as much as having you this close to me.* "No."

She gave the other hand the same thorough inspection. When she finished, she kept the hand in hers. Lightly, idly, she rubbed the tops of his knuckles. "You were lucky. You could have been burned."

"So could you." Compulsively, he stroked his free hand down her spine.

The warmth from the candles caressed the side of her face. The warmth from his hand gliding down her back curled and gathered and grew, deep inside her. "No, not really."

"Yes, dammit, really. I've never seen anything like it. You think more of this house than you do of yourself."

"You're exaggerating."

"Sweetheart, those flames were no exaggeration." He reached out and stroked a finger across her cheek. "When I think of what those flames could have done to this skin—" The horror of his thoughts was apparent in the shakiness of his voice.

"It sounds like you really care."

He took his hand away. Their lovemaking this afternoon was a living, vivid memory. His body clamored to have her again. It would be so easy…so wonderful…so mind-bending. And that was the trouble. He couldn't let his mind be rearranged. He would only hurt her more than he already had. Just now, he'd made a grave mistake by allowing his emotions to get the better of him. Now he had to try to repair the damage. "Of course I do," he said in a casual, offhand way.

"How much, Nico? How much do you care?"

His dark brows drew together with annoyance, at himself and the circumstances that wouldn't allow him to be honest with her. "What kind of question is that?"

"A legitimate one. You see, you confuse me."

"There's nothing to be confused about," he said impatiently.

His sharp reply didn't disturb her. She sensed she was close to the answers she so desperately needed. "Really? Then make me understand how you can kiss me one minute and tell me to leave you alone the next. And how you can make love to me on the beach in the afternoon, then tell me that you'll be leaving the next morning."

Yes, Nico, why don't you do that? He felt the tightrope give a wide swing beneath him, and he reached for brutal honesty to keep him steady. "I kissed you and made love to you because I wanted to, more than I wanted to draw my next breath. I'm leaving because it's best for you."

"That sounds like you think you might hurt me."

"Caitlin..."

"Do you think you'll hurt me?"

He could feel something breaking apart in him, but he continued to fight. With Caitlin, he needed honor, and he had a short supply. He slid his hand along the side of her neck and with a thumb beneath her chin, tilted her face up to his so that she wouldn't miss one word of what he was about to say. "If I don't leave in the next minute, I can almost guarantee that I will."

She studied his stern, closed expression. There was so much she didn't know about him, so much she might never learn. But it was plain she had two choices: accept him as he was, or back away. The struggle on his face and the warning he had given her told her that in his way, he was trying to play fair. Or as much as he could, considering all that had already gone on between them. "You told me yourself that I'm tough. Remember?"

"Yes, but I don't want to put you in the position of having to find out how tough you are."

"Perhaps, Nico, you already have."

It seemed to him at that moment that her eyes could see all the way to his soul. His teeth ground together as the pressure built inside him. "Maybe."

"You can be sure of it."

"No. I'm not sure about anything anymore. Except, Caitlin, that wanting you is eating me up inside."

"Inside?" With a boldness she wouldn't have had this morning, she pushed his sweater up until she could run her palm over his abdomen. "Inside here?"

He couldn't control the shudder of hunger that ripped through him or his reply. "Yes. And lower."

Holding his gaze, she unbuckled his belt and undid his pants. His hand shot out to close over hers in a painful grip. Agony registered on his face and in the rawness in his voice, as if it hurt him to speak, to breathe. "I want you to know, if you go any further, you won't have a choice. Despite all my sins and despite all my crimes, you will be mine."

"Sins, crimes, whatever—my choices are all gone, Nico."

With a harsh, fragmented sound, he yanked her against him and brought his mouth down on hers with an urgent, demanding need. She was right, he thought hazily. Choices had disappeared long ago.

Her arms wrapped around his neck and held him tightly. Someone was trembling; she was sure it was she. But when she arched her back to press her breasts against his chest, a tremor racked his powerful body, and she knew she wasn't alone in this wild, magnificient madness.

Control lost once could be rationalized away. Control lost twice had to be accepted. In the past, control had meant the difference between life and death. Now all his protection was peeling away, leaving him forever defenseless to this woman he held in his arms. He was left with nothing but a fierce passion and an undying love for her.

He backed her against the bed, then lowered her to the cream satin coverlet and followed her down, entering a world of soft hues, sensual textures, and blazing passions.

The chemise had ridden up, revealing narrow pink panties and ivory skin. With a groan, he pressed his face into the softness of her belly.

Hot sweetness flooded through her. She inhaled

sharply and held her breath, waiting for what was to come next, the expectancy a pleasure all its own. Then his tongue darted out to lick at her, and a low, broken moan escaped from her throat.

The honeyed taste and satiny feel of her against the roughness of his tongue was a revelation to him. But the tiny shivers that coursed just beneath her skin brought him special delight. Gently he bit his way across her smooth flat stomach. Not a single mark showed his path—only a trail of fire.

He eased her panties down her legs and off her feet. The picture she made, her hair spread out around her, intensified every emotion he was feeling. She was alluring colors, shapes, and textures. She was woman—his woman—with long lovely legs and the cinnamon triangle of hair at the apex of her thighs. "I need to see all of you," he said, his voice a hoarse, desperate whisper, his endurance almost at an end.

"Yes." She lifted the pink satin chemise over her head, then lay back.

The sight of her struck awe into his soul. The golden hue of her skin had never been more distinctive than it was against the cream coverlet. Her luminosity was almost blinding.

He stripped off his sweater and bent to brush his lips against the hair between her legs. Involuntarily, her muscles contracted and her hips moved, giving him a deep satisfaction and reminding him that the most sensitive, most secret part of her awaited. His hand began to stroke her gently while his mouth fastened on the taut peak of her breast. His hunger for her was almost excruciating, but he was intent on making this the most pleasurable experience of her life, and he set about using all his efforts to that purpose.

She gripped his shoulders as a shudder of rapture tore through her. His every caress and kiss sent wildfire through her veins. He lathed her nipple with his tongue, and she felt as if she was going to spiral away.

Suddenly, urgently, Nico shifted and rose over her. "There's so much I want to do to you and with you," he said, his breathing rapid and uneven.

"Show me."

Caught in a savage tension, he gave a rough laugh. "We're going to need all night."

"We have that, and more."

"Not now. *Now* I've run out of time...." He quickly undressed, moved over and into her. She was ready, but he wasn't. He'd thought he'd known passion before, but he'd been wrong. Once completely sheathed inside her sweet tightness, a wall of fire crashed over him, debilitating him, sucking all strength and air from his body, leaving nothing but a pulsing, merciless need, and he had to pause to catch his breath. For a moment, he was helpless against the incredible onslaught of feelings. Was it remotely possible that it could always be like this? he wondered. The thought was almost impossible to believe. But his answer came when she began to undulate and strain against him. A driving force took possession of him, and he knew that it would always be so.

A floodgate opened, sending unbelievable pleasure in cascades over them, drenching them with ecstasy until they were saturated and could take no more.

The candles burned lower and lower, their flames dancing unnoticed in the heated air. And there was no relief from the rapture. It continued through the night.

Gradually, one by one, the candles guttered down and went out. Finally, at dawn's first light, Nico and

Caitlin fell asleep, tangled together, arms and legs, hearts and minds, bodies and souls.

CAITLIN'S HAIR SPILLED over one bare shoulder in a shining fall as she came up on her elbow and gazed down on Nico's sleeping face. The wariness had come back over him while he slept, but she wasn't concerned. Last night they had shared something extraordinary, and all her doubts and confusion had vanished.

Through his lovemaking, she'd learned that he was a giving, generous, caring person. She'd learned that he could be both gentle and strong, tender and erotically rough. And if when he opened his eyes this morning and looked at her, she saw an expression that was difficult to read, she wouldn't worry. She'd learned he cared for her, and she believed with all her heart that love could grow from caring.

Adoringly, her gaze strayed over him, stopping to study the leanly muscled torso and the broad chest covered with a mat of curly black hair. At times in the night she had lain limply on his chest, fighting for breath and covered in sweat. He had soothed her, murmuring reassurance. And then they had started again.

A brief frown creased her forehead as she noticed the two angry red scars—aberrant marks against the perfection of his sleek, dark skin. The position of his body prevented her from seeing the entire length of the wounds, but she remembered their ridged feel beneath her fingertips. When she thought of the damage the bullets had done to his body, she gave thanks that he had escaped with only scars.

She reached out a hand to smooth a dark lock from his brow. His long thick lashes lifted to reveal warm smiling brown eyes.

"Did I wake you?" she asked.

"Yes. Did you intend to?"

She grinned. "Yes. I decided as long as I was awake, you should be awake, too."

"That's what you decided, was it?"

She nodded, enjoying his morning voice. It had the relaxed, husky timbre of intimacy. "It's nice watching you. You wake gently, as if you're saving your strength for what will come next."

"What do you think will come next?"

A sudden erotic urge flashed through her. "Something wonderful," she murmured, and was taken completely by surprise as he shifted his position, cupped one of her breasts with his long fingers and drew the nipple into his mouth. Her head went back, and her eyelids fluttered closed as an all-consuming heat took possession of her. He tugged and teased at the tormented point until she gasped and cried out. Then he pulled her mouth down to his and kissed her long and deep.

"Good morning," he said when he was done.

She slid down beside him, facing him, and threw her leg over his hip. She didn't know what time it was, and she didn't care. Activity had probably begun in other parts of the house, and decisions were waiting to be made. But she didn't care about that, either. He controlled her. And if he wanted, she'd stay in this bed forever. "Promise me we can always wake up together like this."

A low growl came from his throat. He pushed her over onto her back and surged powerfully and deeply into her, his muscles now coiled, his expression savage with desire. "If I have anything to say about it, we will."

She choked back a cry, wrapped herself around him, and let the wildness begin.

A long time later, the harsh, insistent sound of knocking and a faraway voice pierced through the softness of her dreams. She felt the mattress shift with Nico's weight as he sat up. Rubbing her eyes clear of sleep, she saw that he was pulling on a pair of pants. "Who is it?"

"Ramona. You stay put. You don't want to shock her." He pressed a quick kiss to her mouth, and without taking the time to fasten his pants, he got up and crossed the room. He opened the door only a few inches, angling it so that the view of the bed was shielded.

"Nico, I'm sorry to bother you, but I'm trying to find Caitlin."

Swiftly he tossed various options around in his head, but found none he liked. How in hell could he ease Ramona's mind while protecting the reputation of the woman in his bed? "Caitlin?" he repeated.

"I think I told you that she never eats breakfast, but she usually checks in with me sometime during the morning. When she didn't, I went looking for her. Mr. Haines hasn't seen her, and neither have any of the men. Then I checked her bedroom. Nico, there was a *fire* in there."

He sighed and rubbed the bridge of his nose. The fire couldn't be explained away. "Yes, I know."

"You *know?*"

"I helped her put it out."

"Was she hurt? Where in the world is she?"

"I'm right here, Ramona." Caitlin pulled the door from Nico's grasp and swung it open. "And no, I wasn't hurt."

Ramona's eyes widened as she took in Caitlin, wrapped in nothing but a sheet and standing next to a half-dressed Nico.

"I knocked a candelabrum over in my room last night, and the candles caught the drapes on fire. Luckily, Nico was passing by, and he put it out. Then, of course, I needed a place to sleep."

"Of course," Ramona said.

"We're sorry if we shocked you," Nico told her.

"You didn't shock me," Ramona said gruffly. "I was just worried about Caitlin, that's all."

"Well, I'm sorry I worried you. I should have let you know where I was, but..." She cast a helpless glance at Nico, who merely grinned back at her.

"Never mind," Ramona said, back to her brisk, no-nonsense self. "Now that I know you're all right, I'll get started cleaning up your room."

"Those drapes are heavy," Nico said. "Just leave them, and I'll take care of them."

"Never mind. One of the men will help me. In the meantime, I'll air out another bedroom. I don't think you'll want to sleep in there until the smoke damage has been seen to, do you, Caitlin?"

"No. You're absolutely right."

Ramona nodded and looked at Nico. "Can I assume you won't be leaving this morning?"

"Uh, yes, I won't be leaving this morning."

"Fine. Caitlin, later, when you get ready to move your things, you come and get me if you want help."

"I'll do that," Caitlin said.

Ramona turned on her heel and strode off. Nico shut the door. For perhaps thirty seconds, he and Caitlin stared at each other, then burst out laughing.

"Poor Ramona," he said.

"She'll be all right. She's seen a lot in her life. I'm sure she was more embarrassed than shocked."

"I think I just fell off her list of people she likes," he

said, steering her against the door and at the same time, unzipping his pants.

Caitlin's sheet slipped unnoticed to the floor as she wrapped her arms around his neck and gazed lovingly up at him. "Not at all. You wait. Next time she sees you, she'll be back to normal. In fact, I'm sure she plans to ignore the whole thing, as if it never happened."

"And she's going to prepare another room for you and move all of your things in, so that at night she can think of you in there rather than in here with me."

Caitlin nodded. "You got it."

He pushed his pants down, out of the way. Then with his hands cupping her bare buttocks, he lifted her, sliding her spine up the door until their eyes were level. "But you *will* be in here with me, won't you?"

She circled his body with her legs and threaded her fingers up into his hair. "Unless you kick me out."

"Me?" he said and pushed high into her. "Lord, you've gotta be kidding."

LATER THAT AFTERNOON, Caitlin descended the grand staircase with Nico beside her.

"I'm no expert, but I'm willing to bet this embroidery is going to be expensive to reproduce," Nico was saying regarding the piece of undamaged drapery they had salvaged from Caitlin's bedroom.

Caitlin's happiness was so pervasive, even the damage didn't trouble her. They made the turn on the landing in front of the Tiffany window and started down the last flight of stairs. "I'll shop around. I don't want to have to settle for the *feeling* of the original. If at all possible, I want it to be exactly the same as the original."

"You know, Caitlin," he said, humor threading his voice, "most people involved with restorations are content to use fabrics and furnishings that are of the *type* of the period."

"But this is SwanSea."

Nico smiled wryly. "Right. How could I have forgotten?"

Caitlin laughed. "I admit it. I'm obsessive."

"Be obsessive about me, and I won't mind a bit." One minute he was smiling down at her; the next, he had tensed. "Looks like you have a visitor," he said, indicating the silver-haired man standing just inside the front doors. "Is he the electrical inspector you were waiting for?"

"Could be. I guess I'd better go check."

"I think I'll come with you to meet him if you don't mind."

"Of course I don't."

As she crossed the wide stretch of marble toward the newcomer, Caitlin studied him. An older man, he was fashionably dressed in taupe-colored linen slacks, an open-necked blue shirt and a navy sport coat. Tall and well built, he had hazel eyes and an attractive, slightly weathered face that made it impossible to guess his exact age. She supposed he was one of those fortunate men who seemed to stop aging in their forties and then began again sometime in their sixties. Nico would probably be one of those men, she thought idly.

As she drew near, she realized with amusement that he was studying her as closely as she had been studying him. "I'm Caitlin Deverell, and this is Nico DiFrenza. May I help you?"

"I'm Quinn O'Neill," he said, nodding to Nico and extending his hand to her, "and I'm delighted to meet you."

"How do you do," she said, shaking his hand. "I assume you're the electrical inspector?"

Humor flashed in his eyes. "No, no, I'm afraid not. I'm just a longtime admirer of the house. I'm on holiday in the area, and I thought I'd take the opportunity to stop by."

He spoke without an accent, yet used a European-flavored phrase. Caitlin decided he must have lived overseas for a time. "I'm sorry, Mr. O'Neill, but SwanSea isn't open yet."

He nodded, his expression intent. "I can see that you're in the middle of work. When do you plan to open?"

"Next spring."

"So long?"

His tone carried a hint of wistfulness, and his manner conveyed a warmth that Caitlin responded to.

He grinned. "You'll have to forgive me. I'm really disappointed. I had hoped I could stay here for a few days."

Caitlin was tempted to laugh. Two men with the same wish in such a short time. Apparently she was going to have no trouble booking guests. "You wouldn't want to stay here now, believe me. Things are a real mess. We don't even have electricity at the moment."

"I really wouldn't mind. You see, I stayed here once a long time ago."

Caitlin's interest sharpened. "Really? When?"

"I can't remember exactly...as I said, it was many years ago. But I've always remembered SwanSea as a very special place."

"Were you here visiting my grandfather?"

Quinn nodded. "Jake was a wonderful man. I was sorry to hear of his death."

"Thank you."

Standing beside Caitlin, Nico realized his shoulders

were tensed and his instincts were telling him to be wary. He'd felt this way before in the presence of dangerous men. But he had to wonder, could he trust his instincts in this situation? Or was he simply experiencing the prickly awareness one male feels when another enters his territory? Out of the corner of his eyes, he saw Ramona approaching. She came to a stop near him and listened.

"It would really mean a lot to me if you'd let me stay for a few days," Quinn said. "I promise I wouldn't be a bother."

Caitlin considered the man before her, thinking that it was too bad she was going to have to turn him down. He seemed charming, and his charm was inherent, not forced. She liked him for that. "Mr. O'Neill—"

His smile told her he knew what she was about to say. "You're going to break my heart if you say no."

She laughed ruefully. "You're not making this easy for me."

"Good. Then you'll let me stay?"

"Caitlin pretty much has her hands full," Nico said, speaking up for the first time. "A guest would be out of the question."

"He's right—" she began.

"What's one more person?" Ramona asked.

All three turned toward her in surprise.

Ramona shrugged, uncomfortable beneath the scrutiny. "Heaven knows we have plenty of space, and I always cook for twenty anyway. And you can charge him enough to cover the cost of those new draperies you're going to have to order."

"Ramona's obviously bored," Caitlin said to Nico, her tone wry. "Taking care of you and me has lost its challenge."

"I thought you were going to Boston," Nico said pointedly to Ramona.

"Plans can be changed," she said just as pointedly as she crossed the marble floor to them. "Besides, Mr. O'Neill said he only planned to stay for a few days, and Boston will still be there when I get ready to go. Mr. O'Neill, I'm Ramona Johnson."

Quinn stepped forward and took her hand. "It's a pleasure to meet you. And thank you."

"Nothing to thank me for. Caitlin's is the final decision."

"Are you sure about this, Ramona?" Caitlin asked, and at Ramona's nod, she spread her hands. "Well, if you won't mind the mess, Mr. O'Neill, and Ramona doesn't mind the extra work, I don't suppose there's any reason why you can't stay."

"Thank you, Caitlin," he said seriously. "I'll try not to do anything that would make you regret your decision."

Ramona spoke up. "We'll choose you a bedroom, Mr. O'Neill, and then you can help me prepare it. Caitlin, have you moved your things yet?"

"Not yet, but I will."

"Are you going to need any assistance?"

"I don't think so. Thank you anyway."

"I'll show you the way, Mr. O'Neill."

"Quinn, please."

Nico's gaze followed the two as they ascended the stairs, Quinn moving easily beside Ramona. He was in good condition, Nico reflected, his body lean and muscled. And the uneasy feeling persisted that there was more to Quinn O'Neill than what he'd told Caitlin.

Is he the man Rettig has sent after me? he wondered grimly.

CHAPTER SIX

GOSSAMER CURTAINS of mist drifted across the cliffs. The sounds of the ocean and the gulls were loud in the early-morning quiet.

Quinn watched Caitlin, as he had ever since he'd arrived two days ago, and thought again how lovely she was. Wearing a flowing white dress, she seemed as ethereal as the diaphanous white haze through which she walked.

"Good morning, Caitlin," he called when she drew close enough to hear him.

"Good morning. I didn't know anyone else was up yet."

"At 6:00 a.m., no matter where I am in the world, my eyes pop open. What's your excuse?"

She laughed. "I've always loved this time of day on the cliffs. Even when I was a little girl, I used to climb out of bed and come here. I considered this time and this place my very own piece of heaven before the day began. I never grew out of that feeling. And now with the work going on at the house, I steal this time before the workmen start arriving at eight."

Quinn's expression turned rueful. "And here I've intruded. I'm sorry."

"Oh no, don't be. Actually, I'm glad I ran into you. I didn't see you yesterday. I have a feeling you're taking pains to keep out of the way."

"You were kind enough to let me stay. The least I can do in return is try not to be a bother."

She studied him curiously. "Tell me, has being back at SwanSea lived up to your expectations, or are you disappointed?"

He smiled slowly. "My expectations have been more than fulfilled."

"I'm glad."

"How is your family these days? I've heard rumblings that your uncle Seldon, Senator Deverell, is contemplating a bid for the presidency."

She laughed. "That's right. If he decides to go for it, the experts say he'll win. And Uncle Jacob still holds the title of chairman of the board, but his son Conall pretty much runs Deverell's these days."

"And your mother?"

"She's fine. She's away at the moment."

After a moment, Quinn said, "I think your grandfather made a very wise decision to leave SwanSea to you, Caitlin."

Through the shifting veils of mist, she stared at the house. "Grandfather said that since I was the only Deverell ever to have been born here, I had an extraordinary bond to the house. SwanSea has always been special to the Deverells, but he felt that I was the only one of his four children and two grandchildren who could see what my great-grandfather Edward saw in it. Maybe it was because I spent so many years alone here with only my mother, Ramona and the house for company. The house was almost like a playmate."

"And now you're taking steps to share it with others," Quinn said gently. "That is admirable."

She shrugged. "Not really. My decision involves many things."

"But I'm willing to bet that at the bottom of all those reasons is love of SwanSea."

She nodded and looked back at him. "Sometime I'd like you to tell me about the time you spent here. I enjoy hearing stories about how it used to be."

He turned slightly, so that his expression was partially obscured. "SwanSea's future will shine every bit as bright as its past, Caitlin. I'm confident. Look, there's a fishing boat. Makes a pretty picture, doesn't it, coming out of the mist like that."

She followed his gaze. "It's riding low in the water. I guess they've already gotten their catch. They must have been out for a few days."

FROM HIS BEDROOM WINDOW, Nico also stared at the fishing boat. He'd seen it before, and something about it bothered him, although he couldn't decide what. His gaze returned to Caitlin and the man she was talking to.

Quinn O'Neill disturbed him, too. A lot. If he'd known when he'd felt Caitlin slip out of bed earlier that she would run into Quinn, he would have gone with her. He felt no sense of security that this was the start of Quinn's second full day here and so far he had made no overt moves. Quinn was watching him just as he was watching Quinn. Maybe he was exactly what he seemed, but Nico seriously doubted it. But whatever and whoever Quinn was, he could handle him.

Caitlin was another matter. Nico had no confidence that their situation would be as simple. She'd not only trusted him in her home; now she'd trusted him in her bed. There were times when he felt like the lowest of the low, a first-class bastard. But at night, when they made love, he forgot everything but her. And despite his guilty conscience, whether it was daylight or dark, he knew he'd do everything in his power, honest or dishonest, to keep her with him.

With fresh determination when Caitlin was busy, he had intensified his search of the attic, the most likely place where something from long ago would have been stored.

But he'd made a crucial decision. He could no longer go on without telling Caitlin. He didn't want to hurt her. And no matter her reaction, he didn't want to deceive her.

The mist was lifting; the sun was coming out. Quinn and Caitlin were walking toward the house. Nico's mouth curved with a tender smile as he looked down on Caitlin. No, he thought. He didn't want to hurt her. He wanted only to love her.

CLUSTERS OF GLASS GRAPES hung from the ceiling at different lengths in a fantasy grape arbor created by Louis Comfort Tiffany. Each cluster sheathed a light and cast a iridescent glow over Nico's bedroom that evening. Fresh from the shower, he lay across the end of the bed, his elbow propping up his head, a towel draped over his hips.

A few feet away, Caitlin swept a silver-backed brush through her hair. Her every movement caused light to flow through the folds of the pale gold silk nightgown.

"I can't believe that one hundred rolls of wallpaper were delivered today and not one of them was the right pattern," she was saying.

"Why can't you believe it?" he asked absently, enthralled by her feminine rituals. Each pass of the brush through her hair brought more life and luster to the long strands.

She paused, giving his question thought. "I don't

know. I suppose I expected that because it was Swan-Sea being renovated, everyone involved would give their all." Unexpectedly, the sound of her laughter erupted, spreading a warmth through the room and him. "I guess it was a pretty absurd assumption on my part, wasn't it?"

"I don't think you were that far off base. The men who you have working for you seem very conscientious."

"They are. But then, most of them have grown up around here, and they have relatives who've worked for the family. Some even have ancestors who helped build the house. But the suppliers I'm dealing with long-distance have never seen SwanSea."

"It will all work out," he said softly.

"I know. And we do have the electricity back."

"I didn't mind using candles."

"I didn't, either, now that you mention it." The smile she gave him spoke of a sexual familiarity, and it sent desire tingling through him. Any second now, his decision would become secondary to his desire. And he couldn't let that happen.

"There is something I have to tell you, Caitlin."

She tossed the brush onto a chair, pushed him back on the bed, and slid on top of him, arranging herself so that she lay full length over him. She dropped a kiss on his mouth, then crossing her arms on his chest, she propped her chin on her arms. "You're frowning. Why?"

"Because of what I have to tell you." He smiled with regret. "And Caitlin, I can only think of one thing when you're on top of me."

"What's so bad about that?" she asked and pressed a kiss on his chin.

"Not a damn thing. But..." He shifted out from under her, took a pair of shorts from the wardrobe, and slipped them on.

She sat up and eyed him worriedly. "Whatever this is, it must be bad if you have to get dressed."

His lips twisted. "I'm getting dressed because with the two of us wearing little or nothing, I can't forget, even for a few minutes, how very much I want you."

She sighed. "Okay, Nico, what is it?"

He braced his hands on his hips, searching his mind for some way to make the next few minutes easier for both of them. But there was no way. "Caitlin, I want you to know that I've systematically searched quite a bit of your house. In fact, I chose SwanSea as a place to recuperate because of my search."

The color in her face slowly drained away. *"What?"*

"It's true," he said grimly. "In fact, you caught me in the act one day as I was looking through the desk in the study. Remember?"

"Yes, but you said you were writing a letter to your great-grandmother and you needed a pen."

"A story I had prepared, just in case someone walked in and found me."

She couldn't begin to guess what he was leading up to, but she knew if it were bad, she was vulnerable. Her love for him had left her wide-open. But this couldn't be as bad as it sounded, she thought, refusing to jump to any conclusions. "I don't understand what it is you're trying to tell me."

"Just wait. I'm afraid your confusion is going to get worse. I'd do anything to spare us this, but from this moment on, I'm resolved there will be no more secrets between us."

"You're scaring me, Nico."

He knelt in front of the bed and took her hand. "Don't be afraid. What I'm about to tell you, Caitlin, holds importance only for people long dead and one very sick old woman. Try to remember that."

"All right."

"This concerns your great-grandfather Edward and his firstborn son and legitimate heir, John—my great-grandfather."

"Your *what?*" Shock made her whisper.

His lips briefly compressed. "I understand how hard this must be for you, but hear me out. I told you that Elena is ill and that lately she'd been speaking to me of a time long ago when she was a young woman in Italy. One night, right before I was shot, I made one of my regular visits to her, and she told me something I'd never heard before. In fact, none of the family had ever heard this story. It was so fantastic, we weren't even sure it was true. We're still not."

"What did she tell you?"

"The young man she met and married in 1916, when she was seventeen years old, was John Deverell."

She looked at him oddly. "John died in the war. That's why Edward sought out grandfather." She thought for a minute. "You think John and Elena married?"

"I'm only telling you what Elena told me. Do you know any details about John?"

"No, not really. I'm not sure anyone in the family does."

"Well, the DiFrenzas have never known anything except that Elena's husband was named John. She told me the rest of the story that night. In 1913, when John was eighteen, he left America to go on a grand tour. I gather there were some problems with his father, but she wasn't specific. The war began to break out in Europe, country by country, but John didn't want to return home. He liked being independent. Eventually, he must have been caught up in the fervor of the war because he enlisted in the Italian underground where he was really out of his father's reach. He and Elena met and married, and not too much longer after that, in 1917, he was killed. According to Elena, Edward knew nothing about her or her marriage to John, or that before his death, they had conceived a child. When the child was born, Elena named him Giovanni—John. My grandfather."

Caitlin could only stare at him, staggered by what she was hearing.

"Europe had been ravaged by the war," he said, "and Elena, all alone with her infant son, wrote to Edward of her marriage to John and of the child. She entered her son's name in her family Bible beneath his father's signature, inserted her letter of explanation between its pages along with her marriage certificate, wrapped up the Bible and mailed it off to America. John had told her his father was a hard man, but Elena was confident that with the documentation she was sending him, he wouldn't ignore the fact that he had a grandson, that he would send for them as soon as he received the package. Days turned into months and months into years, and Elena never heard from Edward."

"Why?" Caitlin asked. "Assuming all of this was true, of course."

"I have no idea. Neither does she. But she told me she was so angry and hurt that she took back her maiden name. And after several years, she was able to save money for passage to America. The rest of the story my family knew. She started out sewing in one of those sweatshops, making clothes for a local manufacturer.

But she was smart, and through hard work and luck, she was able to open a little shop of her own. That shop's success eventually led to what is known today as DiFrenza's."

"But if she was so angry, why did she move to the same city Edward lived in?"

He grinned. "If you knew Elena, you'd know that's something she'd do. She's a tiny thing, but she's got enough stubbornness and pride for a dozen big men. She told me she'd never attempted to contact any Deverell, though there must have been times when she could have used an influential and powerful ally. In fact, she told me that all these years, she's viewed the Deverell name with great disdain. She said if they didn't want her in their family, she certainly didn't want them in hers." His grin faded. "But she does want back the Bible that lists the birth of her son along with the signature of her husband."

She gazed at him, her mind whirling.

"After I was shot, I decided to use my convalescent period to ease her mind, come up here and poke around a bit. Besides that, my captain was urging me to get out of town." Watching her, Nico saw an array of emotions reflected on her face. He'd confessed the most important part of his subterfuge, and he hoped she still trusted him. Unfortunately he didn't have a clue as to what she was feeling.

"Nico, why didn't you tell me all of this when you first came here, instead of the lies and the searching behind my back?"

He'd been waiting for the question, and he had no thought of trying to duck it. "Caitlin, what would you have done if I'd shown up on your doorstep and announced that I had a contract on my head, needed a place to recuperate from bullet wounds given to me by a drug lord, and oh, by the way, it was possible that I was related to your family, but I needed to search the house to find the proof."

"I would have slammed the door in your face."

"Right."

"But after we got to know one another—"

"Remember, I wasn't sure if the story was true. I didn't want you to think that I had been using you or that I was trying to take something away from you."

"You did use me," she pointed out with unerring reason.

He was a brave man; courage came easily to him. But telling her the truth about what he'd done had proved to be one of the hardest things he'd ever had to do. The thought that he might lose her made his nerves unsteady. "You have to understand that I deal with life-and-death situations on a daily basis, and this seemed harmless in comparison. Initially I was using you, but I knew my intentions were only to put Elena's mind to rest, not to harm you in any way. And if it makes you feel any better, I started feeling guilty as hell almost immediately."

"But not enough to tell me?"

She wasn't going to be able to understand, he thought, then quickly shook his despair away. No. She *had* to understand, and she *had* to forgive him. He wouldn't let her out of this room until she did.

He rose from his knees and sat beside her on the bed, turning to face her. "By then, I had too much to lose if you didn't believe me. So I put off telling you. And put it off. And put it off. I haven't handled any of this worth a damn, Caitlin. I admit it. I'm a bastard. But I'm a bastard who loves you. No matter what, always remember that."

She felt the breath leave her body. "You love me?"

"More than my own life."

She could hardly believe her ears. "You love me? Why haven't you told me?"

All the love and tenderness he felt for her showed in his smile. "I fought like hell not to love you, but I think I was lost the first minute I laid eyes on you." He paused. "Caitlin, what do you think about what I've just told you about Elena and John?"

"I don't know what to think," she said truthfully. "As a matter of fact, I'm finding it very hard to think at all at the moment." Suddenly she laughed and threw her arms around his neck. "You love me," she said, her voice filled with amazement.

He groaned. "Caitlin, we need to talk more about the Bible and letter I've been searching for."

She put a hand to his face. "Nico, it's natural for me to be astonished by this news. Anyone would feel the same if they had just been told there might be a whole new line to their family tree. But why should we waste any more time talking about something that might not even be true? Especially since I have something very important to tell you."

"Caitlin—"

"I love you, Nico."

He stared at her, stunned. "Do you mean that, or are you just saying it?"

She laughed joyously. "Why would I say something like that if I didn't mean it?"

Bewildered, he raked his hands through his hair. "I don't know."

"Don't you want me to love you?"

"*Want* you to love me? Caitlin—"

The look of utter wonderment on his face made her

act. She stood and gracefully shimmied out of the pale gold silk gown until she stood naked before him. "Make love to me, Nico."

With a low, rough sound of surrender, he reached for her and pulled her down beside him. The lights above them filtered through the colored translucent glass, casting the shapes and deep rose-and-purple colors of grapes over her skin. His mouth began to water as his body hardened.

He bent to taste the wine of the grapes.

CHAPTER SEVEN

HIS ROOM HAD been searched. Nico knew it as soon as he entered his room the next afternoon after a jog. Nothing was out of place; nothing seemed disturbed. But his sixth sense was telling him that his room had been gone through in an extremely professional manner.

Quinn O'Neill. It couldn't be anyone else.

Ever since he'd been here, the work crew had been in and out of the house, and nothing unusual had happened. Besides, Caitlin knew them all. Quinn was the stranger at SwanSea.

He'd already considered the idea that Quinn could be after him. What he hadn't considered was that Quinn could be after Caitlin. It was time to act.

He made a quick trip outside, but Quinn's car was gone. Back upstairs, he called Amarillo.

"I need you to do something for me," he said as soon as he heard his friend on the line.

"Does it involve killing someone?" Amarillo asked with mild interest.

Nico's lips quirked. This was just one of the many times Nico had been thankful that Amarillo was on his side. "I'm not sure yet. Depends on what you find. A man by the name of Quinn O'Neill has shown up here. Use every contact you have, call in favors, beg if you have to, but find out who he is."

"What's he done?"

"My room's been searched. I'm sure he found my badge and gun."

Amarillo's laconic tone disappeared. "Get out of there now, Nico. Your position's been compromised. I told you two days ago that I have a safe place up the coast all ready for you."

"I can't leave him here with Caitlin until I know who he is. Besides, I don't think he's after me. If he was, he would have been supplied with positive identification, photos, the works. But if he's after Caitlin, he might have searched my room to find out who I was and what sort of threat I might be to his plans."

"You mean because he's seen the two of you together?"

"Right."

"I don't like this one bit, Nico."

"Believe me, I'm not jumping for joy myself, but I'll argue with you later. For now, do as I ask. He's driven off somewhere, so I don't have his license number, but here's his description."

CAITLIN'S FACE LIT UP when she saw Nico walk into her study. "I've been wondering where you were and what you were doing."

He leaned across the desk and gave her a kiss. "And I've been wondering how you and I can pull an escape."

"An escape?"

"How would you like to get away from the house for a while? Take a drive. See a movie. Eat lunch somewhere. *Anything.* I'm open to suggestion as long as it's away from here."

She grinned. "Feeling cooped up?"

He straightened. "I'm not sure 'cooped up' is the right phrase. After all, SwanSea is bigger than some countries."

"Not quite," she said with a laugh.

"Well, almost. But I'm definitely restless and in the mood to see something different."

She glanced at the mound of paperwork on her desk and grimaced.

"There's nothing there that can't wait, Caitlin."

Making an instant decision, she pushed away from the desk and stood up. "You're absolutely right. How about going into town? I'd love to show it to you, and I know a great place for lunch."

"Sounds good."

She clapped her hands together, excited. "Okay, now all we have to do is get out of here without anyone stopping me to ask a question."

"Walk fast, don't meet anyone's eyes and keep a straight face. With any luck, we'll be out of here before anyone notices you're gone."

"Good plan. I approve."

Two people called out to her and they received more than a few strange looks, but no one tried to stop them. And by the time they reached the front veranda, their obvious furtiveness had reduced them to giggles.

"We made it," she said joyfully.

Nico's laughter faded as he saw Quinn coming up the steps toward them. "Not quite."

Quinn nodded coolly to Nico, but gave Caitlin a smile. "Hello. What are you two up to?"

"We're running away for the afternoon," Caitlin said in a conspiratorial tone. "But you've got to promise not to tell anyone."

He crossed his heart solemnly. "I promise. Are you running away to any place in particular or just running?"

"Just running," Nico said, not wanting to reveal to Quinn where they'd be.

"We're going into town," Caitlin said.

Quinn shot Nico a look that set off alarm bells in his head. One thing was for sure. Quinn didn't trust Nico any more than Nico trusted him. The search of his room proved that if nothing else. But why?

"I've just returned from there," Quinn said, speaking to Caitlin. "It's a charming place, and I have to say it hasn't changed all that much since the last time I was here."

"When exactly *was* that?" Nico asked. "I don't believe you ever said."

Quinn gave a self-deprecating laugh. "That's because I can't remember. Over the years, my sense of time has become warped."

"What did you do in town?" Caitlin asked.

"Nothing much. Just wandered around. Revisited some of the places I had seen so long ago."

"And it really hasn't changed?" she asked.

"Not in any significant way. Oh, I think there've been one or two coats of paint added, and of course the church is finished now. But it looked to me as if the same families were running the same shops. The fudge even tasted the same. Sinful."

Caitlin laughed. "Ah, you visited the candy store. We'll have to do that, too," she told Nico. "The fudge they make there is to die for."

The phrase sent a chill up his spine. "We'd better get going," Nico said quietly.

"YOU'VE BEEN AWFULLY QUIET," Caitlin said, studying Nico. "Are you upset about something?"

Silently, wearily, he cursed himself. He had forgotten how perceptive she could be. He'd been thinking about Quinn and wondering why he had searched his room. "No, I'm not upset, but I am sorry. I guess I haven't been very good company."

They'd chosen to eat in a converted boathouse at the end of a long pier. Inside the rustic restaurant, old copper gleamed, and lobster traps adorned the walls. Their table was covered by plastic-coated oilcloth and was set by a big picture window. The ocean surrounded them and rolled beneath them.

"You don't have to be good company, Nico," Caitlin said. "Just being with you is enough to make me happy."

His dark eyes narrowed on her. "Has anyone ever told you that you're wonderful?"

She tried unsuccessfully to swallow a sudden lump. "Right at this moment, I can't remember a time."

"Then let me tell you. You're wonderful."

"You're going to make me blush."

He propped his arms on the table and took her hand. "I like it when you blush all over."

"I *don't* blush all over. Maybe a little bit on the cheekbones, but definitely not all over."

"You do, and I'll prove it to you tonight. All I have to do is start kissing you on your—"

"Do you have everything you need?"

They both started and broke away. A small tow-headed boy about five years old was standing by their table.

"My mom sent me over to ask you. She said to say it just like how I said it."

Caitlin smiled. "Hi, Tommy. You know I almost didn't recognize you, you're getting to be so big."

He nodded solemnly. "I know." He stuck his hands deep into the pockets of his overalls and looked at Nico.

"Do you want some of my grandma's blueberry cobbler? It's real good. She baked two panfuls this morning."

"Really? And you recommend this cobbler, do you?"

The boy nodded. "I've already had a bowl. I wanted another, but my mom said no."

Nico grinned. "I guess that's a pretty good recommendation. I'll take a bowl. How about you, Caitlin?"

"Sure, why not? What's an extra five pounds or so?"

"You have to have it with ice cream," Tommy said, "'cause it's better that way."

"We'll trust your judgment," Nico said.

Caitlin groaned. "Make that ten pounds."

Tommy smiled from ear to ear. "I'll go tell my mom."

"Cute kid," Nico said.

"Precious," she said. "As you may have gathered, this is a family business. Tommy's brothers caught the lobster that went into our stew, and his father cooked it."

"It was delicious."

Caitlin took a spoon and crushed a silver-dollar-size mint leaf against the side of her tea glass. "You were good with him. Did you ever think you'd like to have children?"

He arched an eyebrow in surprised. "No, not really. Police work is hard on family life."

"But it doesn't make it impossible. And I gather your family is very important to you."

"Very," he said with a smile "In fact, that's something you and I have in common."

"It's true. Although physically my family is pretty far-flung most of the time, we are very close."

He hesitated, then proceeded carefully. "Except, apparently, for one member."

She looked puzzled. "Who?"

"Your father. I've been wondering about him."

She shrugged. "I've never had one, except biologically of course."

"What happened? Did he leave you and your mother when you were a baby?"

"Try before I was born. It was a hit-and-run sort of affair."

He reached over and clasped her hand in his. "That sounds very bitter. Was it hard on you growing up without a father?"

"No, of course not. I couldn't miss something I never had."

"I'm not sure I believe that."

She grimaced. "Well, to tell you the truth, I'm not sure I do, either. But my mother suffered more than I did, though she never said anything."

"Do you mind talking about this?"

"Not with you. I've never felt the stigma of being illegitimate. It wasn't the badge of dishonor it was in grandfather's day."

"Then why did you and your mother live in such seclusion and isolation at SwanSea for the first six years of your life?"

"I think she needed those years to come to terms with what happened. And we weren't always alone. The family visited often."

"And you loved having SwanSea all to yourself."

She flashed him a grin. "I did, but looking back on it, I can see that Mother was in pain. I guess that's what I resent my unknown father for most—what he did to my mother. *Anyway*," she said brightly, "that's all in the past, and there's something I've been wondering about that very much concerns the present."

"What's that?"

"Well, it's obvious that you're almost fully recovered now."

"I *am* recovered," he said firmly.

She nodded. "Well, I've been thinking about your work and wondering how much longer you can stay."

"Anxious to get rid of me?" he asked, mentally running through his situation. There was still the matter of Nathan Rettig. He was out there somewhere, searching for him. And then there was Quinn. He wasn't about to leave Caitlin alone until he had figured out who Quinn was and what he wanted.

The wry face she made was an attempt to cover her self-consciousness. He'd told her he loved her, but he'd offered no commitment. "You know better than that."

He stood, leaned across the table, and kissed her in full view of the other patrons. Then he sat back down and took her hand again. "I know your work is here and mine is in Boston. I'm not sure how, Caitlin, but we'll work it out. There's no way I'm letting you get away from me. No way."

Until the real thing came along, she thought, she'd take that as a commitment. Reassured, Caitlin smiled, and when Tommy's mother set their ice-cream-ladened cobblers in front of them, she gave a carefree laugh. "This blows my plans to have fudge for dessert."

A half hour later, the warm afternoon breeze rippled the surface of the small deep-water harbor, making the masted sailboats bob and the water glisten like a black-green jewel. Robin's-egg blue, sunshine-yellow, forest-green and deep-red colors adorned the clapboard buildings with their steeply pitched roofs and their geranium-filled window boxes.

"The candy shop is just up ahead," Caitlin said, her arm in Nico's.

"How can you be interested in fudge after that lunch we just had?" He reached down and patted her flat stomach. "Where do you put it all?"

She laughed. "I'm not saying I want to eat the fudge now. But they sell fudge *to go*." She lifted her eyebrows in what was meant to be a significant manner.

He smiled indulgently. Caitlin in a playful mood had a way of melting away his problems. "Ah, I see. *To go*."

"Right. We can get a bag and take it back with us. For *tonight*."

"You and fudge," he murmured. "I can hardly wait."

In a show of mock dismay, she hit her forehead with the heel of her hand. "Oh, no! What am I going to do if you find out that you like the fudge better than you like me?"

The look he gave her was potent with love and wanting. "Not a chance."

"You haven't tasted this fudge yet," she said softly.

"No, but I've tasted you."

"Taste me again," she whispered, leaning against him.

He groaned and bent his head to brush her lips, then dip his tongue into her mouth.

"Let's go home," he murmured.

She felt a small thrill at the fact that he'd unconsciously referred to SwanSea as home. "We will as soon as we get our fudge. Besides, we're here."

"Here?"

"Here," she said, motioning toward a large plate-glass window. "Look, he's about to make a new batch."

On the other side of the window, a pleasant-faced rotund man poured hot fudge onto a cool marble slab.

"That's Paul McGruder," she said, waving to the man. "He owns the shop."

She leaned back against Nico, and he circled his arms around her waist. While they watched, Paul took up a scraper and began lifting the rich dark chocolate and folding it back on itself. He repeated the process again and again.

"Why do I think you've spent a lot of time in front of this window?" Nico asked, his mouth to her ear.

"I have no idea why you would think that." Her tone was innocent, but her expression was rapt.

As the fudge began to thicken, Paul reached for a handful of walnuts and sprinkled them over the glistening surface of the candy. Knowing that he had an audience, he performed his tasks with flourish, slicing through the nuts with the scraper to mix them into the fudge.

Images flowed across the plate-glass window—people strolling behind them along the harbor's edge, the boats, a dog chasing a low-flying bird.

But it was Caitlin's reflection that Nico studied in the glass, enjoying her delight in the candy making. Over the past days, he'd learned that there were many sides to her: the woman who was wild and passionate in his bed, the dreamer and the businesswoman who was bringing SwanSea back to life, the playful flirt, and now the little girl who loved to watch fudge being made. *He loved all the Caitlins.*

"If we don't go home immediately," he whispered in her ear. "I'm going to make love to you right here."

THE NEXT AFTERNOON, Nico surveyed the attic room he had been methodically searching for the last two hours. Caitlin now knew what he was doing and why, but he wasn't at all happy about his activities, and he'd made a vow to himself. There were more attic rooms, but this was the last he planned to go through.

He believed the rambling story Elena had told him; he'd made her a promise, and he'd tried to fulfill that promise to the best of his ability. But he owed Caitlin his loyalty. And this would be the last time he would dig through her family's possessions. His investigation ended here.

Without enthusiasm, he knelt before yet another dusty trunk and inserted a pick into the old lock, gently manipulating the rusty mechanism until it sprang open. Lifting the lid, he delved into the contents.

Quilts, old letters, shoes, lace, odds and ends. He had pulled half the contents onto the floor when he saw the package. Wrapped in plain brown paper and tied with string, the package bore a postmark more than seventy years old.

"Oh, hell," he murmured.

With the minimum of tearing and ripping, he slipped off the string and the paper, then let out a long shaky breath as he stared at the contents of the package. "Oh, *hell*," he said again, this time with force and meaning.

Reluctantly, he checked the entry in the Bible and scanned the marriage license. He'd found the proof Elena wanted.

For one wild moment, he was tempted to destroy it, he was so concerned about how Caitlin would take the news. They'd both become distracted last night, and he hadn't had a chance to say everything he had planned to say.

Reason, plus loyalty and love for Elena, quickly reasserted themselves. The news would make Elena happy. Whatever other waves the news created, he vowed, he was going to move heaven and earth to make sure that nothing changed between him and Caitlin.

Slowly, he replaced the contents of the trunk along with the package, shut the lid, and went to find her.

"HI," CAITLIN SAID, meeting Nico just outside her study. "I was coming to find you."

"Through with your work?"

She nodded.

"Good, because—"

"Nico?" Ramona called, coming down the hall. "There's a phone call for you."

"You can take it in my study," Caitlin said. "I'll wait for you in the drawing room."

"No." He took her hand. "I don't mind you being there."

In the study, he picked up the phone. "Rill?"

"Yeah, I'm afraid I've got some bad news. I've just been notified that two of Rettig's men were spotted in your area."

"Damn."

"Now listen. The local police may be first-rate for all I know, and we'll fill them in out of courtesy, but I want our people to handle this."

"I agree."

"Good. Stay put. I'll be there in—"

"Hold it. Let's think this through before we jump the gun. If they've found me, why haven't they acted?"

"I don't know," Amarillo said tightly, "but if it will make you feel any better, I'll ask them right after I cuff them."

Nico glanced at Caitlin and saw her gazing at him anxiously. He pulled her against him. "Give me to-night, Rill, and I'll call you tomorrow." A long stretch of silence followed. "I mean it, Rill."

"You're taking a big chance, Nico."

"I know, but I'm not the only one involved."

"You mean Caitlin? We can protect her, too."

"We may have to, but I want more information before I make a decision. Something's not right. Have you gotten that other information I wanted?"

"Give me a call back in an hour. I should have it by then."

"Good, because I'll be basing my decision on it."

Nico hung up the phone and looked at her.

"What is it?"

He leaned back on the desk, pulled her between his outstretched legs, and began the story. "The name of the man I was investigating before he shot me is Nathan Rettig. I've just been told that two of his men have been spotted in the area. I have to assume they've tracked me here."

"Nico, no—"

"Don't worry. They're obviously waiting for something. Perhaps Rettig himself. I'm something he wouldn't want to leave to his minions. I've been able to heavily curtail his operation, although I haven't been able to get anything to stick. I'm like a thorn in his side, and he wants me bad."

"Maybe their being in the village is a coincidence," she said, clutching at straws.

"There are no coincidences where Rettig and his men are concerned. If it's not me that's brought them to the village, it's something to do with drug trafficking. Hell, for all I know, it could be both me and the drugs. But whatever the reason, I've got to find out."

"Leave it alone, Nico. Let someone else go after him this time."

He felt an incredible sadness as he met her troubled gaze. He knew he couldn't do as she asked, and he didn't even want to.

She read his thoughts and wrapped her arms around

herself to still the shudder she could feel spreading in her. Nico in danger hadn't been a reality to her before now.

His hand strayed to the side of her head and brushed a silky wave. "I'm so sorry, honey."

"For what?" she asked, startled.

"For bringing danger into your safe world. I never meant to, you've got to believe me."

"I do."

"But you're scared."

"Yes," she said in a small voice.

"It's nothing to be ashamed of. When you've lived all your life in safety, it's hard to cope with danger, except in the abstract. Try not to worry. I'm going to do everything in my power to make sure the danger doesn't touch you."

"And what are you going to do to protect yourself?"

He smiled. "The same. Everything in my power. I don't have a death wish, Caitlin. Especially now that I've found you."

She felt her eyes fill with tears and blinked them away. "So what are your plans?"

"I should get out of here, but there's someone here at SwanSea I don't trust, and I'm too concerned about you to leave just yet."

"Me?"

"Caitlin, it's Quinn O'Neill."

"Quinn?" she asked, surprised.

"He disturbs me. He seems to watch you all the time. But there are other things. For a retired man on vacation, he takes great care to blend into the woodwork. He watches, but he doesn't want anyone watching him."

"Maybe that's just his personality."

"I don't think so. But in any case, I thought you

should know. I'm having Rill, the man who just called, check him out right now. I'm only sorry I didn't do it the first day Quinn came here."

"Why didn't you if you were suspicious?"

"Because I was all tangled up with you," he said huskily, "and I couldn't be sure why my instincts were telling me to be on guard. I could have been just jealous of the man."

"Oh, Nico."

He put his arm around her, pressed his mouth to the top of her head, and breathed in the special scent that was Caitlin.

"Nico, I just thought of something!" She pulled away and looked up at him, her eyes wide with alarm. "When we met Quinn on the front veranda yesterday afternoon, he said the village hadn't changed much except for a few coats of paint and the fact that the church was finished."

"Go on."

"Mr. Haines mentioned the other day that they built the church twenty-five or twenty-six years ago. That means that Quinn must have been here during that time."

Nico nodded. "Sounds like it."

"But don't you see? He said he was here visiting Grandfather. Grandfather didn't live here during that time. He and Arabella were in Europe. The house was closed up."

"Are you sure?"

"Absolutely. Quinn lied to me."

Nico's mouth tightened. "Let's go for a walk. By the time we get back, Rill should have that information."

THE SUN WAS SETTING behind the great house, the color of the ocean darkening, but the scene was lost on the two men who stood on the bluff talking intently.

"So now you know," Quinn said, carefully watching Nico's face for reaction. "I thought I could come here, stay a while, then leave without anyone being the wiser."

"That sounds familiar," Nico said. It was no wonder something in him had recognized that Quinn should be handled with care. The two of them were much alike.

Quinn slipped his hands into his trouser pockets and rocked back on his heels. "You have my life in your hands...so to speak. What are you going to do?"

"My main concern is that Caitlin not be hurt. If you leave now, she won't be."

"And if I do leave, I have your word that you'll keep silent?" Quinn asked without expression.

"You have my word."

"I wasn't ready to leave yet, but—"

"This afternoon would be a good time, but I'll accept in the morning."

Quinn studied Nico's hard face. He'd had many opportunities to observe him since he'd come to SwanSea, and he'd concluded that Nico was not a man he'd want to cross. But Nico was also a man he could admire without any reservations. A wry grin creased his face. "Your partner must have dug real deep to find me."

"There's nothing and no one Amarillo can't find if he sets his mind to it."

"Well, I'm going to have to make a few calls to see that it doesn't happen again."

"That might be a good idea."

Quinn nodded, knowing there was nothing left to say. He turned slightly, preparing to leave, when his attention was caught. "That's odd," he said.

"What?" Nico jerked his head around to the ocean and followed Quinn's gaze. "You mean that fishing boat?"

"Yes. It's riding low in the water, which should indicate they have their catch for the day. But there's no seagulls around the boat. Fish always draw seagulls."

"That *is* odd," Nico said thoughtfully.

When Caitlin had first rounded the corner of the house and seen Nico and Quinn out on the cliff, she'd had a sudden whimsical thought that she was viewing a scene out of an old western. The two men were standing as if they were facing off, their postures radiating tension. She'd wondered if her intrusion would defuse the situation or make it worse. In the end, she'd decided to let the two men play it out themselves, and as she watched, she saw the tension gradually fade away.

As he walked back to the house, Quinn saw Caitlin, hesitated, then continued toward her. "Caitlin, I'm glad to see you. I was on my way to find you."

"Oh?"

His composure faltered only slightly in the face of her obvious coolness. "I wanted to personally thank you for allowing me to stay at SwanSea. I plan to thank Ramona, too, of course."

She glanced over his shoulder to the cliff and Nico, then looked back at him. "Then you're leaving?"

"Yes, I'm afraid I have to. I'll pack tonight and start out in the morning, but I probably won't see you again before I go."

She didn't know whether Nico was still suspicious of Quinn, but his leaving was probably best. Still, she was curious. "Do you plan to continue your vacation somewhere else?"

"I think I've had enough vacation for a while. I need to get on with my retirement plans—decide what I'm going to do with the rest of my life."

She brushed a strand of hair from her eyes. "You know, you really don't look old enough to retire."

Without waiting for her to offer her hand, he reached out and took it. "Thank you. That's a very nice compliment, but I'm ready to retire, believe me. And I just want to say that it was a pleasure meeting you. You're a lovely young woman. Goodbye, Caitlin."

"Goodbye." She stared after him, wondering why she felt disturbed about his leaving. She felt the warmth of Nico's body behind her and turned to look up at him. "Quinn says he's going in the morning. Did he tell you?"

"Yes."

"Well? Tell me what happened. What did you find out about him?"

"I was wrong. He's not a problem or a threat to us."

Her gaze strayed in the direction Quinn had gone. Something about him troubled her, but she didn't know what. "Are you sure?"

"Yes, I'm sure."

"But what about the timing of his other stay here?"

"He said himself he couldn't remember exactly. He must have been mistaken about the church."

"I suppose that's possible. That was a long time ago, and he's apparently traveled much of the world. He's bound to have seen a lot of churches."

He made an abrupt gesture with his hand. "Well, at any rate, I'm not worried about Quinn anymore, but I am still worried about Rettig. I need to leave, Caitlin."

"Oh, no." She reached out for him. Her hand found the solid strength of his chest. "Please don't go."

He covered her hand with his. "I have to, Caitlin. If Rettig knows where I am, my leaving will draw him away from here and you. If he doesn't know, it will eliminate the possibility that he'll find out."

He was a man accustomed to action and danger, she thought, but she wasn't. She loved him, and the thought that someone wanted to hurt him was unbearable. "I'm afraid for you."

He smiled with understanding. She'd never be afraid for herself. "I'll be safer away from here, Caitlin. If I stayed, my main concern would be you."

"Instead of watching out for yourself."

He nodded. He knew from the resignation in her voice that he'd given her the one argument she wouldn't try to take apart.

Her shoulders slumped. "Then I guess I'll have to let you go, won't I?"

He drew her to him until he could feel her soft curves against him. "We're going to be all right, Caitlin. I promise you. We're going to be all right."

The wind took his words, mixed them with the sound of the sea, and carried them up to the cloud that drifted across the sun and shadowed SwanSea.

CHAPTER EIGHT

CAITLIN HELD A MATCH to the wick of the last tall cream-colored candle. When the flame burned steadily, she turned.

Nico lay waiting for her on the bed. The pale white-gold light flowed over the muscular angles and planes of his masculine nudity, giving his skin the texture of velvet and muting the two red scars on his left side.

"Don't come back to me with any more scars," she whispered.

"I won't." He studied the way the candlelight behind her shone through the gold of her long silk gown, outlining her shape, making her appear at once dreamlike and incredibly desirable. "You're beautiful."

"I'm serious, Nico."

"Does that mean you wouldn't want me to come back to you if I happened to take another bullet?"

"I couldn't bear it."

"What?"

"If you didn't come back to me." Her strained voice betrayed the fragile state of her nerves

In one fluid motion, he rose from the bed and went to her, framing her face between his hands. "I'll come back, Caitlin. There aren't enough bullets in the world to stop me."

"Promise me."

"I promise."

He drew her to the bed and down to the satin coverlet until they lay side by side.

"Do you believe me?" he asked, smoothing her hair away from her face.

"Yes."

"From this moment on, the things I tell you will always be the truth. I will never intentionally hurt you. I will never lie to you."

She reached out and touched his face, then let her fingers slowly drift down the hard length of his arm to entwine with his. "I'm going to miss you so much."

"We won't be apart long—that's another promise. I have the feeling that this case is close to being solved. I feel it." He lifted their joined hands to his mouth, kissed the back of her fingertips, then laid her hand between them so that he could push the gold silk strap from her shoulder. The gown loosened from her breast, and he brushed his fingers across the tops of the high flesh. "So soft," he murmured.

He trembled through her. "I didn't think it was possible to want someone the way I want you."

His eyes glittered with a dark fire, and he bent his head to suck a silk-covered nipple to life. His loins ached for her, as did his heart. But now was for finding new ways to make love to her, for driving himself inside her until he couldn't think, couldn't hear, couldn't see—then beginning again. Now was the time for making love to her until she asked him to stop. She'd never done that, he prayed she never would.

He pulled and tugged at the nipple with a gentle, persistent ferocity until she writhed against him, mindlessly, helplessly.

There was a thundering in her brain, a fire low in her

belly. She reached between them to grasp him and heard him draw in a ragged breath. With a delicate pressure, she stroked his length. His hands clenched the sheets, but he said nothing. She continued experimenting, learning the pressure that would make him groan aloud, the caressing touch that would make him roll his head from side to side against the pillow.

It was a time of heated enchantment for her. But soon his body drew taut, and she heard thickly spoken words rumble up from his chest. "You'd better stop."

"I don't want to stop. I like the feel of you." The pad of her finger found a particularly interesting spot and lingered.

"Ah..." His body jerked. "Lord, Caitlin!" He took her wrist, stilling the excruciating and wondrous motion of her hand. "I can make you stop," he said raggedly.

"By holding my wrist?"

"No."

She felt him slip his hands beneath her gown and touch her in a knowing, caressing way that soon had her moving against him once again, this time more urgently. He'd turned the tables on her.

"You're amazing," she said, gasping. "Magical. You make me burn...want...instantly, with just a touch."

"That's good." He slid his finger over her moist soft flesh—rubbing, pressing.

"Yes." Her heart was pumping so hard she was barely able to breathe. "That's good...very good...and it's bad."

"Bad?" He kissed her neck, then closed his teeth around her earlobe and nibbled. "Surely not."

His breath was hot on her skin, fueling the flames rising within her. "Yes. Bad because you make me hurt so much for you. I get to the point where I'll do anything to have you inside me."

With fraying control, he glided his fingers into her.

She closed her eyes, savoring the sensation of hundreds of pleasures that throbbed, tingled and pulsed.

"Are you at that point yet?" he asked, his mouth against her ear.

"Yes," she whispered in an agony of desire. "Oh, Nico, yes!"

"And what will you do?"

Her green-gold eyes were alight with an inner fever as she opened them and looked up at him. "Whatever you want."

A hard shudder ripped through him. "You don't have to do a thing. I'll take care of everything."

Holding her tightly, he rolled onto his back and lifted her over him. His strong arms supported her weight as she positioned herself and then slowly, softly slid down over him measure by measure until they were completely joined. A hoarse sound of satisfaction wrenched from his chest.

Above him, Caitlin shifted, maneuvering him deeper inside her. Already she could feel herself beginning to pulse toward the brink of release, and she began to move. But his hands flexed tightly on her buttocks, forcing her to a slower rhythm, guiding her to rock against him, to make circling movements with her hips.

She tilted her head back and moaned, feeling as though the pleasure might split her apart. Both straps had dropped off her shoulder, and the top of her gold silk gown had slipped down to the very edge of her nipples, barely covering the tips of the tight rose peaks.

Looking up at her, Nico's breath caught at the incredibly erotic picture she made. Gold silk, ivory skin, cinnamon hair—surrounded by white-gold light. The sight almost pushed him over the edge, but with superhuman strength and resolve, he pulled back.

She could feel the moment for which she yearned approaching. She leaned down to him so that her hands were braced on either side of him. Her nipples broke free of the gown and pressed into the thick black hair of his chest. Her hair fell like an exotic concealing veil around them. "You feel like hard, hot satin inside me," she whispered.

Her words set him on fire, and the start of the tiny inner convulsions of the muscles surrounding him stole away his sanity. He pushed high into her and surrendered himself to the night, the candlelight and her.

THE MIST BEGAN to lift from the sea at dawn. Nico observed the scene from the balcony of his bedroom. In a little while he would wake Caitlin and say goodbye. For now, though, he was content to watch the day appear little by little.

He didn't want to leave.

It was a given that he didn't want to say goodbye to Caitlin; every minute he spent away from her would be painful.

What surprised him was the realization that he was going to hate to leave SwanSea. He'd come to know all its odd little quirks, all its nooks and crannies, all the personalities the house could convey. He'd grown accustomed to this view—the rolling green lawn, the cliffs, the sea, the island, the boats... Hell. He was being ridiculous. How could you miss a house?

He'd feel better about leaving if he knew exactly what was going on with Rettig. If Rettig knew he was here at SwanSea, why hadn't he tried something? And if Rettig didn't know, then what the hell were his men doing in the area?

Nico frowned. Through the thinning mist he could just make out the island. The *island.* Suddenly, something in his mind clicked. "Well, I'll be damned," he muttered softly. "So that's what they're doing."

It was all so simple. The fishing boats that rode low in the water had no seagulls following them because their load was not fish. They carried something heavy to mask the fact that they also carried cocaine. Rettig had to be using the island as a dropping-off place for the drugs. His Canadian connections would come down and pick them up.

His adrenaline surged, sending his heart pumping at a furiously excited pace. He'd bet his seat on the board of DiFrenza's that he was right. As sure as he was about this, though, he knew what he had at the moment was only a theory. Up to this point, he hadn't been able to make any charges stick to Rettig. This time he would get absolute proof.

With one last glance at the island, he left the balcony to return to the bedroom and Caitlin. Perching on the side of the bed, he leaned over her and rained kisses over her smooth warm face.

Coming up from a cloud of sleep, she smiled softly. "It's nice being kissed awake," she murmured huskily.

"It's tolerable from my perspective too."

Her eyes slowly opened. "Good morning."

"Good morning." He kissed her, gently, lingeringly.

She blinked sleepily as he drew away. "Is it morning, by the way?"

"All the signs are pointing to it: sun, blue sky—"

She groaned and threw her arm over her eyes. "That means you're leaving."

He pulled her arm away from her face, chuckling. "I've changed my mind."

"What?" she asked, her eyes flying open. "Really?"

He nodded. "I've come up with a theory that requires my presence here. Besides, I'd feel better being here, protecting you."

He pulled back, and she pushed herself up, arranging the pillows behind her. "Why would you think I'm in danger?"

"There's a possibility that I didn't want to mention to you yesterday. Instead of trying for me and possibly failing, Rettig's men might take you hostage and use you against me. I've asked Rill to send men up to protect you. Now I'll tell him not to."

"I don't need protecting."

"Maybe you don't," he said softly, stroking her arm, "but I look at you, and everything in me wants to watch over you. And what's more, I don't see that instinct ever going away. I'm sorry."

She touched his face. "What's going on, Nico?"

"Rettig," he said succinctly. "I think I've finally figured what his men are doing here. The island."

"SwanSea's island?"

He nodded. "They're using the fishing industry of the area as a cover and the island as a drop-off and pick-up point. They fill up their specially equipped boats with something heavy to make it look as if they have a full load and are through fishing for the day. But their main cargo is cocaine. They bring it up the coast, mingling in with the regular fishing boats whenever possible. Then they drop the drugs off at the island. Sometime later, probably the next moonless night, Rettig's Canadian connections come down, load up their own boat, and take the stuff back to Canada. It's been working like a charm. They just forgot one little thing: Seagulls aren't attracted to weights. They should have thrown a few fish in, just for drill."

The idea of the island's being used for drug running was disturbing but secondary compared to her concern for Nico. She searched his face for some sign of his intentions. "So you're going to stay here and do what?"

"Don't worry, I don't plan to do anything stupid. I'm just going to keep a closer eye on the island and see if I can pick up a pattern."

"Nico—"

He touched her face. "Try to understand, Caitlin. I feel very proprietary toward Rettig. This is something I have to do. I started it, and I'm going to finish it."

"I understand what it's like to have a burning drive to succeed at something. I think all the Deverells have it; it takes a different form in each of us. But my understanding doesn't make it any easier for me to see you put your life on the line."

"Hey." He leaned over her, forming a tent of warmth and strength over her with his body. "I thought I told you, nothing's going to happen to me."

"You're not bulletproof, Nico."

He closed his eyes for a moment, trying to decide what he could possibly say that would reassure her. In the end, he decided there was nothing. "I have to do this, Caitlin, and I have to do it my way."

"I know, but that doesn't mean I have to like it."

"Causing you pain or worry hurts me more than Rettig's bullets did."

She slid her arms around his neck. "Don't spend one more minute worrying about me. Because of my love for you, my worry is bearable."

She glowed with a beauty within, he thought, and if

he lived to be a hundred, he'd never deserve her. "I want to make love to you. I need to feel you against me. I need to try to make you forget, a least for a little while, that you're upset and hurting because of me."

"I need the very same thing," she whispered.

RAMONA BURST into the study where Caitlin was working, her face wreathed in a big smile. "Caitlin, your mother just drove up! Mr. Haines is out front helping her with her bags now."

"Great!" Jumping to her feet, she threw her pen down and turned to Nico. "Now you can meet her."

Nico had been lounging in a chair near Caitlin's desk, reading a biography of Winston Churchill. "I thought she was in Egypt."

"No, India. Now she's here."

"That's Julia," Ramona said fondly, backing out the door. "Are you two coming?"

"Of course."

She held her hand toward Nico, and he had no choice but to go with her. It wasn't that he didn't want to meet Caitlin's mother. He did. But he'd hoped to be able to put off their meeting until his problems had been settled and he was able to come down from his tightrope.

Julia Deverell was just walking in the front door as they entered the grand hall. Caitlin broke away from Nico and ran across the marble floor.

Julia threw her arms around her daughter, enveloping her in a hug and a cloud of Opium perfume. "Darling, it's so wonderful to see you. How are you?"

Caitlin drew away and gazed happily at her mother. She was as lovely as ever, her ash-brown hair falling to her shoulder in a stylishly casual fashion, her face free of any makeup, her slender figure clothed in a dark blue silk tank top and a purple, blue and turquoise peasant skirt. Sandals, an armful of clanky silver bracelets and a beautiful large purple rope necklace completed the outfit. She never gave any thought to what she wore, Caitlin thought proudly, but she always looked sophisticated and elegant. "I'm terrific. How about you?"

"Couldn't be better, now that I'm back home with you. Ramona, how are you surviving the renovation?" Julia asked, bestowing a hug on the older woman.

Ramona gave a dismissive shrug. "Caitlin's doing all the work."

Julia smiled at her daughter. "I'm dying to see what you've done to the place so far."

"And I can't wait to show you. But first there's someone I want you to meet." Caitlin beckoned to Nico who had been standing to one side, watching the reunion.

But before Caitlin could perform the introduction, Mr. Haines and several of his men struggled through the door, each carrying an armload of luggage.

"Thank you, Mr. Haines. Why don't you just leave it all there." Julia gracefully waved a hand toward the door. "When I find out what bedroom Caitlin wants me in, I'll give you a call."

"Very well, Miss Deverell. And it's good to have you back."

Julia bestowed a breathtaking smile on the man. "Thank you. Caitlin, wait until you see what I brought you from India. Oh, who's this?" she asked, noticing Nico for the first time.

"This is a very special person in my life—Nico DiFrenza."

With a surprised look at her daughter's radiant face, Julia extended her hand. "It's very nice to meet you,

Nico. You know, I really must stop staying away so long. I miss too much."

"Miss Deverell," he said, shaking her hand.

"Please, call me Julia. I have a feeling we're going to be getting to know each other quite well."

He grinned. "Yes, I think so. And it will be my pleasure. I can see now that Caitlin comes by her beauty quite naturally."

Humor flashed in Julia's green eyes. "I'm going to like you, aren't I?"

"Elena DiFrenza is Nico's great-grandmother," Caitlin said.

Julia lifted her brows ever so slightly. "Does that mean in the future we'll be able to get our clothes discount?"

Nico laughed. "I'm sure something can be worked out."

"Oh," Ramona said in a suddenly strange voice. "Here's Quinn, about to leave us."

Everyone turned toward the man who was standing, stone still, in the center of the grand hall, his gaze fixed on Julia.

"*Quinn!*" Julia whispered.

Caitlin glanced at her mother and saw that all color had drained from her face. "Mother? Do you know Quinn?"

Julia, pale and motionless, stared at Quinn as if he were a ghost.

It was Quinn who finally moved. He put down his bags and walked slowly to her. "Hello, Julia," he said quietly.

"Mother? Are you all right?"

With a look at Caitlin, Quinn took Julia's arm. "Your mother and I are going into the salon and talk a while."

Dumbfounded, Caitlin gazed after Quinn and her mother as they disappeared through a doorway. "That's the oddest thing I ever saw. They—" She broke off abruptly, because suddenly she knew… With an exclamation, she turned to Nico and received another shock. There was no surprise on his face.

"Quinn is my father, isn't he?"

"Yes."

"And you knew."

"Yes."

Caitlin felt as if the world had just been cut loose from its moorings and was spinning wildly through space. "I don't understand."

He took her arm, much as Quinn had taken Julia's, and tried to think of the nearest room where they could have privacy and she could sit down. "Let's go back to the study. Ramona, I wonder if we could trouble you for some tea."

Gazing worriedly at Caitlin, Ramona nodded her head. "Of course."

On the long walk back, Caitlin was silent. Nico let her be, knowing that soon enough the numbness would wear off.

He closed the study door behind them and watched while Caitlin made her way to her desk. Instead of sitting down, she rounded on him. "What's he doing here?"

"He told me he'd just wanted to come see you."

"Me? Now?" Her laugh rang hollowly in the golden room. "Where's he been for the last twenty-six years, and why hasn't he come to see Mom in all that time?"

"You'll have to ask *him*." Her eyes widened with a pain that nearly tore him apart. "I'm sorry, Caitlin, but it's his story to tell."

"The person you had check on Quinn, he told you about him, didn't he? You knew all about this yesterday."

"The report I received gave me information on Quinn's background. When I talked with him on the bluff, he told me the rest, but he asked me not to tell you."

"*He* asked you! Nico, he's a stranger to you. You're supposed to be in love with me. You should have told me."

Nico reached out and tried to take her into his arms, but she shrugged him away. Frustrated, he ran his hand around the back of his neck. "Caitlin, Quinn didn't want to see you hurt. As a matter of fact, he told me that's why he searched my room. He saw how you felt about me and was worried about the type of man he thought I was. And of course he was absolutely right."

"What an extremely *fatherly* thing to do!"

"Caitlin—" A knock on the door interrupted. Nico opened the door and took the tea tray from Ramona.

"How are you, honey?" Ramona asked Caitlin.

"Did you know, too?" she asked accusingly.

"No. But I suspected. I once saw an old photograph your mother kept in a drawer. He was a young man then, and the picture was taken from a distance." She shrugged. "I don't know. When Quinn showed up, the similarity between him and the man in the photograph struck me."

"But why did you ask him to stay?" she asked, a small cry in her voice.

Ramona clasped her hands tightly together. "I just thought it was the thing to do. I still do."

"But why?"

"Julia. You've said it yourself many times. She's

been like a butterfly, flitting from place to place, looking for something. I personally have always believed she was looking for *someone*. Your father, I think."

Tears filled Caitlin's eyes and she sank back against the desk. "How is Mom?"

"I don't know. I'm about to take her a tray of tea, too."

Caitlin nodded. "Please…I'd like to be alone now."

"No," Nico said. "I'm staying with you."

"Just leave."

"She'll be all right," Ramona said to him. "She needs a little time. Come with me to the kitchen, and I'll make you a cup of tea. Caitlin? You drink the tea I've brought, you hear? Nico and I will be in the kitchen if you need us."

"Caitlin?" he said, his tone pleading with her to ask him to stay.

She said nothing. And soon she was alone in the golden room she'd always thought so warm, she wrapped her arms around herself and wondered why she felt so cold.

CHAPTER NINE

SHE SOUGHT THE SUNSHINE and the sea. The heat of the sun and the power and unending rhythm of the ocean had always seemed to her a part of SwanSea and of her. She had a favorite seat—a rock that warmed in the afternoon and was lapped by waves at high tide.

It was there Quinn found her.

Somehow, he knew she would regard it an invasion of privacy if he tried to sit on the rock with her, so he stood on the sand, gazing at his daughter, his heart hurting for her, for him, for so many wasted years.

"I'd like to talk with you, Caitlin." Her gaze remained on the horizon. "Your mother's worried about you, and she wanted to come, but I asked her not to. I felt that it was my place to try and make you understand."

"Does that mean Mom understands?"

His words were cautious. This wasn't a simple situation; there would be no simple solution. "It's not something that's easily understood with just a few hours of discussion, but let me put it this way—Julia now understands more than she did."

She turned her head, and the expression in her eyes was flint hard. "Did you lie to her the way you lied to me when you told me that you had visited grandfather here?"

"You're right, Caitlin. That was a lie. It was an expedient lie, but a lie nevertheless. More than anything, I wanted the opportunity to be around you for a few days, so that I could see you and come to know you in some small way." His voice broke, and he stopped to clear his throat. "I was so hungry to know my daughter."

The charming facade he'd kept in place since he'd been here had dropped away. Now Caitlin saw signs of vulnerability that deepened the lines of his face, and she realized it was the first time she'd seen him show any real emotion. Apparently he was adept at facades. Nico had been right when he'd said Quinn had taken great care to blend into the woodwork. She looked back at the sea. "I really don't want to talk to you. Your explanations should go to Mom, not me."

"They have, and they will continue to," he said gently. "But whether you'll admit it or not, you're angry and hurt, and I don't blame you. Perhaps, though, you could simply sit there and listen to me."

Her posture was stiff, full of dignity and pain, and he felt an ache of pride and sadness in his chest as he gazed at the lovely young woman who was his daughter.

His eyes stung, and the muscles of his throat throbbed from the effort of holding back almost twenty-seven years of tears. But it wasn't the time to cry. He owed her so much, and an explanation was first and foremost. "You see, Caitlin, I met your mother twenty-seven years ago. Most of the house was closed up at that time, but Julia and her brothers had a habit of coming up from Boston from time to time to check on SwanSea and enjoy the solitude and the house where they had been raised. I was on vacation, wandering around the village, and met your mother by accident on afternoon.

"It was 1962, Caitlin, an extraordinary time. John F. Kennedy was president. Already that year John Glenn had become the first American to orbit the earth. The Peace Corps had just been established, and young people were going off to foreign countries to help those less fortunate. I felt I too could make a difference, perhaps even accomplish great things."

Caitlin had slowly turned toward him. He had at least captured her interest, he thought, however unwilling that interest was. "I was twenty-five years old with a master's degree in world economics and had a great desire to do something with my knowledge other than make money. I was eager and idealistic, and I'd agreed to take a very difficult, secret position with the government." He sighed, thinking that living the past had been a hell of a lot easier than trying to explain it. "In the fall of 1962, the Cuban missile crisis shook the world, and the following November, President Kennedy was killed. I'd been doing the work for over a year by then, and I'd lost my idealism. But by that time, it was too late. I was in something I couldn't get out of..."

Quinn's voice trailed off. His gaze was fixed on the horizon, but Caitlin sensed he was seeing something inside him. She waited, wanting in spite of herself to hear more about the events that had affected her mother and her father, the events that had shaped her life before she had been born.

"I loved your mother, Caitlin, you must believe that. We were together for two intense, glorious weeks. By the end of that time, I couldn't bear the thought of leaving her, but I had no choice. Everything was ready and in place for me to be slipped into a certain volatile situation. What's more, I couldn't tell her why I was leaving. One night while she slept, I left. It must have been devastating for her."

For the first time Caitlin spoke. "When I was a little girl, I used to ask where my father was. She told me my father had gone away. I asked why, and she said she had no answers, but some things weren't meant to be. She also said that she thought she must have loved you more than you loved her. I just didn't see how that was possible."

"It wasn't." Deep sorrow etched his face and aged him before her eyes. "Originally I thought I'd be back within five years. I held on to the thought that I'd see her again, and every night I'd pray that when we met again, she'd still have me. But the operation became so involved—and, by the way, so successful—I couldn't leave. I was placed in such a strategic position that if I'd pulled out, it would have meant the death of many other agents." He met her eyes. "It was a bitter pill for me. In reality, no one could really stop me from leaving, but I knew that my happiness would come at great sacrifice to others. I just couldn't do it. And there was also the very real possibility that I would be followed out of that life and into the one I truly wanted. There would have been danger for Julia, and as it turns out now, for you. Attempts to contact her could have also met with the same result. Until just recently, I didn't feel free to make inquiries. That's when I discovered I had a daughter."

She digested that. "You didn't know about me?"

"No."

"I always wondered."

"If I had known…" His voice trailed off, and he took a deep breath.

"Are you through with your work now?"

"Oh, yes," he said most definitely. "I'm really retired."

So now she knew. Finally all of her questions had been answered, but she still felt empty and flat. "Tell me, do you feel you made a difference?"

He thought for a moment. "Yes. Yes, Caitlin, I do. But I wish with all my heart I'd left it to someone else to make the difference."

The sound of the surf and the gulls couldn't disquise the fact that conversation ceased while seconds stretched to minutes.

"I have a favor to ask of you, Caitlin," he said when it became clear she wouldn't say more. "I'd like to stay here a while longer to give Julia and myself a chance to become reacquainted."

"Is that what Mom wants?"

"I hope so. I've suggested it, and I'm hoping she'll agree."

"As far as I'm concerned, it's whatever she wants."

"What about you, Caitlin? Is it too much to ask that we could get to know each other better?"

"Yes," she said after a long pause, "I think it is. You chose your path, and I grew up without a father. Now you've suddenly reappeared. Okay, fine. But I'm not affected. I see no reason why I would need a father at this point in my life."

LATE THAT NIGHT, Nico opened the door of Caitlin's bedroom. He found her lying back against a pile of pillows, reading through a folder of correspondence. A jade-green silk chemise stopped at the middle of her thighs, and her long legs stretched out in front of her, crossed at the ankles. She looked very relaxed, very beautiful, very unattainable.

"What are you reading?" He grimaced at his unintentionally harsh tone. He'd wanted to ask what she was doing in this room instead of his bedroom, his bed. But at the last minute, he'd decided he was afraid to hear her answer.

For some reason, Caitlin had begun to shake as soon as he'd walked into the room. As calmly as possible, she set aside the letter she'd been reading and self-consciously pulled at the hem of the chemise. "It's from an interior-decorating magazine, requesting an interview with me. They want to plan an entire issue featuring SwanSea."

"Are you going to agree?"

"Maybe." She eyed him through a thick fringe of dark lashes. Suddenly it dawned on her that it was two o'clock in the morning and he was wearing black jeans and a black sweater. "You've been out to the island, haven't you?"

"Yes."

She sat up. "Have you lost your mind? There's a full moon tonight."

"That's why I went. I figured there wouldn't be any activity out there, and I was right."

"Still, you never should have gone. How did you get out there anyway?"

"I used one of the speedboats. In case you didn't know, there're three speedboats down at the boathouse that have been refurbished to date."

She gazed at him broodingly. "I knew."

Damn. This wasn't what he wanted to talk about. "I took the smallest boat."

"And?"

"I found evidence of activity, but nothing I could use to pin on Rettig."

"So what are you going to do?"

"Keep watching. Caitlin..." His voice dropped and roughened. "What are you doing in here? Why aren't you in my room? Our room?"

She subsided against the pillows and linked her fingers together. "I decided I didn't want to be there tonight."

"And what about tomorrow night?" he asked, trying to be civilized. He wanted to jerk her into his arms and make love to her until she had no energy left to be upset with him. "Where do you think you'll want to be then?"

"I don't know."

He sat down beside her on the bed. She started to scramble off the other side, but he caught her wrist, keeping her where she was. "Caitlin, I know you're hurt and confused, but please don't stay away from me. Let's work it out together."

She should have been quicker; she should never have let him get this close. His presence had a way of endangering her equilibrium. She tried to jerk away, but he held her tight.

"I'm not confused, Nico. As a matter of fact, it all seems crystal clear to me. I feel your first consideration should have been to me, not honoring some pledge to Quinn that you wouldn't tell me." Tears formed in her eyes, making them glisten like jewels.

"You were my first consideration, honey. I was trying to protect you."

"I don't need protecting, dammit! I've told you time and time again."

"Oh, right. You're a Deverell. You're tough. Well, big deal, Caitlin. I'm not impressed."

"I don't care."

"Well, I do, and it just seemed to me that having a father appear out of the blue like that wasn't something that should be sprung on you."

"You mean like it was?"

"Exactly. And as I told you, it was Quinn's story to tell."

She gazed down at her hands. "You think I'm being unreasonable, don't you?"

"No, not at all. You've received a tremendous shock. I just don't think you've let yourself feel that shock yet."

"Then let me, Nico. Just back off and let me."

He stared at her for a long minute, then sighed. "I can't. I wish I could do as you ask, but I can't. I have this great urge to cushion all your shocks and blows for you."

"You just don't listen to me, do you?" she cried.

"I always listen to you, but I admitted to you days ago that I'm a bastard. Remember I also said in spite of all my sins and crimes, I love you. And because I do, I'm enough of a bastard to stay here in your room if you won't come back to mine." He took her arms and twisted her around and down until she lay on the bed.

She struggled against him. "Nico, I don't want to do this. Let's talk—"

"No. If we talk, you'll have a chance to argue with me, and an argument will only drive another wedge between us. I'm not willing to take that chance. You mean too much to me."

He pressed his mouth to hers, intending to do no more than gently brush his lips against hers, comfort her, let her know how much he loved her. But he quickly realized that wasn't what either of them wanted. He could feel the tension changing in her as she grew softer, more pliable, and it made him want to join with her in love and fire and know the feeling of coming apart in her arms.

Impatiently, he stripped off her panties and entered her.

But once sheathed to the hilt in her, he stilled and met her eyes. "Tell me you want me." His words were a demand, but his tone was begging.

She arched up to him and grasped his buttocks with her hands, trying to pull him deeper. "I want you. Lord, how I want you."

He began to move inside her, hard and fast, bringing to her and to him a burning, a wildness, a great love.

DARK CLOUDS BOILED on the horizon; razor-edged white lightning streaked out of the heavens and bolted straight down to the water. The wind had picked up and blew cool against Caitlin's face. She could see the storm far out at sea and knew it would be sweeping in over the land soon. She'd go in then, but not until.

Sitting on the thick green carpet of grass, she clasped her hands around her knees and lifted her face to the wind, inhaling the energy and the freshness of air that had never before touched land. There was an exhilaration to a storm at SwanSea that she'd never felt anywhere else.

She heard a jangle of silver, caught a whiff of Opium, and her mother dropped to the grass beside her. "I love watching storms," she murmured, without looking around.

"I know," Julia said ruefully. "I can remember more than once trying to find you during a storm, only to discover you standing out here, the wind and the rain whipping around you. You were such a fierce little thing. I always had the feeling you felt that you and SwanSea together could weather anything."

Caitlin couldn't help but smile, because she had felt exactly that way. "I've grown up. I'm older and wiser now."

"But yet I still find you out here."

"The storm isn't here yet." She turned to her mother. With her smooth, unlined skin and windtossed hair, Julia still looked as lovely as a young girl, Caitlin thought. "How *are* you, Mom? We really haven't had a chance to talk."

"I think I'm gradually getting over the shock. How about you?"

"The same. I've caught glimpses of you and Quinn over the last two days. How are things going?"

Julia shrugged. "I don't know. I'm enjoying this time with him, but..."

"But?"

"It's too soon to tell. We've been apart for a great many years. And when you think about it, we were really together only two weeks."

"Ramona told me she's always felt you were searching for someone, that that's why you've traveled so much."

"If I have, it hasn't been conscious." Her lips pursed thoughtfully. "Do you know that Quinn and I have discovered we were often in the same country at the same time? A lot of times even in the same city. If we'd turned a particular corner at a particular moment, we might have seen each other. It's ironic."

"I think it's sad," Caitlin said.

"That, too. At any rate, whatever happens, I'm glad I finally know why he left me."

"You thought he'd left you because he didn't love you enough to stay. You had to have been bitter about that, but if you were, you did a beautiful job of keeping it from me."

"Oh, I was definitely bitter for a while." She laughed shortly. "I am human, darling. But then you came along, and I knew that no matter what, I'd thank Quinn my whole life long for you."

Tears welled into Caitlin's eyes. "I really love you, Mom, and I admire you so much."

Julia made a short, dismissing sound. "You put me in the shade, my darling daughter. I would never even have considered attempting what you are doing here with SwanSea." She reached out and stroked Caitlin's hair. "Quinn told me that you have the same color hair his mother had. I always wondered where that gorgeous cinnamon shade came from." She smiled gently and searched for some sign of what Caitlin was feeling. "I'm worried about you. I want you to know that I understand your hesitancy about Quinn. After all, you must have felt terribly abandoned all these years."

The odd need to comfort her mother wasn't new, she realized. She'd known the urge when she was growing up, and now she knew why. "I had you and the family and just about all the love any one person could handle."

Julia sighed, knowing Caitlin wasn't ready to address the issue of her father. "I won't press you, darling, but I hope that in the future you'll find a way to make peace with Quinn. He needs you, and I think if you'll let yourself, you'll come to realize that you need him. But…Nico…"

Caitlin groaned. "Mother."

"Yes, I know. You'd like me to stay out of it, and I'm going to. I just want to say that over the last couple of days, I've really grown to like him, and it's obvious to me that he loves and cares about you a great deal. Don't hold it against him because he didn't tell you about Quinn. I think it's completely natural and honorable that he should feel Quinn or I should be the one to break such enormous news to you."

"I know," she murmured. The storm was closer now. Caitlin could smell the salt and sulfurous scent in the wind and could feel the electric charge on her skin. The storm would be violent and short. "I know," she said again.

BY MIDNIGHT, the storm had blown over. She and Swan-Sea had survived another storm, Caitlin reflected. Usually the thought exhilarated her, but tonight, as she wandered restlessly around Nico's bedroom waiting for him, she felt strangely flat. The melodic refrain of "Someone to Watch Over Me" was playing on her tape recorder. It reminded her of the night she had stood wrapped in enchantment and Nico's arms while the song had flowed around them, and the memory made her feel even more restless.

Disturbed, she opened the bedroom's French windows and gazed up at the overcast sky. Every once in a while, the moon would break free of the clouds and shine with a silver luminosity. But its freedom lasted mere moments, and then new clouds formed a shroud.

The words of the song drifted through the haze of her thoughts: "…someone to watch over me."

To try to shield someone you love from being hurt was a part of loving. Nico tried to watch over her; she worried about him. This man Rettig had nearly killed him, and now it appeared Rettig was close again.

Suddenly, her gaze flew back to the overcast sky. "Oh, my Lord," she whispered. "Nico's gone out to the island."

She left the room, her single thought to help Nico. It was only the sight of Quinn quietly leaving her mother's room that stopped her cold.

When Quinn glanced around and saw her, his first

reaction was guilt that Caitlin had seen him coming from Julia's room so late at night. He quickly banished the feeling. "I'm sorry if this upsets you, Caitlin, but your mother and I owe you no explanation."

"You're right," she said quietly. "Excuse me."

She started past him, but he caught her arm. "Wait a minute. There's something wrong. I can tell it by your face. What is it? Where are you going?"

She pulled against his hold, but surprisingly his grip tightened. "Quinn, I don't have time for this. Let me go."

"I may be retired, Caitlin, but all my agent instincts are still in place. What is it? Is Nico in trouble?"

She made a sound halfway between anger and a sob. "Yes. He's gone out to the island."

Quinn's eyes narrowed. "The island. Of course. I thought there was something strange… What is it? Drugs?"

She nodded, almost frantic. "Now will you let me go?"

"Yes, but I'm coming with you."

"No—"

"I'm coming with you, Caitlin, but first we need to stop by my room."

A short time later, the two of them were in a speedboat, plowing through the dark waves toward the island—Quinn at the wheel, Caitlin beside him. Before this, she reflected, she'd seen only the pleasant, charming side of him. The past twenty minutes had shown her the steel that had apparently made him so important to the government.

The sea was wild tonight. Spray dampened her skin, blackness enveloped them. She knew these waters well, but she had to admit that she was glad Quinn was with her.

"It shouldn't be too much farther," she called.

He shut off the engines. "We'll paddle in from here. We don't want to alert anyone we're coming."

She nodded and said a fervent prayer that Nico was all right.

CHAPTER TEN

THE FLASHLIGHTS on the table cast broad beams of light on the two men standing in the center of the pitch-black room. Crouched behind the dust-covered couch, Nico listened, unable to believe his good luck. Not only was Rettig here but also Rettig's main Canadian contact, Marcus Kozera. The two men had never been seen together.

"This island couldn't be better," Kozera was saying. "We've made two successful runs, but tonight is our biggest shipment yet, and I wanted to be here to check it out for myself. It's good."

"I told you so," Rettig said with satisfaction. "It's never used, isolated from normal shipping routes, and hell, it even has this house on it." He laughed.

"What about DiFrenza? I'm going to sleep a lot better at night when he's finally dead and buried."

"There've been too many people around that house for a regular hit. This time, I want it to look like an accident, so there aren't a bunch of cops swarming around afterward. He's running longer distances now. Within the next few days, he should have an established route. It'll be easy to take him out then."

"Good."

Rettig laughed. "Right before I kill him I'm going to thank him for leading us to this island."

Behind the couch, Nico tensed, his hand tightening on his gun.

A man's voice burst suddenly into the room, tinny and loud, through a walkie-talkie. "Rettig?"

"Yeah?"

"We've got a woman and a man here. Seems they were trying to crash the party."

"Who are they?"

"Never saw them before in my life, but I'd sure like to get to know *her*."

A cold sweat broke out over Nico. Caitlin and Quinn—it had to bc. Dammit. All this situation needed was another complication. He was going to have to rearrange his plans fast. Nothing could happen to Caitlin…

"Bring them here," Rettig said. "Kozera, you know anything about this?"

"No, but I don't like it."

"Don't worry about it. We'll take care of them. Besides, the risk is why we make so damn much money."

Before Kozera could answer, the door opened.

"Don't hurt her," Nico heard Quinn say. Nico brought his gun up into firing position. Carefully, he peered over the couch. He could just make out the forms of Caitlin and Quinn. The darkness and Rettig and Kozera's movements made it risky for him to get off a shot—and the terrifying chance that he might hit Caitlin kept him still.

"I'm fine," Caitlin said, trying to reassure Quinn. The last time she'd gotten a good look at him, there'd been blood trickling down the side of his face. The man who had come up behind them had struck Quinn for trying to protect her.

"Where'd you find them, Larry?" Rettig asked.

"Josh radioed me from the boat that he'd spotted these two heading toward the beach on the east side of the island. I made it a point to be there when they beached."

"Good job. So…who are *you?*"

Be careful what you say, Nico silently coaxed Caitlin. He wasn't sure if revealing she was a Deverell would make matters worse or not, but it would be fatal if she asked what they'd done with him.

It was Quinn who answered Rettig. "I'm Quinn O'Neill, and this is my daughter, Caitlin. Our boat conked out on us, and we were trying to find some shelter until morning."

"They're lying," Kozera said.

"Use your head," Rettig snapped with irritation. "Why would they walk into a situation like this?"

"He had a gun," Larry said.

Rettig's tone turned ominous. "Really?"

"Sharks," Caitlin said quickly and managed a shudder. "I've seen all the *Jaws* movies. I wanted to be prepared. Look, if you'll just let us go, we'll—"

Kozera laughed. "You'll what? Paddle your way back to wherever you came from and use the first phone you find to call the police? I don't think so."

"You talk too much, Kozera," Rettig said coldly. "It doesn't matter where they came from or where they think they're going." He drew his gun. "Larry, get back out there and guard the shipment. We won't be much longer. We'll take care of these two, and then we'll join you."

Larry left the cottage. Behind the couch, Nico prepared to make his move.

Caitlin could feel herself trembling, but there was too much to think about to be sidetracked by fear. Desperately she tried to rule out all emotion that could block clear thinking. She would never know where Nico was unless they could get out of here alive. She thought her knowledge of the island would give her and Quinn the advantage, but first they had to get away. "Maybe we could make a deal," she began.

Rettig's teeth flashed in the darkness. "I'd love to, sweetheart, but unfortunately I have pressing business. And business always comes first." He cocked his gun.

"No!" With blind instinct she started toward the gun.

"Get out of here, Caitlin!" Quinn yelled as he shoved her out of the way and hurled himself past her at the two men.

As Caitlin lost her balance and crashed to the floor, Rettig's gun went off, and Nico vaulted the sofa and launched himself toward Kozera and Rettig. He swung the butt of his gun against Rettig's temple and followed up with a karate chop to Kozera's neck.

In less than a minute, it was over, and Nico was reaching for Caitlin. "My God, are you all right?"

"Yes." Her elbow ached, having caught most of her weight when she had fallen, but it didn't seem important. "I'm so glad you're here. I was so afraid for you. Oh heavens, what about Quinn?"

"Quinn?" Nico asked, cradling Caitlin against his chest.

"He got me, but it's just a flesh wound." His voice was calm and steady.

"You're shot?" Caitlin said, struggling to see, but Quinn was lying in the shadows.

"Stay where you are," he said. "I'll be all right. You were wonderful, by the way."

"Not as wonderful as you," she said, meaning it with all her heart.

"Nico, sorry you had to take those two out by yourself."

Nico stroked Caitlin's hair, wishing he could see her more clearly. He'd known a terrible rage when Rettig had pointed his gun at her. "No problem."

"So I noticed," Quinn said, his tone dry.

Nico could tell that Quinn was making a terrible effort to keep his words even. The man was in trouble, he thought, and he'd bet money it was more than a flesh wound. "Save your strength. Don't try to move. We'll get you out of here as fast as we can."

The door opened, and a flashlight beam panned around the room. "Nico?" a deep voice called.

"About time you got here," Nico said sharply.

Footsteps crossed the floor toward them. "Give me a break. There were two boats out there, you know, with two men on each of them. That makes *four* in case you've forgotten how to add. Of course, I did have an advantage, being from Texas and all."

The flashlight swept the floor, finding Quinn, then the two men who lay incapacitated on the floor. When the light reached Nico and Caitlin, it bypassed Nico and went straight to Caitlin. She dropped her eyes from the glare of the light and saw the pointed toes of a pair of snakeskin cowboy boots.

"Is this Caitlin?" the deep voice asked.

"Yes, and get that damned light off us."

The light stayed perfectly steady. "Glad to meet you, ma'am. Amarillo Smith at your service."

THE BLADES of the helicopter sliced powerfully through the air, making a loud rushing sound as it squatted on the beach, waiting for its passengers. Holding Quinn's hand, Caitlin bent over his stretcher. "We've contacted Julia. She'll meet you at the hospital."

"That's very kind of you." He tried to pat her hand and grimaced with pain. "You're not to worry about me. It's nothing, you know."

"I know." She was surprised to find her eyes filling with tears. On the other side of him, Nico applied a pressure bandage to the wound in Quinn's chest. "Quinn, when the hospital lets you go, I want you to come back to SwanSea to recuperate. Ramona and I can look after you. I'm sure Mom will be there too. SwanSea can be a little hectic with all the work that's going on, but Nico was able to regain his strength there, and so will you."

"Are you sure, Caitlin?" Quinn asked.

She wiped at her eyes and smiled down at him. "I'm sure." A quick glance told her that the medics were ready to put him aboard the helicopter. She pressed a kiss to his forehead. "I'll see you soon."

The helicopter lifted off into the approaching dawn. Nico took a firm grip on her arms and turned her to face him. "It was very brave of you to come out here after me, Caitlin, and maybe I'll appreciate it after I get over remembering how damned scared I was when I saw the danger you'd walked into. But if you ever do anything that stupid again, I will strangle you."

He kissed her with a ferocity that showed her how much he loved her. When he broke off the kiss, it was a moment before their breathing returned to normal.

"Let's go home," he said. "Rill can clean things up here. There's something there I have to show you."

IN FRONT OF ONE of the attic windows, Caitlin chose a spot that was just beginning to warm with the sun and sank to the floor. Not too far away, Nico lifted the lid of a trunk and rummaged through it.

Caitlin watched him curiously as he lifted a loosely wrapped package from the trunk, walked to her, and dropped down beside her. "Here it is—Elena's bible. Inside you'll find her letter of explanation, along with her marriage certificate."

"Then it's all true."

"I'm afraid there's no doubt."

"Afraid? Why?"

"Caitlin, I want to assure you that the DiFrenzas want nothing from the Deverells. I know that's hard for you to believe, and your family will probably find it impossible to believe. Very few people have as much money as the Deverells, but we have more than we'll ever need in our lifetime, with enough left over for the generations to come.

"Remember that first night when I said I wouldn't be able to afford to stay here? I said that out of habit. Ever since I graduated from law school, I've made it a point to live on my salary. But that doesn't mean I don't have enough money to give you everything you'll ever want." She made a dismissive motion with her hand, but he hurried on. "And it's not the Deverell name, either. My family has proudly carried the name of DiFrenza for generations. We will continue to do so."

"Nico—"

Unconsciously, he shifted closer to her, anxious to make her understand. "But it's Elena, don't you see? Stubbornly, she's held on to her secret all these years. But now she's ill, and she wanted us to know what happened. I promised her I would try to find this package, and for her sake, I'm glad I did. It's evidence that she and a young man named John Deverell once loved and dreamed of a future together. Now she can live out what time remains of her life in peace.

"But this changes nothing for you and me. As a lawyer, I can tell you that your inheritance is absolutely safe, but if it will make you feel any better, I'll sign a prenuptial agreement giving up all claim to SwanSea and your money."

She felt an aching lump of tenderness grow in her throat. "Aren't you overlooking something? Forget the money. You're a *Deverell*, Nico. You're part of SwanSea. You're Edward's great-great-grandson."

"I haven't overlooked that, but it won't affect us. We're second or third half cousins, once removed—or something like that."

"That's not what I mean. I think we're missing something very significant here. My grandfather once told me that Edward's two burning obsessions were SwanSea and having a large family. Who knows what really happened back then, but whatever did, our side of the family never knew about you, and your side of the family never knew about us. But now, through our marriage and our children, we will restore the line that was broken so long ago."

"Does that mean…?"

"Nico, a few hours ago, I was staring into the barrel of a loaded gun, and I didn't know if you were dead or alive. Compared to that, everything else pales. Except the love I have for you." She laughed. "My grandfather would get the biggest kick out of this. And I think this news is wonderful. I can't wait to tell the rest of the family."

Relief flowed through his body with a force that had him trembling, and he didn't even notice that his face was damp from tears of joy. "Thank God," he said softly. "Thank God."

For the moment, the idea of Edward, his dreams and

his house weren't real or important to him. Maybe someday they would be, but for now, only the woman before him had meaning and importance. "Will you marry me, Caitlin?"

"Yes, my darling, I will marry you. Here at SwanSea, with both our families around us. We'll hire an entire army of doctors, nurses, planes, ambulances—whatever it takes—but I want our very special guest to be Elena."

"That would be absolutely right and perfect," he whispered.

For a moment, he allowed himself to bask in the warmth and love of Caitlin's eyes. There had been times in the last few terrifying hours when he'd thought he would lose her. But there she was, warm and generous, giving and loving. He leaned forward and kissed her gently. There had been enough words. He wanted to show her how much he loved her, how all the days of his life, he would cherish and adore her.

Caitlin slipped her tongue between his lips, deepening the kiss and lying back on the sun-heated floor, pulling him with her. She felt swamped by a tidal wave of love and happiness. Her world had once consisted of her family and SwanSea. Now Nico was in her world, filling it to bursting.

Perhaps they'd been luckier than the Deverells and the DiFrenzas that had gone before them. Somehow, they'd been able to hold their dream. They had survived the events of last night, and now another day was beginning. Soon the workmen would arrive, and later she would visit her father. But for now, she and Nico badly needed the passion and fire that only they could give each other.

The morning sun continued to rise, its streams of

light surrounding the two lovers with warmth. And outside, in the sun's golden rays, the windows shone, as if the great house SwanSea were smiling.

SWANSEA PLACE: DECEIT

PREFACE

SwanSea 1898

LIGHTS GLIMMERED in every window of SwanSea. Inside, dance music reverberated through the elegant rooms and hallways. And in the ballroom exquisitely dressed couples whirled gaily, the women's jewels flashing like fire.

A quarter of a mile away, on a lonely windswept cliff, Leonora Deverell could hear the strains of the waltz as she paced in the iron gazebo.

Where was he?

Pausing a moment, she glanced up at the big yellow moon that hung over SwanSea and tried to judge the time. At least an hour had passed since the grandfather clock in the foyer had struck midnight. Anxiously she clasped her hands together. The carriage was waiting for them, their bags already in it. John's nurse had packed all of his clothes and toys, and if she were following the schedule, had probably already tucked him comfortably into the carriage. It would be a long, tiring journey for the three-year-old, and Leonora hoped he would sleep all the way to Boston where they would board the ship for Europe.

Where was he?

Be calm, she told herself. Everything was going to be fine. For the first time in her life she had discovered love. She was happy and full of anticipation for the future.

Suddenly she heard footsteps and eagerly turned. But at the sight of her husband standing before her, she went cold all over.

"Leonora, it is time for you to come back to the ball now. It is almost over and you will want to bid our guests goodnight."

Their only illumination was moonlight, but she had no trouble making out the glittering anger in his cobalt blue eyes. "Edward, I—"

"You will have to change back into your ball gown, of course. I am not sure our guests would understand if you were wearing a traveling suit."

He was so tall, so big, so hard. In the four years they had been married, she had never crossed him, but her love for Wyatt had given her a courage she had never known before. "I cannot live with you any longer, Edward. I have tried to make our marriage work, but you care nothing for me. There is no love between us, and I feel as if I am withering from the lack of it." She paused. "Edward, I am leaving you."

"No, Leonora, you are not." He thrust out his hand toward her, the gesture an order. "Come with me. Your maid is waiting to help you change. If we're quick enough, no one need ever know about this."

"That's all you care about, isn't it?" she asked, despair making her voice quiver. "Appearances. Gaining acceptance into society."

"I don't have time to discuss this with you."

"You *never* have time to discuss *anything* with me, Edward. I thought all men were like that until I met Wyatt."

His teeth came together with a snap. "Wyatt Redmond is an impoverished painter I *hired* to paint your portrait. Surely you wouldn't make a fool out of yourself over a nobody like him."

"He isn't a nobody," she said, tears clogging her throat. "He is the man I love."

"He can offer you nothing."

"He can offer me everything that matters."

For a brief moment, a look of genuine bewilderment crossed his face. "I don't understand. I have given you everything you desired. The grandest house in America. Beautiful clothes. Why, the gown you wore tonight was designed by Worth of Paris, and you have one of the finest collections of jewelry in the country." His finger flicked the topaz, ivory and gold lily she wore on her lapel.

She stiffened, afraid for a moment he would realize the lily was not among the many pieces of jewelry he had given her. Then she realized it no longer mattered.

"Those were the things *you* desired, Edward. They were possessions for your possession. I wanted only your love."

"Love?" His tone indicted he thought her insane.

"I am leaving, Edward, and you cannot stop me."

His hand snaked out and closed on her wrist. "You will not take my son."

She had feared discovery for this very reason. Edward was obsessed with having children, and John was the only child she had been able to give him. She swallowed. "Of course John will go with me. I am his mother."

"What kind of mother would want to take her son from his father? What kind of mother would expose her son to the adulterous relationship she has with her lover?

I tell you, I will not have it. I absolutely will not allow the scandal. No, Leonora. John stays with me." Edward leaned closer and closer still. His face almost touching hers, he cruelly tightened his hold on her wrist, bruising her soft flesh. "Think about this very carefully, Leonora. Because the only way you will leave me is if you are dead."

She stared at him, stricken.

And neither of them noticed that behind them, the lights of SwanSea were going out, one by one.

ONE

Present Day

HE POSITIONED HIMSELF unobtrusively among the onlookers of the photographic shoot and fixed his steel-gray gaze on the world-famous model, Liana Marchall. She was the epitome of serenity and beauty as she stood at the top of the marble stairs beneath the tall, stained-glass Tiffany window that suggested the living form of a peacock's head and body.

The peacock motif continued in a mosaic representing the vivid plumage of the tail. It trailed down the grand stairway and onto the floor of the great hall where he stood. It was breathtaking, but it was nothing in comparison to the woman, he reflected, using utter objectivity.

She was a living work of art. She lacked only two things to make her perfect: a heart and a soul.

His fingers idly rubbed the white-on-white *RZ* monogram on his shirt's cuff while he studied the people with whom she was working. Through inquiries, he had learned that the photographer, Clay Phillips, was relatively unknown and was here only because the great Jean-Paul Savion, one of the top fashion photographers in the business, had come down with a virus on his last trip to the Middle East and had been forced to remain at his home in Paris.

His mouth quirked. *What a shame.*

"How's it going, Rosalyn?" he heard Clay call up to the middle-aged woman who had been brushing extra color onto Liana's perfect cheekbones. "Are you finished?"

Stroking her skin had been like stroking the inside of a flower petal. His fingers flexed, and he slipped his hands into the pockets of his tailor-made gray slacks.

Rosalyn stepped back and critically eyed Liana's face, then reached up and combed a shining strand of wheat-colored hair into place. "Yes," she said finally and somewhat disappointedly, "I'm finished."

"Great," Clay said. The corner of his mouth twitched slightly, and he rubbed the area immediately below his belt.

The man's stomach had to be in knots, he thought. Before this, Clay Phillips had only worked under Savion. He had to view this opportunity as a huge, almost miraculous break.

"Steve, bring the key light down two stops and move that wind machine exactly three inches to the right and set it on low. Got it?"

"Got it," the younger man named Steve said laconically. He wore a pair of bleached-out blue jeans, a nondescript T-shirt, and his hair long and slightly curly.

He was good at his job, he thought, observing him, *but he didn't look prosperous enough to be Liana's type.* The photographer could be another story, though. Maybe Liana had decided her star would be lifted even higher if she helped another photographer achieve fame.

Suddenly Clay lifted his head and swept his gaze

around the great hall as if he were searching the air. "What in the hell is that awful music?"

"Gershwin," Steve said, then grinned. "George Gershwin."

"Gershwin? Where's our music? U2? The Rolling Stones? The Beatles? Sara, did you check into this?"

Clay's abrupt question was directed at the young woman who knelt beside him, loading film into one of his many cameras. She flipped a long, sleek swag of red hair behind her shoulder. "The management said positively no rock music," she said quietly.

Clay frowned. "What decade are these people living in?"

"I asked something like that and was told that this is SwanSea."

"What does that mean?"

"Offhand I'd say it means no rock music," Steve said dryly, sending a wink in Sara's direction. She smiled shyly back.

"Oh," Clay said, his tone and gaze indicating his mind was already on something else, namely his model.

Who could blame him, he wondered cynically.

Clay gestured to Sara and pointed at the camera he wanted her to hand him. "Good, then let's go to work, Liana, darling, are you ready?"

"Yes," Liana said, relieved that the waiting was over.

Oblivious to the frenzy of activity at the base of the staircase, Liana clasped the silk chiffon skirt of her strapless haute-couture gown between her fingertips. With each movement, the dress appeared to change color, one moment a teal blue, the next, a shimmering green. Rather than seeing an actual color, a person received an impression of the two colors that was much like the iridescent eye of a peacock feather. The fabric had been specially woven to produce this effect and was a compliment to the Tiffany window, the marble mosaic of the staircase and Liana's famous teal-colored eyes.

The first straining notes of "Rhapsody in Blue" began to rise. With the material still clasped in her hands, she spread her arms in a V above and behind her head and started her descent, crossing back and forth across the staircase.

As she glided downward, the blue-green silk chiffon fluttered like wings, making her appear as if she were some exotic bird about to take flight.

Below her, Clay scrambled to take shot after shot. "Beautiful, wonderful. Can you raise your arms more? Now lower them. Look down. Good. Over your shoulder—"

Liana, lost in the image she and Clay were creating, followed his instructions to the letter. She'd done it a thousand times. These were her favorite moments, when she could forget Liana, the woman, and focus on Liana, the model, and how best she could sell whatever product her face and her body were showcasing. In this instance, it was the idea of elegance and glamour that would be produced by the combination of her, the dress and SwanSea.

All at once, a light crashed to the floor, jerking her from her state of concentration. Electricity flashed and hot glass flew outward. With one high-heeled shoe poised midair for the next step, Liana hesitated, glancing to see what had happened.

Her gaze collided with a pair of steel-gray eyes, and for a moment everything stood still. As her lips formed the name, *Richard,* darkness rushed in to circle her, she lost her balance, her heel twisted and she began to fall.

YOUR PARTICIPATION IS REQUESTED!

Dear Reader,

Since you are a lover of fiction – we would like to get to know you!

Inside you will find a short Reader's Survey. Sharing your answers with us will help our editorial staff understand who you are and what activities you enjoy.

To thank you for your participation, we would like to send you 2 books and a gift – **ABSOLUTELY FREE!**

Enjoy your gifts with our appreciation,

Pam Powers

SEE INSIDE FOR READER'S SURVEY

The Reader Service — Here's How It Works:

Accepting your 2 free books and gift places you under no obligation to buy anything. You may keep the books and gift and return the shipping statement marked "cancel." If you do not cancel, about a month later we'll send you 3 additional books and bill you just $4.99 each in the U.S., or $5.49 each in Canada, plus 25¢ shipping & handling per book and applicable taxes if any.* That's the complete price and — compared to cover prices starting from $5.99 each in the U.S. and $6.99 each in Canada — it's quite a bargain! You may cancel at any time, but if you choose to continue, every month we'll send you 3 more books, which you may either purchase at the discount price or return to us and cancel your subscription.

*Terms and prices subject to change without notice. Sales tax applicable in N.Y. Canadian residents will be charged applicable provincial taxes and GST.

If offer card is missing write to: The Reader Service, 3010 Walden Ave., P.O. Box 1867, Buffalo, NY 14240-1867

BUSINESS REPLY MAIL

FIRST-CLASS MAIL PERMIT NO. 717-003 BUFFALO, NY

POSTAGE WILL BE PAID BY ADDRESSEE

NO POSTAGE
NECESSARY
IF MAILED
IN THE
UNITED STATES

THE READER SERVICE
3010 WALDEN AVE
PO BOX 1341
BUFFALO NY 14240-8571

Her knee struck the marble, pain shot through her. There would be more pain to come, she thought vaguely, and held out her hands in an attempt to protect herself. Then hard arms caught her against a solidly muscled chest, a masculine scent of musk and spices enveloped her, and she knew that though she was no longer in danger from harming herself on the marble staircase, she would not be as lucky with Richard Zagan.

"You might as well open those beautiful eyes, Liana, because I'm not going away. Not this minute, at any rate."

She didn't remember his voice having such a sharp, cutting edge, she thought hazily. But then again, maybe, on that last day in Paris, it had. She braced herself as if she were about to smash into a brick wall going a hundred miles an hour and did as he said.

The years had given his face a hard, cynical cast. His dark brown hair appeared as crisp and vital as ever, but the silver at the temples was new, and the muscles she could feel in his arms and chest suggested an even greater strength than before. All in all, he was still the most attractive man she had ever known.

Her gaze touched on the sardonic curl of his lips, then returned to the steel-gray eyes. "Hello, Richard."

"So you do remember me? I wasn't sure. I thought perhaps you'd had so many victims in the past eleven years that the first one might have slipped your mind."

"Are you hurt, Liana?" Clay asked, stooped down beside them and taking her hand. "I nearly had a heart attack, watching you fall."

Sara, Rosalyn and Steve stood anxiously in a circle around them.

"Lord, Liana, I'm sorry," Steve said. "I got caught up

in watching you and I guess I leaned against the light. I should have known better."

"It's all right." She pushed away from Richard and sat up. "I'm okay." Her voice was shaking. Though she wasn't surprised, she tried to rectify the matter with her next words. "My knee hurts a little, but I'm fine." Good, she thought. She sounded stronger.

Richard jerked the long skirt up to look at her knee. It was bruised and bloodied.

Liana groaned in dismay. "Oh, no, the dress has blood on it."

"To hell with the dress," Richard muttered, gently feeling the area around the open wound. "What about broken bones?"

"He's right, darling," Clay said and missed the sharp look Richard shot him at the word *darling*. "Can you extend your leg?"

"I think so." Trying not to grimace, she stretched the leg outward.

"Does that hurt?" Clay asked.

"Not too bad."

Richard had been watching her closely. "You may not have any broken bones, but the human body wasn't made for bouncing off marble. You need to see a doctor."

"No, really—"

Clay looked up at Sara. "Check and see if they can get a doctor out here quickly."

"Clay, really, it's nothing."

"When the doctor tells me that, I'll believe you." He pressed her arm with his hand. "You're very valuable to us, Liana."

Abruptly Richard scooped her into his arms and stood. "I'll take you up to your room."

"No!" The jolt of her fall and the initial shock of seeing Richard had worn off. Now she had to deal with the hard, cold fact that Richard was actually here at Swan-Sea. Not only that, he was holding her, and all her senses were clamoring as if it were eleven years ago and she and Richard were back in Paris. It would never do. She couldn't allow the situation to continue. She'd heard the alarm contained in her outburst. Fortunately, over the years she'd learned to adopt a mood at the drop of a hat, and now she wrapped herself in calm as easily as if it were a designer gown. "Please put me down, Richard. I can walk."

He tightened his arms around her and started down the stairs. "You can prove that after the doctor looks at you. Until then, you should stay off the knee."

Surprise at Richard's proprietary manner with Liana held Clay still for a moment, but he caught his breath quickly and said, "Wait a minute. Do you know this man, Liana?"

She looked at Clay without seeing him. It was taking every ounce of her energy to retain her calm demeanor and to fight the steadily growing panic inside her. The warmth and strength of Richard's body was sapping her will. Instinct was telling her to slide her arms around his neck and melt against him. Logic and reason were telling her that would be an exceedingly dangerous thing for her to do.

"Liana?" Clay asked.

Richard gazed down at her. "Yes, Liana. I'm waiting to hear what you're going to say, too. I'm sure you'll use *old* as a modifier, but I can't even guess what noun you'll choose."

Clay planted his fists at his sides. "What's he talking about?"

"Richard is an old...acquaintance."

Richard laughed flatly. "The easy way out. I suppose I should have known."

His hard, sarcastic tone was beginning to hurt more than her knee. "Dammit, Richard, put me down."

"So you've learned to curse. I'm overcome with admiration, not to mention curiosity. What else have you learned?"

"Richard—"

"For instance, have you learned any really hot lovemaking tricks? Now that would really impress me."

She darted an embarrassed glance at Clay as warmth flared in her cheeks.

"Are you ready to let me take you up to your room without protest now?"

She noted his satisfied expression with a flash of anger. "You embarrassed me on purpose."

"I do everything on purpose these days, Liana. Now be a good girl and tell your photographer that I'm not abducting you against your will. Or would you like me to embarrass you some more?"

She briefly closed her eyes. "It's all right, Clay. I'll be more comfortable in my room. Just send the doctor up when he comes."

"Very good," Richard said with mocking approval. "Now what room are you in?"

"Thirty-three."

"How convenient. I'm just down the hall."

LIANA had immediately fallen in love with her room at SwanSea. Light and airy, it overlooked a wide green lawn and the endless sea beyond and had been decorated in harmonious colors and soft textures. Even the strong shapes of the light-toned furniture were softened by inlays and floral decorations.

The bed's four tall posters rose in graceful swirls of carved satinwood. Swags of seafoam green chiffon looped from the top of one poster to the next, then spilled down to the floor to form diaphanous pools.

Until now Liana had felt the mood of the room was soothing. But that was before Richard had invaded its space.

He carefully settled her on the couch, then stood back and eyed her critically. "Raise your skirt."

She started. "I beg your pardon."

His lips twisted. "Don't flatter yourself, Liana. If I wanted to take you to bed, I would. For now, I just want you to lift your skirt off your knee so that the material won't become stuck to the wound."

She didn't trust him or his motives and knew he should be treated with the utmost caution, but his constant taunting had stretched her nerves to the limit. "Look, Richard," she began, the cadence of her words deliberately slow to ensure the steadiness of her voice, "you saved me from falling down the stairs. You've carried me up here. I'm grateful."

"Be still my heart. Liana Marchall is grateful to me."

Her teeth ground together. "*But* I'd appreciate it if you would leave now. I'll be fine until the doctor arrives."

He leaned down to look her in the eye. "You're close to the top of the list of the ten most desirable women in the world, Liana. That's a unique power all its own. But you'll never have enough power to dismiss me. Not again."

"I didn't mean—"

"Oh, yes, sweetheart, you did mean. You were trying to get rid of me, but this time, it won't work—not unless I'm ready to leave." He straightened, spun on his heels, and headed for the bathroom.

Liana pressed her hand to her heart to restrain its wild beating. It was a vain attempt. *This had to be another of her sweet, unbearable nightmares.* Her dreams of Richard over the years had sometimes been so real that, when she woke, she would roll over, absolutely sure that she would find him beside her. Always there would be nothing but an empty pillow.

But now he was here; she was undoubtedly wide-awake, and her memories and dreams were nothing in comparison to the vital, entirely compelling, masculine reality of him.

He returned to the room with a wet washcloth, knelt in front of her, and cupped his left hand behind her knee. With a light delicate touch so at odds with such a tough man, he sponged the blood away from the broken skin. "This isn't too bad," he murmured.

She stared down at his bent head. She wasn't surprised to find his hair still thick and glossy, but she was surprised that her fingers tingled to touch it. "What are you doing here at SwanSea, Richard?"

His steel-gray gaze sliced up to her, cold and impenetrable.

Her throat moved convulsively. "I just wondered. I mean, you're a very important man. Your company has grown twenty times bigger since..." Her voice trailed off.

"You've kept track of me?"

"It's not hard to do. Over the years, I've occasionally picked up the business section of the newspaper. Sometimes there'd be an article about you."

And then there'd been that time, six years ago, right

after her father's death when she'd attempted to see him. She'd gone straight from the funeral to the airport and booked herself on the next flight to New York. Immediately upon landing in New York, she'd called his office, only to be told by his secretary that he was on his honeymoon.

"Save yourself some anguish, Liana. You have nothing to do with my being here."

"I didn't think—"

His knowing smile made the words abruptly die in her throat. That was *exactly* what she had thought.

"I came because of the auction of art nouveau works that will be held in a few days."

"Are you a collector?"

He nodded. "And there are quite a few noteworthy paintings up for sale." His gruff, harsh tone was startling in its contrast to the incredibly gentle way he ministered to her knee. "And I'll save you the effort of asking the next question. Yes, I knew you were going to be here."

Her muscles tightened with alarm; her words rushed out in a whisper. "Then, why?"

"I didn't find out about the fact that you would be here until after I'd booked my reservations. But I decided very quickly it didn't matter, that I'd be damned if I'd let you ruin my first vacation in years and the chance at the paintings." He gave her knee a final pat with the cloth, then surged to his feet. "Besides, Liana, it's a small world. We were bound to run into each other sooner or later."

She wondered what he'd say if he knew the lengths to which she'd gone to make sure they didn't end up in the same place at the same time. "You're right. It doesn't matter. Besides, SwanSea is a large resort. I'm sure we're both going to be busy with different agendas."

She was no more at a disadvantage with him looming above her than she had been when he'd been kneeling in front of her, but she was relieved when he disappeared into the bathroom to return the washcloth. His absence was a chance for her pulse to return to normal. Unfortunately as soon as he walked back into the room, it began to race again.

His smile, a slash of white teeth, told her he knew how he affected her. "Are you here at SwanSea alone?"

"No, I'm here with Clay and the others."

"I figured that out, Liana."

"Then—?"

"Are you and Clay lovers?"

He hurled the question at her with such speed and force, it took her a moment to recover from its impact. "He's the photographer in charge of this shoot. I hardly know him."

"Really. Yet he called you darling. What do you call him?"

"Clay."

He smiled. "I remember when you were in awe of photographers. But, of course, back then, they had the power to make you a star, and you wanted to become a star more than anything. Right? Including more than you wanted me."

She absorbed the salvo with hardly a flinch and congratulated herself.

He continued without mercy. "Not that one should exclude the other. Except when one used the method you chose—going from my bed to Savion's. Damn awkward, Liana." With each word, his voice deteriorated until it was an abrasive rasp. "And of course, there were the things you said. I'm sure you recall, especially the part about you really not loving me at all."

"Clay is the photographer on this assignment," she repeated stonily, "nothing more."

"I see. So you and he aren't lovers unlike you and Savion, who are." His shrug indicated the subject was of supreme indifference to him. "I wondered, that's all, since Clay was very concerned about you, and I didn't see Savion around."

She glanced away. "Jean-Paul is ill. Otherwise he would have been here."

"Oh, I would have bet on that. I'm sure it would take something of catastrophic proportions to keep him away from you."

"If he'd come, his interest would have been only in the assignment." Her teeth snapped together as she emphasized each word. It mattered that he believe her, she realized, and wondered why. After all, it was much too late. "We're all here to work. The opening of SwanSea is a gala event, and this layout will appear worldwide in all the important fashion, society and news magazines."

"More fame and fortune."

"And more hard work."

"I have no doubt. But then I also have no doubt that you receive a great deal of pleasure from what you do. After all, you and Savion work together most of the time, don't you?"

He was playing a game with her, and she was losing badly. It seemed to her she could feel her nerves fraying, one by one, a condition that absolutely had to be kept from him. If he sensed her weakness where he was concerned, he would close in for the kill. She didn't answer him.

"Tell me something, Liana. I'm curious."

She eyed him warily. "About what?"

"*Have* you learned any hot lovemaking tricks?" He heard her indrawn gasp of breath and went on. "Even when you were a novice you could turn me inside out and make me jump through hoops. What are you like in bed now?"

"It's something you'll never know, Richard."

The smile he gave chilled and transfixed her. So much so, she was unable to move, unable to breathe, unable to stop the painful hammering of her heart against her ribs. When the knock on the door came, she jumped.

One dark brow shot up. "Careful, Liana. That skin of yours is much too pretty to jump out of, especially when it could be put to so many other good uses."

LIANA CLIMBED carefully into bed and gratefully sank back against the pillows. Richard had stood silently and observantly by as the doctor had examined her, then applied antibiotic cream and wrapped a large, white gauze bandage around her knee. Thankfully for her peace of mind, he had left with the doctor. After that, visits from Clay, Sara, Rosalyn and Steve had had to be endured.

Alone at last she found her thoughts only increased her tension and anxiety.

Richard was actually here. They had talked. He had held her. Lord, help her!

When she had known Richard eleven years ago in Paris, he had been a gentle and caring man. Now he was hard, cynical and cruel. He used razor-edged words, and he made no careless moves.

But if he'd changed, she reflected, so had she.

She was no longer the idealistic, naive young girl she had been at eighteen. At twenty-nine, she was much wiser. She was also so full of pain she couldn't stand to be touched.

She felt as if her skin was too sensitive, and contact with anyone would hurt, violate, or scar her. The idea was all in her mind, of course. She was touched all the time, by hairdressers, makeup artists, designers and photographers. It was her salvation that she had learned to escape to another place in her mind and block them out.

Suddenly chills of fear shivered through her. She wrapped her arms around her body, but no matter how tightly she hugged herself, she couldn't stop remembering the unexpected encounter with Richard and her reaction to him. The chills worsened.

No real damage had been done, she reassured herself over and over again. But cold fear gripped her, and she knew that if there was another encounter, she might not be able to block him out.

Maybe, if she was lucky, she could avoid him. At any rate, it was something to hope and work for.

But how was she going to deal with the fact that she was responsible for the man he had become?

SWANSEA was quiet. Most of the lights in the great house were out. Its guests were resting. Except for one.

Richard leaned back against the doorjamb of the open French doors of his room, his eyes squeezed shut, his jaw tightly clenched. A breeze came off the ocean, fanning him, but it neither cooled him nor dried the sheen of sweat covering his body.

Night sweats. They were brought on by the pain of the past, the uncertainty of the present and the fear of not knowing how the hell he was going to get through the next day, much less the rest of his life. They often came on him like this when he couldn't sleep and when all he could think of was Liana.

Liana. She had haunted him for eleven years, and in that time he had found that being haunted by her was worse than any ghost. Ghosts were illusory. If you saw one, you might not even be sure of what it was you were looking at.

But Liana. No matter where he went, she was there. As one of the most photographed models in the world, her picture graced countless magazine covers. Every newsstand he passed, every coffee table he sat at, every doctor's waiting room he went into usually held at least one magazine with her picture gracing its cover. Her wide teal eyes would stare out at him, taunting him, reminding him of the one question that drove him to work twenty-hour days.

Success had become the god he worshiped. But nothing was ever enough. There was always one more business triumph to achieve. One more possession to buy.

Yet the emptiness remained. And the question persisted.

Why hadn't she loved him?

TWO

LIANA ROSE EARLY and ordered room service, then slowly dressed and ate a leisurely breakfast. Her purpose was to have ample time to compose herself. When she finally left her room, she wanted her nerves well hidden beneath the cool facade of the supermodel. If she should meet Richard, she wanted no hint of how he affected her to show. It wasn't a perfect plan, she acknowledged, but it was all she could think of for the moment.

At the knock on her bedroom door, Liana's hand jerked, toppling the delicate china cup onto its side and sending hot coffee spilling over the pristine white tablecloth. So much for her plan, she thought with disgust. She hastily righted the cup and snatched up the linen napkin to blot as much as she could of the cup's contents.

When the second knock came, she sighed and threw down the napkin. "Coming."

She used the short walk to the door to prepare herself for whoever might be on the other side. Hopefully, it was Clay or Sara, checking to see if she was ready for today's shoot. Surely it wouldn't be Richard. He hated her. If over the years, she'd had any doubts, their encounter last night had eliminated them.

Still she didn't kid herself. Trying to avoid him would

accomplish only so much. Their situation was volatile and unpredictable, and she had to be ready for anything. Half expecting to meet steel-gray eyes, she opened the door and was astonished to find a beautiful young woman with cinnamon-colored hair and lovely green-gold eyes.

"Good morning. I'm Caitlin Deverell-DiFrenza. I hope I'm not disturbing you."

Liana recognized the name immediately. Caitlin Deverell-DiFrenza was the owner of SwanSea. "No, not at all. Please come in."

Caitlin entered and cast an automatic, all-seeing glance around the room. The disorder on the serving table propelled her to the phone where she dialed a number. There were no push-button phones at SwanSea, only beautifully designed decorator phones that blended with each room's elegant decor.

"Please send fresh table linen and a carafe of coffee to room thirty-three." A magnificent emerald wedding ring set flashed on Caitlin's hand as she hung up the phone.

"That wasn't necessary," Liana said, "but thank you."

"You're more than welcome. I want my guests to have the best service possible."

Uncertain why Caitlin was in her room, Liana waved her hand toward the sofa. "Would you care to sit down?"

"No, thank you. I don't want to keep you. It's just that I heard about your accident last night, and I was worried."

"Don't be. It's really nothing more than a bad scrape."

"Are you sure?"

Liana smiled. "I use to get scrapes worse than this when I was a little girl. There was a big oak tree in our backyard in Des Moines that I couldn't resist climbing.

Unfortunately there's that silly law about what goes up must come down. I came down a lot."

Caitlin nodded solemnly. "I'm familiar with that law. SwanSea has some great trees."

Liana grinned, feeling some of her tension fade. Caitlin, who had more money than Liana was ever likely to see in her lifetime, was one of the most down-to-earth people she'd ever met. "But the urge to climb that tree was nothing in comparison to my fervent desire to learn to roller-skate. I spent hours on my skates out in front of our house. You know, I don't think I ever skated the full length of our sidewalk without falling."

Caitlin laughed. "Well, I'm relieved you weren't hurt more seriously. You could have been so easily, you know. I was very concerned last night when I heard about your fall, but I thought it would be best if I didn't bother you. But when I saw Clay Phillips downstairs this morning, having breakfast with one of his assistants, the lovely redheaded girl—?"

"Sara."

"Yes, and you weren't with them, so I decided to come up."

"I'm glad you did. It gives me the opportunity to tell you how beautiful your hotel is."

A strange expression came over Caitlin's face. "Hotel—yes, I guess it is." She grimaced. "I've spent months working to that end, but it's funny, I still don't see SwanSea as a hotel. I wonder if I'll ever get over the mind-set that this is my home and the people who've come here are my personal guests."

"Why should you get over it? I understand that SwanSea *was* your home. Besides, that attitude is exactly why you'll have a great success. Believe me, I've stayed in some of the finest hotels all over the world, but I've never been in one with more warmth and character than SwanSea."

Caitlin clapped her hands together with delight. "Wonderful. You've boosted my confidence a hundred percent, and I needed that. You wouldn't believe the problems that have cropped up in the last few days."

She'd believe the problems, Liana thought, but she didn't believe that Caitlin needed a boost of confidence. She radiated a strength and a happiness and a feeling that she could handle anything. Liana envied her.

Caitlin shrugged lightly. "Oh, well, I expected as much for the opening. And as long as my guests don't suffer, I don't mind." She clasped her hands together and eyed Liana intently. "Now, do you have everything you need?"

"Everything. Your staff is wonderful."

"I'm glad to hear it, but I don't want you to hesitate to call if you should need anything at all. If we don't have it, we will do our best to get it."

"I'll remember that," Liana said with a smile.

BY LATE THAT AFTERNOON, Liana was wondering if Caitlin could send out for a bottle of energy for her. She'd spent hours under the sun and hot lights in first one evening gown and then another. As they'd moved from one outdoor location to another, it had seemed to her that Clay had been unusually demanding. She understood, though. This was the first major assignment he'd done on his own without the supervision of Jean-Paul, and he wanted everything to be perfect.

But she longed for Jean-Paul. Together they had always made a certain magic on film, and they had an unspoken communication between them that had made any photo assignment pleasurable. Richard had been right in that at least.

"Hell, we've lost our light." Clay plowed his fingers through his hair, the lines of his body set with displeasure and tension. "All right," he said with a sigh. "That's it for today. I'll let everyone know the shooting schedule for tomorrow."

Liana retreated inside an aluminum-framed tent and slipped out of the green beaded gown she'd worn for the last series of shots.

Sara joined her and took the gown. "You were wonderful, Liana."

"Thanks," she said, giving the girl a smile. Although she hadn't met Sara before this trip, Liana thought she was very nice and eager to learn all aspects of the business. She plucked the hairpins from her hair. The tight coil at the base of her neck loosened, then opened, sending a shining, straight mass of wheat-colored hair down her back.

"How's your knee?" Sara asked.

"Not too bad." In truth, standing on it all day had made the dull ache of the bruise turn to a throb. "I'm thankful that I'm here to model evening gowns. The long skirts cover the bandage. If we were doing street-length dresses or bathing suits, *you* would have been the one out there in front of the cameras, with the reflectors throwing heat and light onto you."

Sara's eyes widened. "No way could I do a big assignment like this one. Besides, I'm really happiest behind the camera." She ran her hand over the gown, caressing the beaded work, then carefully hung it up.

Liana pulled on a pair of shorts and a tank top and breathed a sigh of relief at the cool comfort of the outfit. "Clay has done layouts with you before, hasn't he?"

"Only small stuff. Nothing on this scale. Are you going back to the hotel now?"

She should get off her knee for a while, Liana thought, but the prospect of an empty room was unappealing, and the beauty of the grounds was pulling at her. "I think I'll take a short walk. I'm a little stiff, and the exercise will feel good."

Sara laughed quietly. "Exercise never feels good. A hot bath is more my speed and that's just where I'm heading. Maybe I'll even be able to catch a nap before dinner. Have you heard? We have to dress for dinner."

Liana smiled. "Yes, I did hear that."

"But do you know why?" Sara asked as they left the tent.

"I guess I hadn't really thought about it. Why?"

"This is SwanSea."

"What?"

"I asked one of the *very* dignified employees why we had to dress for dinner, and I was told with extreme politeness that this is SwanSea." She grinned, then shrugged. "See you later."

LIANA ENDED UP at the gazebo that stood on the windswept point overlooking the sea. The gazebo was made of iron bent in fluid arabesques. A fresh coat of white paint and new green-and-blue cotton ducking covers for the bench cushions made it a lovely retreat, but Liana thought she sensed an air of sadness and loneliness about the gazebo.

She rested a knee on the cushion and leaned against the railing, reflecting that she didn't mind the strange atmosphere. Sadness and loneliness were emotions with which she was all too familiar. She was used to being by herself; she had long ago made the conscious decision not to get too close to anyone. And it had been years since she'd thought of the irony that one of the most visible women of the decade was also one of the most isolated.

The money she earned modeling gave her security. The sense that she earned her money through hard work gave her satisfaction. But she accepted only the assignments she wanted, and arranged her schedule to suit herself. And when she reached the point where the feel of people's hands on her was just beginning to penetrate through her mind block, she'd retreat to the countryside of France where she had a cottage and no one but Jean-Paul Savion had the address.

Her success had ensured her freedom from people and their demands; it was the main reason why her career was so important to her.

"You know what I remember most about your legs?"

She spun at the sound of Richard's voice, her heart beating wildly. He wore an icy blue shirt paired with taupe-colored slacks, and she'd never seen him look more virile and attractive. Or more dangerous.

He raked his gaze up the long length of her bare legs. "I remember how they seemed to go on forever," he continued, "and how tightly they gripped my waist when we made love. And when you climaxed—"

"Shut up, Richard."

His smile seemed almost genuine, she thought with a distant part of her mind, but she knew better. A smile was an indication of friendliness or affection. He felt neither of those things for her.

"You always did look nice in shorts," he said. "But then you've got the kind of body that shows off clothes to their best advantage. Still, I always liked you better without—"

"Shut *up,* Richard."

He bounded up the steps into the gazebo. Before she had time to prepare herself, he was beside her. Suddenly she felt trapped, as if there were no place for her to run. In fact, all she had to do was step around him and leave. She started to, but the sudden softness of his voice stopped her.

"Relax, Liana. Words can't hurt, you know. Not unless the person at whom they're directed cares, and you certainly don't." He waited a heartbeat, then asked in an even softer voice, "Do you?"

"No, of course not."

"No, I didn't think so." His gaze dropped to the bandage wrapped around her knee. "How is it?"

"Fine."

"Have you applied more antibiotic cream and changed the bandage as the doctor told you to?"

"Not yet."

"But you will, won't you?"

"Of course."

He threw a quick glance around the gazebo. "What are you doing here?"

She had been on the verge of leaving again, but this time it was the puzzlement in his voice that stopped her. "You mean at SwanSea?"

"No. What are you doing here in the gazebo? You're all alone. The sun is about to set; it will be dark soon, not to mention cooler." He waved his hand toward her. "And all you're wearing is that skimpy outfit."

There were reasons for everything he mentioned, but she chose to tell him only one. "I love the sea. I have ever since the first time I saw it."

He drew closer. "When was that?"

She took a step away. "I guess the first time was when my father took my mother and me on a vacation to California." As always when she thought of her father, conflicting emotions besieged her. Unconsciously she stiffened her spine. "At any rate, I don't suppose it's so unusual for a girl who grew up in Des Moines, Iowa, to love the sea."

"No, I don't suppose it's so unusual."

His stare was analytical, his voice low-key, yet the friction in the air was palpable. She had the feeling that if she threw a match into the air between them, it would burst into flame spontaneously.

"It was always hard for me to picture you being from Des Moines," he said after a moment. "You're much too exotic."

"Des Moines was a wonderful place to grow up," she said, automatically defensive, though not directly answering him.

"But you left."

She shrugged. "I couldn't have gotten as far as I have in modeling if I'd stayed there. Pictures and spreads from my local modeling went to New York. Then my portfolio appealed to several designers in Paris. As luck would have it, one of the designers chose me for a runway show before any New York clients could line me up. The job in Paris was a gold-plated opportunity, and I took it." She'd had to. She'd been desperate for the money.

"I guess that pretty much must be the story of your life, right? Taking opportunities—no matter who gets hurt." He paused. "Or was I the only one you stepped on as you climbed your way to the top?"

"I have to go."

His hand encircled her arm as she moved past him. It was the contact of his hand on her skin more than his grip that halted her in her tracks. She gasped at the heat, at the hurt.

He released her immediately. "I didn't grab you that hard."

Silently, with an instinctive need to soothe, she rubbed her arm where he had touched.

Frowning, he moved a few steps away. After another puzzled glance at her, he fixed his gaze on the horizon. "So what's it like to have the world's greatest designers create one-of-a-kind gowns for you?"

"The gowns weren't designed for me," she said, happier about speaking of something that didn't affect her emotionally. "They were designed for SwanSea. Each designer was inspired by an aspect of SwanSea, whether it was a color, a texture, a pattern, or, with some, even just a feeling. Then they created a gown that would complement that aspect or conjure up the feeling that had inspired them."

"Maybe. At least that's what the press release said. But when they designed the gowns, they knew you were the model who would be wearing them. I'm willing to bet that a large portion of their inspiration came from you."

"The gowns aren't for me," she repeated firmly. "Any model could wear them. And they're to be auctioned off at the end of this two-week opening celebration. The proceeds will go to charity."

"Still, the ones I've seen you in so far look as if they'd been made solely for you. Especially the teal gown you were wearing last evening."

"You've seen me in other gowns? You saw me modeling today?" How could she have been unaware of him watching her? she wondered, disturbed at the thought.

"I caught an occasional glimpse of you here and there. It was hard not to. You seemed to be everywhere."

"I only remember three locations."

"Whatever," he said in a tone that expressed boredom with the subject, then took her by surprise by abruptly turning toward her. "Has it been worth it, Liana? Doing everything you've had to do to achieve your success?"

"Yes," she replied without hesitation, understanding that they were talking about two different things, but also understanding that it would make no difference if he knew. She'd left a deep scar in him. She was well acquainted with scars. She had her own to deal with.

Suddenly the imaginary match lit.

He reached out and grasped her face between the long fingers of his hand. "This face," he muttered. "This damnably beautiful face."

Her fragile shield of composure disintegrated with his touch, and in its place, a treacherous need sprang up, softening the urge to recoil and run. "It's ugly," she whispered.

"Yeah." He burst out with a hard laugh. "So ugly its image is permanently burned on the inside of the brain of every man who's ever seen it."

He stepped closer, his body brushing against hers, and her nerves reacted, coming alive, crackling with pleasure and pain. "You're exaggerating. There's nothing remotely attractive about me. My hair is board straight."

"It's thick, and silky, and just the right length to wind around a man's body."

Something molten and debilitating coiled through her. "My lips are too big—"

"They're full and sensuous and make a man fantasize about what it would be like to have his lips sealed to them for about a month."

"You're wrong." She stopped, cleared an obstruction from her dry throat, and tried again. "My eyebrows feather instead of going in a straight line."

"They make a man wonder if there's something not quite tame beneath that perfect control you project."

Somehow she managed to continue to draw air into her lungs, but the air seared her insides like a desert wind, leaving her struggling for breath. Frantically she searched for something else to say. "My eyes are an odd color and too far apart."

"They're arresting and impossible to look away from."

"My jaw is too strong."

"Yeah, but look how well it fits into my hand."

"My skin—"

"Catches all available light. I'm sure Savion has told you it's what makes you a dream to photograph. I'm sure he's also told you that your skin is so soft, stroking it makes a fire start in his belly. And, honey, I bet he strokes you a lot. He'd have to be crazy not to."

His thumb and finger had begun to rub her jaw, and as he spoke, they worked up to her cheeks, pressing harder and harder until it seemed as if he were trying to scrub something off her skin. She wasn't sure he was aware of the pressure he was exerting, but she was very aware she would be in serious trouble if she couldn't regain command of her emotions.

She tried to imagine that the two of them were doing a layout for sportswear or perfume, that he was a model with whom she was merely posing. It didn't work. Not at all.

"Your face," he whispered fiercely. "Your mouth, your eyes, you skin. Your *damned* sexy body."

"Richard..." The ruthlessness of his expression frightened her, excited her.

"It's all right," he muttered. "I'm immune."

And then he brought his mouth down hard on hers, and it was just as she had known all along. She couldn't block him out.

Kissing him again after all this time was like drowning. She felt as if a force were pulling her down, down, to somewhere deep and dark, where there was no escape. The force was Richard. She wasn't sure of the place. She wasn't sure if she cared.

She should fight, she thought hazily. There were reasons why she shouldn't be melting against him like she was. There were reasons why she should push against him and break away. He hated her. He wanted to hurt, then destroy her.

But what he didn't know was that she couldn't be hurt any more. She was all filled up with pain. And she'd destroyed herself eleven years ago when she'd walked out on him. Her career might be a success, but she was a complete and total failure. As a person. As a woman.

Nevertheless, she should fight.

His lips found the indentation behind her earlobe, and he brushed his tongue down the groove that ran behind her ear and partway down the side of her throat. A moan escaped her; a thrill shivered through her. Oh, Lord, he had remembered. She was very sure he'd had many women since their weeks together in Paris, yet he had remembered that one secret, special spot. He wasn't playing fair.

She should definitely fight.

But being in his arms after all these years overrode everything. The pleasure was simply too intense. All of her protective layers were peeling away one by one.

He made little sucking motions up her neck, tasting her, deliberately arousing her, and he had the satisfaction of feeling her go limp in his arms. At least in this one thing she hadn't changed. And neither had he, he thought angrily, as he felt himself grow hard with desire.

He slipped his hand beneath the tank top, and closed his hand around her breast. A shudder ripped through him. The *feel* of her hadn't changed, either. As was true so long ago, her breast more than filled his hand. He'd always found something terribly erotic in the fact that she was so soft, yet so firm. And the way her nipples grew tight and stiff made him burn with an overpowering hunger.

In the past eleven years, he'd found no woman as intriguing, no woman nearly as satisfying. Liana was unique. And he wanted to break her neck because of it.

He caressed her roughly, but she was like a person deprived for too long of the essential elements of life. Nothing was too much. She wanted more and then more still. And so when he lowered her to her back on the softly cushioned bench she made no protest. And when he bent to pull her nipple into his mouth, she could only throw her head back at the ecstasy of the sensations that coursed through her.

"Richard, oh, Richard..."

"Yes," he said raggedly, his mouth wet on her breast. "Call my name. Make me think you want me."

"I do," she cried. "Oh, Lord, I do."

Ravenously he tugged at her nipple. The fact that he used neither gentleness nor care only heightened the intensity of the act and drew both of them toward the point where everything but the ecstasy would disappear. He switched his attention to the other breast. Half over her, he felt her hips lift. She'd probably done this sort of thing so often, it was second nature to her, he reflected, bitterness welling up in him. He wedged his knee between her legs and pushed upward. The sound that was ripped from her triggered a response in his mind, his heart, his gut.

His body blazed with passion, but his mind dispassionately sought caution.

He was a man torn, a man possessed. A man driven to have this one woman.

A man with a solitary unanswered question.

"You still respond like a woman who's giving herself totally to a man," he said roughly. "Are you, Liana? Are you willing to give yourself totally to me?"

His voice sounded as if he were far away from her, she thought, but that couldn't be. His weight was pressing her into the cushions, his body heat was burning through her clothes to her skin. "Yes."

He laved his tongue around a nipple. "You're lying."

She felt feverish, achy, and wasn't sure she had understood him correctly. "What?"

He nipped at her and heard her tiny cry. The roar of the ocean mixed with his heartbeat and thundered in his ears. She was like a siren, trying to lure him to his destruction with a bewitching sweetness and an insidious seductiveness.

The thing was, he'd been to hell and back and lived to tell about it. There was absolutely nothing she could do to him.

He told himself this, and he believed it.

He shoved his hand beneath the hem of her shorts and the elastic edge of her panties until he found the moist warmth he was seeking. He almost lost control then, and for a moment, he forgot what he had been about to say. He plunged his tongue deep into her mouth, and lower, his fingers imitated the motion of his tongue.

The memory of what it was like to be inside her came rushing back, and he was gripped by a heat and need so intense, it seemed his life would be threatened, making him the liar.

"I want you," she whispered against his ear, forgetting time, place and reason. "I want you so badly."

He drew a deep painful breath and tried to clear his head. Passion had never been their problem. Apparently it still wasn't. She could turn him on like no one else. But...

He jerked his hand from her shorts. Their faces were so close, their ragged breaths intermingled, but he didn't notice. He was too busy looking at the desire in her eyes.

"I could take you, couldn't I? Couldn't I, Liana?" he said louder. "Right here. Right now."

"Yes," she said on a sob and turned her head away.

Her answer fanned the flames inside him until he wasn't sure he could control them. But he had to reject her. It was the smart thing to do. "I was twenty-nine when we met. I'd had my share of women, but you were the hottest I'd ever had. I thought you were the most incredible thing that had ever happened to me. When I wasn't making love to you, I was thinking how lucky I was."

As he watched, her passion slowly faded to be replaced by bewilderment. And with the cooling of her passion, he felt stronger. Still, he couldn't quite make himself move away from her. "You were so sweet," he said, the memory thickening his voice in spite of his intentions. "I couldn't get enough of you. If there'd been some way to take you intravenously, I would have done it. What a high—a constant stream of you, pumping through my veins. If we'd stayed together long enough, I might have found a way." Abruptly he pushed away from her and sat up. "I guess I should really thank you. You saved me from becoming addicted to you."

Liana pulled the tank top down to cover her nakedness, but she stayed where she was, too weakened by what had just happened to move. "What are you saying, Richard?"

"I'm saying that I've been inoculated against you." His mouth twisted cruelly. "I may be the only man in the world who is. I wonder if science would be interested in using my blood to make a vaccine against you."

Her stomach churned sickeningly. She closed her eyes, certain she was going to throw up.

"What do you think, Liana? Should I volunteer my blood? I might even get the Nobel Prize." Her unresponsiveness didn't faze him. He felt driven, unable to stop the bitter, hateful words. "Another man might fall for the way you give yourself during lovemaking, but I'm in the unique position to know that you have no heart, no soul." At a small sound of distress from her, he bent and pressed a hard kiss to her lips. "Don't worry," he whispered. "I'm not saying we won't eventually go to bed together. There's nothing wrong with the purely physical as long as it's kept in perspective. Right?"

After a moment, she felt his weight leave the cushion, then heard the retreat of his footsteps as he left the gazebo. Tears slipped from beneath her lashes and slid slowly down her cheek, and her only thought was that she'd been right about this gazebo. There was an incredible sadness here.

RICHARD TURNED on the cold faucet and stepped into the etched glass shower stall. He didn't flinch as the icy water hit him. He braced his arms against the tiled wall, welcoming the frigid temperature as it washed over his body, numbing his body and his mind. He stayed and he stayed, until, when he finally turned off the water, he was satisfied that he couldn't feel a thing.

THREE

LIANA BRUSHED HER fingers across the brooch pinned to the bodice of her evening gown and wished herself anywhere but the dining room of SwanSea. She'd almost stayed in her room. After her encounter with Richard in the gazebo that afternoon, the last thing she had wanted to do was face a large group of people. Even now she could feel their curious stares, as harmful to her as physical blows.

Jewel-like flower lamps by Tiffany lighted the room. The long graceful leaves of potted palms stirred ever so slightly in the gentle currents of air. In the background, a string quartet played pleasantly, soothingly. Startling white linen tablecloths draped tables ladened with glistening silver, gleaming china, and sparkling crystal. Tall white candles added their golden flames to the elegant ambience, and bowls filled with velvet-petaled roses emitted a faint sweet scent.

She had to get out of here.

"Are you all right, Liana?"

An unaccountable desperation was working in her, urging her to bolt from the table, and it was only her years of discipline that came to her rescue. Calmly she looked across the expanse of white linen at Sara, and not even the merciless eye of a camera lens could have detected the effort it cost her. "I'm fine, thank you."

"It's my fault. I worked you too hard today," Clay said, sitting in the chair to her right. "After that fall you took last night, I probably should have canceled today's schedule. Jean-Paul will have my hide if he hears about this."

She reached over and patted his hand. "I'm getting tired of telling you people I'm fine. Just believe me. And about Jean-Paul, you know as well as I do how ruthless he can be when it comes to getting the pictures he wants. He would understand."

Clay's mouth twisted wryly. "You're right about him being ruthless—when it comes to his profession at any rate. Have some champagne. It will make you feel better."

In the hopes that he'd drop the subject of her well-being, she raised the fluted glass to her lips and let a small sip of the cool, bubbly wine slide down her throat. It felt good.

"Champagne seems to fit SwanSea, doesn't it?" asked Rosalyn, striking in a pale rose dress that grazed her ankles. "I mean the glamour of this place is incredible."

Steve shrugged his shoulders against the unaccustomed weight of a dinner jacket, then with a grimace ran a finger inside the buttoned collar of his white dress shirt. "This place is damned hard on your eyes, if you ask me."

"Hard on your eyes?" Rosalyn asked with disbelief.

"Everywhere you look, there's something fantastic. That sort of thing can damage your eyesight after a while." Still squirming uncomfortably, he crossed his long, blue jean–clad legs beneath the table.

Rosalyn laughed. "You can drop the jaded, world-weary act, Steve. I know better. I can't believe how lucky we are to be at this opening. The house isn't full yet, but by the night of the ball, I understand everyone who's anyone in New York society will be here. Liana, have you picked up any information about the socialites who are coming?"

Hearing her name, Liana pulled herself back from the distant place in her mind to which she'd retreated. She shouldn't have been there anyway. Richard had been there, and it had been springtime in Paris. "I'm sorry, what did you say?"

Sara, demure and lovely in a long, gold shirtwaist, used her champagne glass to gesture toward Rosalyn. "She's been busy picking up gossip."

Rosalyn suddenly gasped with admiration. "Look, Liana. There's that man who caught you last night when you fell."

She looked, not because she wanted to, but because Richard's very presence demanded that she do so. He was standing in the arched doorway, self-assured and at ease, carrying on a casual conversation with an attractive younger woman who stood beside him. She saw his gaze idly sweep the room, then stop cold on her and narrow. Something sharp pierced her heart. The candlelight blurred, the music dimmed.

"Who *is* he anyway?" Clay asked.

"Richard Zagan," she whispered. His mouth curved into a slow, hard smile, telling her he'd read her lips.

Her fingers sought out the brooch, its familiar textures and shapes acting as a worry stone. Odd, she thought, how this inanimate object could comfort her. But she'd loved it from the first moment she'd seen it—an exquisite lily with carved ivory petals, topaz stamen and gold-and-green enameled stem and leaves.

"What a *beautiful* brooch."

The sound of a friendly voice gave Liana strength to tear her gaze from Richard, and she turned her attention to Caitlin who had just come up to their table. "Thank you."

"You're welcome." Caitlin gave her a smile, then addressed the entire table. "How is everyone tonight? Are you all enjoying yourselves?"

"Absolutely," Rosalyn said. "We've never had more luxurious working conditions."

"Usually we're on some atoll that isn't even on the charts," Steve mumbled, fidgeting in his chair.

"And that's in the dead of winter," Rosalyn added. "If the weather's cold, you can always find us on some beach. Tell me, is it true that the Trumps will be coming to the ball?"

Liana heard Caitlin laugh, but her reply to Rosalyn somehow blended into a muted white sound. Richard was no longer at the door. Lord, where *was* he? She cast a surreptitious glance around the dining room. He was here somewhere. The surface of her skin felt too exposed, her soul too unprotected, for him not to be.

Then she saw him seated at a corner table that gave him an unobstructed view of her. He was smiling at his dinner companion, and the woman seemed to be hanging on his every word. But much to Liana's dismay, she found it didn't matter that his attention was elsewhere. Richard didn't have to look at her to affect her. His mere presence made her feel battered and bruised, as if she'd taken another fall down the great marble stairway.

And it would have been much better for her if she had, she reflected. Instead she'd allowed herself to fall under Richard's spell, to be carried away by his kisses and caresses, to forget their past. Any one of those things had the potential to be fatal, and she'd done all three.

She should leave SwanSea. It would solve everything. She could fly to France and retreat for a while to her cottage. It would be so easy. She sighed, bringing herself to a mental halt. Unfortunately for her—at least in this instance—she was too disciplined, too professional to leave an assignment.

"That is a stunning gown, Liana," Caitlin said. "Should I know the designer?"

"What?" she asked dumbly, then quickly recovered. Her dress was a deceptively uncomplicated midnight blue dress of silk and chiffon. The sheer material draped from its right lower side upward to the top left of the bodice. From there, a single sheer panel swept over her shoulder and dropped down her back to the floor-length hem. "The dress is by a friend of mine, but he's not well known yet."

"He will be soon though," Sara said in her quiet voice. "And every dress of his Liana wears in public increases the odds of his success."

"I can see that it would," Caitlin said thoughtfully. "You know, my sister-in-law, Angelica DiFrenza, might be interested in his clothes for DiFrenza's. She'll be here for the ball. I'll introduce you, and you can put them in touch."

"I'll be glad to," she murmured.

It was a sense of self-preservation that made her check to see if Richard was still sitting in the same place as he'd been when she had looked the last time. But her need to safeguard herself disappeared as her gaze collided with his. The heat and the hatred of his expression lacerated her, opening wounds she had worked hard to keep closed. She reached for her champagne glass. "Did your friend design the brooch, too, Liana?"

Liana took another cooling, sustaining drink before she answered Caitlin. "No, the brooch was a gift from another friend."

A frown of concentration knit Caitlin's brow as she stared at the brooch. "I just wondered. The lily design seems so familiar."

"I'm sure it does. It's of the art nouveau period."

"Do you know who the artist was?"

"I was told it was Rene Lalique."

"Really? That's very interesting. I just wish I knew why I think I've seen it before."

"Lalique must have used the lily as a theme many times, but with different variations."

"Yes, I guess you're right." Caitlin raised her head, and a smile suddenly lit her face. "Oh, how wonderful, my husband is finally here."

Everyone at the table followed her gaze toward the doorway and the handsome man with black hair and olive-toned skin.

Caitlin waved at him and mouthed, *I'll be right there,* to him. He nodded, and she turned back to the occupants of the table. "I wasn't sure he was going to make it tonight. He and his partner have had to be in Boston all week."

"Is that his partner with him?" Sara asked, indicating the tall, lean, sandy-haired man standing with Nico DiFrenza, his hands stuffed casually into the pants of his Western cut evening suit. "He looks interesting."

Caitlin laughed. "Women usually use the word fatal in reference to him. And yes, that's Nico's partner, Amarillo Smith."

"He's wearing boots," Rosalyn said with slight amazement.

"Of course," Caitlin said. "Well, they're waiting for me. It was lovely talking with you. Enjoy your dinner."

Clay spoke for everyone. "Thank you, I'm sure we will."

"I wonder what she would have said if she'd seen my tennis shoes," Steve added after Caitlin left.

Rosalyn's eyebrows rose. "Not to mention your jeans."

Liana watched with a pang of envy as Caitlin's husband enfolded her in his arms and kissed her. "I'm sure she wouldn't have said a thing."

"She did seem nice, didn't she?" Sara said.

Liana unconsciously sought out Richard. To her dismay, his attention was still focused on her. "Is there any more champagne?" she asked.

Rosalyn tilted her head and stared at Liana. "I've never seen you drink on a photo shoot before."

Liana forced a smile. "But we're at SwanSea, and as you said, it seems proper."

"I agree," Clay said, summoning a waiter.

DINNER WAS ALMOST OVER, but Liana couldn't remember eating a thing. It seemed to her that Richard had watched every move she had made, every breath she had drawn.

Several of the dining room doors that led out onto a large terrace were open. Occasionally she had seen the embroidered silk drapes billow as a breeze slid into the room. But even though no one else at the table seemed uncomfortable, she felt overly warm, disoriented, light-headed.

Music and conversation blurred into a muted wall of noise and flowed over her without making an impression. She reached for her champagne glass and was surprised to find it empty.

"Let me refill that for you," Clay murmured, even while he was doing so.

She drank without acknowledging his courtesy. Was it guilt over Richard that was making her so edgy? she wondered. Or was it the need that, unbidden, rose up in her every time she saw him? *No.* She stopped that train of thought in its tracks. She would acknowledge the guilt, but not the need.

She'd lived with the guilt of her deceit for the past eleven years, and with the help of a strong system of defense mechanisms, she had survived.

But this need—she had to forget about it. Even though there had been many times when she had awakened aching for him over the years, her desire had always been easily quenched by the hard, cold realization that she had been dreaming and he wasn't there beside her and never would be again.

But she wasn't dreaming now. He was a short walk away from her, and she had learned this afternoon that she had no defense against him.

"I have to get out of here," she mumbled, pushing back the chair and struggling to her feet.

Clay jerked around, startled. "Liana, what's wrong?"

Her hand shot out to the high back of the chair to steady herself. "Nothing. I just need some air."

"Would you like me to go with you?" Steve asked.

Another time she might have smiled at his eagerness to leave the formality of the dining room. Another time she might have couched her rejection in a softer tone. But not this time, not with Richard staring at her from across the room. "No, I'd rather be alone."

LIGHTS PLACED unobtrusively beneath shrubs and in grasses guided Liana along unfamiliar paths as she walked farther and farther from the house. She stumbled occasionally, but quickly regained her footing and kept going. She had no destination in mind. It was more a matter of going *away from* than *to.*

She finally stopped when she reached the edge of the cliff. Here, the ocean's roar was louder, the moon and stars brighter, the mood of the night blacker, more isolated. She drew a deep breath and felt herself sway.

"Be careful!" a deep voice said from behind her.

She turned quickly and almost fell. "Richard!"

He grasped her arms to steady her. "You're drunk."

What was the use of denying it? "The champagne was very good." And you, she thought, were completely unnerving. "What are you doing out here?"

"I followed you."

The idea that he had deliberately sought her out panicked her. Plus there were his fingers wrapped around her arms. She tried to break away from him, but his grip didn't ease. "What about the woman you were having dinner with? You just *left* her?"

He frowned as if he were having trouble comprehending her train of thought. "Margaret? She's my administrative assistant. We had some business to discuss, but she's back in her room working now."

She put a hand to her swimming head. "I thought you were here on vacation."

"I've never quite developed the knack of complete relaxation. Some people call me driven." A private thought firmed his mouth into a hard line. "Come away from the edge of the cliff, Liana. You might think it's the answer, but in the end, you wouldn't be happy with the way you looked smashed on the rocks below."

The ground seemed to be rising and falling beneath her feet. Her mind was having trouble operating in the midst of such dizzying motion. Richard was the only thing around her at the moment that was steady and unchanging. She had the greatest urge to hold on to him for dear life, but their past made that impossible. "What are you talking about?"

"Nothing important," he said, casually moving her back from the edge.

His hand on her bare arm was causing internal damage she might not be able to repair. "I really need you to take your hand off me, Richard," she said as clearly and as firmly as she could.

His brows rose, but he released her, then adopted an indifferent tone. "So, when did you become an alcoholic?"

The shock of the question nearly made her lose her balance. "What an incredible thing to say."

"Not so incredible when you consider how much you had to drink tonight."

"It was only champagne."

"I know, but I seem to remember that you never could drink much of it. One glass and you'd be light-headed. If I needed confirmation that you hadn't changed, I guess I have it."

"I guess you do," she said dully. Moonlight slanted over his face, its silver light emphasizing the cold set of his expression. He represented a great menace to her, but she found she couldn't look at him without wanting him. She turned away and fixed her gaze on the phosphorescent shimmer of the dark sea. "Why did you follow me?"

"It's easy to follow someone who looks like you do, Liana."

He moved closer, and then closer still, until she could feel the warmth of his hard body up and down her back, and a new type of intoxication invaded her bloodstream. She closed her eyes. "Go away, Richard."

He bent his head, put his mouth against her ear. "You know what else I remembered as I sat there and watched you tonight?"

His breath was warm on the delicate shell of her ear. She no longer heard the ocean's roar, only his voice, quiet and intimate. "I don't want to know."

"But I want to tell you. It's about that afternoon in Paris when we discovered another way to use champagne."

His words conjured up the day for her with clear, perfect recall. She swayed back against him, and he slid his arms around her waist. As a lover would do. Or as a man trying to set a trap for her.

"Remember, Liana? We ordered cases and cases of champagne. The waiters who delivered them to our room couldn't imagine how we were going to drink all of those bottles, just the two of us, and unchilled bottles at that. They didn't even try to hide how crazy they thought we were, did they? But we didn't care. Remember how we laughed?"

She remembered too well—the joy and the sunshine that temporarily had hidden the reality of why she was with him, the feeling on that afternoon that no one else in the world could possibly be experiencing the same intensity and passion as she was.

"When they left, we emptied the bottles into the bathtub, undressed, and got in."

He licked a spot on her neck, then kissed it. A shudder raced through her, and her head fell back against his chest. *"Richard."*

He went on, his words thicker, huskier. "We made love all afternoon. Looking back on it, I don't think it was so much the champagne that made me drunk as it was drinking it from your skin. I own several wineries now, but not one of them produces a wine that tastes half as good or as potent as what we bathed in that day."

Suddenly he spun her around, and the desire she saw burning in the gray depths of his eyes made her gasp and go weak at the knees.

"What do you think, Liana? Would you like to take a champagne bath with me again? We both know more now. We've had more experience. We could make that champagne boil."

She jerked away and lashed out at him, desperate to hurt him as he was hurting her. "How's your wife, Richard?"

He didn't even blink. "You mean my *ex*-wife? She's happy and healthy and living a very rich life with my money. Which was the whole idea in the first place."

She couldn't believe what she was hearing. "She married you for your money?"

"Of course."

"And you knew?"

He nodded, his gaze never leaving her. "Since I'd already experienced a relationship with deceit, I thought one without deceit might work. One where both parties knew what they were getting. Her, my money. Me, a hostess and sometime companion." He shrugged. "In the end, it was worth the money she wanted to get rid of her."

A chilling wind sent her gown swirling out around her, an undulating midnight-blue cloud in a midnight-black world. Her throat burned with emotion too raw to express. "I've got to go." She turned sharply and started off down the path.

"Wait."

She felt his hand close around her arm and whirled on him like a wounded animal. "Don't touch me! I can't stand it!"

Puzzlement scored his face as he stared at her. "I couldn't have hurt you, Liana."

That was really funny, she thought, but found she couldn't laugh. "Just leave me alone." She turned again, wanting to put as much distance between them as possible, but she didn't get very far before the heel of her shoe came down on a pebble and she stumbled.

Somehow Richard was there to catch her, disgust in his voice. "Lord, you can't even walk." He swept her up into his arms and started back toward the house.

A violent storm of turmoil closed in around her. His strength, his scent, his overwhelming masculinity—his trap had closed around her. "I can make it on my own," she insisted.

"Obviously not, Liana. You're drunk."

She was sure she was, but there was more than wine working in her. Her world was spinning out of control, she didn't know how to stop it, and suddenly she was too tired to try. She went limp against him, winding her arm around his shoulder and resting her head against his chest.

"There," he said. "That's better."

No, she thought. It wasn't better. It was simply the only choice she could make at the moment. She could detect no tenderness or caring in the way that he held her, but she was too weary to worry about his motives. "Can we just stop our hostility for tonight?" she murmured.

"A truce?" he asked mockingly. "What an imaginative idea."

The lights were brighter now; they were drawing closer to the house. She sighed softly, her breath exhaling against the strong column of his throat. "Can't you let it go? Even for a short while."

His arms tightened, pulling her even closer against him. "I don't know."

"Just for tonight. I can't fight you any more tonight."

"Then don't."

There was something in his voice that made her add, "I also can't make love with you."

"Who said anything about love, Liana? I can't recall that I did."

What was the use? she wondered despondently. She should have known better than to try to reason with him, but she supposed being held in his arms had warped her judgment. In the future, she'd remember. Their past made reason impossible.

"Put me down, Richard," she said as they approached the back of the house. "I don't want anyone to see you carrying me."

"Worried that your glossy image will be destroyed if someone sees you drunk?"

"I'm not drunk." And she wasn't anymore. The wind and Richard had whipped all effects of the wine from her.

"Don't worry. No one will see you. By accident, I discovered a back route the other day." He shifted her weight slightly and opened a small rear door that led into one of the back halls of the house. Once inside, he carried her to a service elevator that transported them to the third floor. Only when they were outside her door did he allow her to stand.

"Well, here you are, more or less safe, more or less sound. For now." He waited for some sort of retort from her.

But she sagged back against the door and her sleepy eyes dropped closed. He frowned. Strands of her pale wheat-colored hair had come loose from their coil and lay in enchanting tendrils against her cheek and shoulders. Thick dark lashes threw shadows over the flawless, nearly translucent skin of her cheeks. Her breasts rose and fell above the low neckline of her gown as she breathed.

She made him furious.

Why the hell did she have to be so beautiful? And why was she so damned tired? And most of all, why, out in the bluff, had she screamed at him when he'd grasped her arms? The most obvious answer was that she was repulsed by his touch. Except, she had appeared traumatized, and he had been reminded of a small wounded animal trying to protect itself. "Where's your key, Liana?"

The sudden sound of his voice shattered the lulled state of suspension into which she'd fallen. Her eyes flew open, and she automatically reached into the bodice of her evening gown and pulled it out.

His hand made a fist around the metal warmed by her body, and his eyes darkened. "Do you always carry your key between your breasts?"

"When I don't want to bother with a purse."

He stared broodingly at her for a moment. "Would you flinch away from me if I touched your breasts?"

Their confrontation on the bluff had drained all her energies. The simple truth was the only possible answer. "Yes."

Holding her eyes, he lifted his hand and stroked a petal's outer rim of the lily pinned over her heart. The topaz center glimmered golden. "It might be worth it."

"You'd like to see me flinch?"

"Given my preference, I'd rather see you under me, hot as hell and wild out of your mind."

Helplessly, she shook her head. "Why do you say things like that?"

"Maybe because it's so damned much fun getting a reaction out of you."

"Fun? You're having fun?"

"Oh, absolutely," he said grimly. He inserted the key into the lock and opened her door.

The light beside the tall, silk shrouded bed cast a warm glow into the room. The bed and the oblivion it offered beckoned, but from experience Liana knew that sometimes even sleep wouldn't let her forget. She heard the door click closed behind her. Instinct told her he hadn't left.

"You're going to need help undressing." He walked up behind her and quickly, easily unzipped her dress.

She gasped and barely managed to grab the dress to her before it fell to the floor. Holding it tightly to her breasts, she felt exposed. She took several steps away from him, then swung around. "Don't ever do that again!"

He shoved his jacket aside and planted a hand on his hip. "You know, you're as confusing as hell, lady. This time, at least, I was only trying to help."

"Don't make a big thing out of it, Richard. I don't like to be undressed, that's all."

"Your men must hate that a lot, but then again, maybe it's just one more thing that fascinates them about you.

I know you sure as hell have my attention. This afternoon you dissolved like sugar for me. Tonight, you can't even stand my hands on you."

"This conversation is pointless. You and I are pointless."

"Pointless, Liana? Well, you're probably right. But then what difference does it make when we're having so much fun."

She drew a deep, steadying breath. She had to get him out of her room before she broke down. "Richard, the past is past. It accomplishes nothing to dredge it up. I'm here to work. You're here for a holiday. I think it's best if we avoid each other."

"You came to that decision all by yourself, did you? Very good, sweetheart. There's just one thing. A small thing really."

She didn't want to know. That's why she couldn't figure out why she asked. "What?"

"I still want to touch your breasts, quite badly as it happens. And you might as well know something else, I don't want to stop there. You asked for a truce, Liana, but we haven't even really gotten started, and a cessation of anything between us is unacceptable to me at this point in time. *I'll* tell you when we'll stop. *I'll* tell you when we'll begin." His eyes glittered hard as diamonds as he raked his gaze over her. "Good night, Liana. Sleep well."

FOUR

LIANA WOKE the next morning with a headache and a stiff knee. Neither was enough to keep her from the day's shooting; she couldn't ever remember missing work.

Today would be the first time.

After the tumult of yesterday, she simply wasn't capable of facing anyone, much less the camera. Projecting the cool, poised look she was known for would be impossible.

Clay would probably go up like a rocket when she told him, and although she wouldn't let his reaction change her mind, she dreaded what she was about to do. She reached for the phone and dialed Clay's room number. "Good morning," she said when he answered. "This is Liana."

"Good morning, Liana."

He'd been expecting her call—the strange impression flashed on and off in her mind like a lightbulb. "Listen, I'm sorry, but I'm not going to be able to work today."

"Oh? What's wrong?"

He sounded very calm, very reasonable, she thought, somewhat amazed. But then again, he probably knew to the ounce how much she'd had to drink last night since he'd been filling her glass. "Nothing is really wrong. I think I just need some rest."

"That's probably a good idea. Take it easy today."

"I feel really guilty about this delay, but—"

"Hey, don't feel bad. Fortunately our schedule has some flexibility built into it. Trust me, this won't hurt the shoot at all, and the crew will bless you."

She blinked. "Well, okay, then. Thanks, Clay. I'll work extra hard tomorrow."

"Just promise me you'll relax today."

"I will, and thanks again. Goodbye." She hung up the phone and gave a sigh of relief. The hardest part was over. Now all she had to do was decide how she was going to spend this day.

She needed to be alone, to repair her nerves and rebuild her mental strength, but finding space where she could be alone would be easier said than done.

To stay in her room all day would stifle her. And mingling with the guests at the hotel was out. She wouldn't be able to bear their stares, their attempts at conversation, their requests for autographs. No, she had to get away from the hotel.

She could take one of the rental cars and drive up the coast, but somehow exploring SwanSea's grounds appealed to her more, and she'd noticed that not many people were taking advantage of the grounds that lay beyond the pool house and the tennis courts. She quickly dressed, slipping a violet cotton camisole over her head and tucking it into the waistband of a violet-and-periwinkle circular skirt. With sandals completing the outfit and her hair in a thick braid down her back, she left the room.

IN HIS SUITE, Richard disgustedly flung his razor into the bathroom sink and leaned toward the mirror to view the tiny amount of blood oozing from the nick on his jaw. Too much caffeine, he supposed. Now that he thought about it, he seemed to remember the doctor, during his last checkup, bluntly telling him to cut down on the coffee. Oh, well.

Splashing water on his face, he cleaned the last vestiges of shaving cream from his cheeks and throat, then reached for a towel. A minute later, he strode into the bedroom where he downed yet more coffee, and as a concession to his churning stomach, ate a cold piece of toast.

A fitful night's sleep had driven him from his bed early. He'd worked a while, read the paper, and dressed. What now? he wondered, definitely edgy and restless.

He hadn't had a vacation in eleven years, and he was learning that relaxing was certainly easier said than done. As a matter of fact, it took a great deal of determination. SwanSea offered any number of activities, but somehow nothing was holding his interest.

Just being here was a social advantage, and the business contacts he could make, if he were so inclined, held great potential. The prospect of the art auction was also something to anticipate. Even though his collection was purely for investment purposes, he had developed something of an appreciation for art over the years.

Still, taking everything into consideration, he couldn't help but ask himself what the hell he was doing here.

Suddenly he laughed out loud—a cutting, self-mocking laugh that turned back on him—because, deep down, he knew exactly what he was doing here. He'd known since the first moment he'd learned Liana would be here.

He was set on a course, which he could not alter and from which he could not deviate. And if destruction lay in his path, so be it.

He strolled onto the balcony and surveyed the grounds. A woman with a wheat-colored braid down the center of her back caught his attention.

"Wait up, Liana!"

Liana turned to look back toward the house and saw Steve hurrying to catch up with her. She sighed. She supposed she'd been lucky to get this far without someone stopping her.

"Hi," she said to him when he drew even with her. "Haven't you heard? You've got the day off."

He grinned. "I heard, but I made Clay say it to me twice just to be sure."

She laughed lightly. "So what are you going to do with your unexpected vacation?"

"I haven't decided yet." He glanced down at the toes of his aged tennis shoes, then over her shoulders, and finally looked at her. "Listen, Liana, there's something I want to tell you."

"Okay," she said, wondering at his uneasiness. She had known him for about a year now, and normally. Steve was the epitome of an easygoing, self-confident young man.

"It's about your accident."

"What accident?" she asked blankly.

"When you fell down the stairway."

"Oh. Okay, what about it?"

He planted a hand on one narrow jeans-clad hip. "Well, I've been thinking about it. At first I thought I must have inadvertently brushed against the light in some way to make it fall, but now I'm not so sure. I think it's possible that the light could have been rigged to fall."

Her eyes widened in surprise. "Why would anyone do that?"

He shrugged. "I don't know, but I checked out the light and one of its legs... Well, it just looks possible, that's all." He shrugged again. "I felt you needed to be aware that maybe the accident wasn't an accident after all."

"That doesn't make sense. What would anyone gain by causing it to fall? Everyone involved wants this shoot to be a success."

"That's true," he admitted grudgingly.

She lay a hand on his shoulder. "Steve, you need this day off more than I do."

"Maybe, but do me a favor and be careful. And you might spend some time thinking about who would like to see you hurt."

She shook her head. "I don't have to think. There's no one."

"Liana—"

"Steve, I appreciate your concern, but this wonderful place must have your imagination working overtime. I know it does mine."

He hesitated, then broke into a reluctant grin. "I guess you're right. Sorry, I didn't mean to upset you."

"You didn't. In fact, it makes me feel good that you were worried about me. But enough's enough. Go have a good time. Lord knows, Clay will work us hard enough tomorrow."

"You're right about that. Okay then, see you later. Just don't take any more falls."

"I promise."

Liana watched Steve walk back toward the house, then for some unexplainable reason, she lifted her gaze to a third-floor balcony. Richard stood there, watching her.

Her mind went blank, instinct took over. She turned and ran.

LEONORA DEVERELL. Born 1877. Died 1898.

Liana lightly brushed her fingers over the letters, the only decoration on the small, simple, boxlike house that was Leonora Deverell's crypt. An oversize, heavy-looking concrete urn stood to the left side of the doors, empty. There should be flowers in it, she thought.

She knew from reading various articles on SwanSea that Leonora Deverell had been SwanSea's first mistress, and she seemed to recall that Leonora had been seventeen when she had married the wealthy, powerful Edward Deverell. A year later, her son, John, had been born. Then three years later, Leonora, after a sudden, brief illness, had died.

"How sad," she murmured.

"What's sad?" Richard asked.

She slowly turned, accepting completely that he was there. Running form him would have been an invitation to a man like Richard, and she'd called herself a fool many times during the past two hours for doing just that. But if she'd learned one thing over the years, it was that once something had happened, it couldn't be undone.

She had known he would come. In a way, she'd been waiting.

And where he was, there was danger for her.

With pulses racing, she met his gaze squarely. "What took you so long?"

He smiled. "SwanSea is a pretty big place, and by the time I got downstairs, there was no sign of you."

That's how she'd wanted it. She'd struck out blindly, away from the people, away from him. She'd walked across rolling green meadows dotted by wild aster and goldenrod. Bluebirds and blackbirds had swooped above her, darting between tall pines and majestic firs. At one point, two white-tailed deer darted across her path. She'd been enchanted by everything she saw, but she hadn't remained at any one place for longer than a few minutes. Leonora's crypt had been the only sight that had enticed her to come closer, to linger.

She should have kept moving.

"So how did you find me?"

"I looked in the most isolated places."

A nod acknowledged his discernment.

"So what do you find so sad?" he repeated.

"The fact that Leonora Deverell died at such a young age."

"It happened over ninety years ago, Liana."

"I don't care how long ago it happened, it's still sad. Leonora had a little boy and a husband who loved her very much." All the things she as a young girl had once yearned for, but had had to face that she would never have.

"How do you know her husband loved her?" he asked with amusement.

She shrugged and conceded. "It's an assumption."

"Based on what?" When she didn't answer, he went on, "I'm not trying to get into an argument with you, Liana. I'm just really interested in what has given you the idea that a man you never knew loved his wife."

She was sure his reasons for asking *were* argumentative, but in this instance, she didn't care. Perhaps if she put her feelings into words, it would help her understand why she was so drawn to this forlorn, forgotten place. "Well, first of all, Leonora was the first Deverell to die after SwanSea was built, so Edward had a choice of where he could locate the family cemetery. He placed her crypt as far away as possible from the house so that he wouldn't have to see it and be reminded of his pain."

"I don't know many people who would place a cemetery where they could look out the windows of their house and see it," he said dryly. "It's just too depressing."

"Maybe. But look where the rest of the family plots are." With a wave of her hand, she indicated a larger, more impressive crypt and several tall, elaborately carved gravestones placed some distance away. "He kept Leonora's apart."

He cocked an eyebrow. "Because he thought her so special?"

"I think so."

"Then, why is his crypt bigger than hers?"

"Her death was unexpected. The workmen would have had to throw this up literally almost overnight." She poked at the base of the crypt with her toe. "See? The masonry is crumbling. Shoddy workmanship. And look at this." She reached for the big heavy lock on the two doors and tugged. "This is almost rusted through. A good tug would break it."

"*Why* are you so interested in this place?"

"I don't know," she said, equally baffled. "SwanSea has such a unique character and atmosphere to it. I sensed sadness in the gazebo, and here I sense tragedy." Her head turned in the direction of the house, though she couldn't see it. "There have been times of shadows as well as times of sunlight here."

His amusement took on an edge of fascination. "Are you normally so sensitive to places?"

She shrugged. "I can't remember another place affecting me as much. It's almost as if I were familiar with SwanSea before I ever came here."

He gazed at her, baffled. "I would never have thought you such a romantic."

"A romantic?" She shook her head. "I'm definitely not." The two most important men in her life—her father and Richard—had seen to that. They had extinguished all traces of the starry-eyed dreams in her and in return had brought her immeasurable heartache. She glanced back at the crypt and the markings on it. "Leonora. It's a pretty name, don't you think?"

"Yes, but then so is Liana."

He trailed his fingers down her cheek. The touch was so light, she barely felt it, yet small frissons of heat coursed through her, causing equal parts pain and pleasure. How on earth could she have gotten so caught up with the life of a long-dead woman, she wondered suddenly, when her own life demanded such energy and effort from her?

"I looked up the name Liana once," he said. "It's from a French word meaning to bind, to wrap around—you know, sort of like a creeping vine that strangles the life out of something. I remember thinking at the time how appropriate the name was for you."

Color flushed her skin. He just wouldn't let up. "My mother chose my name. She was French and died when I was very young."

"I didn't know that. But then if I tossed everything I *don't* know about you into the Seine, the river would flood Paris."

She had begun to feel an oppressive weight, and it had nothing to do with the cemetery. With no particular direction in mind, she began to walk, and he fell in beside her.

"Is your father alive?" he asked.

"No, he's dead now, too." What irony, she thought, that he didn't know. But then again, what did it matter? She was all alone, and that was the way she liked it. She didn't want to be bound to anyone every again. Most of all, she didn't want to be responsible for anyone else's pain. She glanced at him. He'd obviously learned his own protective defenses, and they appeared quite formidable. There didn't look to be a soft, unprotected place in him. She would be willing to bet that he allowed nothing to affect him emotionally.

They had both learned well. How very pathetic.

Suddenly she wondered if he had anyone close to him. "What about your parents? I don't believe you ever mentioned them."

"They're alive and happily retired."

"Retired from what?"

"My father owned a drugstore in Chicago. He worked hard all his life, but never could seem to get anywhere."

"Did it ever occur to you that the one drugstore might be all he wanted?"

He slipped his hands into his trouser pockets and bent his head, studying the ground in front of him as they walked. "Just lately it has."

"But you were unable to understand that when you were younger?"

"I'm still not sure I do entirely. I seem to be driven to acquire. Businesses. Art." He cut his eyes to her. "Other things."

"Do you think this drive stems from the fact that your father owned only one drugstore?"

He hesitated. "Partly." Then he added, "I've bought my parents a place in Florida. They're content." He seemed to shrug, then his head came up and he looked at her. "So why aren't you working today? Did you wake up with a headache?"

"Yes," she said, deciding to let him think she had a hangover. It was easier to go with his perception of her than fight it. All at once, a sense of desolation swamped her. The sad ending to Leonora's promising young life. Richard's festering hatred. Her own interminable sadness. It was all too much.

Abruptly, she changed directions and headed back toward the house. With Richard doggedly following her footsteps as he seemed bent on doing, she thought grimly, it would be better to be around people. Hopefully he would soon lose interest in her. Maybe he would even come to understand that it would be better for him to put their past behind him. As she had.

Sure, Liana. Sure.

SHE DIDN'T BELIEVE for a minute that Richard had lost interest in her, Liana reflected the next morning. It was more as if he had put her on hold while he spent the afternoon playing golf. But he had been in the dining room last night, again with his attractive assistant, Margaret, and he had watched her every bit as intently as he had the night before. This time she coped without the champagne.

And now this morning, as early as it was, a crowd of people had gathered on the front steps of SwanSea, the first site of the day's shooting. Liana, dressed in a wrapper, sat before a makeshift table while Rosalyn laid out makeup, combs and brushes.

Usually by this time in a day's shoot, her concentration was firmly in place. This morning, though, her thoughts were scattered. Leonora and her lonely resting place still bothered her and she didn't know why.

She chided herself. What a foolish thing to get upset about. She was being far too impressionable, too open to sentiment. It wasn't like her, and she needed to put a stop to it immediately.

She glanced up at the impressive facade of SwanSea. There was no doubt that it was magnificent, but she couldn't help wondering how Leonora had felt about SwanSea as a home. Living in a small, cozy house as she did, she would have a hard time viewing such a huge place as a home. Had it been just as overwhelming to Leonora as a seventeen-year-old bride? All at once she remembered another Leonora—

"Which dress is first, love?" Rosalyn asked her.

"What? Oh, the gold."

"I saw that one," Rosalyn said, reaching for the pot of foundation. "It's gorgeous, but then all the gowns are. I've overheard several ladies plotting their strategies for the auction."

Liana smiled. "It should be interesting."

Rosalyn applied a light base of foundation to Liana's cheeks, then a cream rouge. "You think we'll see any cat fights?"

"Here? No way. SwanSea is much too dignified."

Rosalyn made a sound halfway between a snort and a laugh. "Listen, sweetie, women and their love of beautiful clothes are the same no matter where they are. You mark my words. It's going to get down and dirty at the auction, and I for one can't wait." She broke the seal on a new jar of loose powder and screwed open the top, then she dipped a puff into the powder and held it toward Liana's face.

But Liana turned toward Sara, who was sauntering up to them.

"Clay's ready for you, Liana."

Liana smiled. "Thanks, Sara. I won't be much longer."

Rosalyn peered at her own image in the mirror. "We're leaving her hair straight for this shot," she said to Sara and idly dusted a sprinkling of powder over her own face. "All I have to do is brush it."

"Okay, I'll tell Clay. You know what? He's in a good mood. He should take more days off. If you call taking pictures of me a day off."

Rosalyn laughed. "Sounds like a busman's holiday to me."

"And for you, it doesn't sound like a day off," Liana said. "Besides, I thought you didn't like to have your picture taken."

"I don't, but it was all in fun. I even got to wear some of your designer gowns."

"Really?"

"Oh, don't worry. I was very careful with them."

"Sara, you don't have to reassure me. They're not *my* gowns."

Suddenly Rosalyn made a sound of pain, dropped the puff, and clutched at her face.

Liana looked up at her. "Rosalyn, what's wrong?"

"My face," she gasped. "It burns!"

Alarmed, Liana jumped up and guided Rosalyn into the chair. Even as she did, she could see red blisters rising on Rosalyn's face. "My Lord, she must be having some sort of allergic reaction. Sara, go see if there's a doctor registered."

"It's the powder," Rosalyn cried.

"Try not to touch yourself," Liana glanced frantically around and spied two ladies standing nearby.

"Quick, run to the hotel and tell them we need cold, wet cloths immediately."

Steve came rushing up. "Sara yelled that something's wrong with Rosalyn as she raced by. What is it?"

Liana took one look at the worsening blisters on Rosalyn's face. "God, Steve, go call an ambulance. Now!"

Fifteen minutes later, Liana was watching the ambulance with Rosalyn in it roar off. "I need to be there for her," she said to no one in particular. "I'd better get dressed."

"Just a minute." Steve restrained her with a hand on her arm. "I heard you tell the paramedics that she'd had an allergic reaction to face powder. What exactly happened?"

"I'd like to know that myself," Richard said, coming up to them.

Her already distressed state was worsened by the sight of Richard. Intellectually, she knew that he was staying here at SwanSea. She was even on the alert against a sudden appearance by him. But she still couldn't get used to *him*—the flesh and blood presence of the man.

"I'd like to hear the story again, myself," Clay said, joining them.

Agitated and anxious to be with Rosalyn, Liana gazed at the three men around her. "I've already told you. She had an allergic reaction to the face powder."

Clay walked to the table behind them and picked up the still open jar. The paramedics had peeled off the label that listed the ingredients and had taken it with them. "Is this what she normally uses?"

"Yes, except normally she uses it on me, not on herself."

"Had she put any on you yet?" Richard asked, scrutinizing her face with narrowed eyes.

"No, she was just about to."

"What about when we last worked day before yesterday?" Steve asked. "Did she use it on you then?"

"No," she said, exasperation and impatience giving the word emphasis. "It was a new jar. She had just broken the seal."

"Could it have been tampered with in some way?" Richard asked.

"I don't see how," Clay answered, eyeing the seal that still lay on the table.

"And I don't see why," Liana said. "Look, it was an allergic reaction, plain and simple. Sometimes it just happens."

"Maybe something went wrong at the factory with the batch," Steve said.

Clay nodded. "I know a chemist I can send this to for an analysis. I'll take it into town right now and get it off to him."

"Fine. Do what you want. But I'm going to the hospital and see about Rosalyn."

Richard caught up with her just inside the massive front doors of SwanSea and grabbed her upper arm. "Wait a minute. You shouldn't go just yet."

She looked down at his hand on her arm, and he immediately released her. "Rosalyn is my friend, Richard. We've worked together for quite some time, and I want to be there for her."

"I understand that, but I also can see how shaken you are."

She wrapped her arms around herself. "It was an awful thing to watch happen."

"It would have been ever worse to have it happen to you."

"Hearing that isn't helping me, Richard."

"Okay, okay. All I'm saying is that you should give yourself some time before you drive into town."

She had thought all hope long dead in her, but she found herself saying, "It almost sounds as if you're concerned about me."

He stiffened; his voice mocked. "I just want to make sure you stay in one piece until we go to bed together."

Anger and hurt whipped color into her cheeks. "It's not going to happen."

"It has to, Liana."

She felt a cold shiver that affected her like heat. "Look, believe whatever you like, but I have to see about Rosalyn now."

"Then, I'll let you go. For now."

FIVE

THE DESIGNER GOWN arched through the air, a beautiful streamer of shiny sequins and orange-and-gold chiffon.

Sara caught the gown, her eyes wide with astonishment.

Liana's mouth twisted wryly, knowing what the younger girl was thinking. Anything less than careful handling for such a gown would be called sacrilege by some. "Sorry. Clay took so long with that last shot. I'd begun to feel like the dress was plastered to me. I had to get it off. I didn't harm it, did I?"

After a brief inspection of the gown, Sara shook her head. "The gown's fine." She began to fold the one-of-a-kind creation with tissue paper. "Clay's been hell on wheels the last two days, hasn't he?" she asked, darting a glance at Liana.

"He's just trying to do the best possible work he can." Why was she defending him, she wondered as she reached for her jeans and a T-shirt. Clay had been almost unbearable to work with, pushing her and everyone else to the limit.

With the breakneck speed she had learned backstage at runway shows, she threw on her clothes. She wanted to get *away* from SwanSea. Nothing had gone right since she had been here, but then in all fairness, she had only herself to blame, not SwanSea. She had let imagination and emotions rule, and as a result, she'd had control over almost nothing that had happened.

She could pack up and go home, she thought for the one hundredth time, and as always, she discarded the idea. There was something keeping her here, and it was time to admit to herself that it was something that went beyond her feeling of responsibility for the assignment.

The obvious answer was Richard, but unable to cope with the volatile repercussions of that particular idea, she rejected it. Suddenly the image of the small concrete burial house on that windswept hill came to her. How very odd, she thought. Was she losing her mind?

"I can understand Clay trying to do a super job," Sara was saying, "but nothing any of us has done has been good enough for him."

It was true, Liana reflected. Under normal circumstances, she could have coped, but these circumstances were anything *but* normal. The past two days had been hard on her, both physically and mentally. She had tried time after time to retreat into her mind, but all her usual blocking devices had proved useless. Too many hands had touched her. Too many people had stared.

Today, it had reached the point that if Clay had told her to strike one more pose or to smile one more time, she would have cracked. As it was, she was hanging on to her composure by a thread.

With cream and tissue, she wiped off every last bit of makeup, then quickly ran a brush through her hair.

"Are you all right?" Sara asked abruptly.

No, she thought. She was far from all right. "Of course. Why wouldn't I be?"

"It's just that you've looked pretty frazzled since we've been here."

The younger girl seemed so solemn, Liana had to grin. "Are you afraid you're going to have to step in for me?"

Sara started. "Goodness no! I know what a professional you are. It would take something pretty awful to keep you from work."

Funny, Liana thought. Lately, she'd been thinking that it would take very little. The idea of retiring was becoming more and more desirable. "Well, don't worry. I have every intention of finishing this shoot. Now I'd better be on my way."

"Where are you going?"

"Into town to visit Rosalyn."

"You saw her yesterday, too, didn't you?"

Liana nodded.

"I've been meaning to get in to see her myself, but I've been so busy. Tell her hello for me, will you?"

"Sure will."

The sun was setting as Liana walked briskly toward the parking lot. Over the years, she'd found that an engrossed expression and a purposeful stride would deter all but the most ardent of her admirers. And it almost worked.

She was nearly to the rental car when she heard Richard ask, "You're certainly in a hurry. Is there a fire somewhere?"

Her heart leaped and an inconsequential thought fluttered through her head—she certainly couldn't categorize Richard as one of her admirers.

She turned and, as always, became momentarily helpless at the sight of him. They hadn't spoken to or seen each other in two days, but she had known he was still at SwanSea. She had actually *felt* his presence. And feeling him without seeing him had been irritating, maddening, and had made her very, very skittish.

He smiled. "Missed me?"

"Have you been gone?"

Her pose of arrogance made her beauty that much more remarkable, and he felt a quickening of warmth deep in his gut. "That's good, Liana. Very good. No, I've been right here."

"Really? I can't remember seeing you."

"That's because I've been closed up in my suite. Something came up with one of my companies, and I've had a series of meetings that have lasted well into the night."

"Everything all right now?" Why in the world was she asking? It wasn't as if she cared.

"Everything's fine," he said. "Where are you going?"

She wasn't used to accounting to anyone for her time. But she had told Sara, and she would tell him if it would get her away from him quicker. "I'm going into town to see Rosalyn."

"Your friend who used the face powder, right? How is she?"

"I'm glad to say she's getting better every day."

"That came very close to being you in the hospital, you know. Have you thought about that?"

Of course she had. And the idea had stolen several hours of sleep from her. "It was a freaky thing to have happened. Fortunately Rosalyn didn't suffer that much. They were able to stop the burning almost immediately, and the doctor is certain that the blisters won't leave disfiguring marks."

"How long will the blisters last?"

"About a week. They'll leave red marks for a little while longer, but they say there are salves that will help the discolorations."

"Wasn't it lucky she put that powder on her instead of on you?"

She crossed her arms over her breasts. "Lucky for me, not for her. I feel awful for her."

"I'm sure everyone does, but still, the shoot hasn't been held up, has it?"

She sighed. She would answer this last question, she decided, and then she'd go. "No, it hasn't. I've been doing my own makeup, and Sara's helped when I've needed her. Clay's talked of flying someone in from New York, but I don't know whether he will or not."

"At least he won't have to fly in a new model. That really would have screwed things up, wouldn't it?"

Her brow furrowed. "Is there something you're trying to say, Richard?"

He tilted his head to one side, studying her. "Actually I wasn't. Normally if I want to say something, there's no *trying* about it." Suddenly an altogether unexpected teasing glint came into his eyes. "Although now that I think about it, have you considered the possibility that someone's after your job?"

Steve had told her he felt it possible that the light could have been rigged to fall—the light that had initially distracted her and led to her tumble down the marble stairway. If Richard hadn't been there to catch her, she could have suffered broken bones or even much worse. Then they would have had to replace her or cancel the assignment, which they wouldn't do. She had talked Steve out of the notion, but what if—*no.* It just couldn't be true. There was simply no one she could think of who would want to harm her.

She looked up at Richard and saw him watching her intently.

"Where were you just then?"

The question, gently asked, almost took her off guard. Almost. "Nowhere."

He cocked his head to the other side as if viewing her from another angle might show him something he hadn't seen before. "I've missed you."

An incredulous look spread across her face. "Missed me? You mean you've missed taunting me."

"You're absolutely right," he said. What gentleness there had been in his tone was gone now. He moved closer, his body pushing her back against the car. "It hasn't been all taunting, has it? I mean I have followed through once or twice. And by the way, there's something you should know. Up to now it has been merely a warm-up."

She felt his arousal press into her, and heat flared low in her stomach. "For God's sakes, Richard, we're in the middle of a parking lot!"

"We could go to your room if you like. Or mine. Or that garden over there."

She pushed against him. "I've already told you that I'm on my way into town."

"You could change your mind. You've done it in the past."

"Leave me alone, Richard."

"I'm afraid that's impossible. Only the fact that I've been so busy has kept me from coming to your room."

An unwanted excitement sprang to life in her. "Dammit, Richard—"

"One morning I found myself outside your room at 4:00 a.m." The desire in his voice stoked the fire growing inside her. "You'll never know how close I came to bribing someone to open your door for me."

"The staff here is too well trained," she said, a tinge of desperation in her tone. "They wouldn't have accepted a bribe."

"For the amount of money I was willing to pay, Liana, *someone* would have accepted. You see, I wanted you very badly that night, as badly as I want you now."

She stifled a moan. "I've got to go."

"There's no need to run," he said, his voice husky, his lower body rubbing against hers. "Our going to bed together would involve only pleasure this time. There would be none of those sticky, complicated emotions that got in the way before."

She couldn't look away from him. He was hard, heartless and bitter, and at the same time, he radiated a masculinity and a magnetism that absolutely undid her. And always, swirled between these two realities like the icing between two layers of cake, her memories of him as he had been in Paris seduced her. She should guard herself against him, and Lord knows she had tried...

She loved him. It was at that moment as she gazed up at him that she knew. Dear heaven, she *loved* him!

The thought sent terror clear through to her bones. She shoved him away and wrenched open the door. Quickly she slid into the car, pulled the door closed, and started the engine.

Richard remained where he was, disturbed because she had gotten away from him before he was ready to let her go and vaguely troubled because he couldn't entirely explain her abrupt behavior. There had been an expression on her face—

In the next moment, he instinctively jumped to the side as her car hurtled past him, though the car hadn't been aimed at him. With increasing speed and squealing tires, she drove out of the parking lot and down the long drive.

Richard's gaze remained on Liana's car as it receded into the distance, and he didn't notice that a man had walked up to him until he spoke.

"Was that Liana Marchall who just drove out of here like a bat out of hell?"

Tense and worried, Richard snarled at him. "Yeah, why?"

The man's brow lifted in mild reaction. "No reason. It's just that I hope she's not going to be driving like that all the way into town, that's all."

"Why?"

"I just came from that direction. Apparently a construction truck lost part of its load. There's all kinds of junk—nails, boards, cinderblocks—strewn over the road for about a quarter of a mile."

"Damn!" Richard was nearly to his car when he thought to yell over his shoulders, "Thanks for the information."

SHE KNEW she was driving too fast, but she couldn't seem to make herself care enough to slow down. She was too keyed up, too disturbed, and she lay the blame solely at Richard's feet. She couldn't look at him without things happening inside her.

Needs. Fears. Wants. Guilts. Passion.

She had been in a constant state of mental confusion and emotional turmoil for days now.

A field stretched to her right, and on the other side of the road, a cliff dropped some distance to the rocks and ocean below it. The wind had her hair flying about her head and into her face and eyes. Impatiently she brushed at her face and was vaguely surprised to find her fingertips come away dampened with tears. She choked back a sob.

She felt as if she were fighting a losing battle. Every time she saw Richard, she had the urge to go into his arms and have him hold her forever. Then in the next minute, she would want to run as far as possible from him. By turns she would have to fight the urge to beg his forgiveness, and bite her tongue to keep from telling him to go to hell.

Now she realized she was in love with him, in fact had never stopped loving him.

Oh, Lord, it all seemed so futile. What was she going to do?

She had driven over the debris before she realized it. The steering wheel jerked in her hands. Then she heard the slap of the rubber of her left front tire—*whop whop whop*—as it hit the asphalt.

The car veered out of control and into the left lane. Adrenaline surged in her veins. Frantically she jammed her foot against the brake pedal. The care went into a slide, turning sideways, skidding toward the edge of the cliff.

Just catching up to her, Richard went cold with fear as he saw what was happening. Even worse for him, there was absolutely nothing he could do to help her. To his horrified eyes, her car seemed to move in slow motion. It floated across the road and onto the gravel surface of the road's shoulder as it headed smoothly, yet with deadly certainty, toward the cliff's edge.

The car came to a stop. Liana's eyes were squeezed tightly shut and stayed shut until she felt sure the car wouldn't move again.

When she finally opened them, she looked out over

the hood of her car and saw nothing but sky and open space. Very carefully, she drew in a deep breath. She glanced out her right window. Following the line drawn by the cliff's edge, she judged that all four tires were on solid ground. With an exclamation, she dropped her forehead to the steering wheel.

Richard jerked the passenger door open and hauled her out of the car. "Dear God, Liana! Are you hurt?"

"No." She pressed her fingers to her forehead. "What are you doing here?"

"I followed you."

A wave of dizziness washed over her. "You're really going to have to stop doing that."

His hard gaze took in her ashen face and her eyes filled with shock. The idea that she'd been frightened, that she'd nearly gone off that cliff, made him absolutely crazy. "It's a damned good thing I did follow you."

"Why?" She looked at him again, still puzzling over why he was here. "You didn't do anything to help."

That she was right made him all the more angry. "You crazy fool! What were you trying to do? Kill yourself?"

"No, Richard. I'm sure I can leave that to you." She congratulated herself on her quick comeback.

"You damn sure can if you pull this kind of a stunt again."

A wave of nausea came and went. Maybe it hadn't been such a good answer after all. "One of my tires went flat."

"No kidding." He uttered a curse and pulled her against him. "Dammit, Liana, you're shaking."

She hadn't noticed. And now all she could focus on was the heat engendered by being in his arms. For the moment, she allowed herself the heat. She needed it.

He waited until he could feel the tremors in her body subside, then gently cupped her jaw and tilted her face up so that he could study it. "Are you really all right?"

"Yes." Moistening her dry lips with a sweep of her tongue, she stepped out of his grasp. "Thank you."

Staring at her in the growing darkness, he searched for some sign of what she was feeling. But it was like a beautiful curtain had come down over her, concealing all emotion. Recalling those terrifying seconds when he had watched her car skid out of control toward the cliff, he had the strangest urge to shake her. He couldn't remember ever being as scared as he had been at that moment. On some level, he was still scared. *He had to take some action.*

He strode toward the car, reached in the open door and wrenched the keys from the ignition.

"What are you doing?" she asked.

He slammed the door shut and locked it. "We'll leave it here. I'll send someone from the hotel to change the tire and drive it back."

"I can change the tire," she said, the protest automatic.

"So can I, Liana, but I'm not going to and neither are you." He grasped her arm and forcefully helped her into the passenger seat of his car.

From her point of view, it wasn't a second too soon—her strength had just deserted her.

MUSIC DRIFTED out the opened window of the main salon, rose like warm, soft air and entered Richard's bedroom through his open balcony doors. He glanced at the bedside clock. Ten-thirty. After-dinner drinks were being served downstairs. People were laughing, dancing, enjoying themselves, but he wasn't tempted to join them.

Nerves were layered on top of nerves. Muscles were coiled to the point of pain. He craved something, but he didn't know what.

Liana was just down the hall.

He gnawed on a thumbnail, restless, unable to relax. He'd notified the sheriff's department of the litter on the road and had received reassurances that the matter would be taken care of. He'd also made arrangements for Liana's rental car to be driven back to the hotel.

He rubbed his bare chest and threw a discontented stare around the room. For once, there were no company fires he had to put out, no messages from frantic executives to be answered. Earlier in the day, he had even sent Margaret back to New York. He spied his briefcase sitting on the desk and thought of the papers it held. He was halfway across the room before he stopped himself. Generating work *wasn't* what he wanted to do tonight.

He grabbed a shirt from the wardrobe and slipped it on. Without bothering with the buttons, he headed out of his room and down the hall. He didn't have far to walk. At room thirty-three, he stopped. In a last-ditch effort to force reason on himself, he stared at the numbers.

Thirty-three. Thirty-three. Thirty-three.

Hell! This deliberation was doing no good. His mind was already made up and had been for some time.

A few moments after he knocked, Liana opened the door. From the looks of her, she had just come out of a bath. The hem of her teal-blue satin robe brushed her upper thigh. A matching ribbon held the pale blond mass of hair on top of her head. Silky baby tendrils curled along her hairline, the ends of the ribbon trailed to her shoulder. Her skin was flushed and glowing.

She appeared soft and sensual with a touching vulnerability. Every man's dream. And his very own personal nightmare. Heaven help him.

Without waiting for an invitation, he walked into the room. "I thought I should check on you."

"Why?" she asked, slightly breathless. She hadn't expected to see him again tonight, but now that he was here, so extraordinarily sexy in hip-molding black slacks and opened gray shirt, she knew she had hoped he would come. But this wasn't a good situation. Just by entering her room, he had charged the air with danger and excitement.

"Chalk it up to my being bored as hell. Or to the fact that you nearly died today, and I thought looking in on you might be the thing to do."

"That's nice of you, Richard, but not at all necessary." She saw his eyes lower to her breasts, and to her horror realized her nipples had hardened at the sight of him.

"Have you eaten?" he asked, a slight thickness entering his voice.

Nervously she tightened the belt of her robe, then immediately regretted the action. Her aroused state was even more apparent with the satin stretched across her breasts. She clamped down on her emotions. "I'm not hungry."

"I am, but not for food."

Warmth suffused her, and to her chagrin, color came up under her skin.

"Invite me to sit down, Liana."

The knowledge that he knew exactly how he was affecting her gave her yet another reason to dig in her heels and resist the temptation to do as he asked. "No."

He threw a glance over his shoulder at the big four-poster bed. "Then invite me into your bed."

She touched her forehead and found it damp. It was residual moisture from the shower, she assured herself, not perspiration. "I don't think so."

"Why not?"

"Nothing pleasant happens when we spend time together."

"Ah, now, Liana, I don't think that's quite true. Besides which, if it is true, I think it's time we try to change it."

His voice had soft, coaxing tones in it, and she felt her body inclining toward the sound and him. She straightened. "Why?"

"Because the memory of what we once had together is there between us."

She shook her head. "Richard—"

"I'm talking about what we shared in bed. Don't tell me you don't remember."

If only she could forget! Sometimes she was almost able to convince herself that her mind had played tricks on her and that nothing could possibly be that wonderful. When they had made love, they had rearranged the solar system.

"Sex is not the only memory between us," she said, her voice softer than she would have wished.

He lifted his hand and reached toward her. She automatically dodged, jerking her head back.

He smiled, waited a heartbeat, and took hold of one end of a satin ribbon. "But like the adults we are, we've put all that behind us, haven't we?"

He was probing, and she should tell him that naturally she had put their past behind her. But there had been so many lies, and suddenly she was incapable of telling him one more—for now at any rate.

"Let's make new memories," he said very softly, fingering the satiny texture of the ribbon. "Right now."

Her knees went weak, her throat dried.

He took a step back and waved his hand toward the bed. Without pushing, pulling, or forcing her in any way, and without any more words, he was asking her to come to bed with him. There were so many things she could do at this moment, and all of them flashed through her mind like a videotape on fast forward. But in the end, she knew she would do only one thing.

As if mesmerized she crossed the room. He went with her, and when he sat down on the side of the bed, she did, too.

He noted her wariness, yet deep in her eyes, there was also a glittering of need that told him she wanted him as much as he wanted her. Her breasts lifted and pushed against the satin with every nervous breath she took. Lord, he needed to proceed so carefully with her. But how could he? Desire wound in his gut, sending signals of urgency to every part of his body. He allowed seconds to pass until he felt in command again. "Tell me something, Liana."

She blinked with surprise. She had half expected him to grab her to him and pull her down onto the bed. "What is it you want to know?"

The phrasing of her response reminded him of another question, the one that had haunted him night and day since she had left him. *Why in the hell didn't you love me as I loved you?*

He closed down that dark, tortured part of his mind where the question resided before it could break free and reach his lips. "I want to know—do I hurt you when I touch you?"

She tried to swallow and felt an unfamiliar rawness. "Every single time," she whispered.

A look of genuine perplexity crossed his face. "How? I know I'm not always gentle, but—"

"Your touch burns right through my skin. Sometimes, hours after you've left, I can still feel the burning."

His expression changed, becoming understanding and satisfied. "Don't be anxious. We'll take it easy, let you get used to the touching a little at a time." He reached up and slowly drew the ribbon from her hair. A cloud of pale hair came tumbling down and settled around her shoulders. Combing his fingers through the silky strands, he whispered, "I promise you something. By the end of this night, you won't remember what it's like not to have my hands on you. And the burning will be so much a part of you, you'll miss it if it's not there."

For a moment, she knew real fear. "That sounds like a threat."

He wrapped his hand around her neck and slid his thumb up the center of her throat, then back down until it rested right over the larynx. Holding her gaze with his, he pressed slightly. "This is what I would do if I wanted to threaten you."

She felt a portion of her air cut off; astonishingly she wasn't afraid. She had to guess the reason was stubbornness on her part. She knew it couldn't be trust.

Several seconds passed, then he eased the pressure and made a small circle over the area with the thumb, waiting until the fear disappeared and the need returned. "All right?"

She nodded.

With a smile, he dropped his gaze to the full sweetness of her mouth, then returned to the incredible teal of her eyes. He slid his hand down the center of her body to the valley between her breasts, then inside the robe and covered one full luscious mound. "*This* is what I would do if I wanted to make love to you." His thumb flicked across the stiffened nipple, sending electrically charged sparks to all corners of her body. Leaning forward, he brushed a soft kiss across her mouth. "Guess which one I want to do."

A soft moan escaped from between her parted lips.

At the defenseless spot where he previously had applied the pressure, he bent his head and licked, tasting the sweetness of her skin, breathing deeply of her natural perfume. As if he'd ingested an intoxicant, he grew light-headed.

Pulling away, he gazed at her. "Answer me, Liana," he demanded gruffly. "Tell me which one I want to do."

She shuddered; her words came with great effort. "I know you hate me."

He pushed her robe off one shoulder, baring her breast to his hungry gaze. He was aching for her and going this slowly was killing him. But there were compensations, such as the sight of the tiny, delicate rose-colored nipple of her breast that seemed to be begging for his attention again. He took the nipple between his fingers and thumb and tugged. "Does that feel like hate?"

She quivered with pleasure and closed her eyes. "Richard..."

He tugged again. "Does it?"

A fog of desire had closed in around her. Her hands shot out to his shoulders to steady herself. "No, it feels like...like wonderful."

"Wonderful? I want it to feel like *burning*." He pushed her back on the bed and her robe fell open. Her nakedness was nearly his undoing. Her slim, ivory body was all he had remembered and then more. And he was about to have her. "Tell me when it feels like burning, Liana." His mouth came down onto the same tortured, throbbing nipple.

The burning started, searing into her, taking all the air in her lungs and her common sense with it. Heaven help her, she thought. She loved him—this man with the steel gray eyes and the hardened heart. For now she didn't want to think about the past that had been or the regrets that would come. She wanted only, mindlessly, to feel.

Her fingers stroked up into his hair. "I need you inside me."

A growling sound came from deep in his throat and he skimmed his hand over the flat plane of her stomach, through the pale, blond curls, and into the sweet warmth of her. "You mean like that?" he asked hoarsely right before he deepened the kiss, thrusting his tongue into the depths of her mouth.

Without waiting for an answer, he began to stroke her with his fingers, finding the place that sent streams of fire spiraling into her. She feared for her sanity. She'd been deprived for so long, and now the pleasure was almost too intense to bear.

"Is this what you want?" he asked huskily. "Is this what you meant?"

Pressure built; heat wound tighter and tighter inside her. His fingers caressed and invaded, creating sensations that she could not describe. And all the while he murmured words of encouragement, although she really couldn't say what they were exactly. Suddenly her body jerked, then her back arched off the bed, and she cried out.

He continued the stroking, never once pausing, but he quickly shifted and pressed his mouth to her taut stomach. And a savage shudder racked him as, with his lips, he felt the contractions of her release within her womb.

When she subsided, he undressed, then lifted and settled her against the pillows. He stretched out beside her and gently brushed a haze of hair from her face. "You never answered my question. Did I give you what you wanted?"

She turned her head and looked at him. His whole body was taut; the power of his desire evident in his hard masculinity. For the first time she smiled. "No. I want *you* inside me." She trailed her hand across his thigh to close her hand around him.

Her action took him by surprise, and a surge of desire made him momentarily weak. He closed his eyes and dropped his head back onto the pillow.

She rotated onto her side and nuzzled his throat with her mouth. "It's been so long since I've felt you filling me until I couldn't take any more of you. It's a feeling of being whole and full and complete." She looked down at her hand, reveling in the feel and the power of him. She gently squeezed. "I want *you,* Richard. *You.*"

With a loud, ragged groan, he rolled quickly between her legs and rose up on his elbows to look down at her. The teal color of her eyes had darkened almost to black. Her lips were reddened and swollen. He lifted slightly so that he could view her breasts. Stiffened points rose from the swollen mounds. With great precision, he lowered his chest on top of hers until he had positioned his nipples against hers.

She gasped. "Richard, please..."

Her plea lanced straight into him and pierced the most primitive part of him. He'd thought of this moment for so long; he wanted to draw the lovemaking out, to savor each of the little sounds she made, each of her pleas. But his body was betraying him and soon he would be the one begging. Every muscle he possessed had tightened until he was gripped by an agony of passion from head to toe.

Flexing his hips, he pressed against the already pulsating feminine nub. Hot pleasure scored through her. She caught her breath, her mouth slightly open.

His jaw clenched at the sight, and he remembered the feel of her womb's contractions against his mouth. He felt as if he were dying. "I guess I'm going to have to give you what you want, aren't I?"

She wrapped her legs around his back and cupped his buttocks with her hands. "Yes, Richard. Yes."

He drew back, then surged into her with a hard, powerful thrust.

After so long. After so long. The refrain hammered in his brain.

Once positioned in her, he tried to pause, to clear his mind. But thought-shattering sensations made it impossible. Then she lifted her hips to take him deeper. What small intellect that had remained fled, and an elemental wildness took over. He plunged into her, fast, rhythmically, desperate to put out the fire in his gut.

Yet he wanted her with him every step of the way as he took them both into the inferno, and so from somewhere he found a control he hadn't known he possessed. He was determined to teach her a new definition of burning, and when she stiffened and cried out, he knew he had succeeded.

Then he let himself go, and much to his surprise, learned the definition for himself.

SIX

LIANA LAY QUIETLY, watching the draperies shift in the night breeze, pale and ghostlike. She was alone. Richard had made love to her twice, and then without a word, he had left.

But every aspect of the hours he had spent here in this bed with her was etched indelibly into her mind and heart. Their lovemaking had made all her memories pale. When they had come together tonight, the world had combusted and everything around them had gone up in flames. And they had been in the center of the conflagration, holding each other tightly, straining together, crying out their shared ecstasy.

Yet here she was alone.

It seemed she was destined to live with only memories.

Had she really been so stupid as to hope for something more? The answer came swiftly. Yes, she had. Without her being conscious of it, hope had begun to grow at the moment she realized she still loved him.

She admired what he had accomplished professionally. Her heart ached for the pain she knew she had made him suffer. Her desire for him knew no bounds. If he felt even a particle of what she felt...

No. To hope, even unconsciously, had been a mistake. She should have known better.

She squeezed her eyes shut, seeking resolve. If she had learned one thing over the years, it was that second-guessing her actions did no good, and in this instance, she had done enough rehashing.

She had to think with her head, not her heart.

She understood what had happened all those years ago in Paris; she didn't understand what had happened here tonight. But she accepted that nothing that had occurred between her and Richard, either in Paris or here at SwanSea, could be undone.

She knew he didn't love her. Maybe taking her to bed had been his own particular brand of revenge. Maybe now that he had his revenge, he would leave her alone.

She paused, realizing how dispassionate she sounded.She should be pleased, but she knew the truth. She might be eleven years older, eleven years wiser, but she was still as head over heels in love with Richard as she had been in Paris.

The sun would be rising in a few hours, and she had no idea what the day would bring. There was one thing she *did* know, however. Whatever happened, she did not regret tonight.

RICHARD LAY SPRAWLED across his bed. His sweat-soaked clothes were stuck to his skin; beneath his skin, pain ran like a raging river. A war was going on inside him, a war in which he was fighting himself. A war in which no matter the outcome, he couldn't win.

He swore aloud and rolled over onto his back. Nerve endings were screaming for him to rush back to Liana and bury himself in her as far as he could. But pride and an unyielding stubbornness kept him where he was. It was important to him that *he* had been the one to do the leaving tonight.

And after all, he told himself, he had had her. He didn't need her again.

He had already won one crucial battle—he had been able to force himself to pull away from the soft sweetness of her body and come back to this lonely room. True, every step he'd taken away from her had been like walking barefoot across broken glass, but the point was he had done it. If he went back to her now, it would be a defeat.

All he had to do was make it through the rest of the night without her, and then he would be all right.

There was just one thing: how in the hell was he supposed to do it?

And if somehow he managed to accomplish it, how would he get through tomorrow?

With a groan he rolled off the bed and went in search of his running shoes. A long, hard run until dawn would do the trick.

A PREMATURE DARKNESS had come over SwanSea. Clouds that ranged in color from pewter to slate scudded across the sky, pushed by winds that carried the sure promise of a storm.

As Liana ran through the sculpture garden, the rose silk of her cape billowed out behind her, revealing the gray chiffon of the designer gown beneath.

"Double back, Liana," Clay called, snapping picture after picture. "Good, now go on to that next sculpture."

Off to the side, Richard watched broodingly as Liana stopped at a bronze form of Diana. The tall, leggy goddess had been sculpted with her garment flying out behind her as she paused midflight to look over her shoulder at a pursuer only she could see. Without being told, Liana emulated the goddess's pose. With her pearl gray gown and the rose cape swirling around her, Liana held the edges of the cape's hood and looked fearfully over her shoulder as if someone were chasing her.

This was the first time Richard had watched her work for any length of time, and he was struck by how demanding, both physically and mentally, her work was. He knew for a fact how little sleep she had gotten, yet there was no sign of how tired she had to be. She was able to strike the most difficult, awkward pose and make it look natural.

Amazing, he thought, recalling how hot and wildly responsive she had been the night before. Today she was as cool and as composed as the bronze statue she stood beside. She was exquisite in the long cape and gown, but last night, naked and flushed with passion, she had come to life and her beauty had transcended anything he had believed possible.

"Good, Liana, good," Clay said. "Now open the cape a little more so we can see the dress. Okay, lift the skirt slightly. More. More. Give me another angle, tilt your head. Good."

A pulse in Richard's temple throbbed. Clay's instructions to Liana were getting to him. Even if the man was her photographer, he had no right to order her around as he did. How could she stand it? She seemed to have all the patience in the world, whereas just the constant click and whir of the cameras were irritating him, grating against already raw nerves.

"Good," Clay called. "Now look this way."

She did and her gaze encountered Sara, kneeling as

usual beside Clay, watching her intently. Sara smiled at her. For some reason, the act broke Liana's concentration, and the mood and attitude she had been adopting evaporated.

Clay cursed.

"Sorry," Liana said automatically.

Sara rose gracefully to her feet and walked over to her. "It was my fault. You were just doing so great, I couldn't help myself."

Liana's reply to the young girl lodged in her throat as she looked over Sara's shoulder and saw Richard for the first time.

"Liana? Forgive me?"

"Don't worry about it," she murmured.

"Get into your next gown, Liana," Clay said. "I want to use this pre-storm atmosphere as long as I can."

"In a minute."

"In a min—?" He broke off as he followed her gaze to Richard. He frowned, then shrugged. "Okay, go ahead. I need to check my film and change cameras anyway. But *only* a minute. Sara, Steve, let's talk about the next series of shots."

Richard crossed the distance that separated them, took Liana's hand, and led her behind the changing tent where they were out of sight from the others.

Liana shivered. Violent, galvanic air surrounded them, but the weather had nothing to do with the electric current that seemed to arc about Richard. He carried his own energy field, and faced with such a force, she could only wait.

He stared at her for a long moment with eyes as dark as the clouds above them. Finally he flicked the wide ribbons that tied the cape closed at her neck. "You look as if you just stepped out of a turn-of-the-century scene.

"That was the idea. A romantic look for a romantic setting."

"Romantic." He repeated the word thoughtfully. "You're certainly the right model for the job. Wearing that gown and cape, you have the perfect blend of femininity, fragility and melting sensuality. But romance, Liana, is an ideal that doesn't exist."

"Maybe that's your belief," she said, hurt by his attitude, "but there are other people out there in the world who want very much to believe that beauty, adventure, and love—perhaps even chivalric love—exist, the kind you read about in storybooks. And if that belief is strong enough, who's to say that somewhere it doesn't exist?"

He gave a harsh laugh. "There's no such thing as love, Liana. You know that as well as I do. But beauty sure as hell exists. A man has only to look at you to know that. But it is what's beneath that beauty of yours that bothers me, and has for quite a while."

Despair gripped her; her love for him really was hopeless. "Was there something you wanted, Richard?"

His smile was quick and not a smile at all. "Of course. Last night should have told you that."

There had been no tenderness in his lovemaking, she reflected wearily. Why had she thought he might show her tenderness now? "Richard..."

"How much longer are you going to be doing this?" he asked abruptly.

"I don't know. That's up to Clay and the weather."

He scowled. "I don't mean today. I mean, how much longer is the whole shoot scheduled to last?"

"We've done just about half of the gowns."

"You'll be here until the end of the week?"

"Yes. The final shots won't be taken until the ball.

The next day they'll auction off the gowns." She hesitated. "Why do you ask?"

"No particular reason. I was just curious."

The strange gray light of the approaching storm emphasized the fierce, angry expression of his face. She half turned away from him, finding it easier to look at the wildly churning sea. "How long do *you* plan to stay?"

"About the same length of time." He stared broodingly at her profile. The hood of the cape had blown off her head. The wind whipped at her hair and her skirts. Feathery streamers of her hair brushed at his face, the chiffon and silk of her skirts wrapped around his legs. Lightning flashed far out over the sea, a silver bolt momentarily connecting sky and sea. He saw her flinch in surprise. He took a handful of her hair in his fist, turned her, and brought his mouth down on hers in a plundering kiss.

The pleasure hit Liana immediately. Then the relief. He might not love her, but at least he wanted her.

She sagged against him and wrapped her arms around his neck. Clay's voice as he gave directions on the other side of the tent faded until she could hear only the soft, heated sounds that she herself was making.

Richard drew her closer, more relaxed now that she was in his arms. His tongue stroked hers with a hunger that vaguely astonished him. He couldn't remember ever kissing another woman the way he kissed Liana. Last night, there had been very few moments when he hadn't been kissing her—and there had been no part of her he had left untasted. He craved that same experience now, her taste, her feel.

Restless and needy, he moved his pelvis against her. *This wasn't going to be enough.* In fact, he felt as if he might come apart if he couldn't...

He slipped his hand inside the cape, down into the strapless dress, and wrapped his hand around her breast. As he did, he felt her shift slightly, making it easier for him to hold her. A hard shudder of satisfaction raced through his body. Her breast was made to fit in his hand. *His hand needed the touch of her.*

The smell of rain was in the air now. The smell of her was in his head. Lord, he had to have her!

Sara peeped around the corner of the changing tent. "Liana?"

Richard glanced over his shoulder. But he didn't release Liana, and he was unable to force himself to move his hand. His broad back shielded Liana, and all the girl would be able to see was that he had been kissing their star model.

"What is it?" he asked gruffly, all the while compulsively kneading Liana. She softly moaned, and he realized his arm around her was all that was keeping her upright. If they were only alone, he would sink with her to the ground, pull her skirts up out of the way, and take her there and then. Just the thought swamped him with heat. *"What the hell is it?"*

"Uh, we're moving the equipment out to the bluff. Clay wants to try to get a picture of Liana there with the lightning behind her."

"I'll be there in a minute," Liana mumbled, willing to say anything to make Sara leave. Reality was slipping away from her.

"She said in a minute," Richard snapped to Sara and watched until she retreated.

Thumbing her nipple, Richard looked down at Liana. Her eyes were closed, her mouth slightly parted. Fresh desire surged through him. And fresh anger. "Why do you let that man order you around?"

Liana's lids slowly lifted. "Because he's in charge of this assignment. I work for him."

"I keep forgetting, don't I? How important your job and the money you earn is to you. Tell me, Liana. If I hired you to work for me and paid you twice, hell, three times what you're getting to do this job, would you do what *I* tell you?"

She swallowed, her attention torn between his words and his hand that continued to caress her breast and tease her nipple. "What you're talking about is making me a prostitute."

"That's *your* perception of my offer."

"Is it an offer?"

"Would you do what I tell you? Anything?"

"Not for money."

"What then?" he asked gruffly, pulling her closer against him. "Tell me. I'll find it, I'll buy it, I'll get it somehow."

You already have it, she wanted to say. *You have my love.* Instead, somehow, from somewhere, she summoned strength and jerked away from him.

He flexed the fingers of the hand that had just held her, then slowly rolled them into his palm until his hand was a fist. "Go back to work, Liana," he said in a low rough voice. "Do what Clay tells you to do. Earn more money. Give the world more of you. But no one will ever know you like I do. And no one will ever have you like I plan to have you."

CLAY NEVER got the picture he wanted on the bluff. Shortly after Richard stalked away, the storm hit. Drenched to her skin, Liana made her way back to her room and took a hot shower. Then she lit a fire in the fireplace, climbed naked into bed, and fell into a deep sleep. She awoke a few hours later and heard the rain pelting against the windowpanes. She got up and added more logs to the fire, then climbed back into bed and snuggled down into the covers. Warm and rested, she watched the shadows dance on the wall, thrown there by the light of the fire.

She didn't stir, not even when lightning lit the room and thunder rolled and boomed overhead, not even when the door to her room opened and Richard entered.

He closed the door behind him. "Your door was unlocked."

"Yes."

He engaged the lock, then walked to the bed. "Were you waiting for me?"

"Yes."

Slowly he began to undress. He unbuttoned his shirt, shrugged out of it, and let it fall to the floor. The fire's light immediately caressed his newly exposed skin, threading in and out of the mat of dark hair that covered his chest, and turning his shoulders and abdomen a warm bronze color. He stepped out of his shoes and reached for the waistband of his slacks. His every movement sent muscles rippling beneath his skin, thrilling her.

The sheer maleness of him overwhelmed her. She itched to run her hands over the strong lines of him, to feel the heat of his body against hers, to inhale his clean masculine scent. When he pushed his slacks over his hips and down his legs, her mouth went dry. He wore no underwear; he was already fully aroused.

He slipped under the covers and took her into his arms. "Are you ready?"

"Yes."

He rose over her and cupped her buttocks with his hands, then with a thrust, buried himself in her. The possession was slow, hot and greater than either of them had ever known before. But that was only the first time, and after that, they lost count. He stayed inside her all night long. Even when they were just resting, he never once separated from her.

They spoke very little. The pleasurable things they did to each other said everything. SwanSea sheltered them; the storm outside never touched them.

They had their own storm, a storm of passion and desire so intense, that daybreak found them in an exhausted slumber, arms and legs entwined, their bodies still fused together.

LIANA HEARD the ringing of the phone through clouds of sleep, and at first she couldn't connect the sound with an action she should take.

Richard provided a clue. "Don't answer it," he said, his mouth somewhere near her ear.

Against her will, her mind began to work. "I should. It's probably Clay about today's shooting schedule."

He made a disgruntled sound and lazily flexed his hips against her. She felt him begin to grow deep within her, and she smiled softly. She pressed her lips against his throat and whispered, "If I don't answer it, he'll send someone to find out if there's something wrong."

With a muttered oath, he reached out a long arm to wrest the telephone from its cradle. The ringing stopped. Gazing down at her, he raised up on one elbow and pressed the receiver into the pillow. "Tell him you're going to be late this morning."

"Richard—"

He moved in and out of her, bringing her body awake and filling her with a liquid warmth.

"Tell him. All right?" he asked, continuing his lazy thrusting.

Her eyes beginning to glaze with passion, she nodded. He placed the receiver against her ear. Caught and held by the heat in his eyes, she murmured, "I'm going to be a little late this morning."

"Clay's not going to like that," an amused voice said.

Her mind instantly cleared. "Jean-Paul!"

Richard ceased all motion.

"I thought you were never going to answer the phone," Jean-Paul said. "Did I catch you in the shower?"

Richard pulled out of her, rolled to the other side of the bed, and threw his forearm over his eyes.

"Liana?"

"Yes, I'm here." A look at Richard's face told her he had retreated both physically and mentally from her. She felt empty and alone. She wanted to touch him, but she had the feeling that if she tried, his body would deflect her hand.

"Liana, you sound strange. Are you all right?"

"I'm fine, Jean-Paul. How are you?"

Richard surged off the bed and to his feet. "Could you hold on a minute, Jean-Paul?"

"Certainly, *chérie.* Unfortunately, I have nothing but time on my hands."

Richard rounded the bed and stepped into his slacks. She covered the mouthpiece of the phone with her hand. "Please stay, Richard. Don't go."

He yanked his zipper up and fastened the waistband of his pants. "I need fresh air. A lot of it."

"Richard—"

He jerked up his shirt from the floor and held it clenched in his fist. "If you're going to talk to him, Liana, I'm not staying."

"He's been sick," she said, trying to reason with him. "I want to find out how he's doing."

"That's very, very touching, but I'm out of here." He crossed the room and opened the door.

"Wait! I won't talk long. I promise."

The door slammed shut after him, and she sank back against the pillows. Her hand shook as she lifted the receiver to her ear. "I'm sorry to keep you waiting, Jean-Paul. I was in the shower."

"You never could lie worth a damn. You want to tell me about it?"

"No," she said, her sad gaze on the door. "No. Tell me how you are instead."

THAT NIGHT when Liana opened the door and Richard walked into the room, she wasn't surprised. She had come to realize that—no matter their past, no matter their present disagreements—as long as they were here at SwanSea, they would be lovers.

SwanSea was large; they could easily avoid each other if they chose. But the turbulent emotions and feelings they carried for each other easily converted to passion, and the power of their passion pushed against the walls of the great house, seeking release.

They could not be in this place without being together.

Now when she closed the door after him, the lovely, soothing room filled with tension. Richard's tension. He was wound tighter than a spring, and she knew why. *Jean-Paul.*

He came to a stop in front of the fireplace and gazed

unseeingly at a stack of freshly laid logs. "I gather you finished your phone call?"

"Yes." She paused. "Did you get the air you needed?"

"Yes."

"Richard, I'd like to explain about that phone call—"

He whirled around, his body taut, his expression fierce. "*No!* I don't want to hear one word about that phone call or the person who called you!"

"But—"

"I said *no,* Liana." He came to her and took her face in one big hand. He stared down at her for a long moment, and when he spoke again, his voice was softer, his manner calmer. "I don't even want to hear his name. All right?"

"I won't talk about the phone call if you don't wish. But, Richard, there is something else, something I've decided it's time you knew."

His thumb caressed her jawline, and his heated gaze focused on the fullness of her lips. "Does it have anything to do with tonight and what you want me to do to you when we go to bed?"

Her throat dried up as desire began low in her body. "No. It's about—"

His fingers tightened around her face, and his thumb brushed across her lips. "Then I don't want to hear it."

She wouldn't let him silence her. Not just yet at any rate. "I have to tell you this, Richard."

He slipped his thumb just inside her bottom lip to the soft moistness. "Maybe," he said huskily. "Maybe. But not tonight."

And then he replaced his thumb with his tongue.

SEVEN

LIANA'S SANDALS DANGLED from her fingertips as she made her way across the rock and driftwood-strewn beach the next afternoon. Perhaps because of the rocks, this beach was unoccupied, people choosing the sandier strip of land closer to the house. But Liana found the natural beauty and most especially the isolation of this beach to be exactly what she wanted, and she gave silent thanks that the day's shooting had gone well enough that Clay had called it quits early.

The late-afternoon sun hung low in the sky and cast a golden hue over the glittering sand and glistening dark rocks. Foam-tipped breakers surged onto the sand and lapped at her bare feet. The sight, sound and feel of the cold water soothed her. She had desperately needed this time of solitude and peace before she saw Richard again and a new storm began.

It had come to her quite suddenly last night that it was time Richard knew of the deceit she had perpetrated on him so many years ago. She had tried to tell him, but he hadn't been in a mood to listen, and it had taken only the persuasive powers of his hands and lips to distract her. But now after a day to think over her impulsive decision, she knew she was right.

She wasn't sure what she hoped to accomplish by

telling him. All along she had felt it wouldn't make any difference if he knew. Even that time after her father's death when she had flown to New York with every intention of explaining, she hadn't held much hope that the truth would change things. She still didn't think it would. But seeing him again, being with him, realizing the depth of love she still held for him had convinced her that at the least he had a right to know.

She stopped to pick up a seashell, examined it briefly, then threw it back out to sea.

From his vantage point a short distance down the beach, Richard kept his gaze on her rather than the shell's flight. Long after the shell had disappeared beneath the waves, she stayed where she was, watching the sea. The wind lifted the hem of her loose-fitting sundress and braided itself through her long fall of hair; the dress and her hair were almost the same shade of pale gold. She looked solemn, beautiful and very mysterious.

He would give up a major part of his possessions to know what she was thinking at this exact moment, he thought, then mentally cursed himself for being so stupid. He would never have the key to her. But at least, for this short time at SwanSea, he would have a part of her.

He walked up quietly behind her. "Were you testing your throwing arm, or was there something wrong with that shell?"

Her peace evaporated as soon as she heard his voice. Turning to face him, she reflected that she had given up asking how he was always able to find her when she could so easily elude everyone else. He seemed to have a built-in radar where she was concerned. "It was broken."

"And you're looking for one that's not?"

The question held only idle curiosity, she noted.

Dressed in gray cotton twill slacks and a sky-blue open-necked shirt, he appeared quite relaxed. Her need to believe that they could share an interlude of peace overruled her doubts. Tension slowly drained out of her. "Yes."

"Why?"

By unspoken agreement, they turned as one and began walking. "I wanted to take a shell home as a souvenir," she said. "The sea is so much a part of this place, it seems appropriate."

"I don't know if I agree. I think one of the gowns you've been modeling would be more appropriate. In fact, I'll buy you one."

She laughed lightly. "Thanks, but no thanks. A gown like one of those would only hang in my closet, gathering dust and taking up space."

"I've seen pictures of you at galas, Liana. I know you go out."

"When I attend functions where I will be photographed, designers lend me gowns to wear. It's free publicity for them."

Thinking about what she said, he paused to pick up a piece of driftwood, studied it for a moment, then drew back and hurled it out over the water. "All right then, I'll buy you one of the paintings that will be going up for auction in a few days. That would be better anyway, because I can guarantee that any of those paintings will appreciate in value."

She smiled, thinking of the simple cottage she called home. "Again, thank you, but I really wouldn't have a place to hang anything that valuable."

"Why not? You live in France, don't you?"

"That's right. In the country."

"A château?"

"Not even close." Still smiling, she nodded toward an outcropping of boulders. "Let's sit for a while."

With lithe grace, he levered himself to the highest point, where erosion and nature had joined forces to make a natural seating area, then he bent, clasped his hands around her waist, and easily lifted her to join him.

"All right," he said, after they were settled onto the sun-warmed rock, "tell me about your home."

She stretched out her legs in front of her and leaned back on her hands. "My house is very small, very old and quite simple. But it has a great deal of charm and character, and I love it."

"But you have other homes, right? This country place isn't your only home."

She almost laughed, because he looked so puzzled. "I only need one home. When I'm on assignment, my contract stipulates that a place to stay be provided for me." He was silent for so long, she added, "The difference between the perception of my life and the reality is a chasm as large as the Grand Canyon."

Her remark drew his gaze, and his eyes were so clear, she felt she should be able to see all the way to his soul. But the clarity was deceptive, and unseen barriers blocked her way. "You don't believe me?" she asked, her tone deliberately light.

"I don't have any reason not to." He reached out and brushed back a wind-tossed strand of hair that had fallen across one ivory cheek. "You've changed my mind. I'll buy you jewelry. Maybe aquamarines, or even sapphires, whichever I can find that would come close to the color of your eyes."

She laughed. "Why do you have to buy me anything?"

"I don't *have* to. I *want* to."

Her laughter faded. "You don't owe me a payment of any type, Richard."

"No, you're right, I don't. But you wanted a souvenir, and I'm trying to think of something you'd like."

"I told you what I want. I want a seashell."

"Then I guess I'll have to help you find one."

A feeling warm as the sunshine that surrounded them slowly grew within her. "That would be nice. Thank you."

"You're welcome." His brow suddenly knit. "Now that I think about it, I can't remember ever seeing you wear any jewelry, either here or in photographs. Is there any particular reason why?"

"No, except again, jewelry doesn't really fit in with my lifestyle." She paused. "I own only one piece of jewelry, and I cherish it."

"Did Savion give it to you?"

The sudden tension in his voice cut into the tranquillity they had been sharing like a piece of jagged glass. She rushed to repair their peace. "Jean-Paul has never given me any jewelry."

"Then who?"

"An elderly lady I met in Paris about ten years ago. She was my next-door neighbor in the building where I took my first flat. She was bedridden and had a full-time nurse living with her, but from the moment I met her, we were friends."

"What did she give you?"

"A brooch in the shape of a lily. In fact, I've worn it since I've been here."

He nodded. "That's right, I remember now."

"Leonora—"

"Leonora?"

"That was her name. We got along wonderfully. I

visited with her several times a week. My visits seemed to cheer her up. I don't think she had anyone else, but she told me stories of the man she had loved and their life together." Her eyes narrowed against the light dancing on the water. "She gave up everything for his love."

"Then she was a fool. There is no such thing as love."

She turned her head and met his gaze. "She thought differently. She told me she didn't mind dying, because she had known true happiness and love. Once she mentioned a regret, a major one apparently, but she never explained. She gave me the brooch right before she died."

"Why?"

"I don't know." She didn't want to tell him that Leonora had often said how much the sadness she saw in Liana reminded her of herself as a young woman. And of course she wouldn't tell him how Leonora had told her that one day she, too, would find true love. He would scoff, and she didn't blame him. Love was a subject better left undiscussed between them.

He threaded his fingers through her hair and tilted her head toward him. Then he kissed her, quite softly, quite gently.

"Would you settle for a piece of driftwood?" he murmured.

Bemused by the tenderness of his kiss, she wasn't sure she had heard him correctly. "What?"

"Driftwood. That is, if we can't find a suitable shell."

She smiled. "A piece of driftwood would be nice."

They scoured the beach, and in the end, chose a piece of driftwood for him and a seashell for her. Later, as Liana showered and changed for dinner, she reflected that the afternoon had been a truly happy time, a time she would remember in the years to come as vividly as she recalled the nights of ecstasy they had spent here.

She met Richard downstairs in the dining room, where they enjoyed a long, leisurely dinner. He seemed totally relaxed, and she soaked up his attention. Every time he smiled at her or they shared a laugh, a secret sensation of pleasure tingled through her. But her happiness was moderated by what she knew was to come later—the story she had to tell him. As much as she hated to jar their current harmony in any way, that was just what she had to do.

When they returned to her room, Richard undressed, leaving on only his trousers, and stretched out on the bed. She undressed, too, and put on her robe, but she delayed going to bed. Instead, she wandered around the room, picking up something in one place, putting it down in another, trying to decide how she should begin. She wasn't aware that Richard was watching her until he spoke.

"What's wrong, Liana?"

She glanced over her shoulder at him. "Nothing."

"Then why are you way on the other side of the room? Why aren't you over here with me?"

She smiled briefly, thinking how much easier it would be to go to him, crawl into bed beside him, and give herself up to his incredible lovemaking. She actually took several steps toward him before she could stop herself.

She shook her head. "There's something I need to tell you."

"Later."

"I have a feeling that if I don't tell you now, I never will, and this is something you should hear."

His facial expression went from relaxed to tense in less than a second. "If it's about Savion, I don't want to know."

She walked to the end of the bed and wrapped an arm around one of the sea-green draped posters. "Actually this is about me and what a stupid, naive young woman I was at one time."

He shifted impatiently. "I don't see the point in rehashing the past, Liana."

"This isn't a rehashing, Richard. This will be information that is entirely new to you."

He rubbed his forehead. "I've lived all these years without knowing. I don't see why it's so important now."

An odd thought floated through her mind: he sounded as if he were afraid he would be hurt by what she wanted to tell him. "It's important to me, Richard," she said quietly.

He made a sound of exasperation. "All right, I give up. Let's get this over, whatever it is. Say what you have to say."

This wasn't beginning well, she reflected nervously, but then she hadn't really expected anything else. She ran the tip of her tongue over her lips. Both her throat and her lips felt dry. "I guess I should start with my father."

"Your father?" he said, surprised.

She nodded. "His name was Donald Gordon, and he owned a small textile business that he'd inherited. The name of that business was Gordon and Sons. The Gordon in the title was my grandfather, who founded the company, the Sons was my father."

She waited for Richard to show some sign of recognition, but all he said was, "Why was your father's name different from yours?"

Her fingers fiddled with the diaphanous material that

draped the bedpost. "I decided to take my mother's maiden name for professional purposes."

"So your real name is Liana Gordon?"

"That's right." She pushed away from the bed and slipped her hands into the pockets of her robe. "At any rate, apparently my father wasn't much of a businessman, although I didn't find that out until later. I was finishing high school about the time the business began to fail. Things went from bad to worse until it reached the point where everything rested on the company getting one contract." She paused. "Unfortunately for him, you were going after the same contract and you won."

Richard bolted straight up in bed. *"What?"*

She nodded. "It was the Rhiman Industries contract."

"I remember." He frowned. "That must have been about twelve years ago."

"That's right. My father told me you were young and hungry and had underbid him." Her throat tightened. "He also told me you were unscrupulous."

"What else did he tell you?" he asked in a soft, ominous voice.

"That the only reason you won was because you had cheated to get the contract. Then in the next breath, he told me that he had lost everything. Not too many days later he tried to commit suicide."

He came off the bed and strode to her side. "Good Lord, Liana, suicide?"

Her lips formed a sad smile. "Oh, he didn't succeed. He botched the job, and he was left an invalid." She tried to laugh but it ended up a sob. "So there I was, just out of high school, no real job skills and a mountain of medical bills that grew bigger every day. I had one thing going for me."

"Your face."

"Yes."

He didn't move, but it seemed to her that he had physically withdrawn from her. "You already told me how you got to the Paris designers."

"And thank goodness that happened." She drew a deep breath. "I finished one job and started looking for another. I had made quite a few contacts while I was there, and I thought my chances would be better in Paris than back in the States. Then one day quite by accident, I read in the paper about a young American businessman who was brash enough to come to Paris and try to sell textiles to the French."

His grim expression told her he knew what was coming next, and this time he did move a few steps away from her.

She made a helpless gesture with her hands. "It was pure impulse on my part. To my everlasting regret, I didn't even stop to think things through. I went to your hotel and flirted with one of the young men who worked behind the desk until he found out your schedule for me. Then I arranged to be in the same place at the same time."

"Tell me something, Liana." His tone held a quiet, deadly quality. "How did you know? How did you know that I would take one look at you and fall like a ton of bricks for you?"

"I didn't. It's just that making you fall in love with me was the only way I could think of to hurt you. I had no money, I had no power—"

"You only had your beauty," he finished for her. "Your face, your body, your eyes, the way your skin smelled and tasted—" He broke off and turned away. "I don't want to hear any more."

She put her hand on his arm and tried to make him look at her. He wouldn't budge, and she had to circle him until she was in front of him.

"You have to listen to me."

"I don't *have* to do anything."

Tears sprang into her eyes. "Please. *Please,* Richard. Just listen for a few more minutes."

"Damn you, Liana!"

She lay her palms flat on his chest, feeling as though the contact would somehow help her get through to him. "I fell in love with you."

He gazed down at her, his expression blatantly incredulous. "How can you even say that?"

Tears slipped from her eyes and ran freely down her cheeks. "Because I did fall in love with you, although that obviously wasn't the plan. But, think about it, Richard. We couldn't have had the incredible two weeks we had if—"

He tore away from her. "What the hell difference does it all make now, Liana? That was a long time ago. It's *over.*"

She dashed at the tears with a shaking hand. "Maybe it doesn't make a difference, but I want you to know the whole story."

"Why? To soothe your conscience? To absolve you of guilt?" His voice and hand sliced through the air like a knife. "Forget it, Liana. It's not my job to give absolution."

She couldn't stop her tears, nor could she stop before she'd told him everything. "Try to see it from my point of view. I had fallen in love with the man I believed had destroyed my father. To make matters worse, I had become involved with that man for the sole purpose of destroying him."

"By making me fall in love with you," he said with a flat sarcasm.

"That's right."

"Well, honey, you sure as hell made me fall in *something* with you, but it was more than likely lust, and you didn't come near destroying me."

"I'm glad."

He uttered a disgusted sound and dropped back onto the bed.

"Richard, I *had* to leave you."

"Right. And before you left, you just had to tell me that you didn't love me, in fact had never loved me."

"I told you that so you wouldn't try to stop me. Don't you see? I couldn't bring myself to tell you the truth. I felt trapped and needed to get out quickly. I couldn't go on living with the man who had destroyed my father, nor could I live with the idea of destroying you. But, Richard, don't doubt that I loved you."

"Love." He sneered as he infused the word *love* with contempt. "And of course, your love for me is why you went to Savion. Because you loved *me.* It all makes perfect sense, Liana." He crossed his hands behind his head and stared at the ceiling.

Bands of pain were binding her chest, drawing tighter and tighter, but she went on. "I was hurting, because of what I had done and because of what I thought you had done. I could see no resolution. Jean-Paul provided me with a safe haven. He expected nothing of me—"

His harsh laugh interrupted her.

What was the use, she thought in despair. He didn't want to hear any of this, and now she was sorry she had forced him to listen. She had opened sealed-over wounds and destroyed whatever tenuous relationship they had managed to achieve here at SwanSea.

"Are you finally through?" he asked.

"No," she said slowly. "There's one more thing. Six years ago, my father died, but right before he did, he confessed to me that he had used you as a scapegoat, as a cover for his own incompetence." She laced her fingers together and stared down at them. "You see, he couldn't accept the responsibility for his failure, and he couldn't bear for me to know that he had lost the company that he considered my birthright." For once, Richard didn't say anything; he was staring at the ceiling again. "As soon after the funeral as possible, I caught a plane to New York. I planned to tell you everything and beg your forgiveness. But when I called your office from the airport, I found that you were on your honeymoon. The news, coming right on the heels of my father's death, was devastating to me." Completely miserable, she shrugged. "That's it. You finally know everything."

She waited for a reaction, expecting an explosion of some sort, but his silence continued, stretching, growing, like an impenetrable wall.

"Richard?"

"Come to bed, Liana."

The quiet resignation she heard from him shocked her. "Is that all you have to say?"

He slowly moved his head on the pillow until he could see her, but his eyes appeared dead, without expression. "I'll admit that when you left me eleven years ago it seemed like a big deal. I took it hard. But looking back on that day, it was only my pride that was hurt, nothing more."

"But—"

"There is no love, Liana. Love is only a word people use as a rationalization for passion."

She couldn't think of a thing to say; she felt as if she'd been hit in the stomach.

"Come to bed," he said again.

The room began to spin, the floor tilted precariously. Somehow she made her way to the bed without falling and managed to lie down.

He didn't touch her. She didn't touch him.

She stared unseeingly into the darkness, listening to the quiet, even pattern of Richard's breathing, and the ear-piercing screams in her head.

And when she awoke, she was alone. Again.

THE CLOUD-SHROUDED NIGHT provided little illumination. Richard used the beam of the borrowed flashlight to light his way along unfamiliar paths as he ran. And ran. And ran.

Damn Liana!

What had she expected? That she could tell him that incredibly stupid story and the past eleven years would be erased? The emptiness. The loneliness. The pain.

Or was telling him her way of inflicting even more pain?

Bitterness choked him until he thought he wouldn't be able to go on. But he continued running, through woods, across meadows, trying to exorcise the demon that tormented his soul—the woman who had somehow imbedded herself so deep inside him, he feared for his sanity.

Even if the first part of the story were true, even if she had set out to hurt him by making him fall in love with her because she thought he had cheated her father, why had she left him?

She said that she had fallen in love with him. He didn't believe it. He *couldn't* believe it. The hateful words she had uttered right before she had walked out the door were forever carved into his brain. "I don't love you," she had said. "I've only been playing with you." And then she had gone straight into the arms of Jean-Paul Savion.

Damn her straight to hell.

He ran, and he ran, and he ran.

And when he found himself in front of her door, he opened it, and went to her.

Through the gray light of dawn, he saw that she was awake.

"I think I hate you," he said quietly as he shoved his sweatpants down and thrust desperately into her.

She arched up to receive him, and his mind went blank, as a dark, burning desire took over.

And every time he drove her, he repeated how much he hated her.

EIGHT

THE SOUND OF voices bounced off the rows of paint-ladened canvases, lifted to the high ceiling and returned to fill the long gallery of SwanSea. Liana didn't hear.

Rosalyn, who was newly discharged from the hospital and who had insisted on resuming work, fussed with Liana's hair, trying to achieve the disordered look of the woman in the painting that hung high in the second tier of art on the wall. Liana didn't feel.

Sara tugged at the folds of the blue gown she had donned for this series of pictures. Liana didn't notice.

Steve shoved a light meter toward her face. She didn't flinch.

With great force of will, she had retreated to the place in her mind where their hands, their voices, their gazes didn't intrude. She had determined that she was through with hurting.

Briefly, foolishly, she had opened herself to Richard and, in the process, had allowed herself to become too vulnerable. No more.

Even the fact that Richard was among the spectators gathered around them didn't bother her overly much. She accepted his brooding presence, just as she accepted the fact that he would kiss and hold her again.

She didn't have the strength to refuse his lovemaking; there were times when she wanted him more than she wanted to live one more moment. But she had decided she could enjoy the interlude of their passion with relative safety if she kept her eyes on the rapidly approaching time when they would both leave SwanSea and go their separate ways. In a matter of days she would be alone again in her little house deep in the French countryside. She would be safe there. Until then, she had to protect herself.

"She needs flowers in her hair," Clay said, eyeing her critically.

Rosalyn bent down to a florist box on the floor. "I have them right here."

Sara draped an almost transparent blue stole around her shoulders; Rosalyn began to weave small cream-colored flowers through her hair. Liana endured their attentions patiently, understanding that their aim was to make her look as much like the young women of the art nouveau period as possible—the women with their flaring veils and streaming hair, who had posed for the posters and paintings of the period.

"The wind machine is ready," Steve said to Clay.

Clay looped a camera around his neck and made one last check of its settings. "Okay, now, Liana, I want you to stand on that ladder over there so that I can get both you and the painting in the frame. Can you do that?"

"Of course."

"Good." He patted her arm, then turned his attention to his crew. "Time is getting critical, people. The climax of this shindig, the ball, is tomorrow night, and we've got an awful lot of work to do yet. We can't afford any more delays, so let's all give our best. Liana, the ladder.

Steve, the wind machine. Sara and Rosalyn, get out of the way. Let's go."

Liana stepped onto the first rung of the ladder. As soon as the wind hit her, the featherlight fabric of her gown began to pulsate around her in sinuous swirls and undulations, and she set about to capture the sensual, languid mood of the first painting Clay had chosen to spotlight.

"Go higher," he called.

She stepped onto the next rung and the next. The sturdiness of the ladder allowed her to pose freely without the fear that it would tip over. Holding on to the top of the ladder, she arched backward so that her hair and dress flowed outward with the wind's current.

"Beautiful, beautiful," Clay murmured, snapping away.

She climbed higher, and when she'd gained the next to the highest rung, she released the top of the ladder and threw her hands upward.

The cracking sound barely intruded on her concentration, but then she felt herself begin to slip and she realized the rung she was standing on had broken.

The splitting wood halved and her feet dropped through to the next rung, but her high heels couldn't gain a purchase and she kept slipping. Just as she made a grab for the top of the ladder, her shinbone struck the edge of a crosspiece and pain lanced through her. Onlookers gasped their alarm, her dress ripped, and then she was falling backward to the floor.

When she opened her eyes, she saw a clearly enraged Richard kneeling over her.

"Don't move."

What was he mad about now, she wondered dimly, as Clay's face swam into her view, then Steve's. Both looked worried and concerned—completely different emotions from Richard's.

For some reason the whole thing struck her as funny, and she began to laugh. But the breath had been knocked out of her, and the laugh turned to a cough, then a sob, then a groan.

"Are you in pain, Liana?" Steve asked quickly. "Do you need a doctor?"

"I'm sure she does," Clay said. "Go call for one."

She felt Richard pick up her hand, his fingers stroking it gently. His voice, however, sounded like he had swallowed broken razor blades. "Where the hell did that ladder come from?"

"Right here," Clay said, throwing a strange look over his shoulder at Sara. "We borrowed it from the hotel. Sara went and got it this morning."

"That's right," the younger woman said.

Sara looked pale, Liana thought absently, as she came to stand over her.

"One of the maintenance people told me where the ladders were kept," Sara continued, her words rushing out in a nervous tempo. "I went before we started this morning and took the only one that was there."

"Didn't you look to see if there was anything wrong with it?" Richard asked her. It wasn't until Liana's soft gasp penetrated his agitation that he realized his grip had tightened on her hand. He eased his hold.

"No. I just assumed—"

"Well, you assumed wrong, didn't you?"

Clay's gaze had been going between Richard and Sara, following their conversation. "For heaven sakes, forget the damned ladder. The important thing is Liana." He looked down at her. "How are you, honey?"

Her brief hysterical period had passed; a throbbing ache that seemed to encompass her entire body had set in. "I've been better." She tried to sit up, but grimaced when she felt sharp twinges in various parts of her body.

"Don't move," Clay and Richard said simultaneously.

"Trust me," she said dryly. "If I don't move now, I may never move." Her second attempt to sit up was a success.

Clay reached out a hand to support her back. "You may have broken something, Liana. We need to get you to a doctor."

This conversation sounded vaguely familiar, she thought dryly. She shook her hair out of her face, sending a dull pain through her head and flowers showering to the floor. "Nothing's broken. I've just managed to collect a few more bruises, that's all." She glanced at Richard. "Help me stand."

When he hesitated, she moved to stand by herself.

"Dammit, Liana," he said, reaching out to her.

Once she was on her feet, her knees buckled, but then braced to hold her weight. She fixed a determinedly bright expression on her face. "See? I'm fine."

Richard muttered a curse under her breath. "I'll take you up to your room."

"No, I'm going to continue working. Clay, which dress do you want me in next?"

Clay looked at her as if she had lost her mind. "What?"

She managed a grin. "Why are you so surprised? You're the one who told us how much we have left to do and how little time we have left to do it."

"That was before—"

Richard's fingers closed around her upper arm. "Liana, quit being so stubborn and let me take you upstairs."

She pushed his hand away. "I'm here to work, Richard. I told you that right from the first day." She glanced toward Rosalyn, whose concern for her had made the blotches on her face more pronounced. The quickest way to wipe the anxious look off her face, Liana knew, was to give her some way to feel helpful. "Rosalyn, do you have any aspirin?"

Rosalyn snapped into action. "In the makeup bag. Come on, honey, I'll give you a couple and we'll get you into the next dress."

Clay eyed Sara for a moment, then shrugged. "Okay, people, let's set up for the next shot."

Steve and Sara set to work.

Richard strode down the long gallery toward the door, his brow knit in thought. There seemed to be a lot of bad luck on this shoot, and all of it was being experienced by Liana. It could be a coincidence. Then again...

RICHARD WENT TO several maintenance people before he found the man with whom Sara had spoken. The man wore a uniform with the name Bill monogrammed over the chest pocket. Richard passed a hundred dollar bill to him to assure he would be the only one getting this man's information.

Bill pocketed the money with a smile. "We have more than one ladder, and as I recall, when the lady came to ask me where they were and if she could borrow one, all but two were in use."

"Two? Are you sure?"

Bill nodded. "Sure I'm sure. I told her to help herself."

"Were they both in good repair?"

Bill looked vaguely shocked. "Absolutely, Mr. Zagan. This is SwanSea. We wouldn't tolerate any broken ladders."

LIANA GAVE A SIGH of pure bliss as she sank into the steaming hot water of her bath and rested her head on the rim of the tub. She was exhausted and it felt as if every bone in her body hurt. But at least, she thought, she had the satisfaction of knowing she had managed to complete the day's shooting schedule.

The heat of the water penetrated through to her bones, and slowly her knotted muscles began to loosen. Her mind drifted, and against her will, her thoughts returned to the moment when she had heard the crack of the rung as it broke in two. How was it that the topmost one had broken when the others hadn't? The wood must have been rotten or weak or...

She remembered how Steve had come to her after she had fallen down the grand staircase. He had intimated that the light might have been rigged.

Despite the heated water, she suddenly shivered. The thought that someone might actually be trying to hurt her was incomprehensible. She had discarded the idea once before and she did so again. She didn't have an enemy in the world.

Unless she counted Richard. She discounted that idea as quickly as it had come to her. Richard certainly made a formidable enemy, but causing her physical harm wasn't his style. He might cut her to pieces with slashing words, but he never left any visible scars. And he might give her sexual pleasure so intense she sometimes feared she would die. But after he was through making love to her, she fell into a deep sleep, not into death.

But what if someone else...

She heard the outside hall door to her bedroom open and knew it was Richard. Her first impulse was to speak to him about her doubts, but the impulse was immediately squelched.

She felt threatened and a little frightened, but Richard was the last person to whom she could show any weakness. He had the power to hurt her, the kind of hurt that wouldn't kill or bruise, but would go much deeper and cause irreparable harm.

When he appeared in the doorway, she smiled. "Hello."

He leaned his shoulder against the door frame and crossed one ankle over the other. Staring at her, he felt the familiar stirrings of desire, the powerful, blood-boiling kind that only she could make him feel.

Tonight yet another satin ribbon tied her hair atop her head, this one blue, and its ends mingled with her wheat-colored curls. His gaze dropped below the clear bath water to her breasts and their taut rosy peaks. In two steps, he could have one of them in his mouth, he thought, and Lord knew he needed the succor he would receive.

He forced himself to look at something else. The triangle of pale hair low on her body drew his attention, and then her legs. Just looking at those long, lovely legs and remembering how they felt around him made his gut clench. Every inch of her skin that he could see had a pearlescent sheen to it, and a fragrance, vaguely floral, vaguely haunting, rose from the water and permeated the air. If he didn't do something and quick, he would lose himself in her for the rest of the night.

"Do you always leave your door unlocked?"

The serrated edge of his voice caused her to throw him a wary glance. "Not always."

"You did early this morning. I came back from running and was able to walk right in."

"As I recall, I didn't know you had left." She reached for the soap and washcloth. "I woke up right before you returned."

He remembered. He had been in agony and had desperately needed to assuage that agony in her sweet, firm body. Just as he wanted to do now. His jaw tightened. "What about tonight? Anyone could have walked in."

"But anyone didn't," she said, unwilling to tell him that she had left the door unlocked for him. "You did."

"That lock is there for a reason, Liana. Use it."

She skimmed the soaped cloth down one arm and across her chest. "Is there any particular reason why we are talking about whether or not I lock my door?"

His eyes automatically followed the path of the washcloth, but his mind worked on how he would answer her. He had to be careful. If he were wrong about this half-formed theory that someone was trying to harm her, he could end up looking like a fool. And his number-one priority at the moment was to come out of this affair with her, unscathed and with his dignity and heart intact.

He rolled his shoulders in a nonchalant manner. "I just think that locking your door would be a sensible thing to do. Several unexpected things *have* happened to you lately." His heart picked up a beat as she lathered soap over her breasts. "You know, it's funny. When we were together in Paris, I don't remember you being particularly accident-prone. Of course, that could be because you spent a great deal of time on your back."

She hurled the dripping wet washcloth at him and had the satisfaction of seeing it land with a smack against his face.

It dispersed a portion of the tension he had been feeling. Smiling, he peeled it off him. "I guess you thought I deserved that."

"I guess I did."

His smile grew bigger, and he tossed the cloth back into the tub, where it landed in the water near one drawn-up knee with a plunk. "Okay, maybe I did."

She sighed. "Just say whatever it is you're trying to say, Richard."

He moved away from the door frame and came to perch on the rim of the tub. Gazing down, he dipped his fingers into the water and absently made figure eights. "You've had three accidents since you've been here. I can see one, maybe even two—the fact that the road was littered with debris wasn't your fault—but three just seems a little excessive. And if you consider the face powder..."

Disturbed, she shifted position in the water. She had no way of knowing if he were simply talking to have something to say, or if he might be genuinely concerned. If she thought for one minute that he was concerned... She shut her eyes. *What was she thinking?* And why did she keep having to learn the same lessons over and over again. She might love him with all her heart, but he certainly didn't love her. And if by chance he did hold any concern for her, it was on a strictly superficial level.

"Liana?"

She looked at him again. "I'm clumsy. Things happen."

She was clumsy, he thought, like a bull was dainty. "If you had broken a leg or an arm or a neck today, what would have happened to the shoot?"

That was a question she had already asked herself, but the answer had given her no help as to what might be going on. "Nothing. They would have brought in another model and the shoot would have been completed."

He frowned. "So no one would benefit."

"No." She tilted her head and studied him. To be making idle conversation, he was asking awfully specific questions. She couldn't resist probing, but for her own protection she coated her words with a slightly mocking tone. "You sound worried about me, Richard."

Immediately he went on the defensive. "I wouldn't call it worry, more like curiosity. Sometimes it gets the better of me."

She sank into the water until it came to her chin. "It's hard for me to believe that anything or anyone could get the better of you."

His lips formed a hard smile. "That's the way I like to keep it." He reached beneath the water and scooped up the washcloth. "I bet you're sore," he said, skimming the cloth from her knee, up her thigh and back again.

She blinked at the sudden change of subject. "A little."

"A lot, I'm sure. That was a hard fall you took."

"The hot water's helping."

He put his hand under her calf and lifted it so that he could better see the dark purple bruise that had formed on her shin. His eyes cut to her, his eyebrows arched.

She shrugged. "It doesn't hurt much."

He released her leg without comment and came to his feet. "How much longer are you going to be in here?"

All of a sudden she felt naked, in more ways than one. His strange moods had kept her almost continuously off balance since they had met again here at SwanSea. Tonight she was tired, bruised and uneasy. She wanted to shield herself in some way, even if it was only with a thin layer of clothes. "I'm through," she said and stood.

Water sluiced down her body, sheening her with a luster he found hard to resist. Looking at her, he felt himself harden, but no matter what she said to the contrary, the fall had to have hurt her, and afterward, she had gone on to work ten straight hours. He would have to be a blind man not to see the exhaustion in her eyes.

When she stepped onto the bath mat, he reached for a large thick towel and wrapped it around her, then tucked the end of the towel between her breasts. It took him several moments to realize that his fingers were lingering.

Disturbed, he quickly pulled his hand away. She was too easy to touch, too easy to want. He needed to watch himself more carefully.

"Thanks," she murmured and brushed past him into the bedroom. There she went directly to the bureau inlaid with marquetry work that was set against one wall. From a drawer, she retrieved a candleglow-colored chemise and a matching pair of panties and slipped them on. When she turned to Richard, she found him already in bed, wearing only a pair of black briefs.

Excitement began to pound through her at the thought of the lovemaking that would come, and she realized how foolish she'd been to put anything on. While it was true she felt a little achy and more than a little vulnerable, she knew from past experience that when he took her in his arms, everything would go away except need of him. She crossed the room, slipped into bed beside him, and nestled against him with an unconscious naturalness.

He put his arm around her and drew her closer against him. "You smell like a secret flower garden," he whispered huskily against her hair.

"Secret?" she asked lightly, happier now that he was holding her.

He paused, wondering why he had used that word. Then an image came into his head of her in a breathtakingly lovely garden. She was the flowers, and the flowers were her, and he was the only one who knew her different fragrances. The strange and uncharacteristic image shook him badly.

"Wonderful," he amended. "You smell wonderful. You know," he went on, adopting her light tone with difficulty, "someone might make a fortune if they could bottle the scent of your skin."

She shifted the position of her head on his shoulder so that she could see him better. "I hate to tell you this, but the bath oil I use is available over the counter."

"Maybe what you put in your bath water can be purchased over the counter, but the way the chemistry of your skin reacts to it is unique." He hesitated as a thought occurred to him. "Do you have a flower garden at your house in France?"

"Yes." Now what were they talking about? she wondered, baffled. And why?

He lightly ran his fingers up and down her arm. "Tell me about your house."

"I already have."

"No, I mean *really* tell me about it. What are the rooms like? How have you furnished it?" He needed to be able to think of her there in the years ahead.

She was confused. Why was he here in bed with her if he didn't want to make love to her? The only other time they had been in bed together without making love was last night, but that had been because she had told him about her father's deception and how it had affected their lives. She understood why he wouldn't want to make love to her after hearing that. But why not now? Unless... Unless he was being considerate of her because of her fall.

"Liana?"

"I'm here."

He chuckled, and his hand briefly squeezed her arm. "That's good. So are you going to tell me about your house?"

"Well, there's not a lot to tell. I've furnished it with pieces I've found over the years, pieces of no particular style, but that fit together beautifully because they're simple and comfortable. And I have white lace curtains hanging at the windows. I enjoy the way they look when the windows are open and the breeze catches them." As she talked, she relaxed little by little, until her eyelids grew heavy and drifted shut. "There's a big stone fireplace in the parlor, and in the winter I keep a fire going there. I love cold, rainy afternoons, because that's when I pull a chair up to the fire and read. I love mysteries."

She grew sleepy and her words slowed and softened. "My kitchen is big—cool in the summer, warm in the winter. One of my favorite things to do in the winter is to make a big pot of stew, the kind that takes two days to make, the kind you keep adding ingredients to.... And every plate I have is different from the other."

He heard her trail off as she gave herself up to sleep. The corners of his mouth lifted slightly. A good night's sleep was just what she needed. She'd been under quite a strain this past week or so, what with her work and those damnable accidents. And he was sure his presence on the scene hadn't helped the state of her nerves any.

He adjusted his position so that she rested more comfortably against him. The sound of her soft, even breathing acted as a tranquilizer. In the distance, the eternal surge of the ocean provided a calming white noise. Now that she was asleep, he reflected, he could go to his own room....

He found himself staying. He didn't know why, but he felt a strange sort of contentment. Here in the night, holding Liana, there were no business pressures, no noises that jarred, no need to seek revenge. It was nice. More than nice, actually.

Too bad this contentment wouldn't last. He was scheduled to return to New York in a few days. All too soon the hostilities and struggles that layered a normal business day would resume. A frown creased his face. He supposed Liana would continue with her life, too. Did she have another modeling assignment lined up, he wondered, or would she return to her little house in France?

He stiffened as a thought occurred to him. Would there be more accidents when she left here? Maybe with even more dire results? He wouldn't be there to protect her. His frown deepened. Not that he had been able to protect her here.

But why would someone want to hurt her?

He gazed down at her again. Even in the half-light provided by the moon, he could see how thin and fragile she was. Her weight hardly made an impression on him. How could anyone deliberately set out to hurt her? He paused as he had a new thought. Wasn't that what he had set out to do? But then that was different, he assured himself. The thought of actual physical harm coming to her made him sick to his stomach.

He pressed his head back into the pillow and closed his eyes. *Dammit.* What was happening here? And why did he care so much?

RICHARD WASN'T SURE when he finally fell asleep, just as he wasn't sure what time it was when he was awakened by the feel of Liana's hands on him. She was caressing him with a touch that took him from sleep to wakefulness in seconds.

Her lips brushed across his chest to his nipple, and he stiffened when her tongue flicked the tiny bud. "Liana..." He gasped. "What are you doing?"

Her palm slid down his body, and she took him in her hand. "I want you," she whispered. "Do you mind?"

He groaned, then gritted his teeth as her hand began to rhythmically stroke him and her soft lips skimmed to his other nipple. The sensations were electric, exquisite, overwhelming. She was possessing him, applying just the right amount of pressure at exactly the right moment and place. His head went back into the pillow, and his back arched as his mind tried to deal with what was happening to him. Other women might have done the same thing, but none of them had ever come close to making him feel this searing, heart-pounding pleasure. *Lord.*

He pulled her on top of him, and without guidance, she slipped onto him. His body jerked at the instant, scorching-hot jolt of excitement her act gave him.

She was moaning now as she flexed and circled her hips against him. The fever that gripped his body moved to his brain. Through slitted eyes and the dim light, he could see her pale hair around her head and shoulders. Her breasts, full, taut and tempting swayed with her movements. He reached up and grasped them; the feel of their weight and satiny texture in his hands nearly took him over the edge. He lifted his head to hungrily suck one rigid nipple into his mouth, and the fire leaped higher in his gut.

"Liana," he said on a long drawn out breath, and his head fell back to the pillow. He was going wild with frustration and need. She was in control, and he found he loved it.

Her rhythm became faster. He arched up to her, time and time again, but she couldn't seem to get enough. She urged him on with whispered words and soft erotic sounds, inciting him to meet her demands.

Every breath he drew hurt, and there was an unbearable pressure in him that screamed to be released. Gripping her hips, he drove upward, using all the strength he had. With a distant part of his mind, he heard her cry out, then he, too, was crying out. Shuddering convulsively, he heard his cries go on and on, then waves of fulfillment began to break over him—too potent to be endured, too powerful to live without.

NINE

LIANA STRETCHED LAZILY, bathed by the early-morning sunshine that fell across the bed. When her arm brushed against Richard, she turned her head to look at him. He was still asleep.

Her heart filled to overflowing as she remembered what had happened between them just a few hours ago. Oh, she knew for him the preceding hours had been nothing more than just very good sex; but what he didn't know, would never know, was that she couldn't have made love to him so unreservedly if she didn't love him.

She remembered how in the middle of the night she had awakened clasped in his arms, and with her guard still lowered from her sleep, she had followed a natural urge. What had happened then had been unbelievable, and she would never forget it as long as she lived.

And in spite of their rigorous activities, she felt completely rested.

Following another impulse, she leaned over and planted a gentle kiss at the corner of his mouth. He opened his eyes; the softness in his gaze delighted her.

"Good morning," she murmured with a smile. "How do you feel?"

He lay his palm flat on her stomach and spread his fingers so that he was touching as much of her skin as possible. "I think the question should be, how do you feel?"

She stretched again, her hands above her head, her back arched, her breasts thrusting upward. "I feel *wonderful!*"

Without moving his hand, he stroked his thumb back and forth across the smooth, tender skin of her stomach. "Are you sore?"

"Only slightly," she said, relaxed again, but with her arms still above her head, "and since it came from such a pleasant activity, I don't mind at all."

The gray of his eyes darkened. Her breasts were inviting, perfect mounds, and so near to his mouth. It had been his intent to leave her alone this morning, but temptation overcame him. He bent his head and drew a waiting nipple into his mouth. *Lord.* What a fantastic way to start a day off! Her body gave him both energy and nourishment. Yet there was a problem, he reminded himself. No matter how hard he tried, he couldn't seem to get enough of her.

Last night, he had found something erotic and unbearably exciting about her being in control. But with the cold light of day came the reminder that he didn't like the helpless feeling his need for her gave him.

Her soft moan quickened his pulse, but he did his best to fight back the desire. He had to stop now, or he wouldn't be able to. Their lovemaking in the middle of the night had left him unnerved, and he needed time away from her to rebuild his defenses.

One final time, he drew on her breast. Then one more time.

"That was nice," she murmured a bit breathlessly, when he finally lifted his head. "Why did you stop?"

Wanting her as much as he did, her willingness for him to continue almost undid him. "Don't you have to get up?" he asked brusquely. "I mean, isn't Clay expecting you to be downstairs for the day's shoot?"

She ran her fingers lightly along his jaw and felt the roughness of his morning beard. "Not until later."

His head whipped back. "If I don't keep away from you, I'll give you whisker burns."

"I wouldn't mind."

"Dammit, Liana, your skin will be too red to be photographed." He was grasping at straws and he knew it.

Before, she might have let his irritation stop her. But last night had given her a new courage when it came to their lovemaking, and, she reasoned, the more memories she had to store away, the easier the long years ahead would be for her. "Haven't you ever heard of makeup?" she asked softly.

"Liana—"

"Please, Richard. I want you again."

With a harsh groan, he succumbed. "Then get ready, because you're going to need a ton of makeup—and not just on your face."

They made love, frantically, passionately, and later took a long, lingering shower together. And in spite of it all, they dressed in plenty of time for them to have breakfast.

LIANA HELD RICHARD'S arm as they descended the grand staircase and felt as though she were encompassed in a haze of passion and happiness.

Richard leaned over and whispered. "It's a good thing the shower water turned cold. Otherwise, Clay most certainly would have sent someone to find you, and when they came, you would have been as shriveled as a prune."

"But I'd be a happy prune."

In spite of the people milling in the hallway below them, he drew her to a stop on the next to the last stair and shook his head with wonder. "You're insatiable."

"Are you complaining?" she asked lightly.

"I love it," he murmured, his tone hoarse and thick. "I've already shown you how much I love it twice this morning, and if you'll say the word, I'll take you back upstairs and show you several more times."

A spike of heat lanced through her. "I wish we could, but I have to work."

He remained silent. When was he going to get enough of her? Stop wanting her? Stop needing her? And most of all, how was he going to be able to let her walk out of his life tomorrow?

She shook her head regretfully, seeming to follow his train of thought. "Today's our last day. Tonight's the ball."

He tensed. "Are you telling me you won't have any time to give me today or this evening?"

"That's not what I'm saying at all. I'm positive we'll knock off earlier than usual this afternoon, and the ball doesn't start until nine. In the meantime, though, I do need to work."

"Forget the work."

She looked at him oddly. He actually sounded as if he couldn't stand the thought of them being apart today. "We couldn't do anything together, anyway, Richard. You'll be busy with the art auction. That's why you came, remember?"

"I remember exactly why I came," he snapped, then stopped before he made a fool of himself. What was wrong with him? He actually sounded petulant because she wouldn't spend the day with him. To make matters worse, his body was already starving for her again. He *had* to get a grip on his emotions; being apart from her would be the best thing for him. Maybe he wouldn't even see her again before he left tomorrow.

But there were the accidents. He hadn't forgotten the possibility that someone was trying to harm her—or worse.

"Then you understand—"

He held up his hand. "Enough. You've convinced me."

She laughed. "Well, darn."

"You *wanted* me to talk you out of working?"

"No." She slipped her arms around his waist and looked up at him with an unconsciously provocative smile. "But I liked that you were trying to."

He groaned, half serious, half good-natured. "All I've got to say is that you're lucky we're surrounded by people."

"Why? What would you do?"

"Believe me, my mind is churning with ideas."

She laughed again.

"There's just one thing, Liana. Be careful today. Make sure anything you stand on is solid and well built. Don't even drink anything unless you see someone else pour a glass from the same container and drink it. Also, be extra careful about your makeup."

She gazed searchingly at him. "You're worried about me?"

His grin was meant to disarm. "I just don't want any more scars on that lovely body of yours. When I see bruises, I feel as if I have to handle you carefully."

His easy manner relaxed her. She grinned back. "Oh,

really? I hadn't noticed you handling me with any particular care. As a matter of fact, I distinctly remember—"

He leaned down and kissed her quiet. When he finished, she forgot what they had been talking about. "We better get to the dining room," she murmured, "or we're going to cause a scandal right here on the stairway."

He laughed, turning her so that they could take the final steps to the immense entry hall. "I'm sure SwanSea's walls have seen much more scandalous events."

"You're probably right," she said, then noticed Caitlin speaking with a group of people. Her wave produced a smile and a friendly nod of acknowledgment from Caitlin.

"Caitlin will be running six different ways today in preparation for tonight's ball," she said as they threaded their way around yet another group. SwanSea was at capacity.

"And don't forget the auction. Speaking of which, are you sure you won't let me buy you one of the paintings?"

"I'm sure. I told you—"

Richard stopped, his expression instantly hostile.

Curious, Liana followed his gaze. Jean-Paul Savion was walking toward them.

Her mouth fell open; she'd thought he was still ill and at his home in Paris.

But she wasn't the only woman in the hall who stared.

Dressed as always in his trademark black, Jean-Paul was a tall man, with heavy-lidded dark eyes and long black hair, pulled back and secured at the nape of his neck. SwanSea was filled with celebrities for the weekend, but Jean-Paul had a presence that tended to halt women in their tracks.

When he reached them, he leaned down to her and

kissed first one cheek, then the other. "Hello, *chérie*. Surprised?"

"Stunned, frankly. I thought you were too ill to travel."

"As you can see, I have recovered."

Actually, he didn't look at all recovered, she thought, but had no chance to say so.

He turned to Richard and raised his eyebrows in a manner both imperious and inquiring.

She couldn't imagine a worse time for this particular meeting to happen, she thought. But then again, she would be hard-pressed to come up with a good time. She tried to steel herself as best she could for what was to come. "Jean-Paul, this is Richard Zagan. Richard, Jean-Paul Savion."

Neither man made a move to shake hands, and each regarded the other with blatant antagonism and contempt.

Richard was the first to speak. "If you two will excuse me, I have a full day ahead of me."

She grabbed his arm. "But I thought we were going to have breakfast."

Richard pointedly fixed his gaze on Jean-Paul. "All at once, I've lost my appetite." And without another word, he whirled and stalked off.

Liana stared after him, unaware that her heart was in her eyes.

Jean-Paul regained her attention by taking her hand and tucking it into the crook of his arm. "I, personally, could eat a horse. Do you suppose, Liana, that they serve horse here?"

She gave a sigh, inaudible to all but the man beside her. "I'm sure all you have to do is ask, Jean-Paul."

SHE SIGNALED to the hovering waiter, then leaned back in her chair as he whisked her plate away. "All right,

Jean-Paul. I've eaten. You've eaten. You've given me your latest medical report. You've told me about your flight over on the Concorde, about the young girl you met and you think might be interesting to photograph. You've even told me about the small plane you rented to fly you from New York to here. Now, don't you think it's about time you tell me why you're here?"

He tossed his napkin onto the table and reached into the pocket of his black jacket for a long, slim cheroot and a gold lighter. Only after he had lit the cheroot and replaced the lighter did he answer her. "I am here because of you, *chérie.*"

"Me? I don't understand."

"Steve placed a call to me after you fell down the grand staircase. He seemed to think that the light could have been rigged to fall."

She rolled her shoulders uneasily. "I know. He told me, but the idea seemed so preposterous—"

"I thought so, too. I thought so, that is, until he called me and told me about Rosalyn's unfortunate reaction to the face powder. Except for a fluke, *chérie,* that powder would have been applied to your face."

"It was a strange allergic reaction. Chances are, if she had put it on my face, nothing would have happened."

He drew deeply on the cheroot, then exhaled a long stream of smoke. "Maybe you are right, maybe you are not. My guess is you are not."

She twisted in her seat. She should have been comforted by the fact that Jean-Paul was here and now she had someone to whom she could tell her fears. But she could only think about how furious Richard had been when he had seen Jean-Paul.

"It was Steve's call yesterday," he went on, "informing me of your fall from the ladder, that finally sent me to DeGaulle to catch the first available Concorde to the United States."

"Steve shouldn't have—"

"Steve did absolutely the right thing. The only thing that would have been better is if you, Liana, had called me yourself."

She fell silent.

Through a veil of smoke, he studied her. "I have never seen you more radiant," he said carefully. "I really hope you are going to tell me that Richard Zagan is not the cause."

"I'm afraid he is."

"Mon Dieu! Has he been here the whole time?"

She nodded. "At first the tension between us was thick enough to cut with a knife. Then—" she shrugged "—things just exploded."

"Exploded." His face twisted with anger, and he savagely put out the cheroot in a crystal ashtray. "The question is—are you going to get caught in the fallout?"

She met his gaze levelly. "Without a doubt."

"Then put an end to it, Liana. Put an end to it right now."

"It will end on its own soon enough."

He took in the set features of her face and sighed. "Then I guess while you are still radiant, I should photograph you."

"You're not going to take the shoot over from Clay are you? Not when we're so close to being finished."

"No, I'm not here to take over. But I *will* observe the final shoot today."

She shook her head. "You can't. It will shake Clay's confidence."

He leaned forward and jabbed the table with a finger. "Who the hell *cares* about Clay's confidence? What is important is that you remain safe."

"You can't do it, Jean-Paul. You know you can't. It wouldn't bother you one iota if another photographer watched over your shoulder. But then there are only a handful of photographers in the world as good as you. Clay will come apart if he thinks you're checking up on him."

"I *trained* him, Liana. He has had me present in the studio many times before."

"This is different. You trusted him enough to let him take this important assignment on his own, and he's done a very good job. Let him finish it."

"Merde!" Jean-Paul flung himself back against the chair.

She looked at him. "You know I'm right in this."

He held up a hand. "All right, all right. Maybe my presence will be enough to deter any more *accidents*. But, Liana, if I hear that so much as a hair on your head is harmed today, I will shut down not only the shoot, but this entire place."

His concern drew a smile from her, her first since she had seen him. "You look tired. Why don't you go up to your room and lie down?"

He rubbed his hand across his eyes. "I hate to admit it, but I think I'll have to do exactly that. This virus hasn't completely left my system yet."

She stood, walked around the table, and kissed his cheek. "Get some rest. I'll see you this evening."

THE DARK CLOUDS that gathered on the horizon during the afternoon set the mood for Clay, Liana and the rest of the crew, and when the thunder, lightning and rain came, the stormy atmosphere seemed right.

Even though Jean-Paul was as good as his word and did not show up at the conservatory where they were shooting, the knowledge that he had arrived was enough to affect everyone. Clay's nerves were evident in every order he gave, and his tension spread to the rest of the crew.

As for herself, Liana's strain increased by the minute. Richard's advice was always in the back of her mind. But how could she be on guard against the unexpected? And how could she tolerate the thought that there was someone who actually wanted to hurt her? By late afternoon, she had reached the point where she jumped every time anyone spoke to her.

She could attribute two of the accidents to herself, she decided. If she hadn't lost her concentration, she wouldn't have fallen down the stairs; and if she hadn't been driving so fast, she would have seen the debris. That left the ladder and the face powder. Wood rotted, it was as simple as that. And as for the powder, they would have to wait for the chemical analysis to determine what had gone wrong with it.

She loved Jean-Paul, but she wished with all her heart he hadn't come. She wanted these last hours with Richard to be spent happily, not in anger.

By the end of the afternoon, when Clay called, "That's all until tonight," Liana was more than ready to stop. She was tired, irritated, jittery, and unable to endure one more trauma, whether it be a touch or a loud voice.

She ducked behind the changing screen and quickly put on flats, taupe slacks and a bright red cotton, short-sleeved sweater. The rain had slackened to a fine mist, and she had ever intention of taking a walk. But when she emerged, Richard was waiting for her, and one look told her he was still as angry as he had been that morning.

His eyes glinted like ice crystals. "I really didn't expect to see you here."

His sarcasm had the same effect on her as the sound of nails on a chalkboard. "Where did you think I'd be?"

"With Savion, of course. After all, the two of you have been apart almost two weeks. I supposed he would want some *private* time with you. At the very least, I thought he would be here."

"Well, you were wrong on both counts, weren't you? Does that tell you anything?"

"What should it tell me?"

"Oh, I don't know. How about that your suspicions regarding Jean-Paul and me are wrong, in fact, have *always* been wrong?"

"Who has suspicions?" he asked harshly. "I have hard, cold knowledge, sweetheart. Remember? I was there when you went from my bed to his in one very short afternoon."

"I did no such thing!"

He stepped closer, invading and taking control of the air she was trying to pull into her lungs.

"Are you denying that you lived with Savion?"

In her peripheral vision she caught a glimpse of Sara and Clay, unabashedly eaves-dropping, but she was too upset for their presence to matter. "Yes, Richard, I did live with him. He took me in when I had no other place to go."

"Excuse me? What was wrong with where you'd been staying?"

"*You* were there. And I've already told you why I had to leave."

"Yeah. Right. Because you had fallen in love with me. I almost have that part straight. What still bothers me—only a little, you understand—is *why,* loving me as you say you did, you became Savion's lover."

"Dammit, I was *never* Jean-Paul's lover! I've told you that time and again."

"Then, dammit, why can't I believe you?"

"Because you're a fool!"

He raised his hand, and she instinctively recoiled, unsure whether he meant to strike her or caress her. Either act at this moment would have been intolerable to her. Suddenly he turned and walked swiftly from the conservatory.

The overwhelming need to escape seized her—she wanted to go somewhere, *anywhere* that was quiet, isolated, peaceful. She wheeled and ran out the back door of the conservatory.

It was growing darker, but she struck out across the grounds.

Damn Richard! One way or the other he had dominated her entire life. It had to stop. The deceit of her father had altered and affected both of their lives. But Richard knew everything now. Why couldn't he understand her side, see more clearly? *Why couldn't he love her?*

She had admitted her foolishness and her stupidity. Their only chance lay in his ability and willingness to let go of the past, but he refused. He seemed blocked about Jean-Paul.

The mist should have cooled her anger. The fast pace she walked should have relieved some of her tension. But she found herself growing more and more agitated. In her mind, *he* was the one who was now being foolish and stupid.

Some time later, she came to a stop in front of Leonora Deverell's crypt and blinked. What on earth was she doing here? Through the increasing darkness, she stared at the letters that spelled Leonora's name. Strangely, her mind went back in years and distance to Paris and another Leonora she had met about a year after she had left Richard. When she had told him that the Leonora she had known there had given up everything for love, he had said he didn't believe in love.

Still, he had shown concern for her safety last night. And today he had been *jealous.* Good heavens! Why hadn't she seen it before? He was wildly jealous of Jean-Paul, even after all these years. He *had* to care!

Hope once more sprang to life within her, but she tried to remain cautious. She had gone through so many highs and lows since she had been here at SwanSea, she wasn't sure how much more she could take.

But Richard had shown tenderness and concern for her. And time and again, he had made love to her as if starving for her. *And* he had displayed unreasonable jealousy. If those weren't the signs of a man in love, what were? Even if he didn't know it.

She had to go to him. Somehow she had to get through is hurt and pride and reach his heart. She would go to him now.

Something sharp struck the back of her head. Leonora's name blurred in front of her eyes, and her knees buckled. She fell to the ground and heard an odd creaking sound of rusty hinges. Fighting against the darkness that threatened to suck her down into it, she tried to make sense of what was happening. But steel-muscled arms gripped her around the waist and dragged her across wet grass, up steps, into a building, finally leaning her against a concrete wall.

Even as she heard the creaking sound again, she struggled to get up. But dizziness overcame her, and she lost her footing. Once more she was falling, and she couldn't stop. She tumbled down a short series of steps, halting only when she struck the side of her head against the hard floor.

Unconsciousness claimed her.

And she didn't hear the scraping of the heavy concrete urn as it was rolled in front of the crypt's doors, sealing her in.

TEN

CLAY SMILED, FEELING a huge sense of relief as he turned away from the crypt and started back to the hotel. At last, something he had done had worked. And in the end, it had been luck rather than elaborate planning that had helped him achieve the goal of putting Liana out of commission long enough to have Sara replace her as the model on this shoot.

Knowing that his time was running out, he'd been racking his brain, trying to decide what he could do next. Jean-Paul's arrival had had him convinced he should abandon his plans. Then two things happened. During his quick visit with Savion this morning, he had seen that the great man wasn't as well as he would like everyone to believe. Then Liana and Zagan had had that argument. Afterwards, Liana had been so upset, she hadn't even noticed him following her. And luck had again been with him when she had gone to the cemetery, and he had happened to notice that with very little effort he could break the crypt's rusty lock.

He hadn't really hurt her, of course. She was only stunned. She would spend an uncomfortable night, but that couldn't be helped. By morning, if she hadn't been found, he would "discover" her. She would be fine, just fine.

Naturally it would have been better if one of the

other little accidents he had planned for her had been successful. If she had broken an arm when she had fallen down the stairs, for instance, or if she had used the face powder and developed a rash, he would have had more of an opportunity to photograph Sara.

Yet the ball was the culmination of SwanSea's grand opening and that would work to his advantage. Once the shots he planned to take tonight were seen, he would be able to persuade the publications involved to use a greater number of them than those previously taken. He could even help matters along by exposing several rolls of film, thereby losing quite a few of Liana's shots.

Yes, that's what he would do.

RICHARD PULLED the phone away from his ear and glared at it. Liana still wasn't answering in her room. Either she hadn't returned, or she was ignoring the messages he was leaving with the hotel operator. He slammed the phone back into its cradle.

He supposed he couldn't blame her if she was ignoring his messages. He had hurt her and made her angry, then stormed out of the conservatory.

But that had been a little after six, and it was now nine-thirty. *Where was she?*

He shouldn't have argued with her, he reflected grimly, but just the thought of her and Savion made him deaf, dumb and blind.

He raked his fingers through his hair, disgusted with himself. A new idea had been steadily growing in him, the idea that he was dead wrong—about Liana and Savion being lovers, about allowing the bitterness of the past eleven years to interfere with the present and the future and, most importantly, about there not being any such thing as love.

Dammit, he'd give her ten more minutes, then he was going to go looking for her.

THE PAIN... Liana moaned, her head throbbed; why didn't it stop? Slowly and with great difficulty, she lifted her hand to her forehead and touched something sticky.

She was lying on concrete, she realized, then shivered. Lord, she was cold. She needed to get off the floor. If only her head didn't hurt so much.

Time seemed to pass—she had no idea how much. But she was still on the floor, she noticed. She rolled over and bumped against something concrete...a wall? No, because she could feel a corner biting into her shoulder. She levered herself into a sitting position and skimmed her hand upward, over concrete, then to wood. Wood? Her fingers found the upper edge of what seemed to be a large wooden box and curled over the top. Taking a grip, she tried to pull herself up. But the wood broke off and fell to the floor with a crash. She flinched at the loud noise and slumped back down, the dizziness and pain almost overwhelming.

Where was she?

Then she remembered. The sharp pain at the back of her head, Leonora's name blurring in front of her eyes, someone dragging her into a building. *She was in Leonora's crypt!* And she was leaning against the concrete slab on which Leonora's coffin rested!

A sob escaped her, but she quickly clamped her hand over her mouth to stifle it. Was the person who did this to her in here with her? Her heart slammed against her ribs at the thought, and a new kind of chill gripped her—the chill of terror.

But she refused to give into the fear. She searched the darkness of the small burial house until she was assured that she was alone. Good. What now? Think, Liana. Think.

It wasn't pitch-black, she realized. In fact, she could see a pale sliver of moonlight. The mist must have cleared. The doors! They must be ajar!

It took her several tries before she was able to stand. She stumbled on the stairs, but finally made it to the source of the light.

She pushed against the doors; they didn't budge. Frantically, she pushed harder. Nothing. Something was blocking the doors.

Tears filled her eyes and she slid down the door to the floor. She was entombed with Leonora Deverell.

PROPPED AGAINST a pile of pillows, Jean-Paul glanced at his watch. Dammit, it was after ten. Why hadn't Liana called him? He had left message after message for her, yet he hadn't heard from her. He knew for a fact the work had been over for hours.

There was only one answer: she had to be with Zagan.

With a muffled curse, he reached for a cheroot and lit it.

He had never known what had happened eleven years ago between the two of them. He only knew, no matter what she said, that she hadn't healed from their love affair. Sometimes when she thought he wasn't looking, he would catch a brief glimpse of pain in her eyes. The bastard had better not hurt her again!

Dammit, but this infection made him feel so powerless! He had come here to help her, and look at him! He had been reduced to leaving messages in between his naps. But *what if something had happened to her?*

A knock sounded at the door, and hopeful that it was Liana, he sat up. "Come in."

"Thank you," Richard said, walking in, his tone anything but polite.

Jean-Paul's black eyebrows drew together in a scowl. "What the hell do you want?"

Richard's gaze scanned the room, then came back to rest on Jean-Paul. "I want to know where Liana is."

With an insouciance he hoped would madden Zagan, Jean-Paul settled himself comfortably against the pillows and took a long draw on his cheroot. "Assuming I knew, do you think I would tell you?"

Richard's first impulse was to drag the man from the bed and beat the information out of him. But the other man's obviously weakened condition made that choice impossible; there would be no triumph in winning such a one-sided struggle. Besides, instinct told him winning the mental battle would be the greater victory.

He chose a chair and sat down. "You and Liana are very close, aren't you?"

Jean-Paul bared his teeth in a mockery of a smile. "Very."

"Frankly, I expected to find her here."

"And if you had found her here, what meaning would you have applied to it?"

Richard crossed his legs, resting the ankle of one leg over the knee of the other leg. "That is none of your business."

"Probably not, but I know the answer all the same. Tell me, Zagan, what has Liana told you about us?"

"That you and she have never been lovers."

"Yet I would be willing to wager that you believe we have been and probably still are."

Richard stared impassively at Jean-Paul. He had viewed this man as an adversary for so long that he couldn't bring himself to admit what he was saying had been true up until a short time ago.

Jean-Paul exhaled a long stream of smoke. "I find your attitude truly remarkable. I've known Liana slightly longer than you have, and I've always found that, though she sometimes keeps things to herself, she never lies."

Richard's anger grew—not at Savion, but at the circumstances that had made it possible for this man to know more about Liana than he did. He stood and shoved his hands into his pockets. "Are you going to tell me where she is?"

"Whatever happened between the two of you," Jean-Paul went on in a calm voice as if Richard hadn't spoken, "hurt her badly. When she came to me, she was in pieces. I did the only thing I could do. I gave her work. Night and day, using any excuse I could think of, I photographed her. I wore her out so that she could sleep at night. And when she was awake, I worked her so hard, she sometimes forgot to think of you for minutes at a time. The side benefit was that the haunting, mysterious sadness I captured with those pictures intensified her beauty and catapulted both of us to fame."

"How lucky for you," Richard said woodenly.

"Yes, it was. And for Liana, too. She didn't have you anymore, but she had success. Ironic, isn't it? In some strange way, I might actually owe you a debt of gratitude, which is one of the reasons, Zagan, if I knew where she was, I would tell you. Another reason why I would tell you is that I fear she is in some sort of danger and I don't like the idea of her being out somewhere by herself. It might not be safe, and I'm too damned weak to go looking for her."

A confirmation of his own fears didn't improve Richard's mood. "There's no need for you to look. Now that I know she's not here, I'll find her."

Jean-Paul waited until Richard had almost reached the door before he spoke again. "I put her back together once, Zagan. I don't want to have to do it again."

Richard quietly shut the door after himself.

THE ORCHESTRA SWUNG into the upbeat Gershwin tune, "I've Got Rhythm," and some of the richest, most influential people in America began to dance.

Clay viewed Sara through the lens of his camera and felt a special thrill of satisfaction. Sara had never understood why he loved to photograph her. But he had seen something in her no one else had. An intriguing woman lay beneath the shy child, and in his camera lens, her fresh loveliness would be illuminated for all the world to see.

The magnificent gold and silver ballroom was beginning to fill. At his instructions, Sara was posed against a pillar, wearing a black velvet gown that might have been fitted on Liana, but looked as if it had been made for Sara. She didn't seem happy, he noted, but once they got started, he would be able to cajole her into the right mood. He planned to capture her in her stillness and black gown and frame her with the ball's color and movement.

She was going to do for his career what Liana had done for Jean-Paul's.

"Clay, do you know where Liana is?"

Richard Zagan's voice held a dangerous edge, cutting in on Clay's euphoric mood. A wary glance over his shoulder told him the man was in a black mood. "As it happens, I don't. Now if you would excuse us, we've got work to do."

Richard took Clay by the shoulders and forcibly turned him around. "I'll excuse you after I've gotten the answers I want. Isn't Liana supposed to be modeling tonight?"

"Yes, but as you can see, she didn't show up, so we're having to start without her."

Richard glanced at Sara. She looked pretty, he thought, but not as lovely as Liana would in the same dress. He returned his gaze to Clay. "Have you tried to find Liana?"

Clay felt one corner of his mouth twitch and tried to relax. Nothing could go wrong now. Not when he was so close to achieving his goal. "I don't understand why you're upset. It's obvious what's happened. After your argument with her in the conservatory earlier, she packed up and left."

"She wouldn't have left, knowing how important these last shots were, at least not without telling someone," Sara said, speaking up unexpectedly. "She's too professional."

"I agree," Richard said, "and I repeat my question."

Clay could feel his control slipping and drew a deep breath. "The answer is yes. Steve and Rosalyn insisted on going to look for her. I told them there was nothing to worry about and that I needed them, but—oh, good, there they are now. Steve, I need you to adjust that light—"

"Did you find her?" Richard asked Steve.

The younger man shook his head. "We even had a bellhop let us into her room."

"Her clothes are still there," Rosalyn said, "but there was no sign of her."

Clay wanted to scream. *Why didn't these people just let it go, for God's sake!* Didn't they understand the importance of what he was doing? "Liana will show up when she's ready to."

Richard turned on him. "You just said she'd packed up and left."

Clay threw up his arms. "How do I know where she is? All I know is I've got to get this shoot underway. And if she's not professional enough to show up, there are others who can replace her."

Richard had never liked Clay, and if he hadn't felt every moment was important, he would have decked him. He started to leave, but felt something stopping him. He turned back to Clay. "There's just one more thing. Have you gotten back the analysis of the face powder?"

"Not yet. I probably should follow up to make sure my friend received it. The mail is so unreliable." He turned to Sara and Steve. "In the meantime, people, we've got to get underway."

Ignoring Clay, Steve gazed at Richard. "I'll help you look for her."

"I will, too," Sara said.

Richard shook his head. "Thanks, but I'll find her."

WIND WHISTLED through the iron structure of the gazebo, emphasizing its emptiness. Richard slammed his hand against a wrought-iron support. Dammit! Where was Liana?

Anxiously, he stared out at the night. Fortunately, the sky had cleared and he wasn't having trouble seeing, but the air was cool, and the grass had been damp beneath his feet as he had walked. Was she cold, he wondered. Was she hurt?

His mind refused to take that next awful step of imagination and wonder if she were dead. She *had* to be all right.

Lord, Liana, where are you?

Outside of her hotel room, they had been so few places together. Where would she go? Or, God forbid, where would someone take her? His jaw tightened at the thought. Confidence aside, he would give himself only a short time to find her, and then he would contact the police.

He could hear the music being played in the ballroom. "Embraceable You." He had never noticed before, but it was really a lovely song. If Liana were here, he thought, he would take her in his arms and dance with her. They had never danced, but he knew she would be light, graceful, exquisite to hold. They would dance as long as they both wanted. Then they would make love.

The afternoon he had found her here, he had taken her down to the cushioned bench, kissed her, touched her. That had been his first indication of how much he had still loved her, only he had been too blind to see it then and too proud to admit that love even if he had seen it.

Liana had been right this afternoon. He *was* a fool. If he had acknowledged even a particle of his love, he might have her with him now.

He remembered the puzzled looks Rosalyn and Steve had given him at the confident way he had said he would find Liana. They might wonder where his certainty came from, he thought grimly, but he knew he had no alternative. He *had* to find Liana. He couldn't live the rest of his life without her.

CHILLED TO THE BONE, her head dully aching, Liana sat down on the inner steps of the crypt. She hugged herself for comfort and warmth, unable to remember how it felt not to be cold or have her head hurt.

She also didn't know how long she had been staring at the long, boxy shape of Leonora's coffin just a short distance away.

From the first, she'd been affected by the tragic story of the young Leonora. Her interest hadn't made sense then, nor did it now, but her heart still went out to the woman. Her happiness had been cut so short, and now there was no one left alive who mourned her. Except her, Liana thought. And now she was sharing her burial place.

She touched the dried blood caked at her temple. During the long hours she had been there, she had fought against the pain and the cold, but most of all she had fought against the fear. She supposed under the circumstances it would be natural for her to believe that she was fated to die here. Actually, though, this experience had made Liana want happiness all the more.

The Leonora she had known in Paris had told her that one day she would find true love. Well, she had already found it. She had been foolish enough to let go of that love once, but never again.

She refused to die there. She had too much living to do yet, too much loving. She formed an image in her mind of Richard and concentrated on it with everything that was in her. He was her heart, her life. He would come for her.

A long time later, she heard movement outside. Just for a moment, she had to fight back the terror that the person who had put her in there had come back. But almost as soon as the terror came, it vanished. Somehow she knew it was Richard.

"Liana? Are you in there?"

She scrambled to her feet, almost losing her balance again in her eagerness to get to the doors. "Richard?"

"Liana? Dear God, you *are* in there! Are you all right?"

"Yes, yes, I'm fine."

"Hang on, honey, I'll have you out in just a minute."

There was the sound of the concrete urn being pulled away, then the doors were opened, and Richard stepped inside and swept her into his arms. He crushed her to him, trembling with relief and happiness that he was finally holding her again.

Her skin felt cold, but she was alive and breathing. He felt as if he had just been delivered from a lifetime sentence in hell. He buried his face in her hair and breathed in her scent. He didn't want to let her go, not now, not ever, but finally, supporting her with his hands on her arms, he pulled back and looked down at her. "Are you really all right?"

"I think so," she said, unable to prevent her voice from shaking.

"What happened? Who put you in here?"

"I don't know who. They stunned me by hitting me in the back of the head, then they dragged me in here. I guess water from the rain we had earlier had seeped beneath the doors. When I tried to get up, I slipped down the stairs and hit my head on the floor. I'm not sure how long I was out. What time is it?"

He glanced at the luminescent dial of his watch. "One-thirty in the morning. Lord, Liana, you've been trapped in the crypt all this time?" At her nod, he swung her up into his arms and held her close. "Let's get out of here."

"I can't think of anything I'd like more," she murmured. But as he turned with her, she glanced over his shoulder, unable to resist the compulsion to have one more look at the eternal resting place of Leonora Deverell, the place that could so easily have become her own tomb.

Moonlight illuminated the inside of the crypt with an eerie silver light, enabling her to see that the entire end panel of the coffin had fallen to the ground and opened the interior of the coffin to view.

Her breath caught in her throat.

RICHARD CARRIED Liana clutched closely to his heart and entered SwanSea by the front doors. Because the ball was still going on, he wasn't surprised to see that the entry hall was empty except for a small staff at the desk tucked discreetly off to the side. But he was surprised to see Jean-Paul and Clay come into the hall through a side door, talking heatedly.

"Dammit," Clay was saying, "you gave this assignment to me, now let me do it."

Pale, but determined, Jean-Paul towered over Clay. "As soon as you answer some of my questions."

"I don't have time for this. Sara, Rosalyn and Steve are back in the ballroom waiting for me."

"And where is Liana?"

"How the hell should I know?"

Richard glanced down at Liana. Her eyes were closed, her dark lashes lay against the almost colorless skin of her cheeks. When he found the person who had done this to her... He looked back at the two men. "Here she is." Clay and Jean-Paul both jerked around toward them. Jean-Paul's expression was of utter relief. Clay's expression, very briefly, was of anger.

Jean-Paul rushed toward them. "Mon Dieu, you have found her! Liana, what happened to you? Are you all right?"

She opened her eyes. "You look awful, Jean-Paul. You should be in bed."

"Bah! I have been there all day. I couldn't stand the wait one more moment, so I came down to see what I could do."

Richard's mouth quirked with faint amusement. "You didn't trust me to tell you I had found her, did you?" he asked, still keeping an eye on Clay who had slowly crossed the distance to them.

Jean-Paul's dark brows rose. "And would you have told me?"

"Eventually." Richard smiled briefly before turning his attention to Clay. "How is your shoot going?"

"Fine." Clay cast a disgruntled glance at Jean-Paul. "Or at least it was."

"You knew, didn't you?" Richard's suddenly quiet voice carried such murderous intent, each word was like a knife thrown.

Jean-Paul stilled.

"Knew what?" Clay asked warily.

"Knew where Liana was—because you put her there, didn't you?"

Liana stiffened, and he tightened his arms around her, trying to reassure her. "I'll take you to your room in just a minute," he whispered.

"I had my suspicions," Jean-Paul said, his expression stricken, "but I didn't want to accuse without proof."

"I'm sure you also didn't want to believe that your protégé could do something like this."

"Why?" Liana whispered. "Why, Clay?"

"I didn't want to hurt you," Clay said, his words coming out in a rush, "but I needed for Sara to be the model here. No matter how brilliantly my pictures of you would be, Liana, I could never gain fame by photographing you. You would photograph beautifully in the dark, and everyone in the business knows it. But Sara was an unknown—"

"Did she know what you were doing?" Jean-Paul asked, interrupting, plainly over feeling bad that Clay could have done such a thing. He was angry now, and it showed in the coldness of his black eyes.

"No. She's always been reluctant to let me take pictures of her, but I knew she couldn't refuse if I put her in the position of saving the assignment."

"Did you rig the light to fall?"

"Yes, yes," he said, his impatient tone implying they were asking all the wrong questions. What was important here was his work. "And I added a caustic ingredient to the powder. I just wanted you out of commission for the rest of the shoot, Liana. I didn't want to seriously hurt you."

Richard was having a hard time keeping the rage he felt under control, and because he was, he spoke softly. "What about the nails and boards on the road?"

"No. The only other thing I did was tamper with the ladder. I had the second ladder so that Sara would be sure to take the one whose rung I had broken. You couldn't even tell that I had broken the rung, then glued it back together, could you?" His eyes shone with excitement as he turned back to Jean-Paul. "I want you to see the work I've done tonight, Jean-Paul. I think you'll agree it's extraordinary. I knew that out of everyone, you would be the one to understand. Nothing is more important to you than your work."

"You *damned* fool."

Liana shut her eyes and turned her face into Richard's chest. He was torn. He wanted to rip Clay limb from limb, but Liana was his first consideration. She had been through more than enough already.

"I'll take care of it," Jean-Paul said.

Even though it seemed Jean-Paul sensed some of what he was feeling, Richard's old prejudices automatically reared, making him hesitate. But the woman in his arms and the love he had for her forced him to look at Savion without the blinders of his jealousy, and what he saw reassured him. Savion had a toughness, a fortitude and a gritty type of integrity that transcended the physical strain he was under. Richard finally nodded, accepting that Savion would do whatever was necessary. He loved Liana, too.

But she was going to be *his* wife.

He carried her to the elevator.

ELEVEN

LIANA AWOKE TO a sun-filled room, the softness of the four poster bed, and Richard, lying beside her, gazing at her.

With a gentle smile, she reached out to stroke the stubble of his morning beard. "How long have you been watching me?"

"Most of the night. I didn't want anything more to happen to you." He took her fingers and kissed each tip. "When I think of what you must have gone through..."

"It's over, Richard. Besides, I knew you would find me."

He smiled. "Did you? I don't know where your confidence came from, but somehow I felt I would find you, too. I *had* to find you."

Her face shadowed. "Clay..."

"I've already spoken with Savion this morning. Clay was taken away last night. What happens to him will depend on the courts and maybe even the doctors. But like you said, it's over. It's time for us to go on."

She searched his eyes, saw the warmth and tenderness, and remembered the hope she had felt yesterday evening before Clay had closed her in the crypt. "There are some things I'd like to say to you."

"No, let me go first. Looking back on that day in Paris

when you left, I realize now I should have gone after you. I don't usually let anything get in the way of what I want. But with you, I couldn't think rationally. If I had, I would have realized that what we had together those two weeks was the real thing and you had to have had another reason. But instead of trying to find out that reason, or even trying to change your mind, I set my pride and ego above my happiness and fooled myself into believing I would be fine without you. But Lord was I wrong! I loved you then, Liana, and I love you now." His voice broke. "With all my heart, with all my soul."

She had had hope, but hearing the actualization of her dream stunned her. "You do?"

"If you weren't hurt, I would show you how much."

"I'm fine," she whispered, sliding her arms around his neck. "Show me."

Regretfully, he shook his head. "You've been hurt."

"Your love is the best medicine I could possibly have."

He groaned. For her sake, he shouldn't let her seduce him like this, but he was helpless in the face of his love and his need for her. After the terror and uncertainty of last night, when he hadn't know where she was or in what condition he would find her, he *needed* to make love to her. It would be a celebration of life and of their future. But...

"I love you, Richard," she murmured, unknowingly ending his hesitation.

He kissed her gently, touched her softly. He gathered up all the tenderness, love and passion of which he was capable and poured it over her. He felt her tremble and trembled with her. When her skin heated, his did, too. When she moaned, he followed with one of his own.

They were together in every possible way. Nothing

was forced; everything came naturally. Each moment that passed was treated as precious, each word that was spoken was valued. Like a flower receiving its first spring rain, she soaked up everything he gave her, then blossomed and returned it to him tenfold.

LIANA WAS GONE. Richard knew it even before he came completely awake. Panicked, he sat straight up in bed and shot a look around the room. Empty! She couldn't have left him, not now, now when it seemed they had found happiness. He glanced at the clock. He had only been asleep an hour. What could have happened?

He was standing, zipping up his pants, when she walked out of the bathroom, dressed. The relief he felt was so profound he almost collapsed back onto the bed.

"What's wrong?" she asked, instantly concerned because of the odd expression on his face.

He went to her and took her into his arms. "You're going to have to be patient with me. I'm paranoid where you're concerned. We've been through so much...."

"I understand," she said quietly. "I have the same fears. We're not going to lose what we have ever again."

For her and with effort, he grinned. "I'll work on taking you for granted."

With a laugh, she stood on her tiptoes and kissed him. "Let's not go quite that far."

"It looks like you're going somewhere. Why didn't you wake me?"

"I didn't want to bother you. Besides, I wasn't planning to be gone that long."

"Where *are* you going?" he asked, reaching for a shirt.

Her brow knitted, not at his question, but at an inner

thought. "I need to speak to Caitlin. Something's bothering me, and I'm hoping she can help clear it up."

"Well, wherever you're going, I'm going with you. From now on, that's the rule. We've been apart too long. If you want to go on an out-of-town assignment, I'll go with you. If I have to go out of town on business, you'll go with me. We're never going to be apart again."

His vehemence surprised her and her heart threatened to overflow with happiness. "I'm going to like that rule."

They left the room, hand in hand, and walked down the hall to the elevator. When it glided to a smooth stop on the fourth floor and the doors opened, Caitlin was waiting for them.

She anxiously scanned Liana. "You've had the worst time here, and I feel just awful about it."

Liana laughed lightly. It felt good to laugh so easily and so often. "Don't give it another thought. It wasn't your fault." She glanced at Richard. "Besides, when I look back on my stay here, I guarantee I will remember only the good things that have come out of it."

Caitlin's gaze darted back and forth between Liana and Richard, noting their joined hands, and placing the obvious interpretation on the situation. She slowly smiled. "In that case, I feel better. Now, what was it you wanted to ask me?"

"It's about Leonora Deverell, the first mistress of SwanSea."

"Yes. What about her?"

"Is there a portrait of her somewhere?"

"As a matter of fact, I've only recently had her portrait brought down from the attic and cleaned. I had it hung in my suite. Would you like to see it?"

"Very much."

Liana glanced at Richard. He looked distinctly puzzled, and she squeezed his hand. "I don't want to say anything until I'm sure." The returning squeeze of his hand told her he accepted her wish not to explain further right now. It might have been only a small sign of trust to some, but she knew it was a forerunner of all the faith and confidence that would grow between them in the coming years.

Caitlin led them to a set of double doors at the end of the hall to a suite decorated, like the rest of the hotel, completely in the art nouveau period.

Over the mantel hung a portrait of a young woman with lovely, aristocratic features, wearing a blue dress that frothed around her ankles like a summer cloud. Her soft eyes held a tinge of sadness, but her smile was sweet and hopeful.

Liana smiled back in recognition.

Though many years had passed from the time the portrait had been painted until the time Liana had known her, the woman's sweet smile, her soft eyes, and most of all the aristocratic bone structure of her face had remained the same. "Leonora," she whispered.

Misunderstanding, Caitlin nodded. "That's right."

"Liana," Richard said slowly, his eyes narrowing on the sight of the exquisite lily pinned at the young woman's breast, "that's your brooch."

"Your brooch?" Caitlin said, startled. "You mean *this* is where I'd seen it? But that couldn't be. All of the jewelry has stayed in the family. We haven't sold or given any away. How would you have gotten Leonora's brooch?"

"She gave it to me."

"That's impossible. She died in 1898."

"I knew her, Caitlin."

"You mean this Leonora is the same Leonora who was your neighbor in Paris?" Richard asked. "The old lady who gave you the brooch?"

"That's right. Maybe we'd better sit down while I explain."

She settled onto the settee and waited while Richard came down beside her and Caitlin chose a chair. Then she began.

"Leonora Redmond was one-hundred-and-one years old when I moved in next door to her. She was bedridden, but very alert, and we grew close. She told me that at seventeen she had married an older man because it was expected of her by her family. She had done her duty and tried hard with the marriage, but love between them never grew. Only his business and the great house he had built were important to him.

"One summer, four years after her wedding, her husband hired a young painter to come to the house and paint her portrait. His name was Wyatt Redmond. They fell in love, but Leonora viewed their affair as hopeless and sent the young man away. He left around midsummer and went home to Paris. But once there he quickly came to understand that he would never be able to live without her and booked the first passage back. He told Edward he had returned to finish the portrait, but his real intent was to convince Leonora to leave her husband and run away with him. He had also brought with him a present for her—the lily he had bought in Paris from the workshop of René Lalique. It was the only piece of jewelry she took with her when she left."

Caitlin had been listening closely. "But I still don't

understand. If she fled to Paris with her lover, who is buried in her crypt?"

"No one. I was there, last night, remember?" The thought made her reach over and take Richard's hand again. Before this morning, she hadn't known how comforting it was to hold the hand of the man you loved. "When I awoke on the floor, I tried to hold on to the coffin to help myself up—although at the time I didn't know what it was. But the wood must have been so rotten, it gave way, and I heard it crumble to the floor. When Richard opened the doors, the moonlight streamed in, and I was able to see that the coffin is empty." She paused. "I thought it was love that had made Edward set Leonora's crypt apart from the others. Now I understand. It was bitterness."

"But why would any man go through a mock funeral for his wife," Richard asked, "knowing full well she was still alive?"

"I can answer that part," Caitlin said. "Because of pride. What I know of Edward came from listening to my grandfather, Jake, talk of him. I learned that Edward was a hard, driven man of enormous pride. I'm sure it never occurred to him that Leonora would leave him, and when she did, he would have been quite disconcerted and mortified. His number-one priority would have been not to get her back, but to hide the fact from society that his wife had left him for another man."

"Pride," Richard murmured softly. It seemed he and Edward Deverell had something in common.

"And I know for a fact," Caitlin said, continuing, "that Edward wouldn't have let her take John."

"Who was John?" Richard and Liana asked simultaneously.

"Their only child."

Liana slowly nodded. "That must have been her regret. She never spoke of her child to me, but she did tell me that when her husband died in 1929, she and Wyatt married. Wyatt achieved only a modest success with his painting, but according to Leonora, they lived very happily until his death in the early nineteen-seventies."

"This is a remarkable story, Liana," Caitlin said, shaking her head in amazement. "I can't wait to tell my family. I've learned the most interesting things about my ancestors since I've inherited SwanSea."

"It seems both Edward and Leonora chose to live with deceit all their lives," Liana said thoughtfully, still caught up in the story. Suddenly she turned to Richard and a look of understanding passed between them. They had been through their own years of deceit, but they had been lucky enough to come out on the other side of those years with love.

"In the end, Edward died a lonely man," Caitlin said.

"And Leonora obviously found a peace of sorts and a happiness," Liana said. "But poor John never really knew his mother. To leave your child has to be the hardest decision any woman has to make. Leonora must have been desperate. She must have felt as if she would shrivel up and die if she stayed here at SwanSea."

Caitlin nodded. "Knowing what I know of the hard man Edward was, I would agree with you. At least she would have had the comfort of knowing that Edward would give his son everything she couldn't. It's not a decision you or I would make, but then I don't feel I should judge Leonora. Only she knew what her life was like."

Liana glanced at Richard, and they both came to their feet. "I feel like going for a walk in the sunshine, maybe out to the gazebo. Caitlin, do you think we could have our breakfast served at the gazebo?"

The current mistress of SwanSea smiled. "Well, I seem to recall telling you to ask for anything that you wanted. I'm sure we can manage it. Just tell me that you will come back to SwanSea one day soon."

"You can count on it," Richard said.

HALFWAY BETWEEN the great house of SwanSea and the gazebo, Liana and Richard stopped and turned to each other. The day was clear, the light almost incandescent. The sun bathed the two of them and all of SwanSea in its warmth, making it hard for them to believe there had ever been shadows.

Richard's gaze was adoring and cherishing. "When I think of how easily our lives could have been destroyed by pride and deceit..."

"I know, but it didn't happen. We both came here, scarred and in pain, but we'll be leaving together. We have our love back, and it's deeper and all the stronger for what we've been through."

"Thank God."

A tremor shuddered through him that she felt in her own body.

"I'll never have to spend another lonely night," he said. "You'll be there—your soft voice, your incredible beauty, *you.*"

She smiled, a different smile, a special smile. "There might be a baby there with us, too, one conceived here at SwanSea. Have you thought of that?"

He chuckled. "Thought of it, hoped for it, prayed for it. But if it doesn't happen now or in the future, my life will still be complete. If children come, I will feel that much more blessed, but you are all I'll ever want or need."

The timeless rhythm of the sea surged behind them. She had come to love the sound and this place. But there was also another place. "Can we fly to France? I want to show you my little house."

"We'll spend our honeymoon there, and in the years ahead, if children come, we'll take them there."

"I love you," she whispered to him.

"I love you," he whispered back to her.

AT THE GAZEBO, the wind wound in and out of the decorative ironwork, smoothing across the green-and-blue cushions, picking up a single feather of a tiny sea bird and sweeping it down the steps.

Today, if there were tears heard here, they would be tears of happiness. And there would also be laughter. Most of all, though, there would be love.

Everything you love about romance...
and more!

Please turn the page for Signature Select™
Bonus Features.

SWANSEA LEGACY

4 A conversation with Fayrene Preston

8 About Art Nouveau

10 Sneak Peek: SWANSEA PLACE: THE PROMISE by Fayrene Preston

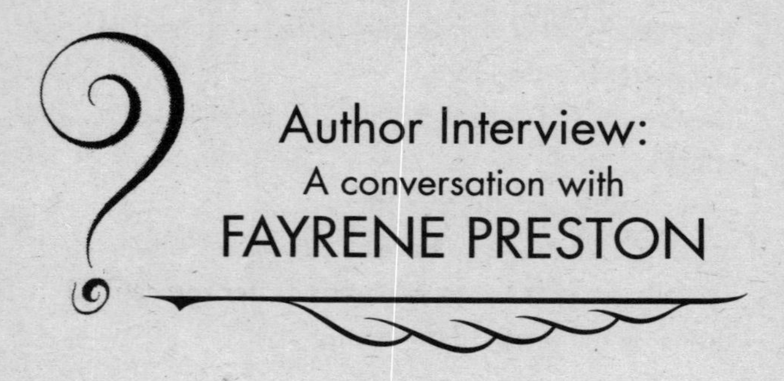

Author Interview:
A conversation with FAYRENE PRESTON

Tell us a bit about how you began your writing career.

My writing career began with my absolute addiction to reading every romance I could get my hands on. At that point, back in the seventies, I hadn't even thought once about writing romance. But I read so fast that I kept running out of books to read. At one point, just to save my sanity, I sat down and began writing a romance. It was for my own enjoyment, never to see the light of day. When the next month's books arrived in the stores, I put my story away, and went back to reading.

It wasn't until several years later, at the suggestion of a friend, that I brought the partially written book out, polished it up a bit and sent it off—"over the transom."

Miracle of miracles, it was bought and published, and I've been writing ever since.

Was there a particular person, place, or thing that inspired these stories?

The idea of writing about a "Great House" appealed to me immensely—the kind of house that's seen generations of the same family, where passion, love and hate have all played out within its walls. So that even a generation later you can almost feel those very same emotions.

What's your writing routine?

Normally I write from 10:00 a.m. to 4:00 p.m., and I have lunch at the computer.

I write the book through once, then rewrite and rewrite until the words tell the story that is in my mind.

How do you research your story?

With the SwanSea books, I researched the era by reading books, not only on Art Nouveau, but also on the Roaring Twenties. I really had the best time.

How do you develop your characters?

This is a hard question for me, basically because it's always different. Sometimes a character comes full-blown to my mind. One day it's not there and the next, it is. There is no explanation for a thing like that. As an author, I simply say a lot of thank-you prayers.

The other way a character grows for me is in layers. Characteristics start layering, one atop another, such as ways of speaking, laughing, loving, smelling, looking, touching. And suddenly a character is born, right smack in the middle of the book.

When you're not writing, what are your favorite activities?

I love to spend time with family and friends. That's first. Going to movies and plays is also lots of fun for me. Plus—and this is a big plus for me—I've never lost my love of reading. I no longer read romance, though, since that's what I write. Instead, I've grown to love fast-moving suspense and mysteries.

If you don't mind, could you tell us a bit about your family?

I'd honestly like nothing better. I have two grown sons, two grandchildren—a seven-year-old precocious little girl and a seventeen-month-old, rambunctious little boy. Better and better, I have another grandchild on the way.

Do you have a favorite book or film?

Well, this question is another hard one for me. I have so many. The great classic film *Casablanca*, of course. I just love the dialogue in that one. One of my current films, believe it or not, is

Step into the Liquid. It's about surfing the big waves, but what attracts me most is the beauty of it and all the colors of blue. It's exciting and soothing at the same time. I also enjoyed *The Bourne Supremacy*.

Any last words to your readers?
Now that's an easy question. I want to say thank-you to my readers. Thank you for your support, your enthusiasm and your loyalty through all the years.

About Art Nouveau

Whether you aspire to decorate your home like the magnificent SwanSea house or you just want to know more about the Art Nouveau style, here are some interesting facts:

* Art Nouveau is French for "new art."

* This decorative style flourished between 1890 and 1910.

* It is characterized by curving and undulating lines, often referred to as whiplash lines.

* Many designs are based on plant forms and depict leaves and flowers in flowing, sinuous lines.

* Art Nouveau encompasses all forms of art and design—architecture, interior design, jewelry, furniture, glassware,

graphic design, painting, pottery, metal-work and textiles.

* Prominent figures associated with the style include:
    * Alphonse Mucha—poster artist
    * Antonio Gaudí—architect
    * Aubrey Beardsley—illustrator
    * Charles Rennie Mackintosh—architect and designer
    * Emile Gallé—glassmaker
    * Gustav Klimt—painter
    * Hector Guimard—architect and designer
    * Henry van de Velde—architect and designer
    * Louis Comfort Tiffany—stained glass artist
    * Louis Sullivan—architect
    * René Lalique—jewelry designer
    * Victor Horta—architect

* Art Nouveau was succeeded by Art Deco.

Here's a sneak peek...

SwanSea Place: The Promise

by

Fayrene Preston

Look for this story in SwanSea Dynasty, *an exciting 2-in-1 volume coming in April 2006 from Signature Select.*

PREFACE

Cambridge, Massachusetts, 1922

THE GRAY LIGHT OF DAWN seeped around the edges of the drapes and into Clarisse Haviland's bedroom. Standing by the bed, belting her rose velvet dressing gown, she frowned at the intruding light. She was not ready for the night to end. She had so few nights left with him….

Jake Deverell stirred beneath the covers. She turned toward the sound of him.

"What are you doing up so early?" he asked huskily, rubbing the sleep from his cobalt-blue eyes.

"I woke up and couldn't go back to sleep."

"Why didn't you wake me?"

"Your last exam is today. I felt you needed your rest."

He groaned good-naturedly. "You sound like my mother."

She swung away, but not fast enough to keep him from seeing that he had hurt her. In a flash he was standing behind her, his big hands cupping her upper arms and drawing her back against him. "I'm sorry, Clarisse. I didn't mean that the way it sounded."

"I know."

He swept her long brown hair free of one shoulder and pressed his lips to the side of her neck.

A sweet warmth flooded through her. But then, he could always evoke a response from her with just the lightest of touches. She laid her head back against him and reached behind her to clasp his hips; muscles flexed beneath her hands, thrilling her.

"I've told you time and again, to me you are ageless," he whispered in her ear.

"To you," she said softly, "because you're gallant. But the truth is I'm thirty-four and you're twenty-two."

He turned her to face him. "Why are you bringing this up now, Clarisse? We've been together almost from the first day I arrived here to attend Harvard."

She smiled softly. "I remember. I glanced up and saw you staring in the window of my shop at the display of my latest hat designs. You looked so serious." And handsome, she added to herself. And tough. That day, something had moved inside her. Something that had felt like excitement and heat combined. Something that had never before moved in her, even when her husband had been alive.

"I was trying to decide which hat to buy for my mother. Then it occurred to me, I could buy them all."

He smiled widened. "Yes, and you did."

"And in doing so, I met you. I had just been through the biggest upheaval of my life, learning that Edward Deverell was my real father, then deciding whether or not to allow the bastard to adopt me."

"Which you did, but only on your terms. You should be proud of yourself, Jake. You bested him."

He grinned affectionately. "Yes, and you have bested me by somehow managing to get me off the subject. Now answer me. Why are you bringing up the difference in our ages?"

"Because within a few days you will be graduating. SwanSea will become your home, and you will take your rightful place in society and begin your new life in earnest."

"Oh, I definitely intend to begin a new life. Unfortunately for Edward Deverell, it won't be the new life he's envisioning. He's given me the two things in the world he most cherishes: his name and his beloved SwanSea—not because of any love he has for me or my mother, but because he hopes I will make his dreams come true." His expression turned cruel. "In the coming years he will be dealt more disappointments than he will be able to bear."

"And what about SwanSea?" she whispered, taken aback by his vehemence.

"SwanSea will never be my home. I view it only as a tool with which to hurt Edward Deverell."

"But they say it's majestic, beautiful."

He glanced down at her, saw her lovely face and her soft blue eyes that held such wisdom, and felt the tension drain from his body. She could always make him feel better. He hugged her, then with a smile set her away from him again. "It's nothing more than an oversize plaything, Clarisse. You and I can play there together."

She shook her head, her expression full of love and regret. "No, Jake. My life is here in Cambridge with my hat shop, and my home is this apartment above the shop. I may be lonely after you leave, but I'll be content."

"You won't be lonely," he said decisively. "If you won't come to see me, I will come to see you. SwanSea is only in the next state, and I imagine I'll be in Boston frequently."

"You say you will come, but—"

He let out an impatient sound and turned away from her. "I can't believe this rotten mood you're in." With the nonchalant grace and power of youth, he strode to the window and jerked back the drapes. The dawn's pale light poured over him, following the long lines of his bronze body, delineating the strong, supple muscles and the taut, corded sinews. Suddenly he snapped his fingers. "I know what I'll do!

I'll *give* you something. Anything. Name it. What do you want?"

She laughed. "Nothing. Absolutely nothing."

"But you've given me so much! I couldn't have made it through these last four years without you, and I insist on giving you a present. I know! I'll choose the present myself. Something wonderful, something—"

"I won't accept, Jake. I'm serious."

He stared at her, perplexed. "But why not?"

"Because no gift could be as wonderful as the time I've spent with you. You think I've given you so much? It's not half what you have given me. The memory of you will stay with me the rest of my life."

"You're being foolish, Clarisse." He made an abrupt gesture that was uniquely his and that conveyed the life and energy in him that was ready to explode. "Never mind. I know what I will do."

He strode to her desk, sat down and drew pen and paper from a drawer. Magnificent in his nakedness, he began to write in sweeping, broad strokes.

She watched him. Perhaps it was the light, she thought. Perhaps it was the moment. But it seemed to her she could see through to his inner self with absolute clarity—the good in him, the faults, the tremendous potential.

He was so very sure of himself. He thought he'd learned everything there was to learn, but he hadn't.

He thought he had the world tamed and that all the rough times were behind him, but there would be more. He thought he was everything he could be now, but it was nothing compared to what he would become.

A thought occurred to her. Jake would have extraordinary children, and she envied the woman who would bear them.

He finished with a flourish, stood and handed her the paper.

She bent her head and read.

I, Jacob Conall Deverall, hereby promise to grant a favor, unconditionally, to the bearer of this letter. In the event something prevents me from granting this favor, be it life or be it death, this promise is hereby binding on my heirs.

So stated in this year of nineteen hundred and twenty-two.

Jacob Conall Deverell

CHAPTER 1

Deverell Building
Boston, Massachusetts
Present day

CONALL JACOB DEVERELL finished reading the note, lifted his head, and pinned the young woman sitting in front of his desk with a hard gaze. "Are you trying to tell me that my grandfather wrote this note to your great-aunt, Clarisse Haviland, and as a result I owe you a favor?"

Sharon Clarisse Graham inclined her head. "That's right."

"You've got to be kidding."

She glanced down at her clasped hands. "Your grandfather, in effect, wrote my great-aunt a promissory note."

"If Jake wrote this—"

"I assure you he did, but we can have an expert analyze the handwriting if you wish."

His expression turned flinty at her interruption.

"—and *if* it was his wish to grant your great-aunt a favor, then it was to your great-aunt that the favor should have gone. The note says nothing about her heirs."

"What the note says is that the promise is binding on *his* heirs and that the favor is to be granted to the *bearer* of the note."

That was what it said, all right, Conall agreed silently, knowing under any other circumstances he would have been amused at the grandiose gesture his grandfather had made as a young man. Jake, at twenty-two, must have been really something, and Clarisse, quite a woman.

Nylon whispered against nylon. Clarisse's great-niece crossed her legs, breaking into his thoughts to remind him that she was a woman to be reckoned with as well, though in quite another way. But he was an accomplished games player in the world of business. He could handle her, though first he had to know what game they were playing and why they were playing it.

He had last seen her ten years before. She had never once in the intervening years tried to see him until today. She wanted money, of course.

"Your reputation in business is one of integrity," she was saying. "It is that integrity I'm counting on when it comes to the honoring of your grandfather's note."

"You're counting on a great deal."

"Oh, I'm well aware of that."

The mockery he saw in her greenish-blue eyes pricked at him. Slowly he closed his hand around the note, crushing it.

"It's a copy," she said softly.

"I don't care if it's an ancient piece of parchment found in the same cave with the Dead Sea Scrolls. There will be no favor granted to you."

She gave a patient sigh and settled more comfortably into the large wing chair. "All right, so much for honor. But what about your family's name?"

He took her quietly posed question as a threat. With his uncle, Senator Seldon Deverell, in the race for the presidency of the United States, he had to proceed carefully until he knew what she was up to. Reporters were nipping like hungry dogs for juicy tidbits on the Deverell family.

He dropped the crumpled note onto the desk and sat back in his chair to study her. When he'd known her, she'd been eighteen, her hair wildly curly, and a free, natural spirit. Now her light brown hair was straight, pulled away from her face and held at her nape by a plain gold barrette. Light, deftly applied makeup enhanced her smooth ivory complexion. Clear fingernail polish covered her short, manicured nails. She wore a severely tailored navy-blue pinstripe suit and a plain white blouse. The hem of the straight skirt covered her knees, even with her sitting.

All in all, her appearance was very proper, he thought. Very professional. Very appropriate for making her way in what she no doubt saw as a man's world.

But her look also had another consequence. It was sexy as hell, understated to the point that it worked on a man's mind, making him wonder what she was hiding beneath the very plain exterior. He was sure she had carefully calculated the whole effect.

He was also sure she had figured to the penny the exorbitant sum of money she planned to try to extort from him.

He watched her hand idly rub the leather handle of her briefcase, an arrogant gesture that conveyed his scrutiny wasn't bothering her and that she was content to wait until he was through. Very, very cool.

The card she had presented him at their meeting had stated she was a certified public accountant for what he knew to be a prestigious accounting firm. Perhaps she wanted the money to start up her own business, or even to buy a partnership in an existing company. The thing was, he didn't care if she said she wanted it for an operation for her poor sainted mother. She wasn't going to get it.

"Since you feel the promise is binding on Jake's heirs, why didn't you go to one of his other heirs—

my father, for instance, or my cousin, Caitlin, or even my uncle, Senator Deverell. You could have caused quite a commotion in my uncle's camp."

"It's not my intention to cause a commotion, and I chose you because you're the most appropriate person for what I want."

She wanted to cause a commotion all right, he reflected cynically, and he knew why she had chosen him. Among other things, with his father retired, Caitlin interested in other things and Seldon in politics, the Deverell business empire was totally and completely under his control. She must want an enormous sum. "Did you know about the relationship between your great-aunt and my grandfather when we were seeing each other?"

"I didn't know about the note, but I did know Jake and Clarisse had been involved."

"Why didn't you mention it?"

Again her eyes mocked him. "When we were together, other things always seemed more important."

A muscle moved in his jaw. "How is it that your family has never tried to cash in on this favor before?"

"I can't speak for my family. Perhaps no one has ever needed it."

"But you do. Need a favor, I mean."

She moved, he couldn't say exactly how. But it was just enough to make him consider that she might not be as at ease as she seemed. "I prefer to think of it as collecting on a promise."

"How long have you had the note?"

"I inherited it last year. Clarisse never had children—in fact, she never remarried—so the note was handed through her younger sister to her daughter, who was my mother, who in turn passed it on to me at her death."

"Is your father still living?"

"He died several years before my mother."

"I'm sorry." His jaw tightened. Dammit. Why had he let himself become sidetracked by personal matters?

He thumped the note with his thumb and middle finger. The crumpled ball of paper shimmied, then stilled. "You know, don't you, that this note would never hold up in court?"

Her chin seemed to rise a notch. "It's a chance I'm willing to take."

She had to be bluffing. She had to know that if she somehow managed to get him into court, a highly unlikely event, he could completely destroy her character.

"Your grandfather was a great man," she said. "I can't imagine you would want his name dragged through court."

"Yours would be there, too, right alongside his."

"And so would yours."

His eyes narrowed. "You must want this very badly."

There was another movement; this time he saw one of her fingers jerk and pull the skin of the hand on which it lay. The gesture bothered him in a way he couldn't put into words.

"Yes," she said quietly, "I do."

He'd had enough. He leaned forward, intense, predatory. "All right, let's quit playing games. I'll bite. How much do you want?"

For a moment she looked startled. "How much?"

He made a sound of impatience. "How much money do you want?"

"I don't want any money from you." Her derisive tone denounced him for jumping to that conclusion.

He blinked. "Then just exactly what is this favor you want?"

"I want you to make me pregnant."

...NOT THE END...

Read more of this story in SwanSea Dynasty, *available from Signature Select in April 2006.*

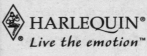

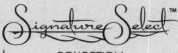

COMING NEXT MONTH

Signature Select Spotlight
IN THE COLD by Jeanie London
Years after a covert mission gone bad, ex-U.S. intelligence agent Claire de Beaupre is discovered alive, with no memory of the brutal torture she endured. Simon Brandauer, head of the agency, must risk Claire's fragile memory to unravel the truth of what happened. But a deadly assassin needs her to *forget*....

Signature Select Saga
BETTING ON GRACE by Debra Salonen
Grace Radonovic is more than a little surprised by her late father's friend's proposal of marriage. But the shady casino owner is more attracted to her dowry than the curvy brunette herself. So when long-lost cousin Nikolai Sarna visits, Grace wonders if *he* is her destiny. But sexy Nick has a secret...one that could land Grace in unexpected danger.

Signature Select Miniseries
BRAVO BRIDES by Christine Rimmer
Two full-length novels starring the beloved Bravo family.... Sisters Jenna and Lacey Bravo have a few snags to unravel...before they tie the knot!

Signature Select Collection
EXCLUSIVE! by Fiona Hood-Stewart, Sharon Kendrick, Jackie Braun
It's a world of Gucci and gossip. Caviar and cattiness. And suddenly everyone is talking about the steamy antics behind the scenes of the Cannes Film Festival. Celebrities are behaving badly... and tabloid reporters are dishing the dirt.

Signature Select Showcase
SWANSEA LEGACY by Fayrene Preston
Caitlin Deverell's great-grandfather had built SwanSea as a mansion that would signal the birth of a dynasty. Decades later, this ancestral home is being launched into a new era as a luxury resort—an event that arouses passion, romance and a century-old mystery.

The Fortunes of Texas: Reunion
THE DEBUTANTE by Elizabeth Bevarly
When Miles Fortune and Lanie Meyers are caught in a compromising position, it's headline news. There's only one way for the playboy rancher and the governor's daughter to save face—pretend to be engaged until after her father's election. But what happens when the charade becomes more fun than intended?